Advance Praise for A L...

"Robin W. Pearson delivers a fresh new voice for Southern fiction, treating readers to an inspiring journey through the complex matters of the heart."

JULIE CANTRELL, *New York Times* and *USA Today* bestselling author

"My mouth watered at the mustard greens and ham hocks. Feels like home. You'll fall in love with Evelyn and Granny B and a cast of memorable characters so rich you won't want the story to end. We can only hope we'll be reading more from Robin W. Pearson!"

CHRIS FABRY, bestselling author of *Under a Cloudless Sky* and *The Promise of Jesse Woods*

"With a deft hand and an unflinching eye, Pearson tackles the cobwebby corners of her characters' lives and in doing so reveals truths that ultimately help us all to heal . . . even when we've convinced ourselves we don't need to."

SARAH LOUDIN THOMAS, author of *Miracle in a Dry Season*

"From the first page, Pearson invites readers into the slow unraveling of truth in her characters' lives as the past and present collide. She writes with both realism and empathy—a powerful combination."

BETH K. VOGT, Christy Award–winning author

"Robin W. Pearson's authentic faith and abundant talent shine through in this wholehearted novel. Bee and Evelyn will stir your heart and stay with you long after the last page of *A Long Time Comin'* is turned."

MARYBETH MAYHEW WHALEN, author of *Only Ever Her*

"With amazing skill and a strong Southern voice, Robin W. Pearson captures the essence of family relationships in her outstanding debut novel, *A Long Time Comin'*. . . . This powerful story will impact and inspire readers who enjoy engaging Southern women's fiction."

CARRIE TURANSKY, award-winning author of *No Ocean too Wide*

"In *A Long Time Comin'* Robin W. Pearson takes readers behind closed doors and into the heart of a family."

ANN H. GABHART, bestselling author of *Angel Sister* and *The Refuge*

"Robin W. Pearson's singular style and fully realized cast of characters ring proudly throughout this novel. Her masterful voice is a welcome addition to the genre of family sagas rooted in hope and faith."

LIZ JOHNSON, bestselling author of *The Red Door Inn*

"The lyrical weaving of family narratives, past and present, is masterful—certainly to be compared with writers such as Sue Monk Kidd and Barbara Kingsolver. . . . Buy this book. It gripped me . . . from page one."

JANET HOLM McHENRY, author of twenty-four books, including the bestseller *PrayerWalk*

"*A Long Time Comin'* is a tender and sweet story of a cantankerous grandmother and her dear family members. It is entertaining yet reveals some hard truths about living and loving. Her characters are charming, endearing, and flawed. I hope we have many years to come of reading Pearson's work."

KATARA PATTON, author

a long time comin'

a novel

Robin W. Pearson

Tyndale House Publishers
Carol Stream, Illinois

Visit Tyndale online at tyndale.com.

Visit Robin W. Pearson's website at robinwpearson.com.

TYNDALE and Tyndale's quill logo are registered trademarks of Tyndale House Publishers.

A Long Time Comin'

Designed by Eva M. Winters

Edited by Caleb Sjogren

Published in association with the literary agency of Books & Such Literary Management, 52 Mission Circle, Suite 122, PMB 170, Santa Rosa, CA 95409.

A Long Time Comin' is a work of fiction. Where real people, events, establishments, organizations, or locales appear, they are used fictitiously. All other elements of the novel are drawn from the author's imagination.

For information about special discounts for bulk purchases, please contact Tyndale House Publishers at csresponse@tyndale.com or call 1-800-323-9400.

ISBN 978-1-4964-4188-1 (HC)
ISBN 978-1-4964-4153-9 (SC)

Printed in the United States of America

25	24	23	22	21	20	19
7	6	5	4	3	2	1

*"... so that they should seek the Lord, in the hope
that they might grope for Him and find Him,
though He is not far from each one of us ..."*

ACTS 17:27

*To my beloved parents
and all those whose joy, healing, answered prayer,
and morning light are a long time comin'*

PART ONE

The Women

Chapter One

June 18

That night when my man eased through the door, his clothes felt and smelled like the summer rain tapping on the roof. There sure aint nothing like a North Carolina rain. He bout scared the breath out of me, but then he grinned and whispered my name in that way he had. I started missing him on the spot cause I figured he'd be gone by the time the first rays of sunlight tickled the floorboards. I slipped to the kitchen anyway and made him a plate since I never could say no to them eyes. To this day when I fry up pork chops, I can still see him gnawing on that bone.

Know what else I see? Me pushing him out that same door not even two hours later. Only the Lord coulda made me do it. And that man made such a fuss! My heart practically thudded to a stop when I heard the children stir. A part of me ached to pull him inside and wrap my arms round him, but my bones said, Bee, there aint no coming back from this. He probly heard my heart pounding in my chest as he stood there with the rain dripping off his brim and his mouth a straight line. His eyes weren't laughing then. And they weren't asking me for nothing either. He just tipped his hat to me—and he sure never looked back. I know. Cause I waited.

But deep inside I could tell he wouldn't come creeping back in a month or so to melt away my anger with them smiles and empty promises and sliding out the door before sunrise. I just wish I coulda told my fool self—Bee, get away from that window and either stop wishing for your husband to come back or stop fearing it. You can't have both.

Beatrice tucked her pencil into the gutter of her worn leather journal and dragged her eyes from the page. She readjusted the thin watch on her left wrist. 10:42. Holding her book to her chest, she hefted herself from the chair. Her bones creaked as they made themselves comfortable in her new upright position by the window of her Spring Hope, North Carolina, home. She strained her neck, aiming to see where the once-graveled road, now paved, turned the corner. Her fingers fiddled with the long gray braid curled across her right shoulder as she imagined his knee-length black coat and matching black felt fedora worn so low it almost covered one eye.

Then, sighing, Beatrice removed the pencil and closed the book altogether. She pulled the strip of rubber from her wrist and snapped it around her diary to secure the pencil. She'd been spending too much time these days looking backwards, getting lost meandering through those long-ago days. "Keep yo' hand to the plow, Bee."

Peeking around the curtain one last time, Beatrice cast a disparaging eye on the Wilson boys in their daddy's car. "Mm-mm, flying down the road like they ain't had no sense." As the noise from their engine faded, she stepped away from the window, retrieved the box from the bed, and laid the journal atop the papers inside. She'd just stow it all in her closet for now. *Too much trouble gettin' out that key to the steamer trunk.*

She shut her closet door and glanced around her bedroom. Sunrays streamed through the parted curtains and struck the mirror. The reflected glare revealed not one speck of dust. It had taken her the better part of a week of stops and starts to scrub her room and the rest of the house with orange-scented Murphy oil soap, and the wood floors seemed to smile at her, they were so shiny. Two fluffed pillows adorned her otherwise-plain light-blue bedcover, the hem of which hung exactly one-half inch from the floor. Nothing needed fixing, straightening, dusting, sweeping, or spraying.

In the front room, Beatrice found something to straighten: the black-and-white photograph of her mam and pap, one of the two framed pictures on the eggshell-colored wall. The back bedroom sat empty, undisturbed. She walked the few steps to the kitchen, but there even the stainless steel sink proved true to its name. Everything was cut, canned, wiped, washed, or stored away. Sighing again, she retrieved the empty clothes basket on the washing machine and tramped from the kitchen out to the clothesline.

The heat slapped her. Beatrice reached toward the first wooden pin and unclipped the underwear. She worked her way down the line, folding the stiff laundry and dropping it into the basket at her feet. She grimaced—*Too heavy a hand with that bleach*—and edged the now-overflowing basket to her right. Panting as much from exertion as from the oppressive heat, Beatrice bent and hoisted the basket to her waist and plodded to the kitchen.

The kitchen clock read 11:17. Beatrice fetched the garden hose from the shed and brought it to the front yard to water the roses her granddaughter had planted by the mailbox for Mother's Day. After she finished dousing the wilting plants and any other hint of vegetation in the yard, she walked to the hose bib. With a squeak of the spigot and a stiff turn of the wrist, she extinguished the stream and detached the hose. She coiled it loosely around her elbow and trooped toward the porch to enter the house by the front door, too tired to go around to the shed. After she dragged her slight frame up the steps, she noticed her water-splattered legs and mud-covered brogans. Shoulders slumped, she eased down the steps—even more slowly this time—to go around back. Worn-out once she reached the door, Beatrice plopped down on the stoop to catch her breath. She couldn't even make it up the one step.

"I told Ev'lyn them flowers was mo' trouble than they's worth." The hose uncoiled on the ground around her ankles.

Some time later, Beatrice pushed herself to her feet with great effort and left the hose in a loose pile, forgotten. She unlaced and removed her shoes before entering the kitchen. Inside, her hot, wet skin greedily sucked in the cool air from the window unit. Refreshed a bit, Beatrice glanced at the clock over the sink: 11:55. *It ain't too early to eat some lunch. I've worked me up quite a hunger.*

The refrigerator yielded just enough pimiento cheese for a nice-size sandwich, and she plucked a Granny Smith apple from the bin in the pantry. Sitting at the table facing down her food, she prepared her stomach to eat.

Lord, You know what I need 'cause You the one who gave it to me and blessed it. Thank You. Amen. She took her time chewing, talking her way through her meal, frequently sipping the water, all the while ordering her stomach to stay in line. And just like many of the people in Beatrice's life, it obeyed.

When it was nearly half past noon, Beatrice slid her bookmark on James 1 and closed her Bible. She ignored the scrape of the chair's feet as she pushed away from the table. She scrubbed her lunch dishes, dried them, put them away, and retreated to her bedroom. There she resisted the urge to flip back the curtain to see whatever busied itself on the other side. Instead, she cast an eye at the clock. Its hands told her, *"Time for a nap."*

Nearly two hours later, refreshed and back on the porch, Beatrice leaned on the cushions and replaited her hair. She wound it, tucked it, and pinned the one long, silver braid into a bun at the nape of her neck. By now, the sun had crept toward the rear of the house, mercifully sparing the front porch. She basked in the nothingness stretching out beyond the yard and the street running in front of it. Then, "My Lord!" she entreated, gripping her side. She hunched over as pain speared her insides, inched around her spine and over her hip, and took hold somewhere in the area around her chest. It stole her breath. She sat still as stone, gripping her dress, eyes squeezed shut.

Seconds . . . a minute . . . forever passed until at last, the fist of pain loosened its hold, finger by finger, and finally let go altogether. The breeze that merely dislodged the heavy air raised chill bumps on her clammy skin. Doctors had warned her, but the suddenness of this spell caught Beatrice off guard. She had half a mind to cancel her afternoon plans, but before the other half caught up, a car crunched into the drive.

Piece by piece Beatrice put herself together, and then she stepped into her house far enough to retrieve her keys and turn the lock. She'd already pushed the heavy baskets laden with clean laundry onto the porch. Wordlessly Beatrice lifted her head a notch as she passed the hand that tried to help and stiffly took the three concrete steps to the ground.

"How you doin' today, Granny B?"

"Same as always." Beatrice looked neither to the right nor the left as she marched to the ancient burgundy metallic Monte Carlo, much as the second hand had ticked away the time. "You can put them two baskets in back." She threw the words over her shoulder as she climbed in. Beatrice drew from her pride rather than from her depleted stores of energy to slam closed her door behind her.

The other door opened and the seat was let down before the driver scooted the laundry baskets across the back. Then he slammed shut his own door and the engine chugged to life. Reverend Farrow turned to his passenger. "Granny B, are you ready?"

Beatrice nodded briskly. "If I ain't now, I ain't never gon' be."

Chapter Two

Now how would her Granny B handle this?

Hands tucked under her head, Evelyn lay on her right side and gazed at Kevin cradling his king-size pillow. She studied her husband's curly brown hair, slightly receding at the temples; his warm, velvety brown skin that didn't quite hide the line bisecting his brow; his long eyelashes almost brushing his cheekbones as he slept; the slightly flared nose that ended right above his heavy mustache and soft, full lips.

"I'm leaving you," she mouthed, practicing so her heart could get used to hearing the words. *But how?*

She couldn't ask Mama for advice. Mama was still bound to Daddy—mind, body, and soul—even though he'd died fifteen years ago. Evelyn definitely couldn't ask Granny B. All her grandmother knew was staying put, even as her husband and children trickled off one by one. It wasn't something she could seek God for. He clung tightly to her even as she tried to pry herself away, holding fast to His promise never to forsake her. No, she was all on her own.

Looking at Kevin made her stomach do flip-flops. And not the fluttery song and dance she'd felt the day she'd spilled caramel macchiato all over his jeans. Then she was all aquiver, laughing with him outside the campus coffee shop. She'd vowed to herself, *Wherever you came from, you're taking me with you, just so I can watch you talk.*

Ten years ago, standing on the sidewalk on the quad, her stomach had moved to the rhythm of his full lips as she'd watched them form complicated words like *book* and *coffee*. Tonight when she looked at his lips, other images came to mind. Painful mental pictures she herself had drawn that had kept her awake.

For the last thirty minutes.

Evelyn flopped onto her back. Her eyes traced the light-green vine that she had spent last summer stenciling below the wood molding. Then she counted the links of the chain that swung from the ceiling fan. Finally she imagined herself plucking the petals from a scarlet daylily planted along their backyard fence. *He loves me . . . He loves me not . . . Go or stay . . . Go or stay . . . Go . . .* Finally the *or* galvanized her into moving.

Before throwing back the covers, Evelyn couldn't resist

caressing his face with her eyes. As if they had a will of their own, her fingers soon followed suit, trailing down to his chin and dancing through his hair, gently, so as not to wake him. But then her mental images overshadowed her heart, and she couldn't stop herself from yanking a curl at his nape.

"Wh-what?" Kevin braced his hands against his pillow and pushed himself up.

Chintz covers thrown back, Evelyn ran her fingers through her own curly, chin-length hair, tousled from all her tossing and turning. She'd been so distracted before bed, she'd forgotten to tie on her silk scarf. "Oh, I'm sorry. I must have bumped you when I got up to use the bathroom."

"Was I snoring?" Kevin, who sounded only two steps away from deep sleep, mumbled the question into his pillow.

Evelyn padded away from the bed. She silently noted the digital clock on the DVR changing from 2:23 to 2:24. Not bothering to turn on the light in the bathroom, she used the moonlight peeking around the curtains as a guide. *"Oof!"*

Careening forward, she caught herself just before dashing her head on the tile wall. Kevin's leather belt peeked out from the slacks and shirt he'd shed before soaking away his stress in the clawfoot tub.

"Ev?"

She squeezed out, "Mmm?" between her clenched teeth.

"Evelyn? You all right?" He definitely sounded more alert. Covers rustled.

"Mmm-hmmm." Evelyn propped herself on the side of the tub and added pressure to her injured, French-tipped toe. She held her breath, listening for, dreading, Kevin's footsteps. She wasn't in the mood to talk at half past two in the morning. What she was in the mood for was smothering her husband and sleeping. Well, maybe she'd smother him first, pee, and then sleep. *And okay, Lord, I'll pray for him then. Just for You.*

A full minute passed before the creaking bed and not-so-gentle snores assured Evelyn the coast was clear, if not quiet. Suddenly resolved, she tiptoed to the large walk-in closet that opened off the bathroom and pulled out the step stool. She stood on the top rung and stretched to reach the topmost shelf. Evelyn pulled down an unused loofah, toothbrush holder, box of Dove soap, and her extra bottle of perfumed shower gel. Then she stepped down, clutching her items to her middle. She walked over to the cabinet, opened the bottom drawer, and withdrew her toothbrush and toiletry bag. Arms now full, she slipped to the back left corner of her closet and let her armload tumble out quietly onto the carpeted floor.

Crouching, Evelyn withdrew a valise tucked under her shirts. Inside it, a plastic bag emblazoned with a red CVS pharmacy logo spilled its contents: a small plastic stick that looked up at her, still showing the same smirking skull and crossbones shaped like a + sign. No lifesaving *or* in sight.

Somewhere in the darkness the tree frog she and Kevin had nicknamed Dave uttered his high-pitched mating call. Evelyn gathered her things and stood. She put each in its place and returned the stool. Finally she plodded back to the mirror and stared at her image captured by the moonlight peeking through the windows. The orange-and-white flowers on her satin pajamas shimmered in the reflection.

So, God, is this Your way of telling me I can't leave my husband?

"Are you with me, Ev?" Kevin touched his wife's shoulder. "Evelyn Lester?"

Gasping, "What?" Evelyn snapped back to the present to find Kevin's six-foot-four-inch frame looming over her in the kitchen. The soapy dish slipped from her hands and clattered against the bottom of the stainless steel sink.

"Where were you?" With one hand Kevin flicked away the suds that had splashed onto his striped Italian cotton shirt. "Anything wrong?"

Everything, her mind screamed. She mumbled, "Nothing. Just thinking."

"About what?"

Evelyn forced a smile and voiced her thoughts, if not the whole truth behind them. "Everything. Nothing." She retrieved the stoneware casserole dish and rinsed it. "Shoot!" She ran her finger along the chip on its edge. Exasperated, she pulled open the cherry cabinet door and dropped the dish in the trash.

"Evelyn! It's just a chip. What are you doing?" Kevin bent to retrieve the platter. *"Ow!"* Hastily he withdrew his hand, but not before Evelyn pinched his fingers as she forced the door closed. "What's the matter with you?"

"I'm throwing it out, Kevin. It's what you do when something is broken." Evelyn edged around him to clear away the detritus from their dinner. Her silence dropped icicles, chilling the kitchen despite the warmth of the summer day.

"Okay. But—?"

She whirled on her husband. Lather dripped from her hands onto the hardwood floor. "But *what*, Kevin?"

"What's wrong with you? You've been stomping around here the last couple of days, barely speaking to me. Pulling my hair when I'm sleeping—"

"I didn't—"

"And now you're throwing away perfectly good dishes and slamming my fingers in the trash can."

Evelyn glared at him, her wet hands clenched at her sides. Kevin didn't blink. "It's me, right?"

"I didn't pull your—"

He trailed his long, tapered fingers down the right side of her face. His voice was a whisper. "Evie, baby."

"Don't." Kevin's *baby* set her jaw as her stomach protested the diminutive use of her name, and she stepped away from the touch that used to thrill her. She dried her hands with the dish towel. "How can you ask me if it's you? Who else would it be? *What* else would it be? It's not like you forgot my birthday or neglected to buy me an anniversary present." She threw the towel on the quartz countertop and stalked from the kitchen.

"But it happened a long time ago, Evie!" Kevin followed Evelyn into the keeping room just off the kitchen to find her staring out the window into the backyard. The Japanese maple they'd planted together last year was finally growing. Its thin red leaves shivered in the breeze. Evelyn's own shoulders, bare in her orange sleeveless shift, drew up as if to ward off the chill.

It. He summed up his devastation of their marriage with a two-letter pronoun. "*It* may have happened a long time ago, but I'm just finding out about *it*. You might as well have slept with her this morning and not six months ago."

Kevin inhaled sharply.

"It's hard to hear it, isn't it? Well, that's how I feel every time I think about you and . . . *her*. *It.* Like I've been punched in the gut."

"But I didn't actually sleep with her. I just—"

Just. Just. Just. Just because your body didn't follow the road your heart had already traveled. Evelyn's insides twisted again. Her forehead broke out in a cold sweat. "*Just* go, Kevin. Don't you have a business trip?"

"Please turn around. I can't talk to your back like this." When Evelyn remained where she was, his demand became an entreaty. "Can't you forgive me? Doesn't God—?"

"Don't talk to me about forgiveness. About God. Unless you're going to tell me what He says about the definition of adultery." Her eyes met his pained stare reflected in the window. "We could talk about *His* faithfulness, *His* truth, but you wouldn't have much to offer to the conversation."

"That's low, Evelyn. I did tell you the truth!"

She finally turned to squarely meet his gaze. "No, you admitted it when I asked you about it, Kevin. After I'd already found out. Tell me—if I'd never stumbled across those text messages, would you have ever told me?"

Kevin raked his hand over his face. "Evie." He moaned her name.

She flew at him. "Don't call me that! Stop calling me that! The man who loves me calls me that! The man I love calls me that!"

One of his large hands wrapped around both of hers and stopped her flailing. His other arm wrapped around her waist and tried to press her close, but she fought him with all she had.

And then she threw up all over his size thirteen wing tips.

Chapter Three

"GAL, WHATCHYOU DOIN' HERE? This ain't yo' time to visit," Beatrice called out to her granddaughter from her front porch. "And whatchyou got there?"

Evelyn unloaded the last of the plants she had stowed in her backseat and turned to the woman who'd shared more than the name Evelyn Beatrice with her. Her grandmother had also passed down a fair share of her strong will. Evelyn drew on that strength now and squared her shoulders as she faced her namesake.

"Hydrangeas. Mama and I thought we'd add some color to this yard." Evelyn moved to hoist the second rectangular planter to her hip and chose instead to work on first one, then the other.

"'Lis'beth know I don't like no flowers round here." Beatrice glared at Evelyn from the bottom step. "Stuff like that just create mo' work for me to do. And they just gon' die anyhow."

"But, Granny B, they'll come back every year, and they'll look pretty right here framing the front porch. It's not that much work because Mama can clip them for you once they grow some. And I can help out more often now I'm not teaching. You can enjoy the beauty without being put out."

Granny B angled her eyes toward the roses struggling for life beside the road. "No muss, no fuss, huh? I done heard all that before. This my yard, and I don't need nobody takin' care of it for me. Hmmmf, plantin' hy-dran-gees to try and pretty up this yard." She spread her wiry arms to encompass her postage stamp–size plot. "All this here dirt, with barely a bit a grass to cut. That ain't even in the neighborhood of good sense."

Back when Beatrice Agnew was raising both herself and her children, the woods crept up practically to the back door. But not today. Those small hands and feet had snatched and trampled the life right out of each tiny weed or blade of grass that had dared to grow. Evelyn now swept the yard, using the rake to leave plenty of lines in the dirt so that Granny B would know she'd done as she'd been told, like her own mama, Elisabeth, had when she was a girl. Sweeping the yard was a part of "settin' things right," what Granny B called cleaning up.

Evelyn had left her grandmother sputtering in the front

18

yard while she'd trudged around back to the small storage shed to retrieve a shovel, rake, and garden hose. "Speaking of fuss." Evelyn leaned the tools against the porch rail while Granny B, still grumbling, stamped off to pick up stray leaves blown over from a neighbor's tree. "Have you reconsidered coming to Mama's birthday party?"

"When I ever change my mind 'bout somethin'? Go with yo' first mind is what I say and what I do."

"If that's your way of saying you're not coming . . ."

"I ain't got no *way* of sayin' nuthin', gal. I done told you and yo' husband I ain't goin' to no party. And I done told 'Lis'beth already, so there ain't no need to brang it up again. I was there for her birth. Cain't get mo' excitin' than that. And you need to sweep the yard first befo' you get to messin' thangs up." Granny B pointed to the part of the yard near the mailbox at the curb. "Anyway, where's yo' husband? Surprised he ain't helpin' you with this. Y'all don't move without the other one movin', too."

"Uh . . . Kevin?" Evelyn grabbed the rake and walked toward the front curb.

"Unless you got some other husband I don't know 'bout." Beatrice used the ever-present cloth draped through the belt of her chambray dress to flick away beads of sweat from her forehead. She lifted her braid draped across her neck and over her shoulder and soaked up the perspiration. The gold cross hanging at the base of her throat glinted in the sunshine.

Evelyn managed to chuckle weakly. She'd come to Spring Hope today to escape Kevin, but he'd chased her there nonetheless. "He's . . . home. Working. But he's going away." Immediately Evelyn wished she could pluck the words from the air between them and tuck them into her pocket.

"Away?" Granny B walked slowly toward her granddaughter, pointing. "You missed that place by the drive, gal. Away where?"

"Europe." Evelyn bit off the word but regretted it since her grandma was likely to sniff out her *Who cares?* attitude. She forced herself to face Granny B. "And South Africa. He'll be gone about three months. So he's going to miss the party." She turned to her task—and another subject. "And since I'm not done, I haven't missed anything yet."

"Europe? *Africa?* Is that why you here, actin' all stiff? You mad 'cause he gon' miss all this birthday goin's-on?"

"I'm not mad!" But realizing that she sounded quite the opposite, Evelyn seized the opportunity Granny B had unwittingly thrown into her lap. "Actually, yes, I guess I am. We've worked hard on all these plans and now he's going to be off for three months, missing everything."

"Well, so am I. Missin' thangs, I mean. So I guess you gon' be mad at me, too." Granny B retreated to the porch. Her hand trembled as she grasped the rail to pull herself up the short flight.

"But we're inviting everybody!" Evelyn rested the rake on her shoulder so she was free to tick off names, starting with her older siblings. "Yolanda and Lionel and their families."

Her mama's birthday celebration at summer's end would mark the first time the family would come together since they'd buried Graham, Evelyn's daddy. Evelyn and Kevin had planned to throw the party at her mama's house in Mount Laurel, where she lived with Jackson, Evelyn's younger brother, about two towns over from Granny B. Yolanda and Lionel were flying in from Boston and Phoenix.

Evelyn moved on to include Granny B's grown children. "Then there's Aunt Ruthena and Uncle Matthew. Little Ed—"

"Edmond gon' be there?" Granny B straightened up. "He's out already?"

"Uh . . . uh, I mean, it's *possible*. We're inviting him . . . or at least his children—"

"Now don't start to lyin', gal." According to Granny B, the back of Little Ed's head was the last she'd seen of her oldest son, nearly twenty years ago. At the time, he was ducking into the bed of his friend's pickup truck, heading out of town right after a load of rib eye steaks had gone missing from the Piggly Wiggly. She crooked an eyebrow at Evelyn. "I didn't know Rikers Island gave out passes for birthday parties."

"I didn't mean that Little Ed was *definitely* coming, just that he *wanted to*. Well, Aunt Sarah told him about it when she saw him on visitors' day . . ." Her words died an unnatural death.

Granny B gave Evelyn plenty of rope to hang herself— and the time to do it. "You been namin' ever'body gon' be at your mama's party; now you stammerin' and stutterin', sayin' *maybe* this or *possibly* that. The truth usually can slip through right easily, but the lie got to be greased up and twisted round to get through yo' lips."

Evelyn ran her fingers through the damp tendrils at the nape of her neck and laughed wryly, thinking about all the oil Kevin had applied to his own lips the past six months. "I'm not lying, Granny B. I'm sure Little Ed wants to come—and who knows what can happen between now and then? Right now, I'm just focused on getting *you* to the dinner, not your children. When is the next time you can see almost everybody in one place?"

"Well, according to yo' aunt Ruthena, the world gon' be endin' soon enough, and we all gon' be together in the sky somewhere. Ain't no need to go rushin' thangs down here." Granny B opened the front door. "Since you determined to do all that work, I'm gon' head back in to the kitchen."

The door creaked shut behind her. Evelyn returned to raking. She knew Granny B had never been one to count her children's fingers and toes. She had just focused on each tiny, hungry mouth—because somehow, someway, she had to feed it. She had screamed, sweat, and pushed her first child into the world when she was fifteen, right in her own bedroom. After Elisabeth came Little Ed, and then she'd miscarried twins. Meant to be third born, they were the first to die.

"That was a real bad day," Granny B had pronounced, shaking her head, when she'd told her granddaughter the story many years ago. Her hands had never paused as they'd cut up tender greens.

"Girl, those are called mustard greens," Mama had explained later when Evelyn had asked.

After the twins came Ruthena, Thomas, Mary, Sarah, and then the last, Milton, born in a blinding rainstorm two months past Granny B's thirtieth birthday. According to her, soon after, Granddaddy Henton flew the coop. One day, all her grandmother had found were his muddy boots by the back door and his crumpled gray hat in her front room. But he did come back more than thirty years later when he visited each month in the form of a Social Security check, paid to Beatrice T. Agnew, widow of H. A. Agnew.

"'Course, that won't never pay his debt. That price only I can pay. Me and Milton," Granny B was heard to say.

As the sun climbed higher in the late-morning sky, Evelyn paid for ever laying eyes on those hydrangeas. But she finally completed the work. She then cleaned off Granny B's tools, replaced them in the shed, and headed to the house. After doffing her shoes on the front porch, she entered Granny B's front room. Furniture polish gave her nose a warm, lemon-scented hello.

"Granny B?"

"Gal, ain't no need to be yellin' fo' me. I cain't be but in so many places in this house." Granny B had moved through the front room, down the short hall, and on to the sunlit kitchen in the back of the house. A breeze from the open window rattled the shade a bit, but Granny B, unflappable, was putting away the broom in the corner to the right of the back door. She removed the cloth from her waist, folded it twice, and placed it atop the small pile of soiled laundry sitting in the basket on the washing machine. She turned her lean, five-foot-one-inch frame in Evelyn's direction. "You done?"

Evelyn nodded, then picked up the thread of conversation she'd begun unraveling an hour ago. "You know you're going to miss out on all the fun."

"Fun? Listenin' to Mary go on 'bout livin' the high life? Puttin' up with Ruthena prayin' for ever'body and layin' on hands? I can see her now: 'Lord, bless this, and Lord, bless that.'" With her eyes rolled back, looking skyward, and her hands waving in the air, Granny B did a fair imitation of her daughter. "With all that blessin' and such, nobody gon' be able to eat, let alone have some *fun*. I ain't got time for all that."

Evelyn chuckled. "You'd render her speechless seeing you there."

"Speechless? *Ruthena?* She hadn't never been speechless. Even when she came slidin' out from tween my legs, she was screamin' and hollerin' 'fo' anybody slapped her on the behind. I was the one who shoulda been carryin' on."

"That birthday party sound 'bout like that grave party you and yo' mama throw every year, only not as much fun. What's gone is gone. If you was me, you'd know there ain't no bringin' him back."

"Him who?"

"I meant *it*. The past." Granny B reached for the broom again and handed it to Evelyn.

24

"We don't plant flowers at the family plot to have fun, Granny B. We honor those things that never die. Like commitment. Love. Tradition." Evelyn grappled for a hold on Granny B's eyes. "Like Mama's birthday, as a matter of fact." Evelyn didn't add, *but not like my marriage.*

"Well, Jesus taught me just 'cause it's a tradition don't make it right. Goin' to that grave ain't 'bout committin' to yo' daddy. That's 'bout you and 'Lis'beth, just like this here party. Now, case closed. I ain't goin'. If you plan to stick round here, then get to work. You can start by sweepin' up in my room."

"While you do what?" Evelyn knew her Granny B just wanted her out of her hair, but she refused to disentangle herself so easily.

Without missing a beat, Granny B reached into the corner to retrieve a wide-brimmed hat hanging on a hook over the washing machine. "Whilst I sweep the backyard. You didn't do too good a job at it this mornin'." That said, she pushed through the screen door into the backyard, letting the door slap shut decisively behind her.

"All this family talk probably got her thinking about Milton." Evelyn moved the wooden ladder-back chair Granny B kept beside her bedroom door, swept the area, and replaced the chair. "Will it ever get better?"

Granny B had had it hard, and there was no way her granddaughter could ever separate her from an ounce of her pain and suffering, not that anyone could. Evelyn believed that every morning, before Granny B got dressed, she put on this suit of armor—not her full armor of God because that never came off. Her past. And she buttoned it up tight. It protected her from all kinds of nasty things, such as healing, redemption, or a cool balm for those festering sores of resentment and sadness. And it also prevented her from taking much pleasure from the faith that she set such store by.

Besides Henton's check, Lis and Evelyn were the only parts of the family who regularly stopped by. Even Kevin kept his distance, despite Beatrice's view that Evelyn was glued to her husband's hip. Under the guise of "settin' things right," she stopped by just to spend time with the crusty piece of bread that was her grandmother. Sometimes during her visits Granny B related some memory of the past, providing small details about this event or that. Evelyn often pictured all those people from her grandmother's past, banging their tiny fists on the inside of her lips, begging for air, but not even Little Ed could pry them open with his strong fingers. Her Granny B wouldn't set them free until she wanted to, and then only for a short spell.

Knowing that what Granny B wanted was a clean bedroom, she checked inside the closet for dust balls. Spying none, Evelyn started to slide the door closed when she noticed a box on the shelf, partially hidden under some of Granny B's sweaters. *Now what could that be?* After spending a moment or two staring at it, Evelyn shrugged away her curiosity and moved on, sweeping by the steamer trunk that had belonged to Granny B's own grandmother and around the heavy cherry dressing table.

In less than five minutes, about three minutes longer than

it should have taken her to clean Granny B's pristine floors, she finished. Looking around the room, Evelyn's gaze settled on the closet. Even though she couldn't see it, the partially covered box niggled at her. She'd cleaned Granny B's room so often she knew what belonged in that closet: her dresses hung on the far right and next to them her skirts. Then the shirts and the blouses. At the far left end her one pair of bleach-stained denim overalls. On the shelf at the top of the closet, her sweaters. At the bottom huddled her shoes, placed according to style and season. That was it. Or at least that should have been it. No shoe boxes and no boxes on the top shelf. Except for this odd box pushed under a stack of sweaters, a box that hadn't been there last month or the month before. Granny B's life maintained a certain order. Everything and everyone had a place. Hence Evelyn's curiosity and her sense of . . . *something*.

Evelyn didn't consider whether she *should* peek inside the box. She wondered only if she *could*, if she had the mettle. Never before had she considered invading Granny B's closely guarded privacy, but for some reason that tucked-away box whispered, *"Evelyn Beatrice Lester,"* using her whole name like her mama did when she wanted her immediate attention, no questions asked. Or maybe it was simply fallout from the truth-seeking missile that had wreaked havoc in her own home the night she happened upon Kevin's phone.

Holding the broom, Evelyn tiptoed on sneakered feet to peek out the back door. Granny B was still sweeping the farthest portion of the yard. After scooting back to the closet,

Evelyn used every bit of her five feet three inches to reach up to the shelf and push aside the sweaters. She placed them in the same order on another part of the shelf, and she picked up the box.

It was solid, a little bigger than a standard shoe box, but not by much. It might have held a pair of boots at some point, not that Evelyn had ever seen Granny B in boots. It was unmarked, a plain, brown rectangle with a slightly nubby texture. She knelt on the floor and shook it a tiny bit, testing its weight and feel. Something inside, several somethings, shifted and moved. *Paper, some kind of paper,* she concluded. Aloud, she hissed, "Why don't I just open it, or am I going to stand here sniffing and shaking?"

Again, the *or* did the job.

Evelyn sucked up some courage along with a deep breath and slowly lifted a corner, half-expecting something to snap off a finger or shower her face with blue paint. When neither happened, she cast a final furtive glance over her shoulder before she removed the lid and set it on the floor. Sitting on her haunches, Evelyn stared at the contents: a leather-bound book with a rubber band encircling it . . . and envelopes. More specifically, letters. Moving aside the book, she picked up one, then another, and saw that they were all addressed in the same neat scrawl, with all the letters straight and skinny and leaning to the left side. She did not recognize the handwriting, and none of the letters had a return address. Quickly leafing through them, Evelyn determined that they were addressed to her aunts and uncles and some to Granny B herself.

Some of the oldest dated back almost fifty years. One was opened, and very carefully, for the seal was neatly broken, with barely a ripple in the surface of the envelope. *Read it?* In answer, Evelyn pulled out the delicate sheets of paper and scanned the last page. *Henton.*

Granddaddy Henton? Evelyn didn't know he could write his name, let alone a letter! Hastily, her fingers shaking, she turned back to the first page and began reading the letter postmarked *June 15 . . .*

"What in hades do you thank you doin'?"

She froze. Granny B glared down at Evelyn from the door of her room.

"Did you hear what I . . . ? I cain't believe . . . Who told you . . . ?" Granny B strode to where her granddaughter was planted on the floor. She snatched the letter, ripping it. As brittle in her fury as its delicate pages, she didn't seem to notice.

Somehow, Evelyn dislodged her voice from where it had curled itself around her toes. "Granny—"

"You get yo' fill?" Granny B muttered between clenched teeth. A tear, unchecked, dripped from her cheek onto her right breast pocket. "I hope so, 'cause I figure yo' bus'ness is done here."

Evelyn tried to formulate a reason for her presence in her grandmother's room, for reading her private things, but all she managed was, "Granny B, I just—"

"You just what?"

She did not, could not, reply.

"Yeah, I just bet 'you just.'" She turned from her. "Get up and get out."

Still, Evelyn crouched there.

"What I say? Do you thank I don't mean it?" Granny B quivered from the ends of her gray hair to her dirt-smudged walking shoes. Suddenly and forcibly moving into action, practically knocking Evelyn down, she snatched up the rest of the letters scattered about her granddaughter's feet. As she gathered them, Granny B murmured, her voice icy taut with emotion, "Cain't I just have somethin' to myself? A little part that's mine? I shoulda burned 'em. That's what I shoulda done. Burned 'em with the rest of the trash all them years ago." Granny B dumped the letters back into the box on top of the leather-bound book. She crushed the lid, stepping on it as she moved to reclaim her possessions. She tucked the box under her arm to keep the lid closed.

"But you didn't burn them. You kept them—and you read them."

Turning in the direction of the voice, Granny B looked surprised to see Evelyn still there and as shocked as Evelyn that she had the nerve to speak. "Who say I read them?"

Evelyn reached out tentatively, but Granny B twisted away, much as Evelyn had fled Kevin's touch a few days before. She was sure, though, that her grandmother had enough composure to keep from throwing up on her feet.

"Granny B, I only—"

"I bet you only . . ."

Even though she had Granny B by at least ten pounds and "towered" over her by two inches, Evelyn recognized and acknowledged the implied threat. Her clasped hands covered her mouth as if to hold in the faltering words explaining the attack on Granny B's privacy, the assault upon Granny B herself. How could Evelyn say that she'd known what she was doing, but she'd thought it was important to do it anyway? It was that same inexplicable compulsion that had led her to Kevin's phone, but what unknown truth had this latest reconnaissance mission revealed?

Before Evelyn could formulate any further response, Granny B stalked from the room, still holding her box of letters. Evelyn moved to follow her, but then she spied the corner of something white peeking out from under the bed. Evelyn gave maybe one second's thought to returning the letter addressed to *Beatrice Agnew* before slipping the envelope in the waistline of her jeans, in the small of her back. She ignored the clamor of her conscience as she ran to catch up with her grandmother.

"Granny B?"

Again, Evelyn didn't look hard or long in the four-room, one-bath house. She found her holding open the front door, facing away from Evelyn, staring outside.

"I just want to say . . . I mean, I know I shouldn't . . . What I mean is, I'm sorry." As Evelyn moved toward the open doorway, a corner of the letter she'd tucked away stabbed her—and Granny B—in the back. "Really, Granny B, I am sorry—"

"Just what is you sorry for, gal? That you got caught? 'Cause I know that you ain't sorry 'bout what you done." Granny B cut her eyes at Evelyn, her voice rising barely above a whisper. "No, you might be sorry, but you ain't really repentant. I can see it all over you. But that's all right. I ain't got to worry 'bout seein' nuthin' else where you concerned. Get out, Ev'lyn."

"But—"

"I. Said. Get. Out." A small piece of her icy facade melted. "I thought you was a bit different, Ev'lyn. I thought you understood what it meant for me to have somethin' of my own. But fo' you to come here . . ." Granny B swallowed and tightly wrapped her composure around herself. "Well, if you gon' treat me with no respect, then I ain't got no time for you. Get out. And don't come back here. Them's some words you don't have to slip somewhere to hide and read 'cause I'm sayin' 'em plain to yo' face."

When Evelyn remained there, Granny B spat, "Is you glued to that spot? Ev'lyn. Get out this room. Leave my home. Don't never come back here again."

Chapter Four

"So, Evie . . . lyn," Kevin stuttered, "you're home early. Did you get kicked out?"

Evelyn hung her large pink-and-black flowered Vera Bradley satchel on the hook beside her drafting table and pulled out her chair. She slid out of her low-heeled mules and tucked her feet under the desk. "Not hardly," she answered woodenly.

"I expected you to stay at the library most of the day." Kevin looked at his wife over his computer screen. "What's that? Is that the mail?"

Yet again, Evelyn had lost her nerve before reading the letter she'd taken from Granny B's house a few weeks before.

She slipped the envelope into the thin top drawer of her three-foot-tall table and pushed the drawer closed. Although Granny B was right at the time about her lack of repentance, she was starting to feel convicted about taking it.

Evelyn spared Kevin a glance before turning toward the mahogany chest of drawers hugging the wall on the left. "Why did you hope I'd be gone all day?"

"I didn't say I *hoped* you'd be gone all day." Kevin spoke slowly and carefully as if he had to fit a quarter in a penny-size slot to pay for each word. "I just thought you'd stay until the library closed, doing research." He glanced up at his computer. "It's barely two thirty."

Evelyn sat down and reached beneath the desktop into the recess holding her manuscript about a boy named Peter. "Any calls?"

"Just Yolanda. We talked about your mom's birthday party until one of her kids broke something and she had to go." He paused for a moment. "She was disappointed that I wouldn't make it."

"I guess you've disappointed a lot of people lately. She should get in line."

Evelyn heard his exhalation as she arranged the colored pencils on her desk, but she resisted the urge to look up. Instead, she persisted in lining up her pencils by brightness and hue, a part of her writing routine. Giving him the silent treatment was a habit she'd recently adopted.

Her life had always closely revolved around God and Kevin. Her day dawned and set with Him and him. Usually she and Kevin started the day with a couples' devotional, even when he traveled. They checked in on each other throughout the day, whenever he had a moment between clients at his marketing firm or when she could pop into the teachers' lounge at Bostwick Elementary. After work and school they met in their home office, where he'd fill her in on his outrageous conversations with clients and she'd bounce ideas off him about Peter and his antics with his imaginary dog, Dominick. They dedicated Sundays and Wednesday evenings to worship and Bible study and ended each day with prayer.

At the first of the year he started spending more time in his home office, and they were together even more. As a young, childless, married couple they had nothing but time and energy for each other. They spent their evenings either one-upping each other in the kitchen or trying out a new eatery or jazz club downtown. Kevin helped her get past her fear of bugs long enough to hike with him one Saturday a month. She bribed him into watching classic movies on Sunday afternoons. At night, they exercised their passion for each other in more intimate, and just as fulfilling, ways. They had a good marriage . . . or so Evelyn thought.

Six weeks ago, she had noticed Kevin's phone charging in their bedroom. Just as she had disconnected it to take downstairs, a text message from "Samantha Jane" highlighted the screen: I know you said it was a mistake, but I miss you.

Evelyn might have hesitated at Granny B's, but she suffered no such compunction before typing in the password for

Kevin's phone, something she'd never before felt the need to do. Dread became horror as she'd followed the trail of messages: Meeting starts at 10 . . . Can you believe Jim? LOL . . . On for lunch? . . . What flight are you on? . . . Is that a new suit? Looking good! Then: Thanks for being there for me when I needed a friend . . . I've always loved talking to you, but I had no idea . . . If you ever need ANYTHING, including me . . . Last night was wonderful, and I have no regrets . . . Love, me . . . I miss you.

Evelyn brushed away a tear and busied herself with the papers on her drafting table until she could steady herself and avoid Kevin's eyes heating the curls on her crown.

"Speaking of calls, when is the last time you talked to Granny B? You didn't go last Saturday. How is she?"

Her grandma had tossed away the title "Mrs. Agnew" years ago. She wore "Granny B" the same way she always wore her comfortable lace-up shoes and single hair braid. Everyone called her by this name, whether tied to her by blood, marriage, or community, from the county sheriff to the cashier at the fish market.

But as far as Evelyn was concerned, Kevin cut all ties when he spent the night in Atlanta with Samantha Washington— Samantha *Jane* Washington. She wasn't Granny B to him anymore. He lost that right—no, he *spit* on that right that "wonderful" night he spit on the right to call her Evie. Even if they had *just* come close to sleeping together before he'd remembered he had a wife at home.

"Evelyn? I said, how is—?"

"The same as always." She finished arranging and rearranging her pencils and setting up her large manuscript pages on the tabletop. She adjusted the light so that it shone directly on the square of space where she designed her story. Evelyn studied her implements and opted for a blood red. A fiery red. The color of her anger and the hook-and-ladder truck Peter and Dominick were watching pass Peter's house on Kirkpatrick Street.

"And how is that?"

She's angry, righteously so. Betrayed! Evelyn raged, not sure if she was describing herself or her Granny B. But she only murmured, "Not different." As far as she knew anyway. She hadn't spoken to her since being kicked out, but Kevin didn't know anything about that.

There were a lot of things he didn't know.

Evelyn threw down her pencil and pushed away from the table. She dragged her eyes upward to meet his. "Kevin. What is it? What do you want from me? You don't really care about my grandmother."

"As much as it hurts hearing you've kicked me out of the exclusive Agnew club, I'm grateful you're finally talking to me. But, Ev, you can't believe I don't care about Gran—Miss Beatrice. Or you."

Before she could respond, they both turned toward the tickety-tap of their Yorkshire terrier's nails on the hardwood floor, descending the stairs. Cocoa rounded the corner into the room and tickety-tickety-tickety-tapped over to her mama. She scratched gently against Evelyn's bare legs. Evelyn reached down and scooped her up, nuzzling her under her chin, snuggling Cocoa close to her heart.

Kevin did not wade across the deep, wide breach. Instead, he stuck a toe in the water, speaking quietly from behind the shelter of his desk, his face partially hidden behind his computer. "Of course I care about Granny B. I love her. She's my family too."

Too, another tiny word that packed a powerful punch. "You don't betray someone you love." A little voice in her wanted to add *hypocrite, but she smothered* it—not because it would hurt him, but because it condemned Evelyn herself for her own crimes and misdemeanors. She cradled Cocoa under her left arm, and with her right she stuffed her pages into a portfolio and dropped her pencils into a carrying case. *Why did I think I could get any work done here with him?*

"Maybe, but you do make mistakes. And the people you love forgive you." Kevin moved out from the protective shelter of his desk as he delved into deeper, murkier waters.

"I'm so sick of hearing you spout off about forgiveness!" Evelyn threw her remaining materials into her bag helter-skelter. "How could you, Kevin? What did I do . . . what *didn't* I do that made you need a relationship with this woman? That's what it was, a relationship, not an 'accident'!"

Cocoa yelped and wriggled from Evelyn's overly tight embrace, hopped onto the floor, and scurried over to the safety of the love seat under the window. Evelyn crossed her arms over her midsection to warm herself in the absence of her pet, trying to calm her now-churning stomach. She prayed there wouldn't be a repeat of their last confrontation.

"We're friends . . . we *were* friends!"

She pounced on the present tense. "So you're *still* friends. Friends? After all this . . . all this . . . this 'I'm sorry; please forgive me'? But you know what? You should never have been friends in the first place, let alone *still*! You *work* together, Kevin. More specifically, she works *for* you. Which means there should never. Have been. A friendship." Evelyn jabbed her index finger in the air, emphasizing each phrase. "It was an *employer-employee* relationship. In fact, she can sue you! That's sounding like a pretty smart thing to do. If you're going to cheat, at least be smart about it."

"Sam didn't work for me. She worked for Eric—"

"Sam. How cute. 'Sam didn't work for me.' But that's all you have to say? *That's* your excuse?" Evelyn huffed. "Wait a minute, *worked*? What do you mean *worked*?"

"You couldn't possibly think we'd still be working together." Kevin raked his right hand down his face, a habit of his that had made her smile not that long ago. "Samantha Jane quit. She's moving to Illinois." He sighed. "And yes, she could sue me, I suppose, but she wouldn't."

Evelyn smirked. "Of course not, because you're such good *friends*." Crushed herself, she could muster no sympathy for his admin's abrupt leave-taking. "A broken heart?"

"She didn't love me, Evie, despite what she said." Kevin stepped closer. Cocoa growled from the couch. Ignoring the dog, he whispered, "And I didn't love her. I love you. You know I do."

She winced at her name and at his nearness. In a voice that was more hiss than hush, Evelyn responded, "What I know is that you left me, if only for a day, a moment. Okay, so you just came this close—" Evelyn held two fingers a millimeter apart—"to having sex with her, but you were unfaithful to me, and you know it. You chose to spend time with her, you gave in to a mutual attraction, you became besties . . ." Her laugh held no humor. "You shared something precious with someone you say you don't even love, Kevin, something you share with me. So how can you really love *me*? And if you do, how can you *not* love her?"

He shook his head, perhaps to clear away the fuzziness created by Evelyn's reasoning, but still he tried to speak. "Ev—"

But she couldn't stand, physically or emotionally, to hear him defend something she considered indefensible. Her empty stomach rebelled against all the emotions roiling around within and without. She backed away from him, shaking her head and holding up a hand to ward him off. Evelyn snatched up her bag and scooped Cocoa from the sofa.

This was the closest she'd been to Kevin in weeks, since she'd thrown up all over his feet. As if willing to risk another pair of shoes to maintain their connection, however fractured and tenuous, he pursued her to their family room. Though he didn't touch Evelyn, he used his considerable size to block her from rushing pell-mell through the room and to the garage.

"Evelyn—"

She drew up short. "If you touch me . . . Please, just—just . . . don't touch me. I don't think I could take it." She shook from head to toe.

"Okay. Okay. But you look terrible." Instead of reaching for her, Kevin held up his hands in surrender and backed toward the kitchen.

Evelyn watched his retreat, thinking of how he used touch to communicate: kissing her nose instead of saying hello; squeezing her knee under the table to let her know his plans for dessert; playing with her hair to show he was listening while she talked about her students; cupping her shoulder in church to indicate he was getting sleepy and needed some gum. Whenever she was within reach, he was reaching for her. She knew it showed incredible restraint for him to back away at that moment and offer:

"Water. I'm getting you some water."

As if that would quench her dry, thirsty places.

"No. Nothing. Wait! Uh, yes, juice. Orange juice, please. With ice?" Evelyn's physical needs overwhelmed her emotional ones, and succumbing, she plonked her things down on the coffee table and fell in a heap into the overstuffed armchair in the corner. She hated to depend on him for anything, but she knew she couldn't take another step, even to help herself.

One minute later she was sipping an icy tumbler of juice. Five minutes after that, her meager stomach contents decided they would stay put, at least for the moment. She rested her head on the tufted back of the chair and closed her eyes.

When she opened them, more than an hour had passed, and a delicious smell wafted from the kitchen. She stretched and sniffed her way in its direction. She peeked around the kitchen door at Kevin.

He stood there with his shirtsleeves rolled up, handsome, focused, in his element in the kitchen as much as he was in the boardroom. And in the bedroom. Looking up from the twelve-inch skillet he was standing over, he gave her a small smile, the gap between his front teeth winking at her a bit, making his perfect, chiseled jawline a little less perfect, a little more approachable. She almost smiled back at him.

Almost.

Instead, she nodded toward the cast-iron pan. "Is that—?"

"Chicken Lester." They locked eyes for a moment.

The first time she'd prepared the dish—a thinly disguised chicken marsala—they were newly married. Kevin had just started his company, and money was very tight, too tight to waste on wine they didn't drink. Instead of splurging on a bottle for a test-case meal, she and Kevin had substituted homemade chicken broth and a cardboard carton of the cheapest mushrooms they could find. They'd dubbed the successful result chicken Lester forever after.

"Hungry?"

She just about shook her head, but her stomach, appeased by the calcium-fortified orange juice an hour earlier, was now fully alert and ready for action. Evelyn nodded. "Can I help you with anything?"

"Almost done. Why don't you freshen up and meet me at the table?"

Evelyn accepted his offer and retreated up the back stairs to the landing and hastened to their bedroom. Getting ready didn't take long, especially after her dry run a couple of weeks ago.

"Evelyn!"

Freshly showered, dressed, and packed, Evelyn quietly took her bags down the front stairs and circled around through the mudroom. She tucked them by the back door leading to the garage. Kevin, busy setting the table in the sunroom on the other side of the kitchen, didn't hear her as she retraced her steps to the second floor so she could descend the back stairs. Evelyn arrived at the table a little out of breath but ready for her last supper.

"You feeling better?" Kevin set down her plate and pulled back her chair. He stood there, obviously waiting for Evelyn to sit down.

"Why don't you go ahead and sit, and I'll bring your plate so we can sit down together?"

"O-okay." Kevin sat—directly to her right instead of across from her at his usual place—and sipped from his water glass. Evelyn centered his plate on his mat before sitting down. Instinctually, she covered his hand with hers, and hands clasped and heads bowed, Kevin asked for God's blessings on their meal.

This is why I have to go, Evelyn thought. *I'll fall back into habits and rituals without thinking about what I'm doing.* Bile rose into her throat. *And I will* not *forget.*

They ate quietly, exchanging a few banal comments. When the meal ended, she crossed her fork and knife on the plate and pushed it away. She clasped her hands under her chin, almost as if to pray, and took a deep breath, but Kevin stopped her as she parted her lips to speak.

"You look beautiful, Evelyn. You really do. Even more than usual."

His light-brown eyes caressed her face, something she didn't think she could ever let his hands do again. All she could think about were his hands touching *Samantha Jane, who missed him.* Avoiding his eyes that looked hungry for her despite the filling meal, Evelyn studied the remains on her dish instead, giving herself and him time to digest both the food and the moment. "Thank you," she murmured. "Kevin—"

"Evelyn." They spoke in unison. He paused, but then he continued instead of letting her speak first, as his father had surely trained his oldest son. "Evelyn, we can make it through this. We just need to take some time, to talk it through. What we have is good. It's based on truth, no matter what it looks like now." He swallowed. When he started to speak again, his voice cracked. "I'm sorry. I am *so* sorry. I don't know how I could have betrayed you by even looking at another woman, let alone getting close enough to . . . to consider having an affair with her, but I do know it will *never happen again.*"

Evelyn blinked to break their connection and focused on the Scripture from 2 Corinthians she had read earlier that day: *"Persecuted, but not abandoned; struck down, but not destroyed."* Her resolve renewed, she met his eyes, and this time she did not waver. She refused to let her condition force her from the table and to the bathroom or worse, to the bedroom with Kevin to forgive and forget. She spoke quickly, definitively. "I'm leaving, Kevin."

"What? What do you mean—?"

"I'm leaving. You. Tonight."

"B-but what about this—?"

"This what? Dinner? It was delicious. Thank you. It was perfectly cooked, and actually, it was well-timed. I couldn't think of a better way to remind myself of what we had, of what you threw away when you nearly *had sex* with that woman." She could feel the heat rising from her toes, working its way up to the collar of her loose, printed shirt.

"You say, 'I know it won't happen again,' but in the same breath you admit you have no idea *how* it happened in the first place. If that's the case, how can you promise you can prevent this from happening again? How can you sit there and tell me our marriage is based on truth? What truth? Whose truth? You lied to me when you hid your attraction to her, and you kept lying for another six months when you hid what happened that night. If I hadn't read those messages, you'd still be lying now with your lips clamped shut on the truth, telling me how much you love me instead of telling me how sorry you are. As far as I'm concerned, you might as well have had sex with her because you wanted to."

Evelyn stood. The napkin resting in her lap dropped to the floor. "How can I trust you?" She wanted to ask him, *How can* we *trust you?*

Kevin's silence didn't answer either question.

"I love you, but I don't believe you. And I can't trust you with my . . . with my heart." Evelyn wasn't sure what had almost slipped through her lips, between the crack in her defenses, but she knew she had to leave before the walls crumbled completely and she said too much. "I don't know where we're headed. All I can do is *feel* right now. I can't think clearly, whether to stay or to go—"

"But you *are* going!" Kevin exploded to his feet, throwing his napkin on the table.

Subconsciously her feet made truth of his words as she backed up a step from him, toward the door, but she continued to face him. "I am going, but . . . but . . . I'm not moving out, at least not . . . not permanently." Evelyn struggled because in her heart, she really did want to go. For good. But her head told her that this was her brokenness talking, her passionate nature. She knew she needed space and time to pray. "I don't want to rush into anything, Kevin, whether it's to work this out or to let my lawyer do it for me."

He inhaled sharply at that, and his eyes widened.

Evelyn sensed he had never entertained that thought, the idea that she would divorce him. He seemed to shrink a few inches, to diminish physically as he swallowed his emotions. She watched him sink into his chair.

"But our house is big enough. I can move to a guest room, to the basement."

Evelyn allowed a tiny smile. "No, Kevin, it's not big enough. I see that tonight. If I stay any longer, we'll be eating by candlelight and making love after dinner, and I'll let that erase what happened without dealing with it. There's too much at stake for me to let that happen."

"Have you prayed about this, Evelyn?"

"Did you and Samantha Jane pray about it?"

He squeezed his eyes closed. One hand covered the other that was curled into a fist. He rested his forehead on his clasped knuckles.

"Really, Kevin, did you?"

He shook his head, once, twice, but he kept his eyes closed, his head bowed, seemingly submitting to God's will even as he resisted his wife's.

"Well, okay then. I'll pray about *us* long and hard. Believe me. I know you have a long trip coming up. When you leave for Europe, I'll return. We both have work to do, and I don't think we'll get much done if we stay here together."

She waited a minute, giving him time to respond, but Kevin said nothing. He just continued to shake his head. She turned away from the tears that seeped from the corners of his eyes.

"Cocoa!" From out of nowhere the dog pitter-pattered to

her and she picked her up. "Good-bye, Kevin. I'll pray for your success and safety." Evelyn turned away.

"Do you really think God will hear you if your heart isn't right?"

Evelyn gasped at the sucker punch. *If* my *heart isn't right.* She gathered her bags she'd stowed by the door and added Cocoa's leash and travel case. She turned back in his direction. It was his turn to stare out the window into the backyard. "You'd better hope so."

With these whispered words Evelyn loaded Cocoa and their things into her Acura SUV. She pressed the button overhead to open the garage door. She backed down the drive and turned her car in the direction of Mount Laurel. To Mama's.

It was time to go home.

Chapter Five

A WEEK INTO HER VISIT, Evelyn determined home wasn't that sweet.

Jackson spent his free time attached to his PlayStation controller, enjoying his last months before college. Her childhood friend Maxine Owens had to leave on a writing assignment. She couldn't picture what Peter would do next in her story because all she saw was Kevin, boarding the flight for Europe. Arm in arm with Samantha Jane. Swapping salted peanut–flavored kisses in business class.

So she wore herself out running here and there. From Harris Teeter with groceries. From her sister's phone calls. From her mama's observing eyes. From thoughts of Granny B.

Today, Evelyn's fleeing feet had led her to Headquarters, the full-service salon Elisabeth—Lis—had opened the year her husband died. Evelyn got there early for their "date" to visit her daddy's grave site, so she hid behind the wood-and-iron screen in the lobby.

Lis strode through the aisles in her three-inch-heeled sandals. She leaned in close to a stylist's ear and graced her with her Southern, yet professional lilt. "Laurie, you must base your client completely before using the chemical. Let me show you, dear." Effortlessly, yet surely mindful of the expensive red pantsuit she was wearing, Lis demonstrated how to liberally spread the coating behind the ears, above the brows, and around the temple, protecting her client from chemical burns. Done, she stripped off the gloves as she depressed the trash can's pedal with a red-tipped toe. Again, she leaned into her stylist.

Evelyn watched her mama's lips move as Laurie bobbed her head up and down and blinked back tears. Then Lis smiled again and moved toward her office nestled in the rear. On her way she chatted with two other clients sitting under cooled hair dryers. Mama hated to see customers idle like cars at a red light. Tired of wasting gas herself, Evelyn gathered her bag and stepped into view.

"Evelyn! Is that you?"

"Girl, you look good!"

"Isn't she though? Just like her sister—"

"And her *mama*."

"Miss Lis didn't tell me you were home . . ."

Evelyn played the role of visiting dignitary as she stopped

to formally introduce herself to Laurie and chat it up with Saundra, John, and the other stylists who had been family to Lis since Graham's death. She shared some Krispy Kreme doughnuts she'd picked up, handed out smiles and promises to visit soon, and wound her way to the back.

Before Evelyn could tap-tap on the partially open door, she heard her mama expel a breath and mutter, "Order dryer caps. Track anti-humectant shipment. Discuss procedures with stylists. Do something with Evelyn."

Evelyn swung open the door. "I have some ideas if you're fresh out."

Lis barely blinked an eye as she set down the pen and notepad. "I was wondering when you'd come out from hiding. Now be careful you don't knock my dress off the hanger. I'm changing out of this pantsuit before we visit your daddy. I'll be ready to go in a minute."

Of course Mama knew I was there. Evelyn stepped in the room and closed the door quietly behind her. The green sundress hanging on the back of the door swung side to side before coming to a stop.

As she watched her mama shuffle papers, Evelyn's eyes zeroed in on a photograph on the corner of Lis's desk. In it, a tuxedoed Graham and Evelyn in a white ball gown posed at the top of a winding staircase. Evelyn was thirteen, a year before Daddy died, on the night she'd tucked her left hand into his right arm so he could usher her into Mount Laurel society. She could still smell his Old Spice. Still feel the taffeta crinkle every step she took. Still hear Mama's voice.

"Now, don't show all your teeth, girl. You know how your eyes close when you smile too big."

"Darn if you didn't show all those pearly whites during that first dance."

Lis's words plucked Evelyn from her reverie.

"That was because Daddy told me, 'Evelyn, you're the most beautiful girl in the world' when we danced that night."

"And you were."

Evelyn felt her forbidden, yet familiar smile stretch toward her earlobes. "Why, Ma—"

"Miss Lis, you asked me to stop in when I was through?" Laurie peeked in. She made the shortened version of Elisabeth's name sound like a *z*.

Evelyn whirled toward the door. This time her mama, too, looked unsettled, like she was caught between a rock and a hard place. Or maybe it irked her to hear her name mispronounced.

"Did you still want to see me?" The stylist stepped deeper into the office.

Lis looked from her daughter to her employee and seemingly opted for the hard place. "Laurie, why don't you throw a load of towels in, unpack the new shampoo, and restock the shelves up front? I'll catch up with you after my date."

Laurie swallowed the directive soaked in the syrup of Lis's mellow drawl. "Yes, ma'am. Good to meet you, Evelyn."

"You, too."

Lis moved Evelyn's photograph to a bookshelf and faced her baby girl.

Evelyn itched beneath her once-over. "What?"

"Nothing. Just admiring that color on you."

"Really? Actually, I thought of you when I bought this dress."

"Re-ally?" Lis's right brow arched delicately as the word dripped from her mouth. "How so? And why don't you come closer so I can see you properly."

The better to criticize you with, my dear. Evelyn crossed in front of the file cabinet and stepped around the desk. "Well, I know how much you like Carolina blue. And you told me A-line dresses complement my figure." *Actually, what you said was "They're good at hiding what you don't want people to see."*

"Well, it won't complement it for long if you keep popping those." Lis nodded toward the Krispy Kreme box.

"Do you dive this deep into Yolanda's or Lionel's business?" Evelyn perched a hip on the edge of the desk.

"Why are you worried about Yolanda or Lionel?"

"Why are you worried about me?"

"Maybe I love you more."

Her employees might have mistaken Lis's pursed lips for a smile, but Evelyn knew better. She snorted. "Maybe you need to love me a little bit less." She plopped the box down where her picture had sat moments before. "Besides, I thought we could celebrate." *And I had a craving for a glazed doughnut.*

"Celebrate what?"

"My visit, of course."

"Oh . . . of course." Lis moved aside some paperwork and

peeked into the box. She smiled sincerely and extracted a glazed lemon-filled doughnut. "Why didn't I think of that?"

Because you're too busy thinking up ways to drive me nuts. Evelyn didn't voice her thoughts but was sure her face spoke volumes, especially to her mother, who was extremely well-read in all things Evelyn.

"Well, speaking of celebrations . . . what about mine? Is your aunt Sarah going to make it? I know they'll have to work around her husband's schedule at the hospital. And gracious, where will all those children sleep? She never goes anywhere without them. Maybe she's afraid they'll run away when she's not looking, though it would serve her right. But don't tell her I said so." She chuckled wryly. "You know, even though she left Spring Hope as soon as she could, I don't think Spring Hope ever left her. Maybe that's why we get along."

Evelyn knew the family still referred to Sarah as the "knee baby"; Mama's youngest sister was barely out of her cloth diapers when Milton arrived. Sarah's husband, Samuel, headed the emergency department at a New York City hospital while she homeschooled their six children.

Elisabeth used her pinkie finger to flick off a bit of glaze from the corner of her crimson mouth. "Yolanda says she can't seem to pin you down these days, so you and Kevin must be trying to keep something big under wraps. What have you two cooked up for my birthday?"

"Kevin?"

"Yes. Kevin. Your husband?" Her eyes pored over her

daughter's face. "Is everything all right? Is his job okay? Believe me, I know how hard it can be to run your own business. Hard on the finances . . . and a marriage."

"There you go again. Are you as concerned about Lionel and Yolanda? Just because my sister and brother are such successful movers and shakers doesn't mean that they're doing any better—or worse—than I am." Evelyn slowly extracted a slightly warm glazed doughnut and chewed hard to ignore the pangs of her conscience. *Of course Kevin and I are doing worse than everybody else. Why else would I be sitting here in Mama's office getting lectured about eating a doughnut? That is, of course, unless Yolanda's husband is a philanderer, too. Or maybe Lionel's wife is fighting some inner demons. Not that anyone would have ever thought Kevin had horns and a tail.*

"Evelyn . . . Evelyn . . . Evelyn. Why are you always comparing yourself? They're my children, same as you." Lis unlocked the bottom left drawer and withdrew a stack of receipts. She started arranging them in three piles on her desk. "I'm just as concerned about them as I am about you. Why wouldn't I be? But I don't have to go through these changes with Yolanda and Lionel. I just ask Lionel, 'Baby, how're things with your wife?' and he says, 'Mama, well, you know Muriel was mad at me last week because I was working too much . . .'" She added a receipt to the second stack and glared at Evelyn. "All you need to do is share with me every now and again—"

At that moment, the door opened and Laurie—Lis's rock—poked her head around the crack. "Uh, excuse me.

I'm finished. Do you want me to take a client off the floor and—?"

"No!" Lis rose, disturbing her neat rectangles.

To Evelyn, Laurie looked as ruffled as the receipts on her mama's desk.

"Just take over the phone from Charlie, will you?"

Laurie nodded silently, her brow furrowed, and backed out of the room.

Evelyn faced her mother. "What's going on with her?"

"So we can talk about Laurie's business, just not yours?"

As Evelyn drew in a deep breath, she thought about Kevin and his big secret, Granny B, and what she herself was carrying around these days. "I don't mean to sound defensive, Mama. I do appreciate your concern. If I needed your help . . . umm-hmm . . . If I had something to tell you, I would." Now, *that* was closer to the truth. Oh, there was so much more than that. So much more that she would not, could not say to Mama. Her mother's look told her she knew it, too. She conjured up a smile and wiggled the dough-nut in the air. "Mama. Listen. I'm great. Kevin is great—everything's great. Now why don't we talk about something else? How does that sound?"

"Great," Mama muttered. She lowered herself to her chair and straightened her bundles. "But you'd probably better quit with the doughnuts while you're ahead, Evelyn. We will be going out to dinner tonight after visiting your daddy's grave."

"M—"

"And speaking of visits . . . what about my mama, Evelyn? When are you planning to visit her?"

So far, she'd sidestepped anything that might reveal last month's Situation (and she'd forever use capital letters when she thought of It, kind of like "the Flood" or "the Fall"). But nothing was easy with Mama. Evelyn shifted from one cheek to the other on the corner of her desk.

Lis licked her doughnut's gooey lemon center. "You've been here almost a week, and you haven't made it to Spring Hope yet."

"Umm . . ."

"'Umm'?"

"Well . . ."

"'Well' what?"

"Well, I—"

The office phone jangled. Lis held up a long finger. "Hold that thought. Headquarters. This is Elisabeth."

Evelyn decided to walk through the door of opportunity and hopped off the desk. She wiggled her fingers good-bye and mouthed, "I'll pick up the flowers." If she left now, she'd have time to lie down for an hour or so before meeting her mother at Hillcrest Cemetery.

She had a feeling she was going to need some reinforcements.

Chapter Six

EVELYN KNEW GRANNY B had buried her the moment she'd stumbled down her three concrete steps and slunk away in her car. Not six feet under the wiry Bermuda grass and a pile of sandy North Carolina soil, but deep down in the back of her mind where she cataloged and closely monitored all the hurts and wrongs done to her. When Evelyn left Headquarters, she knew she'd have to find some way to explain to her mama why Granny B definitely wouldn't attend her birthday party this fall. Why she wouldn't see Granny B anytime soon.

But Lis beat her to it.

"She's dying, Evelyn. Mama is going to die."

Evelyn stared, struck dumb. It would've been a picture-perfect moment—Lis, clad in the heather-green frock, perched on the edge of the wooden bench, the sun a golden halo—if not for the silent stream of tears dripping unchecked into the pot of gardenias in her lap. The tears . . . and the headstones that dotted the Hillcrest Cemetery hillside.

A chattering blue jay broke the silence. Lis swiped at her cheeks, replacing the tears with streaks of dirt. Evelyn swallowed her rising panic and tried not to choke on the news.

"Wait a minute, Mama. Back up. Start over."

Lis took a breath. "You remember Ruby Tagle?" Her voice was deeper, the words spoken more slowly, her accent more pronounced.

"Mama, why—?"

"Girl, just answer the question."

Memories of warm molasses cookies, butter-frosted pound cakes, collard greens and salt pork, and honey-glazed ham washed over her. "Of course I know Ruby Tagle. My friend Maxine's grandmother. Oh, you mean, *she's* dying? But you said—"

"I got a call from her this morning at the shop. Remember? Right before you left. You know, they're pretty close—well, as close as Mama is to anybody, other than you—"

"Are you doing this on purpose?"

"Anyway, Mrs. Tagle is Mama's emergency contact. After Dr. Hedgepeth talked to her, she immediately called me."

"Emergency." She rolled the word around on her tongue. "What emergency?" *Crusty people don't get sick. They just get crustier until God says, "Enough." Right?*

"Thank God he's known our family for so long and is willing to break that hippo law thing."

HIPAA, Evelyn thought automatically but figured this wasn't the time to correct her. And Evelyn sure wasn't ready to thank God for anything yet. "What's wrong with Granny B? Is it a heart problem? You can't just tell me she's dying without telling me what the doctor said. Is this a second opinion? What do we need to do?" Resolve crumbled as panic snowballed and gathered momentum.

"Evelyn, I told you practically all that I know! Mama is . . . she has . . ."

"Cancer?"

"Yes! I mean , . . no. It's . . . She has something called acute myeloid leukemia."

Boy, that's a mouthful. Sounds deadly. "What is that exactly? What do we do now?"

Lis jumped to her feet. The pot hit the ground and rolled against the headstone. *Graham Willis. Son. Husband. Father. Child of God.* "'*We?* What do *we* do?' And just who is 'we,' Evelyn?"

"You, Granny B, me—you know, *we.* What's with that look? If there isn't a 'we,' then why are you telling me? You know I love Granny B, that I want to do whatever I can—"

"And why do I know that, Evelyn? '*We*' haven't given a whit about her, not enough to go see her once the last month or so. You've been 'just too busy,' 'so booked up,' 'had a full itinerary.'" As Lis elucidated all her daughter's excuses, she stepped closer, crushing a white blossom underfoot. "You've been home for a week, and you have not so much as said one word about her. Where was this great love of yours for Mama that you now sit here telling me about? Hmmph, 'What do *we* do now?'"

Now was not the time for Evelyn to explain the Reason she hadn't gone to see her elderly grandmother—for all of a sudden that was what Granny B was: her *elderly* grandmother, an infirm person, not the strapping, healthful, ice-crunching old lady who'd turned her from her home without blinking. No, that terrible Incident had been wiped away with just the whisper of the word *dying*. Now she needed to add sugar cubes to the trough so her mama would drink.

"Okay, listen. No matter what happened in the past, that is exactly what and where it is: the past. You know that people say and do a lot of things . . . things that really don't mean much in the long run or in the short run either. What will mean a lot more is what I—*we*—do right now. You just said yourself that I'm the closest person to her, so it makes sense for me to reach out to her, especially now."

Lis looked away. Evelyn admired her beautiful, dirt-smudged profile before she started searching her pockets. She considered cleaning her mama's face with a slightly crumpled, sugar-crusted napkin from Krispy Kreme, but she handed it to her so she could do it herself.

Lis retrieved a handkerchief from her own pocket. She dabbed at her cheeks and smoothed her ever-perfect coiffure. "You know what makes sense? If you had shown her these past few weeks even a tenth of the concern you're showing now, *we* wouldn't be in this situation. Mama probably would have confided in you, and we would have known how to help her. *We* could have saved her, Evelyn."

She dropped to her knees and stabbed at the dirt with her spade. Lis was much like Granny B: everything had its place, and if it didn't know where to go, she'd put it there, including Evelyn.

Much as Kevin had controlled himself and merely offered her a glass of orange juice, Evelyn silently took the spade from her mama and gently used it to lower the trampled gardenias into the hole. Lis and Evelyn spent the next hour wordlessly planting and cleaning away the dead leaves, bits of trash, and old flowers from the family plots. When they finished, Evelyn distributed a few of the new plants to the graves of Grandpa and Grandma Willis. The tension in their heartstrings gradually loosened.

When Lis moved to stand, Evelyn rose quickly and cupped her elbow. Lis pulled away and rose with little effort, but Evelyn looped her arm through her mama's and edged closer. Together they returned to the bench under the Southern live oak tree. Its roots stretched unseen beneath the headstones.

Lis's eyes drifted far away from Hillcrest. "You know, your grandmother's always watering those hydrangeas."

"She is?"

"You thought she'd let them die, what with all that work planting them? You always seem to have a way with her. At least you used to."

"Mama—"

"When I was down there digging, I thought back to when she used to send all of us out to Booker Perkins's garden. Well, he called it a garden, but it was really this huge plot of land he owned where he grew corn, beans, peas, all kinds of vegetables. Every summer, he'd come by our house at the crack of dawn and load us all up in the back of his truck. Over a few weeks' time, we'd clear that whole piece of land."

"How old were you?"

"When we started going, Sarah wasn't as tall as a tobacco leaf. I'd have the taller ones pick from the highest rows and the rest of us gather up what was left. Little Ed pushed the wagons." She gazed into yesteryear's fields, seemingly unmindful of her fresh flow of tears.

Evelyn didn't know if her mama was mourning what once was or what was to come.

"Thomas was kinda fragile, so he didn't help much. But he'd lead us all in singing or telling stories. He could imitate Mama or Mr. Perkins. Almost anybody. He'd have us all laughing about one thing or another before long, distracting Little Ed from worrying about messing up those pretty hands of his."

"Y'all could laugh in that heat?"

"Girl, that work kept us out of Mama's sight. She would have had us doing something much worse, I know. Besides, we would have plenty enough time later to be around the house as we got the vegetables ready for canning and storing."

"I can see Ruthena out there now, praying for God to help her pick that corn."

Lis swatted a mosquito. "No, Ruthena wasn't out there with us. At least, not after the first picking season or two. She kept her color most of the year 'cause you can't get a whole lot of sun when it's streaming through stained-glass windows."

"Come again?"

"Ruthena spent most of her time in church. Personally, I think her preoccupation with the Lord began with her simple wish to beat the heat—mostly the kind Mama laid on us. Ruthena made friends with the missionary group from church, so they put her to work most days after school and during the summer. She'd be running around delivering plates of food and Bibles to the sick and shut-in. She took prayer cloths to folk, ran errands for the pastor—it was Pastor John back then—dusted off the pulpit and choir hymnals. Ruthena wouldn't show up back at Mama's until long after we were home."

"How did Granny B feel about that?"

"Ruthena wasn't quite as holy then as she is now, so she was much easier to live with. As long as Ruthena didn't try to save everybody, Mama was fine with her work in the church. Besides, membership has its privileges, as they say. Mama got a few free plates of food in her time, and with us working in Mr. Perkins's fields most of the summer and Ruthena doing the Lord's work, all the bases were covered. We stayed out of trouble. Of course, Little Ed didn't cooperate for long."

Lis stood and gracefully stretched her back and neck. "Mama didn't look to God to provide, at least not to provide in the way you think. She didn't believe in letting her burdens down. They kept her warm at night in a way none of us kids could. Mama believed God saved her, but her salvation gave her something to look forward to, not something she got to enjoy here on Earth. You wouldn't find her in church, singing His praises. She stuck to doing His work at home. For her, *we* were the Lord's work."

Without warning, Lis grasped Evelyn's right hand with both of hers. She leaned in to her, blocking out the sun, the branches of the oak tree, the headstones around them. "Evelyn, it's time for us to do the Lord's work now. Mama needs us. Not you or me laying prayer cloths on her or dousing her with oil like Ruthena. But *us*.

"Mama never asked us for anything. I never even heard her ask God for something. We just made the best of what He gave us because it took all of us to survive. Evelyn, I want my mama to stop looking to heaven to end all her pain. I want her to find peace and joy now, on Earth, 'in the land of the living,' like the psalm says. And she can do it if we help her."

Evelyn tried to tug her hand from that inexorable, painful grip.

"She needs a constant presence in her life, someone she can depend on even when she doesn't want to depend on anybody. She's had that in God, but He works through our hands and feet, too. What Mama doesn't need is someone feeling sorry for her, somebody whose main purpose is to clear a guilty conscience . . ." Lis glanced down for a second before again interlocking their eyes. "However well-deserved that guilt may be."

Evelyn didn't curl her fingers around the ones clutching hers, but she stopped pulling away. "I know you feel this need to protect Granny B from me . . . but you need my support just as much as she does. It makes no sense for the two of us to fight like this."

Then Evelyn finally did intertwine their fingers. This time she wouldn't let *her* go. In a lowered voice she importuned, "Please. Just tell me what you need me to do. I can talk to the doctor, run errands for you—anything you need while you're taking care of Granny B. I can pick up prescriptions—"

"I need you to see your Granny B."

Evelyn nodded vigorously. "Oh, of course! I'll extend my trip. I was thinking that next week, once you've had the chance to talk—"

"To-mor-row." Lis peeled away her fingers. Then her two soft, sweetly scented hands gently, yet firmly, cupped her daughter's face. "Tomorrow." With that she stood. "Now, let's get out of this heat and give your daddy some rest."

Chapter Seven

"ARE YOU AWAKE? I assumed you wanted to get a good start on the day. It's getting late."

"Yes, Mama," Evelyn called out wearily to the voice on the other side of her door. But she only squeezed shut her eyes and rolled away from the sunlight. Cocoa greeted her with a slurp. Evelyn wiped her nose and mouth. "Ugh. Down, girl."

Lis poked her head in. "Well, all right then. You'll have to drive my car because Jackson drove yours to work. You know you shouldn't park behind me. And keep that dog out the bed."

Her mama's promise—or threat—of "tomorrow" had played ping-pong with memories of yesterday all night.

Groggy, Evelyn swung her feet to the floor as her mama's carpeted footsteps whispered their retreat. When the room remained in its rightful place, she stumbled to the bathroom and studied her reflection in the mirror. She shook her head slightly at her spiky hair and the dark circles marring the pecan tan under her eyes. "Oh, Aunt Mary would have a fit!"

Evelyn could picture her aunt's flaming lips, arched brows, and bejeweled hands. But it wasn't always that way. Years earlier, as a new divorcée with a young son, Mary had been forced to move back home to Granny B's, an arrangement that had lasted a mere three weeks. "Once in a lifetime was enough for anyone, and I had the nerve to try it twice!" she'd whispered to her niece one day, shucking corn on Granny B's porch. When her son got his football contract with the Seahawks, Mary dropped everything and moved to Seattle, grasping her newfound wealth with both hands.

Evelyn turned away from the mirror and her memories to focus on the battle at hand. She nudged the faucet all the way over to cold, hoping that dose of icy reality would help her get all her ducks in a row, as she mentally rejected one outfit after another. *What do you wear to a war?*

Finally Evelyn decided on a loose, sleeveless sun-splashed shift that provided some maneuvering room. She lacked an iron breastplate, helmet, or protective mask, but the dress fit nicely over her full armor of God to help her brave the trip to Spring Hope.

The sun lit the way to Granny B's. Trees were a green blur as Evelyn watched her speedometer creep from sixty-seven . . . to seventy-one . . . to seventy-five miles per hour. Her desire to be on the other side of the trip surpassed her dread.

What will I find once I arrive? It'd be just like Granny B to pretend Evelyn wasn't there, sweeping over her feet—taking away all her good luck, her aunt Sissy once warned—and go about her usual business. *Oh, Aunt Sissy, how I wish you were here now. I could use some reinforcements!*

Thoughts of Granny B's son Thomas and Sissy, his common-law wife, made her smile. They lived with their four children in Chesterfield, Virginia, where he was a founding partner of a family law firm and she managed the office. When the childless Ruthena first heard about their living situation, she went to her "sisters" for prayer—Sister Smith, Sister Jackson, and Sister Williams—at the Palmer Tabernacle Church of the Living Waters. Evelyn knew they might as well get up from their knees because Sissy wasn't going anywhere, if her twenty-five year-long relationship with Uncle Thomas proved anything. But she also knew Ruthena wouldn't stop driving over from Charlotte to lay oiled, prayerful hands on her sinning brother's head, for according to her, "God don't recognize sin."

No, Evelyn wasn't hoping her aunts and uncles would drive over to Granny B's, at least not today. Who she most wanted—*needed*—to see was a continent away. *Kevin.* She'd scooped him out of every thought and feeling, ignored all his texts, and condemned him for not daring to call. She'd tucked him away in the heart-shaped box where she'd stowed Granny B. He was hidden there alone now, for she'd plucked up Granny B upon hearing her mother's announcement. Even now Evelyn curled her fingers into a fist, fighting the urge to call him.

On autopilot, Evelyn signaled a right turn and exited the highway. She veered right at the top of the ramp and headed west toward Spring Hope. Traffic was unusually heavy, so she slowed, but her thoughts traveled at the speed of light. *Lord, why is Granny B sick? Why did I come home now, right when Granny B and Mama need me? I know You wouldn't have allowed this mess with Kevin and Miss Samantha Jane just to put me on this particular road. How can this be for our good? I need a burning bush!*

Passing newer houses and a couple of stray dogs, Evelyn pulled up just past the mailbox and parked. She stared at the place where Granny B had lived for more than sixty years. Carrot Lane. Not much had really changed since Granny B had raised all her children there. Refreshed but consistent. Same shade of bright white. Same green shutters and porch rails.

"Who's sweeping the yard these days?" Evelyn murmured. Her eyes strained for any sign of life: the movement of a curtain, a shadow, a noise. Part of her hoped that Granny B was downtown somewhere, getting a prescription filled or buying croakers and hush puppies at the fish market. *Nope,* she thought, *today is Thursday. Granny B only gets fish on Mondays when the truck brings them in fresh.*

After ten minutes Evelyn grabbed the bag of Granny Smith apples Mama had sent along, stepped from the car, and strode up the walkway to the front door. She tried to muster an air of confidence in case Granny B was peeping out from some unknown vantage point, but she felt like the rosebushes gasping for their last breath by the curb. *I think I can . . . I think I can . . . I think I can,* she chanted as she chugged up her mental hill. By the time she pulled back the screen door and knocked, she was primed for her Moment of Truth, and she craned to hear those firm, no-nonsense footsteps. But after standing there longer than it would take Granny B to walk around her house three times, she realized she wouldn't hear Granny B's footsteps because the woman wasn't home. She would have left the front door open behind the locked screen. Evelyn sighed and flopped into the wrought iron porch chair. She rubbed an apple on her sleeve, took a bite, and chewed on her options.

Should I take this as a sign? Regroup and come back later or better yet tomorrow? But . . . hey! Granny B's absence is my burning bush! God is telling me to haul butt out of here while I can and let Mama handle things until Granny B and I can iron out our Situation! Clutching her epiphany as she had the apple, Evelyn skipped down the three steps from the porch—

"Where you goin' in such an all-fired hurry?"

—and almost jumped clean out of her skin. Whirling around, she caught sight of her burning bush.

Granny B's eyes seared a hole in Evelyn's forehead. "So, chile, why you standin' there like a possum in the road? Didn't you hear what I said?" She put a hand to her hip.

Evelyn dredged up a husky "Well . . ."

For a minute Evelyn studied Granny B, her eyes hungry for a good look at the woman she'd worried she wouldn't see alive again. As always, she'd donned a simple housedress, with a belt that she could cinch twice around her tiny waist, and pulled back her steel-colored hair severely from her thin face into a braid that curled across one shoulder. Her bare legs ended in familiar, sensible black leather lace-ups.

When Evelyn's eyes crept back up to Granny B's face, past her crossed arms and bony elbows, they locked with her gray ones. Still. Defiant. Fiery. *Triumphant?*

"Since you was leavin' so quick, I guess you came all this way just to sit on my front porch and eat a apple?"

Maybe I did hear those footsteps after all.

"Gal, if you just gon' stand there like a darn statue, you might as well keep on runnin' and git in your car and drive on home. I ain't got time to stand here all day." Granny B spun on her heel and walked around the back of the house.

Evelyn didn't know what Granny B expected, but she followed her, albeit tripping over her two left feet rather than striding confidently as she had before. Gone was the happy little engine that could. By the time she reached the backyard, Granny B had picked up an empty laundry basket and was heading inside through the back door. Wet linen hanging on the clothesline flapped in the morning breeze.

Getting in gear, Evelyn ran to catch the screen door before it slapped her grandmother on her backside. It clapped shut once, twice before she could follow her into the house. Evelyn stood there and stared through the mesh as Granny B set her basket on the washing machine to the left of the door.

On the drive over, Evelyn had worked out how her visit with Granny B would go. She ran through the scenario in her mind as she watched Granny B walk to the right to wash her hands in the kitchen sink. It started with a *"Hello, chile. What brang you here?"* and ended with fried chicken and pound cake. In between they agreed to put the past behind them. So far, however, the only thing Evelyn had gotten right was the word *chile*.

Abruptly her grandmother wheeled away from the sink and caught her staring. Out of words and running out of time, Evelyn stammered, "G-granny B . . ." She swallowed and finished lamely, ". . . you're home."

Granny B pursed her lips. "I reckon I am. But that don't mean I ain't busy. As usual, I got plenty a thangs to do and no time to be wastin'."

No time to be wastin' on me, Evelyn amended silently. "Well, my time is pretty precious, too, but I did set aside some to spend with you. Inside, preferably."

Granny B peered at her granddaughter for a few moments more through half-closed eyes. Just when Evelyn was beginning to think she'd have to say whatever she'd come to say outside, in God's front room, Granny B tsked. "Well, as long as you don't plan on startin' none of yo' mess, and you stay

outta my way, I reckon a *few* precious minutes won't kill me."
She walked to the door and pushed it ajar.

But they might kill me, Evelyn thought as, relieved, she
quickly shimmied through the barely open door, not giving
Granny B the opportunity to change her mind. She glanced
around the kitchen and reacquainted herself with the surroundings. An oak table and four chairs hugged the far right
wall. The water heater and washing machine shared a space
on the left, by the back door. The narrow refrigerator faced
the door and abutted a wall of cabinets. A set of canisters,
a dish towel, and a long-handled spoon were the only items
visible on the pristine countertop. The kitchen walls were
painted off-white, and the hardwood floor was bare, other
than the garbage can squatting near the mat that lay just
inside the door, its *Welcome* long since faded from the passage
of time instead of use. Evelyn noticed what must have been
her mother's handiwork: yellow curtains and a yellow- and
white-striped vinyl tablecloth.

"I see you noticed them there curtains and table coverin'
yo' mama put in here."

Evelyn jumped guiltily.

"I told that gal I didn't want or need those thangs, but
you know how yo' mama is. She just do what she wont to do,
even though this my house." Granny B cut her eyes Evelyn's
way. "Like somebody else I know."

Already she was peeling off the gloves, finger by gnarly
finger. Evelyn murmured something that wasn't agreement
or disagreement. She glanced back at the flapping sheets and

towels to dispel the niggle of irritation and the flutter in her stomach. *What is wrong with me?* Whenever she visited Carrot Lane, she didn't stand around wondering what to do next. She just jumped right in and did what Granny B was doing or something else that always needed doing.

At last, at a loss, she positioned herself by her grandmother at the sink. "What are you working on?"

"Tender greens." Granny B's hands, ever in motion, dunked the green leaves of what Elisabeth called mustard greens in a sink filled almost to the brim.

"What do you need me to do?"

"Nuthin'. I like to do my own greens—"

"I know, Granny B."

Evelyn recalled her grandmother's long-ago pronouncement: *"Nobody gon' break a tooth on no rock or get choked tryin' to chew up no en-tire leaf in my house."*

"So how about I work on the meat? You haven't done that yet, have you?" At the curt shake of Granny B's head, she continued, "And I can separate the bad leaves from the good while you wash them and cut them up." Evelyn knew that this plan was foolproof. At one time, these were her assigned tasks whenever she worked on her greens.

Granny B still seemed to think it over for a minute. Then she instructed her how to season the ham hock with salt, black pepper, and sliced onions and green peppers, her way of granting permission. Those were her last words for a while; they worked without conversation. Granny B kept filling the sink with greens, washing and sifting through them, throwing away the brown leaves that Evelyn missed as she sifted through her own pile of tender greens.

Evelyn was dabbing away sweat from her forehead by the time Granny B had cleaned and cut up all the greens, yet the older woman looked as crisp as a December morning working at the sink. Evelyn didn't complain about the heat—she had learned her lesson about doing that a long time ago—but she took quick sips from a tall glass of ice water from time to time.

Almost two hours later, the ham hock was tender enough to slice with her fork, the way Granny B liked it. She herself had softened up quite a bit, too, as they settled into their old routine of getting the greens ready. Without asking, Evelyn poured the meat and all its juice into the pot with the greens and put the pot lid about three-quarters of the way on top of it. This prevented too much heat from collecting in the pot and causing the greens to boil over. In her peripheral vision she noticed Granny B nod slightly, approving.

But "Coffee?" was all she asked.

Granny B could drink hot coffee even if she was sitting down to lunch with the devil. Determined to meet her halfway, Evelyn accepted her offer. "Does—?"

"It ain't got no caffeine in it."

Evelyn retrieved two cups while her grandma set the ancient percolator on one of the back burners. Granny B never owned any saucers. As Evelyn watched her spoon grounds into the stainless steel pot, she considered how to broach her main reason for coming down today. She also used the time to weigh the pros and cons of bringing up their Situation. Bring It up or let sleeping dogs lie?

By the time they sat down at the kitchen table and Evelyn had creamed and sugared her coffee, Granny B's sleeping dogs were stirring. "So you decided to come back." Always matter-of-fact.

Not sure how to phrase her response, Evelyn sipped her coffee and nodded. "Yep."

"Why you come back? I thought we'd said 'bout all they was to say."

"Not quite."

Granny B braced a weathered arm on the table. The other hand cradled her coffee cup. "So that's all you got to say, Ev'lyn Beatrice? 'Yep' and 'not quite'? That's all you come to say?"

Evelyn stood, thinking she would buy another minute or two pouring a second cup of coffee, but Granny B stopped her with a hand on her arm. "I wouldn't get mo' coffee. They say they ain't no caffeine in it, but you cain't always believe the TV. And I know how you young folks set such store by these doctors."

Evelyn barely heard Granny B's warning about the coffee. Weeks had passed since she had seen, smelled, listened to, argued with, or been frustrated by this woman. Until she'd placed a warning hand on her arm, Evelyn hadn't realized just how much she'd missed having Granny B's steady, guiding touch in her life. And she was faced with the likelihood of losing this *thing* forever if that acute myeloid leukemia had its way. Tears splashed into Evelyn's half-empty cup before she could snort them up. *Why did I ever want to change my name? It's* her *name. Oh, Granny B, how long will I get to hear you say it?*

"I know them tears ain't for me. From where I sit, you the one with a lot goin' on." Granny B sat back in her chair. "What? You finally get up the nerve to apologize? Okay, I accept. Now let me get back to work—I cain't let my greens cook too long on the stove."

Granny B yanked Evelyn from her wading pool of sentimentality and threw her unceremoniously into the deep end of indignation. And that water sure was cold. The greens simmered softly atop the stove, but Evelyn embraced the icy heat of anger. As she wiped away the wetness on her face, she yearned to exclaim, *"Apologize! For what?"* But instead she bit back her retort and surreptitiously wiped away her tears.

"Gal, you hear what I said?"

She gathered herself. "Of course, Granny B. I'm sorry; I was just thinking." *Maybe she'll think that's an apology, and we can move on.* "Did you want more coffee?" She stood to rinse her cup and set it in the sink to dry.

"No, I don't want nuthin'. 'Cept for you to come over here and sit back down."

She sat. They stared into each other's eyes for a solid minute. Her grandma blinked first, which gave her courage to plow ahead. "So, Granny B. What's going on with you?"

"What's going on with *me*?" She put her right hand to her hip and crooked her left index finger in her granddaughter's direction. "You the one need to be answerin' *that* question."

Growing even more frustrated and hot in the warm kitchen, Evelyn blew out a lungful of air. She sat back in the chair. "Now, don't try to turn this around. You know what I'm referring to."

"I ain't turnin' nuthin' round. And you know what I'm *referrin' to*."

"Actually, I don't." *Does she want to know about Kevin's new job? My job?* She plucked and discarded one option after another. Flustered, she changed tactics and loaded the cannon: "Granny B, you should know that I've heard the news."

Evelyn waited for her to light the fuse, but when Granny B only glared at her, she added more gunpowder. "Granny B, why didn't you tell somebody? You knew we'd all be here for you, doing whatever you needed, making sure you were taken care of."

"Me? I got all I need, gal." Granny B rose and stirred the greens. Without taste testing what simmered in the pot, she added a dash of her special seasoning that she kept behind the regular stuff like salt and pepper. "The question is, you got all *you* need?"

"What was it you used to tell me? 'Whatever you hide in the dark will someday come to light'?" Evelyn jumped to her feet. She grabbed her grandmother by one of her wiry shoulders, as much to steady herself as to capture her complete attention.

Granny B squinted at Evelyn as if studying an unknown specimen through the lens of a microscope. "And I would tell you that same thang again. Ain't you a big fat pot callin' the kettle black?"

Once again, she could see defiance, fire, and triumph in Granny B's eyes. But no, she determined, today it would take more than a firm shove to get her out of this house.

"You can talk about pots and pans and kettles all day, Granny B. We can discuss all the utensils in this whole kitchen. But first, I want to hear some truth from you."

"Well, let's just start with you, little Miss Sassafras. Comin' in here and talkin' to me about tellin' the truth. We'll start with you."

The kitchen was heating up. Evelyn threw her hands into the air. "What are you *talking* about?"

All of a sudden the triumph faded from Granny B's eyes. The fire and the defiance warred with each other. Defiance won out, reducing the flames to mere embers. She thrust out her chin and her hand returned to her hip. "I'm talkin' about that baby you carryin', Miss Ev'lyn Beatrice. When was you plannin' to tell the truth about that so we could help *you* and give you what *you* need?"

All Evelyn remembered was a loud *boom!* And then suddenly Granny B was picking her up off the mercifully cool hardwood floor and helping her sit down at the table, stuffing her head between her knees.

"You all right?"

Evelyn nodded slowly but kept her head down and her eyes closed. Neither said anything for five minutes or more.

"How 'bout you sittin' up?" The pressure of Granny B's fingers on her left shoulder turned this suggestion into a command. Granny B placed a cool cloth in her hands. "Here. Take this and put it on the back of your neck."

Eyes closed, Evelyn obeyed.

"Still all right?"

Again she nodded. "Yes, I'm fine." When she finally peeked between her eyelashes, Evelyn saw Granny B to her left, hands tucked inside her apron pockets.

Evelyn didn't bother to ask what had happened because she could think of little else all the time she crouched at the kitchen table. The one question that hammered away at her—the one question that she could not get past—was *How did she know?* With the cold war at home and Kevin's intermittent travel, he had not even realized that she had missed her last two cycles. *How did* Granny B *know?*

"Want some water?"

Granny B's question snapped her back to the present. "Uh, no, nothing. I'm fine."

"You didn't look fine when you was layin' out on that flo' a few minutes ago."

"Well, it's pretty hot in this kitchen, if you haven't noticed." Testing her equilibrium, Evelyn put weight on one foot and then the other.

"I been workin' in this very same hot kitchen for nearly seventy years now, and I ain't never had no faintin' spell," Granny B harrumphed. "And I was pregnant myself many a them years."

How did she know? "What is it with this pregnant stuff? This is the second time you've said something like that." Evelyn could not bring herself to outright deny her pregnancy. It was hard to deny something that she had not completely accepted.

She inhaled deeply and exhaled her words in a great rush as she attempted to redirect the conversation. "Granny B, could you please sit down in the front room with me so we can have a talk?"

"I don't see as we have much to talk about. Unless you ready to start admittin' the truth."

"Well, to hear you tell it, there's nothing more for me to admit."

"That thick waist of yours is doin' the talkin' for you."

Automatically, her hands flew to her nonexistent bulge, partly from some instinctive need to protect it and partly to check for any signs that she was showing even a little bit.

Granny B's eyebrows lifted at her discomfiture. "Ain't no need for you to try and hide nuthin'. I'm surprised 'Lis'beth ain't said somethin' yet. She's had enough babies. She should know the signs, same as me."

Evelyn studied the floor as her hands fluttered to her sides. "She can't tell you about something that she doesn't know."

Granny B raised her eyebrows. "Oohh! So you got yo' own skeletons clankin' in the closet. And you come down here tryin' to free mine."

"I wouldn't consider a pregnancy a 'skeleton.'" Her words were so dry and brittle Evelyn had to be careful not to snap them in two as she spoke. "But don't you have enough to worry about right now?"

"You got yo' own private business, but I just ain't got none. Is that what you sayin'?" Granny B crossed her arms over her chest.

Evelyn almost laughed. "Oh, you have plenty. That's why I came here, to—"

"It really don't matter what you come here to do. You done run out of time." Granny B began hustling her toward the open back door.

Evelyn tried to wrench her arm from her grandmother's viselike grip. "I'm not leaving here until I've said what I came here to say," she managed. Unbelievably, Granny B pushed her even harder, practically dragging her to the door. She was shocked as much by her physical strength—*Isn't this the same woman on the brink of death?*—as by her gall. Verbally throwing her out was much different from using both hands to do it.

"What are you doing, Granny B? Stop this! Is this how you treat people you love? Who are only trying to help you? Maybe that's why Henton left, having to put up with stuff like this day after day."

As if Evelyn had pushed her away, Granny B reeled back and hit the washing machine. The detergent fell over onto its side and powder spilled onto the floor. Granny B glowered at her, her chest heaving. Her anger simmered, threatening to bubble over like the greens on the stove.

"Who are you cooking for, Granny B? Who are you

cleaning for? Who are you waiting to see? Who's going to eat all this food?" Evelyn's hand swept in the direction of the pot. "I'm almost the only one you ever let in here on a regular basis, and now you won't even allow *me* to come. There's no point storing this food in your freezer because your pigheadedness is going to let you die in what . . . ? A few months at most? Or what, do you think that Henton is going to walk in here one day?" Evelyn shook her head slowly. "Well, that ain't gonna happen. You made sure of that, didn't you?"

"I don't know whatchyou talkin' 'bout."

"Oh, you know exactly what."

Uncharacteristically, Granny B retreated. "I 'spect you to be gone when I come back."

"Well, you expect wrong," Evelyn retorted, following her and blocking her escape. "Aren't you tired of running people off? You did it with Granddaddy, you've done it with your children, and you've tried it with me."

"You best move, gal."

Evelyn planted her feet, prepared to wrestle with the angel. "No, I won't let you run me away!"

"You oughta know about runnin' folk off. You been runnin' yo' mama off for years. You wont somebody to talk to? Go home!"

"No!" Then she added, less forcefully, "Please, Granny B." Evelyn swallowed and continued, still more gently. "Don't you think it's about time you talked about it? If you let down that burden . . ."

"What? You wont me to lay my head on yo' shoulder and just cry my fool head off? Tell you all 'bout why that . . . that . . . *ma-an* left me and my chillun, left us here to die like . . ." She gulped down a breath, and with a nod, Granny B answered her own questions. "'Course you do, 'cause you *care* about me."

Then Granny B shook her head. "Well, I won't do it. It ain't none of yo' business why he left." She returned to the washing machine to clean up the spilled detergent.

Evelyn spoke to her back yet again. "You don't have to tell me why Henton left, Granny B. I know the answer to that: You kicked him out. Just like you threw *me* out. But why would you force Henton to leave here, right when you needed him most? You did have seven children to feed and clothe and take care of—"

"You don't have to remind me how many children I had by the time his sorry behind left here. I was there, remember?" Granny B's voice was flat.

Evelyn winced. She softened her voice, hoping to deliver the same message on a pillow instead of a sword. "Why not write him back after all those times he wrote you? I counted— what?—ten or fifteen letters that Henton had written you, right up until he died. Letters to Mama and Thomas, Little Ed—to all of you!"

Granny B remained silent as she braced both hands against the washing machine.

"What about forgiveness?" Evelyn pushed away the memory of Kevin asking that same question. "Believe me, I know

I may be upsetting you, but I think talking about this can help—"

"Upsettin' me? You ain't upsettin' me. You makin' me angry as—!" Granny B reined in her emotions, flexing her fingers. "You thank you have the right to come into *my* house, meddle through *my* thangs, and wont to talk about *forgiveness*, tell me about *my business* . . ."

"Well, you—"

"Well, you, nuthin'. This my house and my life and I'm gon' do with it what I wont." Granny B pushed away from the washing machine and strutted down the hall into her bedroom.

"This is not just your life. It does not involve just you." Anger suffused Evelyn's bones and made her tremble like a leaf in a spring breeze as she tramped after her grandmother. Her fingers shook with it as they reached out to Granny B. Then that same anger curled her outstretched fingers into an impotent fist. "How can you stand there and say that? You have children, grandchildren . . ."

"And how you figure that?" Granny B looked around her as if perplexed. "I don't see nobody else livin' here, payin' no bills." She crouched on one knee and lifted the bedspread. "Hmmpf. Ain't nobody under there. They must all be out on the back porch, waitin' to jump up and yell, 'Surprise!' when I walk outside." Granny B pressed a hand to her side as she straightened.

"They may not be living out here, but they should be living in here, in your heart." She gently tapped her grandma on the left side of her chest with an index finger.

Granny B knocked aside her finger. "Is that where I been livin' since you been gone? In yo' heart? 'Cause you sho' ain't been round here." She reached for the cloth and lemon-scented furniture polish sitting on her dresser. After spraying the rag, she furiously wiped away nonexistent dust.

"As a matter of fact, yes, you have been constantly in my thoughts and in my heart. Just like Henton has lived in yours for more than sixty years."

Granny B threw down the cotton swath. Through clenched teeth she ground out, "Why you keep sayin' that? You thank I care one whit 'bout that man? Yes, Henton *said* I throwed him out. Un-huh." Granny B's head bobbed up and down. "But what kinda man allows hisself to get kicked out his own house—that is, if he really wont to stay in the first place? I tried to kick you out just a few minutes ago, but you still standin' here."

Granny B's eyes bored into her granddaughter's. "Yes, he wrote *letters* to my chillun, tried to reach out to 'em. But I couldn'ta stopped him from seein' 'em if he'd a really wonted to. He knew where they lived, where they was goin' to school. Spring Hope ain't but so big."

Granny B turned away. "If my man had wanted to come back—if he'da wanted to *stay*, ain't nobody coulda done nuthin' to stop him, Ev'lyn."

"But why, Granny B? Why would you want him gone? Back then you had all my aunts and uncles to look after. There's no way you could have wanted to do it all yourself, even knowing what I know about you. And now here you are. You're dying—"

"Dy—!" Granny B raised her finger.

"Yes, Granny B, Mama and I know what Dr. Hedgepeth told you. You. Are. Dying. And yet here you are, still trying—no, fighting—to be alone. To die here alone. Do you really expect Mama and me—any of your children—to let you continue to live and then die that way, the way Henton left you, grieving and alone? Yes, he might have let you push him out, but we won't. *I* won't." Unable to hold herself back any longer, Evelyn's raised voice was cutting; she brandished her words like a weapon.

Granny B crossed her arms and looked beyond Evelyn, at some distant point through the open bedroom door.

"Granny B? Granny B, please. Look at me. I know you like to keep to yourself, but God knows you don't have to depend on just yourself or Mama or me. You're surrounded by your children. Aunt Ruthena and Uncle Matthew would drive over from Charlotte in a heartbeat if they knew—"

Eyes finally meeting Evelyn's, Granny B spewed, "So she can put some of that veg'able oil on my head and pray over me? You thank the same God that done kept me all these years, who took my chillun, and the same God who's gon' kill me gon' just change His mind and save me now? You thank God is just havin' some big laugh 'cause ain't nuthin' else important in this here world that He needs to bother Hisself with?" She looked out the window. "And whatchyou gon' do? You cain't even stand up for more'n two minutes without faintin'. Got a baby on the way. You cain't even take care of yo'self and you gon' try to take care of me?" She looked away and grunted, almost to herself, "Even if you could, I wouldn't have you here. I'm gon' be with Him soon enough."

Evelyn ignored her vituperation, the words that sounded more like a curse than a promise. "Maybe Aunt Mary won't step out of the spotlight long enough to fly here, but Uncle Thomas and Aunt Sissy would love to help. That's what they live and work for—helping. Surely God wants you to experience His goodness here, in the land of the living, not just in heaven. All you have to do is reach out, Granny B. Forgive. What can be so hard in that?" *Yes, Evelyn, what can be so hard?* a little voice prodded and poked her.

Granny B took her time answering. But then finally, in a monotone, she asked, "What can be so hard? What can be so *hard*?" Her voice crept to a whisper. "I reached out for almost twenty years to a man. But that man, the one who came to me in my bed for almost twenty years, that man stole my childhood and much of my life. And what he didn't take, I kept givin' away till I had barely nuthin' left. Well, no more." The angry tears that had gradually pooled in Granny B's eyes slowly gave way, spilling down her cheeks and dropping onto her heaving chest, her sturdy black shoes, and the hardwood floor.

"Now, Henton was long gone 'fo' his body ever left here, when my heart was breakin' over Milton. He didn't stay round long enough to help me. I needed somebody *then*,

Ev'lyn. Sho', I was reachin' out, but not for that man. Never for that man." Granny B didn't seem to be addressing Evelyn.

Evelyn stumbled there, caught up in the image of a young woman left alone to fend for herself and her family. While she paused, Granny B silently walked around her to the door of the bedroom.

"Maybe you got somethin' else to say, but I don't care to hear it, chile. Not right now. If you wont to do somethin' for me, you just get outta my house."

A few seconds later, Evelyn heard the back door bounce a few times until it finally shut for good. Deciding to give Granny B what she had asked for—no, demanded—Evelyn quietly walked dry-eyed and cotton-mouthed through the front room and let herself out.

Evelyn woodenly traversed the quiet two-lane road leading from Granny B's house and eventually merged into the mélange of cars, 18-wheelers, and sport utility vehicles flowing steadily on Highway 64. She didn't want to play music, talk to God, or even hear herself think. Her mother would give her plenty to listen to when she got back to Mount Laurel.

Despite the fact that Granny B was a grown woman who could and did make her own choices, her mama had anointed her with the task of getting Granny B to see reason. Even though her grandma knew what was at stake—life or death—Evelyn knew she'd have to find the words to explain why she'd failed her task, and ultimately, Granny B.

Evelyn snapped on the radio, but just as abruptly she turned it off. Instead, she tuned in to her own regrets as the car pressed ever closer to her temporary home. The soft *ca-chunk, ca-chunk, ca-chunk* of the tires devouring the uneven asphalt vied with the cacophony of what-ifs and should-haves in her mind. Over the din she heard Granny B's mournful voice: *"I reached out for almost twenty years to a man. But that man, the one who came to me in my bed for almost twenty years, that man stole my childhood and much of my life. And what he didn't take, I kept givin' away till I had barely nuthin' left. . . . I needed somebody then, Ev'lyn . . . Sho', I was reachin' out, but not for that man. Never for that man."*

Thing was, Evelyn had always felt within arm's reach of Granny B, even during her four years away at Emory. She couldn't think of a time when she wouldn't willingly take a kick in the pants from her grandmother before she'd accept a word of advice from her own mother—not that she could avoid one or the other anyway. Tonight, she couldn't seem to avoid anything Granny B had said. *"Well, if you gon' treat me with no respect, then I ain't got no time for you. Get out. And don't come back here. . . . Don't never come back here again . . . Don't come back here again . . . Don't come back . . ."*

Evelyn shook her head to clear the voice. Cars were passing her in droves.

Forgive, she herself had had the nerve to say. Forgive! *What a hypocrite, you telling Granny B to forgive Henton,* she accused herself.

But that's different, another, bitter voice reasoned. *Kevin betrayed* you. *You didn't kick him out. He left you a long time ago for Samantha Jane.* Evelyn closed her eyes to the voices, but she couldn't silence them. *He's probably with her now. Why not? You don't want him anymore.*

The first voice cried weakly, *But don't you?*

Honk! Ho-nnnk! Startled, Evelyn met the angry eyes of the driver in the Mini Cooper passing her in the left lane and realized she'd again slowed to a near crawl. Desperate, she pulled over into the breakdown lane to pull herself together.

Seven miles to Mount Laurel, the mileage marker announced. She had driven about thirteen miles from Granny B's house. Yet, parked there in front of the highway sign, she felt thousands of miles from really reaching either her mama or grandma. And millions of miles from Kevin. Evelyn pondered turning the car to head . . . where?

She strained to see through tears streaming from her eyes, dripping from her cheeks, dampening her dress front. "God, I asked You for a sign that I was headed along the right path, but instead You sent me some pigheaded old woman who wouldn't know a sign from You from a pot of tender greens. Now what?"

Evelyn's head flopped against the leather headrest as the ache crept up from the back of her neck and wound over her cranium. But her eyes were open wide enough to see a car careen out of control and cross the median. She had a clear view of her "burning bush"—two tons of steel and plastic— heading straight for her car.

Chapter Eight

FOR THE SECOND TIME in less than twelve hours, Beatrice watched her granddaughter come to. But not on her kitchen floor. This time, Evelyn was stretched out on a rolling cot with lights glaring down in her face. From her spot in the corner of the frigid, sterile room, Beatrice's eyes followed a groggy Evelyn as she conducted a self-inspection. Her bushy silver eyebrows furrowed as her granddaughter's fingers found the bandage pasted squarely across the middle of her forehead.

"Ever'thang still in place?"

Evelyn cried out. Her wide eyes darted across the space to Granny B, sitting in a chair on the left side of the room.

She stood and walked over. She read Evelyn's shock.

Evelyn tried to raise herself to a sitting position. "Wh-what h-happened? Wh-what are you doing here?"

"What am *I* doing here? Well, obviously, I'm here to see you. You need to be explainin' whatch*you* doin' here." She gripped her granddaughter's left arm and hand and helped her sit upright on the bed. The girl's hand shook slightly in her own. "Take it slow, gal."

Beatrice could feel Evelyn watching her every move. *Does this crazy chile think I done somethin' to her?* Her mouth twitched as she propped a pillow behind Evelyn's head and back. "You gon' be all right, gal. Why don't you lay back on this pillow and get yo'self together. You gon' be all right. From what the police can tell, you was parked 'side the road and some fool car slammed right into you." She inclined her head toward Evelyn. "It don't make much sense to me, why you woulda been parked along that highway, but that's what they say happened." Granny B studied Evelyn.

"I was driving home . . . and I pulled beside the road because . . . I felt a bad headache coming on . . . so I decided to pull off to the side . . . right at the turnoff. . . . I sat there for a few minutes . . . then I thought . . . if I could just close my eyes for a moment and lean back on the headrest, I would feel better and I could drive on to Mama's."

Granny B craned her head toward Evelyn as the words tumbled over each other, gaining momentum as the memory of the entire morning's events rushed back. She watched her let down her guard and relax in tiny increments—first the small of her back, then the middle, her shoulders, and finally her head against the pillow.

"So how you feelin'? Anythang hurt? Do I need to get one of them doctors or nurses in here?"

Evelyn slowly moved her arms and wriggled each of her fingers. She shifted her right leg, then her left, rotated her ankles, and curled her toes.

Granny B commented dryly, "In case you wonderin', yo' baby is fine."

"The baby."

Has she not even wondered how this accident affected it . . . her . . . him? "Yes, 'the baby.' You ain't even thought 'bout that baby, have you? I watched you. You gave mo' 'tention to that little toe longer than you gave to whatchyou carryin' round in that belly of yours. You ever gon' ask about it?"

"I haven't . . . I mean, did you . . . ?"

Granny B knew the answer to the question Evelyn couldn't speak. "No, I ain't told nobody. It's still that secret you been workin' so hard to hide." She paused. "It ain't none of my business to tell, though I'm sho yo' mama wouldn't agree with that."

Evelyn closed her eyes and expelled a whoosh of air.

"Well, 'course you never said you was pregnant, but I knew better." Granny B folded back the sheet and tucked it a bit under Evelyn's armpits. "So when yo' mama and I got here, I made sure to tell them doctors 'bout you being pregnant so they wouldn't do nuthin' they shouldn't be doin'."

"Mama's here? Why were you together? Where is she now?"

Seeing her eyes water and the obvious pain she was in, Granny B stopped judging, at least long enough to put Evelyn's whirring mind to rest. "'Lis'beth called me up to find out what had happened to you, why it was takin' you so long to get home. 'Fo' I could explain that you was long gone, somebody called her on her phone. Turned out it was the hospital, sayin' you was here. I guess they got the number from 'Lis'beth's car. I got Ruby and Lerenzo to bring me over, but they can pick me up now I see you fine."

Evelyn's shoulders relaxed. "So where's Mama now?"

"It's not my whereabouts you should worry about." The woman in question pranced into the room before Granny B could answer. "You should be more concerned about *you*. What were you thinking, parking along that road like that?" Lis strode briskly over to the cot and started smoothing down her daughter's hair.

Gruffly Granny B instructed, "'Lis'beth, stop messin' over the girl. You prob'ly makin' her head hurt with all that rubbin'."

Lis threw her a this-is-my-daughter-and-I'll-do-what-I-want-to glare. Continuing to finger-comb her daughter's curly strands, she demanded, "Explain yourself, Evelyn. You could have been killed! Not to say anything about the fact that that crazy driver demolished my car!" She pursed her lips and added under her breath, "My *new* car, at that."

Evelyn brushed away her mama's hand. "Do you mind

if we continue this particular discussion later when I'm not lying on my deathbed?"

"I wouldn't exactly call this your winding sheet." Lis perched on the end of the cot.

Granny B stepped back, silently witnessing the tableau created by the two who never could abide much of each other. Lis fussed over and at her daughter while Evelyn stiff-armed her mother, flicking away her hands and answering her in one-word sentences. Neither looked satisfied; both seemed frustrated. *That chile wish 'Lis'beth would disappear in a puff of smoke . . . and take me with her.*

But the only puff either was rewarded with was a whiff of Dolce & Gabbana's Light Blue as Lis lifted and straightened the starchy white hospital linen crumpled around Evelyn. "Don't worry; you're not in danger of taking your last breath. Doctors say you can go home in the morning. They just want to make sure you don't experience complications." Lis searched the room. "In fact, I should get one of those doctors in here so they can check your eyes with that light or take your pulse or do whatever it is they need to do to give you a clean bill of health."

She turned to Beatrice. "Mama, did you let anybody know she was awake?"

Granny B shook her head curtly. *Who do I look like?*

"I'll see if I can find somebody who can help us out." Lis halted at the door. "But you're going to have to tell me why you were parked beside the road. You couldn't have made it another ten miles to the house before taking a nap?"

After the doors whispered closed behind her, Evelyn retreated to the pillows to accept whatever thin comfort they could provide. "Thank you for not telling her about the baby. That's one discussion I'm not ready for."

"Don't be thankin' me. That's between you and yo' mama, and I ain't in it. But you better tell her—"

"Better tell me what?" Lis emerged suddenly through the doors. Medical personnel squished behind her in loafered feet.

"Uh . . ."

"She needs to tell you the truth," Granny B cut in. "Ain't no need layin' up here hidin' nuthin'. Not when there's folks here to help."

Lis parked herself at the end of the bed as medical staff examined their patient efficiently and thoroughly. "I hope you have sense enough to tell the doctors if something is hurting you, Evelyn."

"Of course I do. I'm fine. Just a headache—and I had that before the accident. That's why I pulled over, to rest my head a bit."

Granny B grunted and ignored Evelyn's look. She let her granddaughter continue her awkward dance along that thin line between fact and fiction. Her face an impassive mask that belied her turbulent thoughts, she watched Evelyn turn this way and that, according to the doctor's directions. She tsk-tsked silently at the sense of their final decision to skip the overnight observation but concluded that these folks were grown. *It ain't none of my business. These here doctors and their* practice *of medicine. Hmmph. These folks can't even heal my big toe, let alone this disease I'm totin' around. I don't blame that girl for bein' ready to leave. I could do a heap better takin' care of her.*

Evelyn signed the release papers and checked out the tag on the nearest white coat. "Is it Dr. LaSalle?"

The doctor looked up at her from her clipboard.

"May I talk to you a minute?"

When Granny B heard Evelyn clear her throat, she leaned over to Lis. "Let's give Ev'lyn a minute to get herself together." She picked up her daughter's purse.

"What?" Lis seemed intent on helping Evelyn inhale and exhale, coaching her through each breath, if need be. Her eyes and ears were pinned to her. It took Beatrice's formidable resolve to overcome her protests and steer her from the room and close the door.

Once they stood on the other side of the double doors, Lis unleashed her frustrations. "Mama, what in the world! Why'd you pull me out like that?"

"'Lis'beth, you need to give that chile some privacy. She can get dressed on her own."

"You think so? I thought she could drive on her own, too, but look where we are."

"Blame that other driver. You need to give her some room to breathe. Y'all like two banty roosters fightin' for control over the same henhouse."

"Nobody's fighting, Mama."

"But you 'bout to."

"You know I don't like hospitals. You remember the last time I was in one like this—"

"Yes, I remember. And I also remember that gal was here with you. That was a hard road for you and her both. It was yo' husband, but that was her daddy." She pointed to a young man in blue scrubs chatting it up with a nurse at the central station. "Why don't you find somebody to help us get her to the car. Ain't that boy free right there?"

Lis glared at her mama, but Beatrice didn't back down, so Lis stalked over to the orderly. Beatrice watched her daughter use her considerable Southern charm on him, and just as he pushed over a wheelchair, the doors to Evelyn's room swooshed open. The doctor and nurse breezed through with barely a nod at either of them. Before the doors could swing to, Granny B and Lis pushed through, followed by the orderly she'd pressed into service.

Beatrice took in Evelyn dressed in her bloodstained dress. "So, gal, you ready to go?"

Evelyn nodded at her grandmother. "As I can be. How are we getting home?"

Lis laughed and coughed simultaneously. "Well, unfortunately, not in my new Infiniti. It's practically totaled. As a matter of fact, it's a miracle you made it out of the accident with just some bumps and bruises and a scrape or two. The other driver suffered several broken bones and had to be admitted."

"Serve him right, since he the cause of all this trouble," Granny B harrumphed under her breath. She pulled Lis out of the way while the orderly helped Evelyn into the chair and arranged her feet.

"Then how are we getting home?"

"The same way *I* got here. You forget about Jackson's car?" Lis thumped her daughter softly on the head and settled Evelyn's purse in her lap.

Wincing, Evelyn managed a small "Oh—"

"The hoopty," Lis and Evelyn said in unison. The "hoopty" was Jackson's pride and joy, a 1985 Chevy Impala that had been around the blocks a few times—quite literally. Lis raised a carefully plucked eyebrow at Evelyn's unspoken complaint. "Remember, Jackson took your car this morning because you'd blocked him in."

Granny B retreated to silent partner status as Evelyn's eyes skittered from hers to Lis's, then to the brown-speckled tile floor.

"I'll take you home and get you settled," Lis explained. "Then I'll see Mama home."

"I'm gon' call Ruby to come back here," Granny B declared. She stopped beside the courtesy phones at the right side of the automatic doors leading outside. One hand held her worn leather bag.

"Don't be silly, Mama. I've got two people to take care of now. So come on. Let's not keep this nice young man waiting." She threw the hospital attendant a radiant smile, which he sheepishly returned. "Now, come *on*, Mama."

Granny B bristled at the command but didn't ask what

two people Lis had in mind. "Well, Ev'lyn, at least you came out in one piece."

The attendant wheeled Evelyn out to the hospital's nearly deserted parking lot. Only the distant moon hovering in the early evening sky greeted them. They easily picked out Jackson's tangerine four-door sedan with rims and profile tires. Granny B opened the back passenger door. "You might wont to stretch out in the backseat, put yo' feet up on the ride home."

"Thanks." Evelyn gave her mama the bag holding her release papers and jewelry. She climbed into the backseat and stretched out.

Beatrice took the bag from Lis. She could tell by her granddaughter's closed eyes that she had no intention of uttering a word during the trip. And neither did she.

Evelyn expected that her semiconscious state during the smooth ride would prevent further interrogation about just why she was parked along the road so close to home. But she didn't expect to wake up parked in front of Granny B's house. She straightened abruptly. Pain stabbed her right behind her eyes. "Mama, I thought you were dropping me off at home first?"

"No, not exactly." She turned from her daughter to stare pointedly at Granny B.

Evelyn sensed something afoot. "What do you mean 'not

exactly'?" She took in Granny B's firm jaw and her mama's determined expression. "What's going on? Why are we stopped here?"

Lis looked straight ahead. "We discussed it and decided it was best that you stay in Spring Hope for the next few days. The doctors want you to have complete bed rest, and I won't be able to take off work to take care of you—"

"I don't need you to take care of me, Mama. I'll be fine at your house. All I need is food, something to drink, and a remote control. Not that I don't appreciate your offer, Granny B." Sarcasm peeked out from behind Evelyn's words like the delicate lace edges on a doily. "But I can get along just fine. Really. I can manage."

Lis readjusted herself in her seat to turn around. "It's not up for discussion, Evelyn. You heard what the doctor said. You have a concussion, and you're going to be stiff and sore for quite a while. The stairs at home would wear you out, and I won't be there to help you get to the bathroom or check in on you during the day."

Evelyn hoped Granny B would offer a word or two in her defense. In *her own* defense. God knew she didn't want someone underfoot, least of all someone she considered public enemy number one. Granny B, however, sat there. So Evelyn sat up straighter in her seat and tried to look the picture of health—bandaged, bruised, bleeding, and all.

"Thank you, Mama." Evelyn cleared her throat. "And, Granny B. But I vote that you drive me home to Mount Laurel. All my work is at your house, all my clothes.

Everything. I won't be in town for that long, and I came here to spend some quality time with you and Jackson—and you, too, Granny B. If you're worried about the stairs, just set me up in Daddy's den. There's a pullout sofa in there and a television. And the den is near the kitchen . . ."

But her mama adamantly shook her head. "No, Evelyn, absolutely not. You wouldn't get any real rest on that sofa, and there still wouldn't be anyone there during the day to help you. And this is just for a few days, until the weekend. When you come home, you'll still have plenty of time to visit with us and get some work done."

Lis sighed. "My goodness, girl, a car just slammed into you—sure, it could've been avoided, but I don't blame you. You're hurt, Evelyn, and you need help. Why are you putting up such a fight?"

Feeling her last line of defense slipping away, hearing her own hotly spoken words thrown in her face, Evelyn turned to Granny B. "You've been sitting there without saying a word. What do you think of this? I'm sure you're not happy about the idea of having an invalid underfoot. You're busy enough. And you need to take care of yourself."

"Oh, so now you're an invalid. A minute ago you felt strong enough to—"

"Hush, 'Lis'beth. Now I sho' ain't gon' say it was *my* idea. But I can stand the comp'ny for a couple days. And I'm sho' the doctor told you why you need to take it easy." Granny B cast a sidewise glance back at Evelyn as she dangled that warning. "I don't thank neither of us have much to say, even though it is my house. Least that's what it say on the deed, last I checked. 'Sides, you can stand on your own two feet. I won't be at your beck and call, contrary to what yo' mama thank. But I will 'spect you to stay out from under me while I get on with thangs."

While Evelyn stared stupidly at the back of Granny B's iron-gray hair, Lis quickly exited the car and opened the back door. She stood there, hand outstretched toward her daughter.

For a moment, Evelyn silently rebuffed the offer of help, but a sudden stab of pain in her left temple finally spurred her to grasp her mother's slender fingers and emerge, albeit ungracefully, from the car. "I cannot believe you are forcing me to do this," she seethed.

"It makes perfect sense. While she's seeing to you, you can talk to her about her own situation. I couldn't have planned it better. Well, maybe without the accident," Lis hissed back. Then she added loudly, "Come on, Evelyn, let's get you settled in the house," as Granny B slammed her door and walked toward them.

The two older women escorted their victim up to the porch and into the front room. Then Granny B directed her assistant to sit Evelyn down on the sofa while she readied the bedroom. "Didn't know I'd be havin' comp'ny," she explained saucily before leaving.

"I'll expect you to do as you're told." Lis propped sofa pillows behind her daughter. "And I mean *everything*. Right, Evelyn?" she added with a raised brow.

A prisoner of war, Evelyn churlishly turned her head to stare out at the woods bathed in the murky evening light.

"We-ll-l . . ." Her mama expelled the word with a lungful of air. "Jackson and I will bring you some clothes and your computer. Is there anything else you think you'll need over the next three or four days? Although I can't imagine you'll have the energy to think clearly enough to write one word during that time."

"Just bring some clothes, please, and the portfolio by my bed. What about Cocoa? And Kevin? I don't want you to tell him anything, upsetting him when he's halfway around the world."

"Well, you not brangin' that little piece of dog here," Granny B grumbled from some unseen spot in the hallway. "I'm likely to sweep her up with the rest of the dust and hairballs on this flo'."

"Now, Mama." To Evelyn, Lis responded, "Jackson can walk Cocoa when he gets home from work. I'm sure she's used to being alone all day anyway." She pointed a crimson-tipped nail in Evelyn's direction. "But she better not have any accidents on my floors or get on my furniture."

"Cocoa is house-trained. You don't have to worry about that, as long as you don't forget to take her out. But what about Kevin—?"

"I'm not planning to call him—and it's not like he calls the house anyway. You can tell him what you want to, even though the truth is always right. Speaking of, I should give

Kevin a piece of my mind for going away for so long, not taking care of you."

"Kevin doesn't have to take care of me."

"And why not? He's your husband, isn't he? Now that you've lost your job, he is paying the bills. I'd say that means he's taking care of you. Wouldn't you agree? Or are you afraid he'd say he was too busy flitting around the world to come see about his wife?"

Evelyn wouldn't admit her mama had stepped on her tail, but she yelped nonetheless. She fought back tears. "For the last time, I did not *lose* my job. I quit. And don't bother explaining Kevin's duties as a husband to me." She sucked in a breath to launch another missile. "Furthermore—"

"'Lis'beth, ain't it 'bout time you got yo'self home? Won't Jackson be lookin' fo' you?" Granny B appeared in the doorway.

Lis looked like she was considering saying something more before Granny B took her arm. "Now I said Ev'lyn could stay here, but I ain't said nuthin' 'bout the rest of y'all. Don't thank y'all gon' be clutterin' up my house, all in the way over the next day or two. This gal gon' be all right. By the sound of things, you ain't helpin' her get no peace and quiet nohow." Granny B directed her daughter from the room to the porch.

"And don't be callin' here all day. I ain't got time to be jibber-jabberin' on no phone," Granny B called out as Elisabeth started the car.

Evelyn listened as Granny B's solid footsteps crossed the

front porch and watched as she entered the front room—or holding cell, as she felt at that moment.

"I told you I ain't gon' be sittin' round here, just waitin' for you to ring some little bell. You know where things are, so you can get up and get 'em. Since there ain't no TV in the bedroom, you just gon' have to stare out that window for entertainment until yo' mama brang you somethin' to do. Or you can come back out here. But don't thank you gon' run up my 'lectric bill while you here burnin' up the TV. As you is just gettin' here, I will brang you somethin' to eat and drink, but I ain't takin' orders. You'll just have to eat what I give you."

With that, she disappeared.

Truth be told, Evelyn had expected a lot less, and if experience proved anything, she'd love whatever flowed from Granny B's kitchen. So she settled in, alternately gazing out the window and dozing. The moon played hide-and-seek with the clouds as nearby crickets called to neighbors. Granny B moved about in the kitchen, clinking pots and rattling utensils, providing a soothing background to Evelyn's what-ifs and maybes. Sighing to herself, she decided to focus on making the best out of the current situation. "Better yet, maybe I need to concentrate on seeing how I can best make it out of here alive."

Granny B came around the corner of the front room, holding a tray laden with food.

Evelyn's fluttery stomach growled in welcome at the appealing aroma.

Granny B set the tray beside her. "There's grits here and

fish. I know it ain't fresh, but I froze it when it was. And a corn muffin with some preserves Ruby made. This cold coffee oughta settle your stomach if you feelin' sick, but you prob'ly oughta drink this prune juice. That should flush any germs and thangs outta yo' system. No tellin' what you done picked up in that hospital, and I don't need you passin' anything on to me."

The juices suddenly flowed in Evelyn's mouth, and her stomach answered with another grumble. She managed a hasty "Thanks" as she picked up the tray and settled it solidly down on her lap. Slathering on some butter and strawberry preserves, she tucked into the corn muffin. She was so knee-deep in eating that she nearly missed the self-satisfied curl of her grandma's lips.

Evelyn lost track of time as she polished off the grits and fish. She sipped a little prune juice and then sat back, full, happy, and ready for a good sleep.

Granny B must have been hovering right outside the room because the moment Evelyn rested her fork on the plate, she emerged. "I see you took no time in finishin' this off. But you didn't drank the coffee or all the prune juice. They would help yo' bowels if you feelin'—"

"I'm fine, Granny B." Evelyn didn't want to ruin the memories of a good meal with more talk about her intestinal tract. "Thank you again for cooking for me. I know you have plenty to do without taking the time to do all this."

Granny B used the napkin to brush away the few crumbs

Evelyn hadn't managed to inhale, then picked up the tray. "Don't be 'spectin' me to do this all day."

Evelyn held up a hand. "I know, I know. You've explained that you won't wait on me hand and foot. But even so, doing what you did . . . taking me in . . ."

"Not that you was reachin' out or nuthin'."

Evelyn grimaced. "But all the same, you reached out to me, and I appreciate it."

"You didn't appreciate it much when yo' mama told you, you was gon' be stayin' here. In fact, you had better thangs to do than put a foot in this house."

"It's not that. But we both know I was the last person you thought you'd be welcoming back—especially within hours of kicking me out." Evelyn added softly, "Again."

"Well, thangs change. If I ain't learned nuthin' else in this life, I've learned that," Granny B pronounced. "You should get some rest and I've got yo' bed all made up now. 'Sides, it's gettin' late and I got some thangs to do before bed. And you know yo' mama will be back 'fo' long, interruptin' me."

Granny B helped Evelyn to her feet. She winced as bruised muscles stretched.

"Maybe if you feelin' better tomorrow, you can get up and come outside a bit and sit in the sun. You won't get better layin' up in that bed all the time. You just gon' get sore on top of everythang else."

"Yes, maybe." Tomorrow seemed like forever away. She could only focus on each difficult step she took to reach the end of Granny B's short hallway. As Evelyn turned toward the extra room, however, Granny B pushed her in the opposite direction, to the right, toward her own room. "What?" Evelyn stopped dead in her tracks. "I thought I was going to bed."

"You is. There's only a twin in that other room, and I 'spect you gon' need some extra space to get comf'table. You gon' take my bed."

"But—"

Granny B's eyes locked with her granddaughter's. "In the state you in, I don't thank you'll be gettin' into much trouble this time round—or do you want to fight it out again? Whatchyou thank?"

Evelyn smiled at Granny B, for the first time in what felt like years. "I 'thank' you right, Granny B." She squeezed the gnarled fingers of the hand cupping her elbow and peered into her grandmother's eyes.

After a moment, Granny B nodded. Then she guided Evelyn the few remaining steps between the door and the double bed. She'd pulled back the cream-colored bedspread to reveal white cotton sheets, ivy leaves sprouting over them, and piled two pillows, one atop the other, on the side of the bed closer to her nightstand, beside the window looking into the front yard. With her help, Evelyn changed into a nightgown. It barely reached her ankles, but its well-worn fabric felt downy to her skin. Granny B stopped well short of tucking her in, but that didn't detract from Evelyn's feelings of being well cared for.

"You gon' be all right?"

113

Evelyn nodded drowsily, barely hearing her parting question, too weary to murmur good-night before Granny B closed the door. She didn't move until the sun poked her between her eyelashes the next morning.

Chapter Nine

Evelyn watched as Granny B gathered laundry. A strong wind tangled up one of her queen-size sheets, and she struggled to unravel it from the line.

Thus began her second full day at Granny B's house. The two previous nights had passed uneventfully. Her mama and Jackson had dropped off the materials she'd requested, and they had spent a couple of hours visiting the evening before—something Granny B was none too thrilled about, by the sound of her grumbling.

Evelyn had talked to Kevin and reassured him that she was all right. She knew it was the right thing to do, but she had kept the conversation to a minimum. Although she wasn't surprised he hadn't offered to hop on the next North Carolina–bound flight, disappointment niggled at her.

Left to her own devices, she carefully avoided any real interaction with Granny B. And true to her word, except for a glass or two of water, she received no special treatment. After that first night of having dinner served to her on a tray, she ate all her meals at the kitchen table opposite a mostly silent, yet relatively pleasant Granny B.

This morning she woke to find Granny B in "her" bedroom.

"Layin' round so much ain't good for you," Granny B told her, raising the blinds. "I was up cookin' meals and washin' clothes for three other children two days after Thomas was born. And I don't mean pushin' a few buttons on no mi-cro-wave or throwin' some stuff in a machine. Gal, I'm talkin' 'bout *work*. Now get up and get some sunshine so you can get to mendin'. That bed pro'bly gettin' hard."

Evelyn didn't tell her that the bed was feeling pretty toasty at the moment and that she'd had every intention of wallowing in it for another hour or two. Instead, she found herself at the sinfully late hour of eight o'clock, bathed and fully dressed, watching Granny B from the kitchen doorway. She pushed open the screen and gingerly walked across the backyard.

Without a word, she held one end of the flapping sheet straight as she removed the clothespins from the other end. As Granny B unpinned each third of the sheet, Evelyn slowly folded that section, working through all the kinks in her shoulders and neck. She made her way toward her grandma until at last the sheet was free and folded, ready to go into the wicker basket at Granny B's feet. They moved to the second row of the clothesline. Granny B removed pins from towels on the far left end of the line. Evelyn gathered the rest of the linen on the far right end.

"I hadn't told anyone about this baby," she said softly. Evelyn had no idea why she decided to pick up the threads of a conversation left dangling days ago, threads they'd severed. She kept her eyes on the lily-white pillowcase in front of her, and Granny B continued to work on her towels. But Evelyn banked on their history. Granny B was like a teakettle on a hot eye: she'd get all steamed up, blow her top, and then cease to boil once removed from the source of the heat.

"I'm not sure I'm even ready to think about it myself, that I'm pregnant. I have no idea how Kevin will react, what with all that's going on between us. He really hasn't been there for me," Evelyn remarked almost to herself. "Anyway, how will I know he'll be there for a baby? And if I haven't even told my husband, how can I tell anybody else?" She quickly glanced to her left before she unpinned the fitted sheet.

"We haven't even thought about having children, not really. Of course, on some level we knew that one day we would or that we *should* but only . . . not right now. I want to work on being a writer, a wife . . . on just being a person. I'm not ready to be somebody's *mother* yet. I'm not even good at being somebody's daughter." Evelyn risked another look

Granny B's way. "Or somebody's *granddaughter*, for that matter. Getting pregnant was not in my plans, and being a single parent most definitely isn't."

"You think dyin' was in mine?"

Startled by her question, Evelyn glanced at Granny B but didn't answer. By this time, Evelyn was a pillowcase and a towel away from her grandmother. She took down the pillowcase and folded it in half lengthwise.

"In my heart I know my Father knows best, but I'd sure like to know what He knows sometimes. Here I am pregnant, out of work, married to a man who seems to be married to his job most of the time . . ." *And to the people who work there.* "I'm alone . . ."

"And you ain't got nobody to reach out to." Granny B folded the last piece of laundry and dropped it into the basket.

She looked at Granny B directly this time. "And I ain't got nobody to reach out to."

Granny B bent down to tuck in the edges of the towels that hung over the side of the laundry basket. "Well, it ain't like women don't have babies every day. I birthed nine of 'em, and I sho' didn't sit around with my head up my butt, wonderin' what to do next. Nobody didn't need to tell me what I needed to do. I just did it." Granny B hefted the basket to her side and directed her steps to the house. "And I did it *alone*."

Evelyn picked up the cloth bag of clothespins and brushed away the bits of grass. Then she clipped it to the line before slowly trailing Granny B. She'd grown accustomed to seeing her ramrod-straight back.

When she opened the back door, Granny B was extracting wet laundry from the washing machine. She watched her separate and shake each piece before tossing it atop the growing pile of sodden clothes in another basket. Her grandma did not acknowledge her presence, not even when she leaned on the wall beside her. "It's not that I'm thinking of *not* having this baby. I'm not thinking much of anything at the moment." When Granny B didn't react, she amplified her thoughts. "I'm just trying to make you understand why I hadn't volunteered the fact that I'm pregnant. Why I didn't say much about it in the hospital."

"Well, you ain't got to worry about explainin' nuthin' to me—it ain't none of my business." Granny B draped a pair of panty hose over the rack above the washer and dryer and closed the washing machine lid. "It's yo' husband you need to be worryin' 'bout. And maybe yo' mama." After heaving the basket from the top of the dryer, she rear-ended the screen door and headed back outside to the line. This time, Evelyn hurried as quickly as her sore body could to catch up with her and maintain the "momentum" of the conversation.

"I'm not 'worried' about Kevin—at least about this baby. Or Mama either, for that matter. Even though I didn't plan it, I can do this on my own . . . with God's help if I need to."

"You young people and your *plans*. You thank everythang's supposed to go by some big *plan* you created. Then, when things don't work out, you run around like crazy chickens, blaming God." She waved her hands above her head. "'What do I do? What do I do?'"

"Speaking of plans, you've had a sudden crimp in your own."

"If you call 'cute my'loid leu-ke-mia a 'crimp,' then unh-huh, I guess I have." She looked up at Evelyn from her crouch by the basket and caught her granddaughter's look. "I might as well say it straight, as you and yo' mama been meddlin' around in my personal business anyhow."

"We—"

"Just hush up, gal." Granny B clipped wet underwear to the line. "Best you own up to it. It ain't like I got somethin' to hide no mo'. Just like you ain't gon' have much to hide in a few mo' months." She paused to appraise Evelyn's mid-section. "Make that a few *weeks*."

Evelyn watched her for a moment, bending and clipping and sidestepping, bending and clipping and sidestepping. "Nothing to hide? It's not like Mama went looking into your private medical files. The information came looking for her."

"Well, my business mighta gone lookin' for her, but here I find you all chin-deep in it." Granny B moved to the second row. She pushed the bag of clothespins down the line, out of her way. "So what? You came over here to Sprang Hope to get into this business of my bein' sick? You wont to know just how long I'm gon' be round, botherin' you folks?"

"No, I'm here to make sure you stay around, botherin' us folks."

Granny B barked. "And just how you s'posed to do that?

You makin' deals with God? Huh, I think He done put enough on my plate, thank you very much."

"Maybe, but your daughter—"

"Which one? 'Lis'beth?" Granny B straightened to eye her granddaughter. "What y'all got cooked up?'

"We don't have anything cooked up." Evelyn took a pair of women's briefs and pinned them to the clothesline. She shook her head. *Just how many pairs of white panties does any woman need?* "The first we heard of your illness came from somebody other than you, and we just want to know what's really going on. You know, like . . . when did you get diagnosed? What are your symptoms? What can we do to help? Have you and your doctor considered a bone marrow transplant or chemotherapy? Mama and I want to make sure you and your doctor are clear on your method of treatment."

"We is." Granny B went back to her bending and clipping and sidestepping, though Evelyn intuited she was also sidestepping a bigger issue.

"You is? I mean, you are?" Suspicious, she let a pair of underwear hang by one leg. "But from what Mrs. Tagle told Mama—"

Granny B's head snapped around. "Ruby? What she know 'bout—?"

Evelyn mentally kicked herself for the slip. "Anyway, that's not the point. It was our understanding that you weren't getting treatment at all. Oh, wait! Are you seeing somebody other than Dr. Hedgepeth? Do you have a specialist we don't know about?"

"No and no."

"No? Then what—?"

"You is full of questions about thangs that ain't none of yo' concern." Granny B finished the underwear and picked up the now-empty basket. "Haven't you learned yo' lesson yet 'bout stickin' yo' nose into other people's situations?" She walked away.

Evelyn tried to make sense of what Granny B had, or rather, had not told her as she stood there.

Evelyn limped back to the house, pulled open the back door, and stepped inside. She didn't have to look for Granny B. She was staring out the kitchen window, sipping from a glass of ice water. Evelyn searched for a way to start.

But before she could wrap her lips around the words, Granny B stated, without preamble, "I know you got somethin' to say as usual. Stop chewin' on them words and spit 'em out."

Evelyn jumped. "Well, since you know so much, you know what I was going to say. 'Cause I have no idea."

Granny B seemed to take her time setting down the glass beside the sink. Then she faced her. "You gon' ask me 'bout what I'm doin' to fight this animal that's eatin' away at my insides. You gon' ask me what my doctor say 'bout all this, what he doin' to *cure* me. You wonderin' why I ain't told nobody nuthin' until now." She waited a beat. "That 'bout it?"

"You're getting there."

"Well." Granny B wearily took the few short steps between the sink and the table. It was then Evelyn realized her grandmother had leaned against the countertop for physical support, not to enjoy the view. "Well." Granny B pulled a chair from the table, lifting it so it did not scrape the floor. She sat with her back to the refrigerator. Her eyes gazed out into the wide space of the backyard, perhaps taking in the clothes flapping on the line or the birds perched on the back fence. While she focused on that unknown spot, she said dryly, "I 'spect you gon' sit down."

Evelyn eased into a chair.

"I don't rightly know why I see fit to tell you 'bout all this, but see'n as how you and yo' mama know so much as it is, I guess I might as well." Granny B reached down into the right front pocket of her plaid housedress and withdrew a lace-trimmed handkerchief. She first wiped away moisture from her forehead and around her mouth, and then she wiped her chin, her neck, and down to the first button of her faded-red housedress. Finally she folded the cloth into a tiny square and returned it to her pocket.

Evelyn itched for her to go on. She had never known Granny B to sit still. "Are you in pain? What made you go see Dr. Hedgepeth in the first place?"

"Looking back on it, I guess I'd been feeling pretty bad for a while," Granny B responded quietly. "I cain't even say what exactly. I didn't really hurt nowhere, but I just got tired and stayed tired. I been gettin' weak—one day, I could barely lift that coffeepot over there on the stove. I dropped it and got coffee all over this here flo'. I had to go sit down two hours 'fo' I could get in here and clean it up. Made such a mess . . ." Granny B *tsked*, fading off, shaking her head slowly.

Evelyn didn't know if she was thinking about the mess or how bad she'd been feeling.

"Most times, I'm all right, but . . ." Granny B let the words crawl until they stopped altogether, which allowed Evelyn to fill in the blank with her own wild imaginings.

"Why didn't you say something, Granny B? Mama never would have allowed you to go to that—"

"'Lowed me?" Granny B snapped. "It was fo' me to decide when or if I would go to the doctor." Granny B expelled a breath. "Well. After 'bout a week or two, I did start feelin' a kinda pain, just this heaviness, this achy-ness down somewhere deep. I waited, but then it seemed like it wouldn't go away, no matter what I tried. So I asked Ruby to carry me to see that Dr. Hedgepeth—who, by the way, don't know more'n my hairy behind 'bout curin' nuthin'." Granny B snorted. "All he did was write down a lot of words and make me take a lot of tests. It didn't make no kinda sense the blood they took from me. It took weeks 'fo' he was finally able to tell me I had this disease."

"Acute myeloid leukemia."

"Yes, that." Granny B swallowed and smiled slightly. "Ain't that a mouthful of nonsense? Hurts 'bout as much to say it as it does to have it." She walked over to the sink and picked up her glass. She drained the water in a slow gulp, and then she upended the glass in the sink. The ice clinked and rattled against the stainless steel.

Evelyn waited until Granny B rinsed her glass and set it on the draining board before she spoke. "But what did Dr. Hedgepeth say?"

"What did he say?" Granny B's raised eyebrows indicated the answer was obvious. "Well, I got it, and they ain't no givin' it back. So it's mine, just like this here house."

"Okay, we know you have leukemia. But I know that you can treat it. What did the doctor say about where we go from here?"

"I know exactly where *I* go from here—to that piece of dirt I done picked out in my backyard." Granny B pointed through the back door.

Evelyn didn't turn to look. "Granny B, that's not what I mean, and you know it!"

"You know, chile, I don't rightly care what you mean. Do you see me askin' you a bunch of questions 'bout that baby you carryin' around? I haven't asked you 'bout when you gon' tell yo' mama or yo' husband, or what you gon' do 'bout bein' pregnant. You know what's right and what's wrong."

Evelyn jumped up and grabbed her grandmother's own words from the air and waved them high. "Aha! So you admit that this is absurd!"

"I ain't admittin' no such thing. I was talkin' about *you*. I've lived long enough to do all manner of foolishness—you got plenty mo' years and mistakes ahead. Now, I ain't asked you what I need to do 'cause I already know. I been runnin' for a while now, thinkin' it won't find me, but this disease know where I live." Granny B rested against the sink and again gazed out the side window. "I accept it now, and I don't need no interference from nobody to make it worse."

"Are you in much pain?" Evelyn dreaded an honest response.

"What kinda question is that to ask me, gal? This ain't really 'bout the pain. I been in pain all my life from one thang or 'nother." She crossed her arms. "But see, *that pain?* I's able to control that. I could see where it was comin' from. Livin' is all 'bout hurtin', at least in my 'sperience. For me, death just gon' brang the end of my pain."

Granny B pressed her lips together for a moment. "But dyin' 'cause of somethin' like this? I cain't control it." She looked at her granddaughter. "I guess I thought like the rest of you that I was just too mean to die. Ain't that somethin'? I guess mean people die, too."

Did I think she'd just keep washing clothes and cooking tender greens through all eternity, while children, grandchildren, and great-grandchildren lived and died? Evelyn didn't know the answer, and she wasn't prepared to respond to Granny B's admission or her apparent acceptance of the inevitable. But she could deal with scientific facts.

"Granny B, you say you can't control dying, but you can. Know how? You get treated. That's what Mama and I are talking about, giving you some sense of empowerment over this—this—this *animal* as you call it." Evelyn's voice rose a bit as she struggled to find the right words, but she remained seated. Her hands clenched with the effort to contain herself.

"Empowerment? You young folks always throwing round

that word like it mean somethin'. You ain't got power from nobody but God. *Self* don't give you nuthin'." Granny growled as she faced Evelyn. "And I'll tell you somethin' else. I won't get power from takin' medicine that gon' leave me bald and cause me to waste away to my bones and make me sicker than this 'cute my'loid mess. And then, after all that, I still got to die. You thank power come like that? Well, it don't. I faced up to dyin'. And it ain't hard really. It may be hard for you and yo' mama and for anybody else to deal with, but I faced it head-on befo'. *I got the power.*"

"What? Your faith?"

"Gal, hush yo' mouth. God been here with me all the time. He ain't goin' nowhere even when I do. What I'm talkin' 'bout don't got nuthin' to do with Ruthena's white man in the sky. It's 'bout what's really goin' on right here in this po' black woman's body. People die, and that's a fact. Ain't no need in delayin' death or makin' me suffer just so y'all can feel like you doin' somethin'."

"But—"

"Uh-uh, no. Now, this my body. Y'all come traipsin' through this house and in my life anytime y'all feel like it. You even get into my personal medical condition, but you won't interfere in this. You cain't strap me to no machine and make me take nuthin', least of all somethin' that come from somebody else. I got this here, gal. *I got the power.*"

"What is wrong with you? Is this leukemia affecting your mind? Are you telling me you're completely refusing treatment, that you're just going to sit back and die to show you're in control or to hurt us the way you hurt after Milton? So you can keep on with this ridiculous resistance to help from somebody else? That's a death wish!"

Evelyn collapsed into her chair, her mouth agape. "What kind of sense does that make? Yes, it's your body. Yes, you say what, how, when, where—we acknowledge you're in control, Granny B. But you don't have to take this stance to show us that you mean business. Okay, you're fed up with the whole lot of us. We'll step back and let you handle your own visits, your own treatments—"

Granny B shook her head. "See, that's what I'm talkin' 'bout. '*You* gon' do this, *you* gon' do that.' Have *I* lost *my* mind? Nobody got to do nuthin', leastwise hurt 'cause a what I done. What y'all young folks say? All I got to do is stay black and die? Well, I got the first part down, and now I'm workin' on the second part."

"Granny B, that's not funny."

"Now we agree on somethin'!" Granny B slapped her hands together.

Evelyn jumped in her seat.

"There ain't nuthin' funny about this, so you gotta know I'm serious. You cain't do nuthin' 'bout this decision, Ev'lyn, so you can rest easy. I'll even tell yo' mama 'bout it so you can just take a load off. I'm not crazy. Talk to my doctor, and he'll tell you. He'll even 'splain that my decision make a whole heap-a sense 'cause that medicine he was gon' give me couldn't do much anyway. Maybe buy me a month or so, but that 'bout all. This leu-ke-mia ain't stoppin' long enough to let nobody off, Ev'lyn. This train's a-movin'." Granny B walked around their chairs to lean against the doorjamb of the back door. "Now, I'm speedin' past eighty years old, and I'm gon' spend my remainin' time doing what I wont, not layin' up sick."

Evelyn took a deep breath. *Does she really think we'll just let her go off and die somewhere like a dog?* She started to silently tick off salient points on her fingers to help Granny B see the light.

"I know you sittin' there wonderin' how you can get me locked up so you can have yo' way."

Evelyn looked up at her. *Okay, forget number three.*

"Fact is, Ev'lyn, I just waited too long to do somethin' about it. By the time I got to the doctor, it was too late. All Dr. Hedgepeth can really do now is waste my time. He cain't do nothin' fo' me. Talk to him—he'll tell you."

"But if that's the case, why did he contact Mrs. Tagle and have her talk to Mama?"

"I didn't say he didn't want me to get chemother'py. He mentioned some kinda medication that might help slow thangs down, but he just say it won't do a heck of a lot of good. You know educated folk. They thank they can use they books to fix ever'body's problems, even though they smart enough to know they cain't." Granny B made a wry face. "Now, I've had plenty-a time to wrap my mind round this. You gon' need some time to do the same." Granny B paused a half beat before adding, "It's kinda whatchyou doin' 'bout yo' baby."

"Would you please stop talking about this baby? The two situations are totally different!"

Granny B calmly studied her over her shoulder. "Oh? Just how so?"

"Well, for one—" Evelyn was about to say that her pregnancy didn't affect anyone else, but it did. "But—" This time she almost pointed out that it was her body. "You see, you—" Again, she clamped her lips together. Then she growled low in her throat like some cornered animal and blurted, "'Cause it is!"

Granny B laughed shortly. "You don't like havin' to justify yo' decisions, do you? You don't thank I have a right to make you 'splain what you doin' 'cause it really don't involve me, does it?" Suddenly sober, Granny B returned her eyes to the view outside. She said quietly, "Sho', I'd like to tell you to take yo' fool head out the sand and grow up. I'd like to tell you, you's somebody's mama now, so act like it. I wish I could tell you it ain't all that bad—after all, you got a husband who's workin'."

She drew a deep breath. "I could point out you got a husband you love, even though he's made you so mad you could spit. And that he loves you. You got a nice house and a family that'll be buttin' in and offerin' help you don't even need. I'd like to tell you all them thangs, but I'm sho' you been thankin' of all this yo'self and you don't need to hear me spoutin' off 'bout what you can see plain befo' you."

Evelyn fought the urge to squirm.

"I respect the fact that you got a head and you can bang

it against that wall over there as much as you wont. You gon' make the decision that's right for *you* 'cause it's *yo'* business, and whatever you do 'bout yo' life is yo' business. 'Cause the decisions you make? You got to be at peace within yo' own skin. You got to live with 'em." Then she whispered, "Or die."

Tears coursed down Evelyn's cheeks by the time Granny B finished telling her all the things she would like to tell her but wouldn't. She wanted to shout, *"You're wrong! Be quiet!"* But then she thought about Kevin and all the decisions she had to make. She held her stomach and choked back a sob.

Granny B continued to stare outside, giving Evelyn time to put her face back together. They remained in those positions for a good while—Granny B by the back door, Evelyn at the table silently weeping, going over argument after useless argument in her head, trying to formulate a response, however inadequate.

But then Evelyn got it.

Granny B did understand this, her need to protect her most private, innermost self. She knew Evelyn's business was *hers*, and she possessed sole ownership of her own and could and should protect it. That's what Granny B had done when she'd come across Evelyn in her room weeks ago. This was how she felt right now when Evelyn was trying to get her to confront something she probably faced every morning when she looked in the mirror. Finally she got it.

Evelyn closed her eyes to hide her shame, but she knew she could not hide the truth. She owned up to it by uttering the only four words she could manage, the only words that might make a difference at the moment.

"Will you forgive me?"

<hr>

After dinner that night, still in the forgiving mood, Evelyn decided to reach out to Kevin. She intended to extend the tiniest of olive branches and let him know how she was faring in the fiery furnace. Granny B had announced after dinner that she had some things to do and had retired to her room, so Evelyn had time on her hands. She hoped they'd talk again, but she thought Granny B's daily Energizer Bunny routine had worn her out, although she would never admit it or alter it in any way.

Quickly, before she could change her mind, Evelyn tapped out: Hey. Just checking in. While she waited for Kevin to answer the text message, she propped her feet on the porch rail and sat back to relish the scenery. She'd settled down on the front porch in the chair directly to the left of the door, close enough to hear Granny B if she called out, not that she expected her to.

It was nearly eight, yet the night air dripped water. Lightning bugs flickered in the twilight and unseen crickets peeped somewhere beyond the expanse of dirt Granny B called her front yard. Evelyn swatted mosquitoes that discovered her hiding on the porch, but she determined they wouldn't spoil her few moments alone, outside the four walls of Granny B's house.

The phone chirped beside her. She almost dropped it on the concrete in her haste to answer it. "Hello? Kevin?"

"Yes. Ev." Kevin's answer was terse, his voice slightly hoarse.

Belatedly, Evelyn realized that it was almost 1 a.m. in London. "Oh, Kevin! I'm sorry! Were you asleep? I forgot that you were five hours ahead." *But now that you're on the phone, you'd better talk to me. I really need to talk, Kevin.*

She heard rustling in the background. At first she pictured him shifting in the bed, rustling the sheets, getting more comfortable. But then she heard voices, and he cleared his throat. When he spoke, it wasn't to her but off to the side, to someone else. *Was it another woman? It's one o'clock in the morning! Were those bedsheets?*

When Kevin spoke to her again, he sounded more alert. "Evelyn? Is there anything wrong? Has something else happened?"

Oh no, no, nothing's wrong. Well, nothing else is wrong, other than the fact that Granny B is dying, and I'm carrying your child. Her words almost cut her lips they were so stiff, brittle. "I hadn't heard from you. I just called to update you."

"What are you talking about, you hadn't heard from me? You told me not to call." His voice was a whisper, but Evelyn could tell that he'd walked away from whatever background noise she'd picked up on when he'd answered the phone.

"Yes, but I thought you might be concerned since I'd had the accident . . ." She swallowed and squeezed her eyes shut, trying to rekindle those feelings that had prompted her to call in the first place. "And I missed you."

Silence spanned the distance between them.

"Kevin? Are you there? Did you hear—?"

"Of course I heard you. And I miss you, too, Evelyn. I just wish you had called earlier. I'm in the middle—" But a voice called his name then.

That is *a woman's voice!*

"I'm sorry. I see you're busy. That's not Samantha Jane, is it?"

"Saman—? Of course not! Evelyn . . ." Thousands of miles of swirling ocean waters couldn't drown out the breath Kevin expelled. "Eric and I are out with some key clients, and they want to wine and dine all night. And of course, I've got an early meeting—"

"Okay, okay, Kevin, I get the message." Evelyn had already tired of the conversation, such as it was. "I didn't really call to get a rundown of your day. I already know how important you are. And you don't owe me an explanation at this point."

"Ev, why don't you dismount from that high horse and—"

"What do you say you go back to your . . . *meeting* . . . and we talk another time? Take care and—"

"Wait, Evelyn! Don't hang up! Back up a minute. You said you wanted to tell me something. What is it?" Kevin's tone became more conciliatory, like he strove to salvage the wreckage of their conversation. He sounded more like the husband who had begged her not to move out than the distracted marketing executive who had answered the phone.

"No, Kevin, don't worry about it. Good luck, have fun with all that stuff that you're really *good* at doing, and we'll talk some other time, when it's more convenient." Full of attitude, Evelyn pushed End. Thinking about it for only a second, she then held the Power Off button. *Why did I really call him anyway? What did I plan to talk about? Would I really hand him the news that I'm pregnant, with him thousands of miles away in some hotel room?*

Evelyn stood and stretched. The lightning bugs and the chirping crickets had lost their allure, thanks to her husband and a few bloodthirsty mosquitoes. She pivoted to head inside. And ran smack into Granny B's steady gaze.

"Oh! Granny B! You scared me!" She covered her heart with her hand. "Where are you going?"

"Outside." Granny B's eyes flickered to the phone. "I hear you talkin'?"

Evelyn waved her phone. "Yeah, I tried to call Kevin."

"You *tried*? He ain't there?" Granny B pushed open the screen and stepped out onto the porch.

"He's there, all right. But he's busy. I told him we could talk tomorrow." Evelyn watched closely as Granny B sat down in the chair she'd just vacated. *Is she moving more stiffly?*

"From what I heard, you told him that you would talk some other time, when it was mo' convenient. And you didn't sound none too happy 'bout it neither."

"Granny B! You were eavesdropping!" Evelyn was shocked not so much that she had, but that she admitted it.

"I ain't did no such thang. I was on my way to the porch and I heard you talkin'. Now, who's Samantha Jane?"

"What else did you hear while you were walking to the door?"

"Nuthin'. You didn't say much more'n that—'fo' you hung up on him." Granny B folded her arms and looked at her granddaughter. "How *is* Kevin?"

"Why do you ask?"

"Prob'ly 'cause you just got off the phone with him, and it seemed like the right thang to do. But if you don't wont to say nuthin' 'bout him—"

"I thought you might have something specific in mind, that's all. Kevin's fine. He's working hard and long, and he loves it. You know he's in Europe?"

"Yeah, you and yo' mama both told me fifty-'leven times. He need to slow down some if he too busy to talk to his wife when she call halfway round the world."

Evelyn started counting lightning bugs. "You would think," she agreed low under her breath.

"Did you call to tell him?"

Evelyn had worked her way up to thirteen. "Hmm? Tell him what?"

Granny B's silence screamed the obvious.

She forsook counting lightning bugs and enumerated the stars instead. She got to number seventeen before she replied, "I don't know why I called. Either way, I didn't tell him. And I thought that subject was one of the things we weren't going to discuss."

Granny B's eyebrows rose. "Who said? Them one of yo' rules?"

136

"I don't have any rules per se. I just thought today we agreed that we'd let the other person live her own life."

"I didn't say I was gon' carry that baby for you." Granny B paused. "So when you gon' tell him?"

Evelyn inhaled deeply and exhaled on a count of ten. "Granny B, I'm not really up for this right now. I'm exhausted, I'm sore, and to be honest with you, I'm pretty ticked off with my husband right now. Please, let's not get into this." She reached for the handle of the screen door. "I'm going to bed, something you were supposed to do ages ago."

"I 'member," Granny B said quietly in the night as if to the dancing lightning bugs, "when I found out I was carryin' Milton. I just sat down and cried. For days. I had missed my mont'ly, so I knew what was goin' on, but I just kept hopin' and wishin'—who knows, I might even've said a prayer or two." Granny B went silent, obviously thinking back. "I just couldn't be pregnant."

Granny B's soft voice halted her granddaughter's exodus more abruptly than any command. Evelyn leaned against the door.

"Early on, I was so tired, I didn't thank I was gon' make it through breakfast. But there was the washin', the cleanin', the cookin'. All them children. And Henton, he wan't no kinda help, not that I wanted his anyway. Many a time I thought about drinkin' some lye or throwin' myself down the back steps. I even considered goin' to visit Mae Sheridan, this woman who could arrange thangs back in those days."

"Granny B! You—" Evelyn was shocked by her admission,

by the ugliness of it. She wondered if her grandmother regretted those feelings after all that she'd been through with Milton. *But does Granny B ever regret anything?*

"Gal, stop catchin' flies and close yo' mouth. You cain't tell me you hadn't tried to wish away yo' baby any less'n I tried to. And why? 'Cause you scared you gon' be raisin' that baby all by yo' lonesome in that big house? Hmmmpf. I learned there was worse thangs to worry 'bout . . ." Granny B propped both her hands on her knees, her elbows bowed out at right angles as she surveyed the darkness in front of her. "I had all them children, each tryin' to get a piece of me, and here I come up with another one."

"So what made you decide to have the baby?"

Granny B studied the darkness for a long time. Finding nothing in the heavy air, she seemed to reach somewhere deep inside for the unvarnished truth. "The steps weren't high enough," she stated flatly.

Evelyn's hands worked to hold her heart in her chest as she took a step back. *"It's Milton's life you're mourning, Granny B?"*

"Don't sound too saintly—is that what you thanking? God gon' send a lightnin' strike, and yo' hair might get burnt?"

But her grandmother didn't duck or cower. And her face didn't reflect fear or self-loathing, let alone anything close to piety, sainthood, or repentance. Evelyn looked away from that vacant expression to catch her breath and mask her own shock and confusion. When she turned back, Granny B was peering out into the yard. Evelyn touched her shoulder. "Granny B?"

"That last pregnancy was the hardest on me. And so was the birthin'. I really thought he was gon' tear me wide open. Maybe he knew from the beginnin' he wan't wonted." Granny B talked more to herself than to Evelyn. Her shrug seemed to shake off the memory. Her sudden movement also shook her granddaughter's hand from her shoulder. "Sit down, gal."

Thrown off-kilter by her change of mood, Evelyn crouched on the top step and half turned to face her.

"If you don't learn nuthin' from me, learn this: Don't go into this with a bunch of second thoughts and hard feelin's. What's done is done, and they ain't no undoin' it. So you might as well stop messin' up yo' mind and go on and tell yo' husband and yo' mama. If you don't, you just makin' it harder on yo'self and this baby." Granny B pursed her lips and muttered, almost to herself, "Secrets ain't no good for nobody." Louder, she pronounced, "Life is God's gift, somethin' I didn't come to appreciate in time."

"You've still got some time, so what about you and your gift, Granny B?" Being who she was, and whose child and grandchild she was, Evelyn felt obligated to hold up the mirror so her grandmother could see herself just as clearly. "I know some people who would be very interested in hearing what you have to say, who deserve to know as much as you say Kevin and Mama deserve to know about mine." She braced herself for reprisal, but the older woman surprised Evelyn. Which shouldn't have surprised her at all.

Granny B inclined her head slightly. "You may have a

point. Gettin' this cleared up now means less confusion later when I'll be too busy dyin' to fight."

Evelyn's heart quickened a beat and her stomach flip-flopped. "So what do you mean? I can tell Mama? You want me to call Aunt—?"

Granny B looked at her, her body bent in a forty-five-degree angle, a hand on each arm of the chair she was using to push herself upright. "So that means you wont me to call yo' husband and tell him yo' news?" She stood completely straight then and reached out toward Evelyn's phone. "Just tell me the number. I'll call him right now. I'm sure Kevin still tryin' to get through since you hung up on him. If he ain't mad yet, he will be in just a minute."

Evelyn laughed so hard, she snorted. Finally she composed herself. Her nose ran, and her stomach ached from the exertion, but it sure felt good. When she looked at Granny B, she saw that she was still inclined toward her with an outstretched hand. "I'll do my own dirty work, thank you very much. You can do yours."

Granny B cracked a smile. The sight of it actually stopped Evelyn's laughter cold. "Well, then. We both need to get to bed. We got a beautiful day to ruin for a lotta folk and not much time to do it in." She let the screen door slam closed behind her. "Good night, chile."

"Good night, Granny B." As Granny B hobbled to her room, Evelyn sat peering into the yard with a lighter heart, her spirit dancing with the lightning bugs.

Chapter Ten

A COOL BREEZE WAFTED through the mesh. Nothing ventured out but a fat black spider spinning a web in the top right corner of the porch. When the screen door creaked open, it skittered into the corner and played dead. Beatrice stepped out and bent to lace up her walking shoes.

Heavy-lidded, peering out at the world that appeared to have as lazy an aim as she, her granddaughter sat up from the lounger and drawled, "Where are you going in this heat?"

Beatrice could tell Evelyn was enjoying her roost, holding an icy glass of *decaffeinated* mint tea. She'd been eyeing her from the doorway for the better part of ten minutes, and the only part of Evelyn that had moved were the damp tendrils of hair on her forehead and the hem of her loose cotton dress when tickled by the wind.

"For a walk. And it ain't that hot." She hid her grunt of pain when she started down the steps. "I need to get out a bit. This house startin' to close in on me."

"Can I go?"

"I don't know. *Can* you?"

"No, I mean, *may I?*"

"No, *I* mean, *can you?*" *This chile gon' make me change my mind 'bout going.* "You thank you can walk?"

"Sure. I mean, I guess."

"You not feelin' too weak 'cause you preg—?"

"Granny B, I said I'll be all right. As hard as you've had me working, this walk will be a nice change of pace."

"But what about—?"

"Granny B! I said I'm okay. Now please, let's go."

Beatrice pointed at Evelyn's feet. "Seems to me like you need to put some shoes on 'fo' we go."

Fifteen minutes later Beatrice turned with a sneaker-clad Evelyn onto Deep River Road. The older woman folded back the brim of her straw hat and squinted up at the trees. Red-breasted robins perched on branches, calling to each other. They strolled down the middle of the deserted road, as there was no sidewalk to speak of and no traffic to impede their trip. Beatrice carried in her left hand a large stick that she kept propped beside her front porch. She swung it to and fro—when she wasn't leaning on it. "Just in case some dog thankin' 'bout doin' somethin' foolish, he might better thank again," she explained.

After forty-five minutes the two neared an intersection where Deep River Road crossed Ann F. Gladwell Way, a road named for a long-dead woman who had taught people in that area how to read. At this crossroads, Deep River Road's asphalt changed to packed dirt. On either side of the four-way, gold- and green-speckled fields stretched for acres. Here, Beatrice turned 360 degrees in the middle of the road. She didn't care that Evelyn stood back, watching, waiting.

At last Beatrice stopped, partially facing the crossroads, her back to Evelyn. She pointed left with her stick. "See that field there? That belong to Booker, who brang me all them veg'ables." She rotated slightly so that her stick encompassed all the land around them. "His daddy owned all this land, and his daddy 'fo' that, but Booker gambled it all away, all 'cept this patch over here."

Beatrice's hand fell to her side and she bore down on the stick. "On summer mornings, I didn't let the rooster finish crowin' 'fo' I had the chillun up and out the house."

"They worked hard."

"You thank that hard work? Keepin' all them chillun fed and clothed, now *that* was hard work. They had it easy. 'Sides, Booker let us keep part of what they brought in, and we ate off that all winter."

"But they were children, Granny B."

"Chillun? And what was I? At the time, 'Lis'beth wan't much younger than I was when I started havin' all them. If

I was old enough to have 'em, then they was old enough to pick a couple veg'ables in the summertime. How did you 'spect me to keep a roof over they heads while they daddy was off seein' the world and makin' a name for hisself? I couldn't do it all. Believe me, I had to do much worse to keep the wolf from the do'."

Beatrice focused on the waving grasses that stretched to meet a copse at the far edge of the property. "And sometimes he got in anyway," she added quietly.

She snatched up her stick and walked in the direction from which they had come. "You gon' let a dyin' woman walk faster than you?" She didn't intend to give Evelyn time to ask any questions. She'd gotten a few steps ahead before speaking again.

"The summers wan't all bad, contrary to what you might be thankin'. Harvestin' didn't take but a few weeks; then Little Ed, Mary, 'Lis'beth, Thomas, Sarah—they'd all run out the house, headin' to who knows where. Sometimes I'd see 'em in the woods 'hind the house, takin' cover from the sun and heat—and from they mama." Beatrice chuckled dryly. "By summer's end, after spendin' part of it workin' in the fields and the rest of it outside playin', they'd all look like little raisins, even Little Ed, who looked more like a banana than a grape at summer's beginnin'. They paid a pretty price tryin' to hide from me, but I guess they figured it was worth it."

At her granddaughter's expression she smiled, although there was little true humor in it. "Yeah, I knew they was tryin' to get away from me. They hated bein' out there in the sun, but they hated bein' round me mo'. Cain't say as I blame 'em 'cause I wan't no fun to be round in them days." She ignored her granddaughter's snort.

When Evelyn finally spoke, she sounded far away to her grandmother, as if she had to muster all her courage to voice her thoughts. "So you didn't really try to keep track of their whereabouts? They just ran wild?"

"Ran wild? No, they wan't runnin' wild. I knew where they was, gener'ly, and yo' mama was always there, standin' in the way tween me and the chillun. Takin' care of 'em when I was down, especially after . . ." She shook herself to disentangle the tiny hands that wanted to hang on to her hemline and drag her back to those long-ago days. She wouldn't have far to go; the pain was always nearby.

"'Lis'beth was meant to be a mama. I was there when she had Lionel. Graham was at work in Raleigh and couldn't get there in time. The way she looked at that baby when he was born, like she couldn't believe he was all hers and at the same time, like she wonted to give'm to me." Beatrice cut her eyes at Evelyn. "The same way she looks at you now."

Again Evelyn snorted.

"The same way I looked at . . ." Beatrice blinked up at the sun and swallowed. ". . . at Little Ed. Somebody was always ready to come back and tell me when he got into somethin'. 'Course you know he always been a thief."

"Granny B!"

"Gal, I knew it from the beginnin'. Just by lookin' at his hands. To be such a little thang, he had some big hands.

When he was a baby, people used to say, 'Man, look at them hands! My, yo' baby got big hands!' Somebody said he was either gon' be a piano player or a thief—and you know we ain't never had no piano."

Evelyn laughed out loud.

"If it ain't the truth, then you can knock me down right where I stand," Beatrice asserted without a trace of a smile. She stood there feeling and looking like she was ready to fight. But then she moved her lips in the direction of a smile, melting away the tension like a scoop of ice cream on a hot sidewalk.

"By the time they made it back home, they was covered in dust and dirt, knees and elbows ashy and scratched from clambering through and over fences. It was by God's grace and mercy they never got blood poisonin', lockjaw, or somethin' worse from all that rusty wire and broken glass. They'd be standin' there with faces pressed up 'gainst my do', hands over they eyes tryin' to see through the rips in the screen, hopin' they looked pitiful enough for me to let 'em in. They didn't mind if I shooed 'em straight to washin' up at the basin 'cause they just wanted to be inside, away from that blazin' sun."

Beatrice's stories danced in the air between the two until at last the women turned onto Carrot Lane. It took them considerably longer to get back. She noticed Evelyn growing stiffer and sorer as the walk dragged on, barely keeping up with her own snail's pace. At the door Evelyn collapsed on the top step, as hot, ashy, and sweaty as Beatrice's children.

"I'll brang you some ice water. Now hush, gal. I might

as well po' you up a glass while I get one for me." Ignoring Evelyn as the girl half rose from her spot, Beatrice extracted her key from the front pocket of her blue- and gray-checkered housedress and opened the door.

She trudged into the house to get Evelyn water, but when she returned, she found her granddaughter asleep on the lounge chair—in practically the same position Beatrice had found her before their walk. "That chile, nuthin' but a baby herself. Ain't a bit of good." She downed the water herself and headed back inside. There, she retrieved the electric window fan she kept behind her bed and set it up on the porch, aiming a soft whir in Evelyn's direction. When she returned to the front room, she gathered her remaining dregs of energy, climbed onto the sofa, stretched out her legs, and promptly dozed off.

More than an hour later Evelyn slowly swam up from sleep.

"Time to come in, gal. That's enough rest for now."

Evelyn stood lazily, yawning. *Funny, Granny B always seems to know how much sleep I need or don't need.* All in all, she did feel refreshed, considering that morning's thousand-mile trek. She stretched and yawned again and noticed that the sun rested lower in the sky. Evelyn opened the screen door and stepped into the front room, turning her back on Granny B's neighbor working in her yard and the faint sounds of children arguing over a ball.

Evelyn ambled on through to the back of the house. She knew where she'd find Granny B. Expecting to see a bushel of raw vegetables that needed cutting, peeling, or shucking or yet another basket of laundry, she stopped short when she turned the corner into the kitchen and found Granny B sitting at an empty table—save for a familiar, oddly shaped brown box.

"What's that?"

"Gal, quit talkin' out the side of yo' mouth and come sit down. We ain't got time for you to play like you don't know what this here is."

"Why's it here, Granny B?" Her heart thump-thumped in her chest. For Evelyn, that box represented the eruption of trouble in her life, much as Eve's first taste of the forbidden fruit.

"Don't start gettin' nervous. I ain't accusin' you of nuthin'—not this time. I got somethin' I need you to do for me."

Evelyn spoke directly to the box. "Does this have anything to do with our conversation last night?"

"Yes, it do." Granny B snapped her fingers in front of her granddaughter's nose.

Trance broken, Evelyn's eyes locked on her grandmother's face. "How so?"

Granny B opened the box and removed a leather book held closed by a rubber band. She plunked it on the floor beneath her chair. Then she poured out the box's contents. Letter upon letter slid onto the table.

Evelyn recognized the handwriting from the letter she still held hostage in her desk at home.

Granny B read as she stacked them, "Ed. Sarah. 'Lis'beth. Ruthena. Mary. Thomas." She sighed. "Milton. . . . All these letters. I wonder what they would mean to the chillun to get a letter like this in the mail, just outta nowhere?"

Evelyn said nothing.

"Yeah, I just wonder." Granny B's fingers riffled through the small tower she'd created. "Well, what's done is done." She snapped back to the present and stood. "Hope an egg salad sandwich is enough for you. You ain't gettin' picky on me, being pregnant and all. I got apple slices and some juice to go 'long with it." Granny B retrieved two plates Evelyn hadn't noticed and set them on the table with a soft clink.

Despite her nervousness, Evelyn's stomach rumbled. Obviously, egg salad still appealed to her and the baby. She reached for a half sandwich. "Thank you," she murmured.

Granny B pushed aside her own plate along with her granddaughter's appreciation. "I sat up in that room thankin' a lot last night 'bout what you said, 'bout tellin' ever'body what's goin' on. I asked myself, 'Should I call? Should I get 'Lis'beth to drive me to ever'body's house so I could tell each one in person?' But I can't really do that, can I?" Granny B looked up from the small pile of letters. "Mary live all the way over in Washington, and that ain't no drive round the block. Little Ed locked up, and I don't fancy visitin' him in no prison, seein' him 'hind bars. Ain't nobody got time for all them phone calls."

She didn't look at Evelyn as she spoke. Granny B's eyes

followed her fingers as they caressed each name before moving on to the next.

"After stayin' up more'n half the night, I decided I would clean out my steamer. When I opened that trunk, there sat this box. I went to set it aside, but somehow . . . I knocked it over, and all these letters come flyin' out. Went all over the place. And that's what made me thank, 'Beatrice, you can write your own letters.' Nobody cain't interrupt me while I'm sayin' what I got to say, and I can save time and money. And then I thought that I might as well send these letters from that no-'count Henton, too, 'cause I guess it ain't right that they won't never see 'em, even if he dead and all. I'd either have to send 'em or burn 'em up. So . . . I guess they might as well read 'em. I mean, it won't kill me, will it?" Granny B smiled stiffly.

"So you're going to write everybody a letter and mail it with the letter from Granddaddy?" Evelyn couldn't imagine Granny B sitting down to write a grocery list, let alone some heartfelt letter telling her children that she was dying. "Why haven't you sent the letters before now?"

"No, I ain't writin' nuthin'. I'm leavin' that to you. And wan't nobody's business before now."

"Me? I thought you said *you* should be the one to tell them."

"I *will* be the one. Will you just hush?" Granny B dug out her handkerchief and wiped beads of perspiration from her brow. "I been thankin' 'bout how Henton got help writin' his letters—he had to, 'cause I ain't never seen him write more'n his name. Barely even that. So then I thought, 'Bee, you can do the same. Put that worr'some girl to work.' If you wont to, you can explain that you're writin' the letter, but that it's really from me. You know, say it right at the very beginnin'. Get it out the way. Then, you just start talkin'—or writin'—usin' my own words."

Granny B jabbed a finger into the table. "Now, my words *exactly*, Ev'lyn. You can clean it up some, but other than that, you say what I wont you to say." Granny B stared at Evelyn for a second. "You hear me?"

Evelyn nodded slowly. "I understand, Granny B. But do you think this is the same as telling them yourself? Isn't this a little impersonal?"

"Impersonal? How much mo' personal I got to be? I'm tellin' 'em somethin', truth be told, they don't really *have* to know, but I figure I oughta. It's gon' be in my words, but I just wont them to understand exactly what I'm sayin', and I know you can help me do that."

"Okaaayy."

"Listen, I don't care if you agree or not. I just wont you to help me. Will you?"

Evelyn could see this meant a lot to her, and she was glad Granny B planned to share such a critical part of her life—her *death*—with the people whom she had effectively shut out for decades. "Of course, Granny B. I'll help you in any way I can. You say you want me to include these, too?" She pointed to the letters on the table between them.

"But I don't wont you to read these. These is private. They ain't got nuthin' to do with me. Or you neither."

Has she noticed there's one missing? "I know. You're right. So when do we start this project? If we start now, we should be able to get them all done by this afternoon." Evelyn lifted the lid on the empty box. "I don't see any paper or—" Suddenly a familiar horn blew outside, and then Evelyn heard a car door slam. *The hoopty?*

Granny B walked toward the noise.

"What's going on?" Evelyn raised her voice to get her grandmother's attention. "Granny B?" Evelyn followed her to the front room. She suspected who it was but not why she was there.

"I called 'Lis'beth, and she come to pick you up. That's her now." After Granny B pulled her bags from the closet by the door, she turned to face Evelyn.

"But what about the letters? I thought you said—"

"You thank I'm gon' say it in a sentence or two? It gon' take me some time to get all my thoughts together. And we both know you got some business of yo' own to straighten out 'fo' you can help me get the wrinkles out of mine." Granny B pushed open the door as her daughter ascended the steps. "'Lis'beth."

Lis looked at Evelyn first, then at Granny B. "Hey. Y'all all right? I wasn't expecting you to call about picking Evelyn up so soon."

"I wasn't expecting it either." Evelyn retrieved her bags.

"I got those. Is everything okay? Something didn't happen, did it?"

"Ain't somethin' always happenin'? We's alive, ain't we?" Granny B blocked her daughter from coming farther into the house and kept Evelyn right where she was. "But I got thangs to do, and this girl all right. She should be able to manage them stairs fine over at yo' house, if that walk we took today mean anythang. So if y'all excuse me, I'm gon' change those sheets on the beds. I'll go 'head and latch this screen door after y'all so nobody cain't come in."

"Well, okay," she answered as if she had a choice. "You know, I could have picked you up in the morning. I had to reschedule a consultation at the salon to come out here, Mama was so determined that I come right this moment."

"You'll have to take that up with her." Evelyn stepped to the door, but not before sneaking in a peck on her grandmother's cheek, something she rarely did in the past but planned to do more often while they still had her on this side of heaven. Evelyn waited until her mother had reached the front step before going through the door herself. "Granny B, I'll see you soon?"

Granny B watched as Lis pranced to the car. She latched the screen door. Her eyes held Evelyn's. "I be in touch."

PART TWO

The Children

Chapter Eleven

Beatrice said Elisabeth and her doll got on like a mother hen and her nest of eggs. Henton had fashioned Hattie Mae's body from cotton ticking and scraps of cloth and her hair of tangled black yarn. The doll's unblinking eyes, one stitched on higher than the other, convinced Elisabeth she could really *see* and *feel* the world.

Hattie Mae had no nose to speak of, and a single pink ribbon formed her mouth. No doubt about it, Hattie Mae was ugly, but she was Elisabeth's baby. Hattie Mae didn't talk back, give her orders, punch her, or steal her last spoonful of grits. Hattie Mae just maintained her same stoic expression, providing a pillow when Elisabeth's pallet got too hard for her to stand at night.

"Gal, if you don't put that doll down and get to scrubbin' them flo's . . . ," her mama would growl. But Elisabeth wouldn't put Hattie Mae down for anything. She would tuck her baby into the waistband of her skirt and get down on her hands and knees and scrub the floors or fold the laundry or clean the washroom. No matter the task, Elisabeth kept Hattie Mae close by.

But as much as Elisabeth loved Hattie Mae, she would have buried her in the backyard in the deepest hole she could find to get her hands on Suzy. Anytime Elisabeth got a chance, she walked slowly past the large storefront window, her eyes glued to Suzy's silky blonde curls; her pert, perfectly centered nose; her pouty crimson lips that matched the merry blush in her cheek; her vapid blue eyes that invited you to love her, cherish her, and hold her dear. Elisabeth had never told anybody about her one-sided love affair with the soulless doll, and her desire for it had mushroomed because she couldn't share it.

Unspoken perhaps, but her love for Suzy had not gone unnoticed. And one Saturday morning, Little Ed took great pleasure letting Elisabeth know just what he knew.

Elisabeth was sweeping the front yard. All the other Agnew children busied themselves with chores—everybody except Little Ed, who sidled up to Elisabeth as she scraped the hard-packed earth by the neighbor's shrubs. Elisabeth sensed him watching her. From time to time, she shifted Hattie Mae to a spot under her waistband that wasn't as hot and sticky. Then suddenly, just a second after she forgot about Little Ed, he snatched Hattie Mae from her hideaway.

He held her aloft. "She sho' is an ugly ol' thang. 'Specially when she up against that white doll you really wont." Little Ed wrinkled his nose, his delicate features scrunched up as he took a whiff of Elisabeth's prized possession, her only possession. "And she stank, too. Don't smell new like I bet that doll in the winda smell."

Elisabeth dropped the rake and tried to reach for Hattie Mae, but Little Ed held her behind his back. "Now, hold on a minute, gal. What's yo' hurry?"

"Little Ed! Give me back Hattie Mae! I wan't botherin' you!" Elisabeth tugged on his right arm and then his left as he switched Hattie Mae from his right hand to his left and back again. "Little Ed—"

He had a slight frame and was two years younger, but he was wiry and lithe, and of course nobody could match him when it came to those hands of his. He flattened his palm and extended his fingers over Elisabeth's nose. She smelled pine needles, sweat, and—*What was that?*—Sulfur8 before he sent her reeling. She lay there wishing the dirt would just swallow him up whole, right where he stood. Dirt to dirt and all that.

"Now that I got yo' 'tention, you might wont to take me up on my offer." Little Ed dangled Hattie Mae by a strand. Her eyes stared at Elisabeth. Her arms hung askew as she swayed back and forth, back and forth.

"What are you talkin' about, Ed? And give me back baby Hattie!"

Little Ed threw the doll at Elisabeth as if Hattie Mae meant nothing to him—because she didn't. "Girl, take that ol' thang. But I could get you somethin' better, let me tell you. Somethin' like that doll—what's her name? Sally? Sadie?" Little Ed turned and strolled away.

She stepped on one of Hattie Mae's tiny arms to chase Little Ed. "It's Suzy. What do you mean, you can get me Suzy?"

"It's like I said: I can get it fo' ya." He sucked in his bottom lip and shrugged. "I know how to get in the sto'."

And so Little Ed had used those dexterous hands of his to jiggle the lock to Mr. Fulton's store and snatch Suzy—not the Suzy who sat gazing out the window, but one of the many boxed up in the back. He had presented her to Elisabeth with a flourish one afternoon while their mama was shopping and their daddy gone who knows where and after the other children had escaped into the woods. "Here you go," he'd announced. "Don't forget to pay me."

Elisabeth had secretly finger-combed Suzy's buoyant curls and smoothed Suzy's black-and-white pin-striped dress with its wide white collar. But she never used her to wipe away her snot and tears after a whupping, never tucked her into the waistband of her skirts, never took her out to work with her . . . because nobody was supposed to know Suzy even existed. Suzy had a pretty comfortable life. Unlike Hattie Mae and Elisabeth.

And Beatrice. One day some fingers gripped Elisabeth's shoulder as she crouched over Suzy on the back stoop, counting the stripes on the doll's skirt. She knew there were thirty-two, but this was about all Suzy was good for. Elisabeth recognized the feel of her mama's knuckles before she ever turned around, her eyes wide and her breath escaping with a "Wha—!"

"I wonder if Jesus walked in here in a leisure suit, would I have much use for Him." Beatrice scoffed. "Or Him for me? I figure He wouldn't get down in this dirt with me or help me clean up one of y'all's messy behinds. Let alone touch the drunks and streetwalkers down on Temple Avenue. Whatchyou thank, 'Lis'beth?"

Elisabeth tucked Suzy under the tent her bent knees created. "Well, I—"

"No, suh, that love you got to hide, that's too good to touch you? It ain't real. It do more harm than good. Give me somebody who can hold me and who I can hold anytime I get good and ready. Look at Thomas." She pointed to the toddler trying to pinch a beetle burrowing into a crack on the bottom step. "He one of the fussiest babies I ever seen. Always cryin' over somethin'. Hangin' on me. But when he see I'm upset, he always reachin' for my face, kissin' my tears.

"Now, Little Ed? He such a pretty child, always grinnin' 'bout somethin' rollin' round in his head. But the only time you gon' find him is when you trip over him in the dark. Ain't much help to you or me, but plenty of trouble." Beatrice slapped at Thomas's hand as it made its way to his mouth, the bug trapped between his thumb and index fingers. Immediately he screwed up his face and worked up a wail.

"You tell me. You wont those roses bloomin cross the street that hide all them thorns or the sour weeds y'all love so much? Jesus wearin' a suit or dusty robes?" She swatted Thomas's backside and ordered, "Hush up now" before nudging him into the yard toward the clothesline. Beatrice and Elisabeth watched him pluck a long green weed and suck on it for a few minutes before she went back inside, leaving her daughter alone with Thomas. And Suzy.

So one day Elisabeth dug a hole for the doll and tossed her in it. Little Ed never asked her what happened. He just spent her twenty-two cents and ate her bologna sandwiches, smiling and winking as he did so.

As far as Elisabeth was concerned, no one else ever knew about Suzy. That was, until her daddy caught up with her, some fifty-odd years later.

Dear Lisbeth, his letter began:

It been a long time. You probly thought youd never hear from me or see me agin. Maybe you never wanted to, seein as how I lef and all. But I hope you care won way or nuther if Im dead or livin and that Im in Jasper. I dint want nobody to find me, but I dint have no money to go but so far. Twinny miles bout as far as I got. Corse B found out, but I trust she dint never tell nobody.

You mite not want to hear it but I ben missin all yall runnin round, playin and yellin, tearin up the

devil. I even miss B. It been a long year babe girl.
Rutheena and them yungern you but you always ben
my babe. Sarah dint care nuthin bout me she was so
yung wen I lef. But you new me. And I new you. You
go for wat you want, jus like you did wit that wite babe
doll you had. I usta see you take her out from hind that
washbord and you jus sit and hold her. You took better
care of her than I did of yall. But you wanted that doll
and somhow you got her. Well I say somhow but that
mean Edmond. That boy wuld do anythang for you.
Rong or rite. He try to hide it tho.

I gess I up and lef outta noware like that doll. But
ther wont much els I culd do. Jus like Edmond my rong
was rite in my hart. B ask me wat good was I doin
you by stayin. I wasnt no daddy to yall and never no
husband to B. I hope yo mama tell you all bout it won
day but nowin B she go to the grave wit it on her lips.
Trust I luv you even tho I aint never told you to yo face.
I jus dint feel it was my place. I hope you hav som real
babes to take care of. Mabe then you see wat it like to
luv somthin so much you got to leave it.

———————

"Sometimes we just wished she would die. Then we could
drink as much as we wanted, play as long as we wanted.
We thought we wouldn't have to pick vegetables or sweep
the yard or clean another thing if she would just go away

or at least just leave us alone for a few days." Lis spoke very softly, yet very deliberately. "Thanks to this leukemia, Mama is finally cooperating, but now I'm hoping she'll stick around a little bit longer. Long enough to fuss at me, ignore me, yell at me, or kick me out of the house. My heart quakes at the thought of her dying and leaving me. Can you make sense out of it, Evelyn?"

Lis registered Evelyn's startled reflection in the window-pane. "I told you when you were little I had eyes in the back of my head."

"Oh, you saw me in the window. Why are you eating chocolate this time of night?" She took her mother's candy bar and closed the foil wrapper. She set it down on a notepad on her father's desk.

It was well past midnight, and until Evelyn appeared, Lis had been standing alone in Graham's den, her nose against the cool glass. Her eyes looked past the clouds scudding across the moon in the inky sky to images indelibly imprinted in her memory.

In her mind, her brothers and sisters ran back and forth on the hard North Carolina clay of Mama's yard. She inhaled the dust their hot, cracked feet kicked up as they skirted between the house and the sidewalk, around the house, and back to the front door. She listened to them argue over whose turn it was to ask Mama for permission to come in for water and held her breath as they held theirs.

They could never tell what Mama's mood was. It changed from day to day, from moment to moment, from bad to worse. Maybe they would get a drink of water and more time to catch june bugs with string. Maybe they'd have to pull weeds. She could still hear Mama say, "Y'all done had 'nough fool time. Get in here and get yo' be-hinds in bed."

Lis reached past Evelyn and retrieved her sweet. She took a large bite. "Why am I eating chocolate? Well, my mama is dyin' and I didn't have any kind of relationship with my daddy. Soon I won't have anybody. No daddy, no mama. Nothing."

She chewed the last of the candy and dropped the crumpled wrapper into the bin beside the desk. "You know, Graham could sit for hours if you let him, just poring over one subject or another. I never could stand to sit down more than five minutes with a book. I don't know how I managed to get through all those hours to get my license to open Headquarters." Lis hoped the change of subject indicated that the previous one was closed.

"How are you feeling?"

Lis didn't feel like diving into that particular pool of emotion. Any unshed tears from earlier in the day bubbled just below the surface, waiting to spring forth and overcome her. Not even the deep tissue massage had helped. She left work with a great hollow in her middle. Talking about her *feelings* wouldn't fill it. Missing Graham wouldn't do it. Thinking about her daddy wouldn't do it. And watching her mama die surely wouldn't do it.

"Girl, I don't want to talk about how I'm feelin'," Lis finally answered in a tremulous voice, her back still to Evelyn.

Tired as she was, her Southern accent weighed down her words rather than dancing lightly through them as it usually did. "Ask me in a few months' time when I'm an orphan— a middle-aged *widowed* orphan at that. Maybe by then I'll know just how I'm feelin'. And by then I'll be *feelin'* plenty."

"But—"

"*But* what about you? You've had a big day, what with tellin' us all about this baby. How did Kevin react to *your* big news?" Lis composed herself enough to turn away from Graham's bookshelf to face the five-foot-three giant in the room. She watched her younger daughter fiddle with the ties of her robe.

"I'm fine."

"You're fine. If you say that one more time . . . ! That's all you been sayin' since you got here, and we all know it's a lie." Lis shook her head. "So we know that *you're* fine, but what about the rest of us? Your sister is feeling some kind of way since she had to hear it from me, and I know *I'm* put out. But I'm just your mama. Kevin's your husband. He must be *angry*."

Lis tried to figure out just where she'd gone wrong, to determine when she had been relegated to the role of second-class citizen. *So she finally came clean,* she stewed. *She's been walking around here for weeks, telling me everything is fine, fine. "No, Mama, nothing's going on," and here she is pregnant. And thinking she can hide it from* me! Internally, she shook her head in disbelief. *This girl! I'm her mama, and she can't tell me she's pregnant.* "So?"

"So . . . what? Isn't a baby good news?" Now Evelyn took a

turn at the window. By this time, a steady breeze had pushed away most of the clouds to reveal a half-moon and a few glistening stars.

"It should be. But I got the impression he didn't know. He rarely called, and you'd think he would have checked on you two after the accident . . . if he'd known." Lis weighed her next words, a rare move for her when it came to Evelyn because they both stayed armed and ready, shooting from the hip and aiming for the heart. "You know I already suspected."

Evelyn whirled around. "What! How did you . . . ? Did Granny B—?"

"No, chile," Lis said, sounding like Beatrice. "I'm a mama too. I picked up on the changes in your body. I tried to give you plenty of opportunities to tell me—making mention of your eating, your weight, asking about your health. . . . Why do you think I insisted you stay with Mama so she could babysit you after the accident? It wasn't just for her sake, though that's what you thought. It hurt that you didn't tell me yourself. I can imagine how Kevin must feel."

Evelyn returned to stargazing. "He doesn't know yet."

"What? So why did you decide to finally tell me?"

Evelyn shrugged and rubbed her hands down her nape. She stretched her neck as if she'd just returned from a long run.

Lis ticked off nearly a minute on Graham's desk clock as she trained her eyes on Evelyn's back.

Evelyn stopped squirming. "Well, you would've found out eventually. Which you did."

"That doesn't answer my question, Evelyn. You're what, ten weeks—?"

"Fifteen . . . and a half."

"Almost sixteen weeks pregnant. Sixteen weeks. Your second trimester! And you've been staying here all this time, and you didn't see fit to tell your own mother that you're carrying her grandchild!" Lis shook her head in wonder. "I just don't understand it, Evelyn. What purpose does it serve to hide this from me, your brothers, your sister, and your husband? At least you told Mama."

"I didn't tell Granny B anything. She told me. But why would I confide in you? My pregnancy would just give you one more thing to worry about, one more thing to worry *me* about. You've been walking around since I got here, talking about, 'Can you afford *this*? Should you be doing *that*? What about your *job*? Did Kevin really go to Europe for work, or did he just up and leave you?' Now you can't honestly say you didn't think that last bit even if you didn't say it out loud. At least to me."

The truth slapped Lis in the face, and it stung. But she retreated to familiar territory and wriggled her toes around in it. "Regardless, girl, I'm your mama. I'm supposed to say stuff like that. If I didn't love you, you think I'd care enough to ask you what you're doing? What am I supposed to think? You come down here without your husband. You don't have a job—"

"I quit my job—"

"—and you act like you don't have to get back for anybody

or anything. The only person you can spare a word for is your Granny B—"

"But isn't that what you wanted? The only thing you could talk about when I got down here was how I'd ignored Granny B all this time, how much she needed me, how I could help her get treatment—"

"But you haven't been too successful with that, now, have you? You've been doing quite a bit of talking for the past few weeks, but Mama hasn't thought about going to see a doctor. And from what she says in this letter of hers, she won't be either. A lot of good you've done."

Lis knew she shouldn't have said it, but she knew she didn't want to take it back either. Stubbornly, she took in Evelyn's look of disbelief. As her daughter hugged herself around her middle, it was painfully obvious what she'd worked to conceal all these weeks. Seeing the shape of her grandbaby and grasping that Evelyn seemed more hurt than angry by her comment, Lis finally relented. "Look, I know you did the best you could. It's just that she's my mama and—"

"And I'm your daughter. Does that mean anything to you? I'm not dying, but shouldn't that mother-and-child thing count at least a little bit?" Evelyn turned away, her voice quaking.

Lis couldn't remember the last time she'd seen her baby girl cry. She took one halting step and then another until she reached her. Awkwardly, she patted her on the back, half-expecting Evelyn to brush her away and leave the room. When Evelyn remained, when she seemed to actually lean into Lis, she repositioned her hand first to her daughter's shoulder before stroking Evelyn's short, spiky do. At a loss for what to say next, she asked the only thing that came to mind. "Why did you cut your hair so short?"

Evelyn withdrew from her mother's touch and the room.

Lis let her go. What should she have said? *It's normal for a happily married woman not to tell her husband she's pregnant. He'll find out eventually. It's okay that you don't think enough of your own mother to tell her you're pregnant. Don't worry about the fact that your grandmother is dying—and that you apparently have done nothing to stop it. Dear, dear, don't cry.*

Lis retreated to her own bedroom, gathering her pink chenille robe closer to her, trying to find a source of warmth. The item in her pocket stopped her short. She pulled out the first letter that had fallen from the long envelope she had opened earlier that afternoon. It was her mama's words, but it most definitely was not her nearly illegible writing. Lis closed her door and collapsed on the chaise. Slowly she flattened the three-page death threat against her lap.

Elisabeth,

    You know, you're my firstborn. There I was, fifteen years old, and you come out all naked and wet, fully expecting me to feed you and clothe you and care for you like I knew what I was doing. I used to look at you and think, "You are a darn fool child, trusting me." But I did it. The good Lord and I . . . well, we raised you. Sometimes I felt I was all by my lonesome, but I know

He was there. But you did some raising yourself. You raised me first—and then you took on the raising of all the rest when . . . well.

You been walking around here, wringing your hands, trying to tend to this problem like you tended to your brothers and sisters. Well, you can't. There just ain't nothing you can do. I know I never been one to offer much in the way of comfort, but let me say this: Rest easy, child. This is my job. This is something I have to do.

That's really all I got to say. This child here keeps saying I need to soften up, but I'm the one who's traveling on this particular road God done laid out for me. And you know I don't care what none of y'all got to say, or I'd have been dead a long time ago. I've got lots more letters to write, so I can't be handing out tissues or holding hands, though I can't really think of one of you who'd shed many tears to see me go. Maybe you'll be crying cause you need company since your children can't seem to stand living too close to you—like my own. I'm telling this child here to hush up because this is my letter.

You know, all my life I had to do something for somebody else—my mam, my husband, my children. Well, this is it. I'm drawing the line. This is what I'm doing for me. If I got all that fancy treatment you wanted, that would be for you and this girl writing this here letter. Writing this ain't really for me, but I figure I could do this and no more.

I think Evelyn has accepted it, and now it's time for you and the rest of them to accept it, too. Really, it don't matter if you do because I'm going to die either way. But you can make this hard or you can make it . . . well, it's not going to be easy, but at least you can make it better. This girl says, "easier." I guess that fits, too. Anyway. I'd appreciate your cooperation, even if you can't help me much.

So what do I have in mind? The doctors say I don't have long, so the time I do have has become precious to me. More precious than I would have thought, and more than I really want to admit to anybody. It's too precious for me to waste time being pumped full of useless medicine that makes me feel worse than I do already. I plan to spend the rest of my time doing what I always do. Maybe you don't see the value in cooking and cleaning and all, but this house and taking care of it are part of me. It's really all I've ever had.

I know you think that's my fault, don't you? If you've read Henton's letter, I'm sure you do. Yes, I made him leave. That's right and true. He says he didn't want to and that he even wanted to come back. But you can best believe I couldn't have kept him from his house if that was all there was to it. You probably want to know why. Well, that's not what this letter is for. What I'm writing about is about me, and I guess a little bit about you.

Elisabeth, this part is hard for me, harder than the dying really. I know there are things you've never heard from me, things you felt you needed to hear while you were growing up. These old newspeople and talk show people call those years the "tender years." They'd have you think children only need to get pats on the back and what they call "understanding."

But I know different. And you know different, too. I know you know because of who you are today. You've made it. By your estimation you found you a nice man, built a beautiful home, and raised four good children. While all praise got to go to God who made you, some of those crumbs got to fall on my table.

No, I didn't coddle you. I didn't say, "There, there, that's all right" when you broke something or made a mess. I let you know how the world really works. I gave you something you could take in and pass on. That's what He charged me to do. It's what my mam didn't do enough of for me, and it hurt me in the long run. If you look deep in yourself, you'll see I'm right, and one day you'll appreciate it.

Well, Elisabeth, that's it. This girl says I need to end this properly, so I will tell you I'm proud of you, and yes, I love you. I think you've done right smart by yourself. I don't see why people need to waste time sitting around getting paid to watch other people sitting around. But you've done good, and I'm happy for you. Let that be some comfort for you, if you need it. I trust you to let me handle my own business. I think I've done fine for myself by myself for a while now. Let it be.

Your mama

Lis stroked Hattie Mae, who now sported hair extensions that draped well past her shoulders. Hattie Mae's knowing eyes still looked out at crazy angles, and her mouth was still a wide, straight line, but she wore an updated dress and shoes, and she had a whole wardrobe to choose from. Her hair still drank in all of Lis's tears—the ones that fell when her husband died and the bitter ones she shed now, as the three pages ripped from the envelope slowly drifted to the floor, one by one.

Chapter Twelve

EDMOND, AGE 11

"Okay, Mary, when I say the word, you ask Booker for one of them squash, the ones he keep way in the back. And just in case he moved them to the front, you pick somethin' else. Just make sho' whatever you pick is way in the back of the truck."

Four-year-old Mary nodded, her eyes big. She drew eighteen-month-old Sarah closer to her.

Little Ed could tell Mary was too scared not to listen. He stroked the baby's curls, playing the role of the kind, fun-loving big brother. He winked and lowered his voice conspiratorially. "And when you see Booker go up to get what it is you ask for, I want you to pinch Sarah—"

"Pinch—?"

"Shh! Not enough to hurt her. Just so she'll scream and I'll know it's time. You got it?"

Sarah must have heard him because she parted her lips as if she would scream right then and there.

Little Ed clamped his hand over her mouth, nearly covering her entire face.

"No!" When her eyes welled up, he rubbed her hair and smiled. Then he softened his tone. "No, baby girl, not right now. Only scream when you see Booker go get that squash. Now, Mary gon' be standin' right there 'side you. She'll let you know when it's time. Okay?"

Sarah rubbed her eyes and pouted.

"Y'all ready?" He looked from one to the other. While the toddler stared at him with wide eyes as if she was counting his teeth every time he opened his mouth, her older sister hesitated just a bit before she nodded.

"What is it, Mary?" Little Ed pretended to be patient, but he wanted to yell. Booker would be moving on to the next street soon.

"Well . . ."

"Well, what?" A bit of impatience oozed through his clenched teeth.

"I'm gon' ask Mr. Booker for the squash. And then Sarah gon' scream . . ."

"Okay . . . ?"

"Where you gon' be? Whatch*you* gon' be doin'?"

"Don't you worry none 'bout that. You just do yo' job,

okay? Now it's an important job—prob'ly the most important." He trained his eyes on Mary's. "So I can count on you?"

This time, she bobbed quickly.

"Good. Let's go." He noted that Booker's truck was idling by the Moore house. "Okay, you take Sarah here," he directed Mary, "and walk up there natural-like, just like Mama sent y'all to get some veg'ables fo' dinner."

Little Ed trotted off, looking back once to make sure Mary and Sarah were following his plan. By the time the girls got to Booker's truck, Little Ed was peeking out from behind the big maple across from the Moores' front yard. He saw the rusty truck pause in its slow trek up Carrot Lane as Mr. Booker waved to the girls in the big rearview mirror. Little Ed grinned when the driver's door creaked open.

"Hey there, Mary, little Sarah!"

"Hi, Mr. Booker."

"Hi, Meestah Bookah," Sarah echoed.

"Y'all need somethin'?" He pushed his hat back on his head and smiled really big and friendly.

"Well . . ." Mary glanced in the direction of Little Ed's tree.

Behind it, Little Ed wished she would speak up.

"Your mama send y'all for some beans or . . . ?"

"Squabs!" Sarah piped up, seemingly proud of her new word.

"Squash?" Mr. Booker looked at Mary. At her barely perceptible nod, he let down the back door and climbed into the truck bed. He didn't have to go too far. The squash sat in baskets right in front.

From Little Ed's lookout spot, everything was going according to plan. Or close enough.

"How many?" Booker's fingers tapped on the yellow squash without moving them.

"Uh—" Mary said woodenly.

"Your mama didn't say how many she wanted? That don't sound like Beatrice."

"Uh . . ."

Sarah beamed. "Twenny hundwed!"

Booker laughed. "Twenty hundred? How about a dozen?"

While Sarah clapped her hands with excitement, Mary began to wail for real. Little Ed ran to the truck and grabbed two handfuls of the first things he saw: half a dozen glossy red apples. He snatched them up.

But Booker seemed to be waiting for him. As he brushed by him, Little Ed noticed the farmer's hands were empty, free of that yellow squash he was supposed to be counting out. Little Ed heard Booker mutter, "Excuse me" and the sound of pounding feet as he took off running. Little Ed winked at an openmouthed Sarah. Mary shut up in a hurry.

His long thin legs carried him far and fast, but not farther or faster than Mr. Booker's. Soon enough, the vendor snatched Little Ed's dingy, white T-shirt. It gave somewhat, but the threads held long enough for Booker to wrap five of his long, thick fingers around Little Ed's scrawny neck and drag him back.

He banged on the door until Beatrice answered it, then related the details of Little Ed's latest escapade, mercifully omitting the parts that Sarah and Mary had played. Booker shrugged off her gruff apology—which was more an acknowledgment of what a sorry so-and-so Little Ed was—and stomped back to his truck.

Little Ed took one look into his mama's face . . . and took off again. He didn't expect her to tear off after him.

She *was* eight months pregnant.

But when he chanced a look back, there she was, on his heels. Little Ed deliberately slowed his pace. He didn't want to get beat, but he didn't want his mama to get hurt either. Strong, fast, devious—and considerate.

In minutes she caught up with him and with a *whop!* sent him flying. "Do I got yo' 'tention?" she hissed.

"Yes, Mama," he heaved.

"And you got the nerve to 'yes, Mama,' me after what you done? Caught stealin' from Booker's truck. You know I got to see that man every week?"

"Yes, Mama." Little Ed knew it was better to give the wrong answers than give no answer at all.

"I cain't believe you!" Mama was hot as fish grease. Anger sizzled and popped from her. She took another swing.

Little Ed ducked.

Beatrice grabbed him by his shirtfront and brought him close enough he caught a nasty whiff of the grits and corned beef hash she'd had for breakfast.

"What I tell you, Ed?"

"Uh—"

"What I tell you?" She shook him with every word.

"You said—"

"I said you bet' not get caught stealin'. You ever hear me say that?"

"Yes, ma'am. But—"

"No buts, Ed. You thank I'm gon' have folks sayin' I ain't raisin' nuthin' but thieves out here?" Beatrice shoved him from her.

"No, ma'am."

"Well, you must, to let Booker catch you with yo' hands wrapped 'round a half-dozen apples."

"Yes, ma'am. I-I-I mean, no, ma'am."

"Yes? No? Say what you mean, boy."

"I mean—"

"You don't mean nuthin'. And you'd have Booker thank you ain't worth nuthin'."

"No, Mama. I just—"

Beatrice shook her head. "Six apples. That what yo' freedom worth?"

This brought Little Ed up short. Up to now, he'd thought all he'd have to do was wait Mama out, let her have her say, maybe get whacked once or twice. *What's this about freedom?*

"Yes, boy. Yo' freedom. You decided you just gon' throw it away for some fruit. How you feel now? You feel like celebratin'?"

"Whatchyou talkin' 'bout, Mama?" Little Ed's voice rose

to a high-pitched squeak. "Booker gon' turn me in? For some apples? I can make it up. I—"

"How you gon' make it up, Edmond? You gon' give him some money you done stole from somebody else? You gon' give him back the apples you dropped in the dirt when Booker dragged yo' ragtail behind back to the house? They ain't nuthin' you gon' do 'cause they ain't nuthin' you *can* do to make it better. Maybe you learn somethin' at that trade school they got for boys like you."

"For some apples? They wan't nuthin' but apples!" Little Ed grabbed his mother by her hands. His eyes pleaded with her. "Mama. Them apples didn't cost more'n a few cents. If Booker gon' let it go, why you gon' turn me in?"

"That 'cause Booker ain't got no sense. He don't know that you gon' be right back in his truck bed next week, stealin' somethin' else. And this time, you gon' do better 'cause you prepared. At least I can say that: you learn from yo' mistakes. You can use that up at that school." Sighing one of her this-gon'-hurt-me-more'n-you sighs, Beatrice withdrew her hand from Little Ed's grasp and turned away from him. She started trudging toward town.

"But, Mama . . ." Little Ed danced along beside her.

"Save yo' breath. You gon' need it tomorrow."

"I got some money hid! I'll go get it and give it to Booker right now. Please, Mama!"

Beatrice stopped short. "You got money, Ed? From where? Who lookin' for it?"

"Nobody! It's mine! I got two dollars, and I ain't never had a chance to use—"

"That's 'cause you just take what you wont."

"No, no. I just ain't found somethin' I wonted to buy, is all. But I'll just give it all to Booker, and I know them beat-up, sour apples ain't worth all that."

"It don't matter what you thank them apples worth. It matter what Booker thank they's worth."

"Yes'm."

Beatrice put her hands to her hips. For a time, she studied the long road stretching toward town. Then she gave equal time studying the short road leading toward their little house before she closed her eyes.

Little Ed held his breath, figuring his mama was praying over his future.

She sighed. "Well, by my figure, it's a longer way to town. And I suppose it really ain't worth that kinda walk." She waved a finger at him. "But you better watch yo'self, Ed. Do what you say you gon' do. Better yet, do what *I* say you gon' do."

"Yes, ma'am! Yes, ma'am! I'll go get my money and take it to Booker!" He took one step before she snatched him back with a hand. His thin shirt gave way completely this time and ripped all the way to the seam at the bottom.

"You just wait a minute, boy." Mama turned Little Ed around, his shirt flapping, hanging from his back. "Ain't no use throwin' good money after bad. You just give me that two dollars. Booker done washed his hands of all this, and it don't make no sense to brang it all up to mind when I see him again. He just gon' gamble it away. Now, remember what God say in Ephesians: Steal no more. Get to work. Do good with those big hands of yours so you can share it with your family."

"Uh . . . okay." Little Ed's forehead wrinkled at her interpretation of the Scriptures.

Mama turned toward the house. Halfway there, she called to Little Ed, whose feet remained rooted to the spot, "You gon' steal somethin', make the beatin' worthwhile. Then you better run like the devil you is. Next time—and don't tell me they ain't gon' be no next time—next time, you bet' not get caught stealing."

Edmond,

I hope this letter cach up wit you afor too long. How you doin boy? You lernt to stay out of trubble yet? It sure can find you. That trubble new ware I lived too—least it did for I moved. I aint got no trubbles now. I aint got much els ether, cep this bed I sleep on an this job. But thats ok wit me. I hope you dont have to give up all you got like I did but findin peace is worth it. Wen I lef, I culdn't see wat was ahead. It was more bout wat I was leavin behind me. Ther aint no scusin my leavin yall like that but we all wulda ben sorry had I stayd one more day.

You need to look after yo famly now. Thays all you got. You like the wind blowin in and out from any direcshun. An I hope you dont never stop blowin. Thay need somthin like you. But you blood. You gotta stick by and thay gone stick by you. No matter wat trubble find you. So treat em rite. Speshully them sistas. I wish I could say look after my babe boy but ther aint no helpin him now. Thats all on B.

I hope to hear from you won day. I live rite here at 23 Reedy Creek in Jasper if you need somware to run. And dont you worry. Trubble dont know me no more.

Henton Agnew

"Well, *Henton Agnew*, trouble sure knows *my* name." His mind engorged, Little Ed folded the letter and stuffed it into his duffel bag. When he'd opened the large envelope from his mama and discovered the two enclosed letters, his hands had unfolded Henton's first, almost of their own volition. But now . . . now, he couldn't handle any more. He set aside his mama's letter for later, when he could savor her words alongside a fritter at Weisel's Bakery. At that moment, he could only chew on Henton's memory like it was a stick of red licorice. His *daddy* had written him a letter. "If I had gotten this then . . ." But it wouldn't have made a difference, this trouble-free place Henton had offered. Little Ed had had a new address for the past fifteen years, away from everything and everybody, but he definitely wouldn't have considered it a safe place. Trouble had found him anyway. Yet so had salvation.

Beatrice seemed to tuck his news under her cloth belt when he'd called her at the beginning of the year. It was like she'd always suspected the prison gates would swing open just as Jesus opened his heart.

"I guess I won't get no mo' collect calls then," she'd commented dryly. "Yo' bill been paid fo'."

Little Ed pictured her sitting on the faded-green velour sofa in the front room, looking through the open door at the street, one hand holding the phone, the other in her lap. Somehow, he'd known she wasn't talking about the charges from the telephone company.

"I know, Mama. Paid in full," he'd responded, smiling into the phone as he ignored the tap on his shoulder warning him there were others in line. Little Ed determined then to save up and return to Spring Hope, maybe by Thanksgiving. It had been too long since he'd been with his mama, and it was time he stepped up as the oldest son in the family and reconnect with his own grown children. And not because Henton had said so.

Little Ed stepped off the Number 15 bus onto the sidewalk running along Fulton Street. He dropped his scuffed green duffel onto the steamy concrete square at his feet. It contained a few pairs of underwear; two crew-neck undershirts; a pair of black slacks; three sets of socks; a toothbrush and a travel-size tube of Crest; a red- and white-striped shirt;

his hairbrush; and the Bible, compliments of the Gideons, the State of New York, and Jacko, a zealous inmate.

Inside the Bible, along with his mama's letter, he had hastily stuffed the last two or three pieces of mail he'd received just that day before they'd released him, a full three months earlier than expected. In the right front pocket of the only pair of jeans he owned crouched $122.00, all the money he had in the world. Unshaven, nearly broke, homeless, Little Ed squinted up at the sun and grinned broadly. Then he picked up his bag and snuggled it right under his left armpit. He wouldn't let some other homeless New Yorker steal his life's possessions, test his newfound faith, and force him to do something that was sure to land him right back in the joint.

Little Ed strutted down Fulton. He stared at the buildings he passed and the people who passed him. Lou's Odds and Ends. Bibi's Hair and Nails. You Rent, You Own! The more things changed, the more things . . . changed. Little Ed's good mood faded as his stride evolved into a plod. Nothing was really the same in his old neighborhood. He ticked off missing pieces as he passed familiar corners, alleys, and streets. Nope, no more Mr. Weisel and his greasy apple fritters that were so good first thing in the morning. Little Ed licked his lips at the thought. And oh, man, what had happened to that old lady over on Bushwick who used to sell flowers and papers? And crazy Al? Who would sell him his weekly paper and daily breakfast burrito?

At the corner of Fulton and Nostrand Avenue, Little Ed reached into his right front pocket and retrieved the small white card Jacko had pressed into his hand after he'd prayed for him.

"Here, man. My sister runs this small hotel, and she'll give you a place to stay. Just show her this, and she'll know you know me."

"And she'll let me stay anyway?" Little Ed had laughed.

"Hey, Tarheel, you better give it up," Jacko had warned. Tarheel was Little Ed's name in prison. His slight drawl informed the inmates he was from down South. "Anyway. She won't charge a lot, and the place really ain't all that, but it beats this establishment."

"But not by much," Little Ed observed as he stared at "Rita's Rooms—$19.95 a night," which squatted between two ten-story buildings. Bars covered all the ground-floor windows, and rust coated the fire escapes. He ignored the glares of the two men huddled on the bottom step who looked like they owned even less in the world than Little Ed, and trudged up the six steps to the door. He pushed the bell to the left of the cracked glass pane and waited. The door buzzed, and a lock clicked. Little Ed felt for just a moment that should he venture through, he wouldn't make it out. At least not without losing a little blood or a few teeth. Feeling foolish, he stepped into the dark, musty foyer, but not before taking one more—last?—look at the sunny sky behind him.

"You lookin' for somebody?"

Little Ed jumped at the deep voice. Behind a set of bars hunkered a woman of some unknown age and origin. *Is this Jacko's sister? Man! What does his mother look like?*

He walked over to the window. "Uh, I'm looking for a room."

"For how long?" The Yoda-like woman squinted up at him.

"Uh, well, I'm not sure. Jacko just told me—"

"Jacko? How do you know Jacko?" another, higher voice called out.

A door that Little Ed hadn't noticed opened beside the window where the first stranger glared out at New York like she'd rather spit on it than take a bite from it. Through it stepped a beautiful golden-skinned woman with auburn hair cascading toward her waist in long waves. Little Ed, who had been staring at bearded, bald, gruff masculine figures for the past fifteen years, offered a quick "Thank You" to God.

"How do you know Jacko?" the vision repeated.

Please, please let this be Rita. He fished out the plain white card from his pocket, flipped it over, and handed it to her. "Are you Rita?" He referred to the name on the front of the building.

Her brown eyes studied the card. "There is no Rita. That's Josefina, the owner. I'm Carolina . . ."

Cah-ro-lee-na. His hope faded as his heartbeat quickened.

". . . Jacko's sister," she finished in the same singsong voice.

Well, all right! Little Ed exulted, feeling the smile creeping back, the one that had practically swallowed his entire face the minute he'd stepped off the Number 15 bus. "Oh, *you're* Jacko's sister. He told me that you would give me—"

"We're booked up." Carolina's flat words abruptly ended Little Ed's daydream of a shower and shave.

"What? But Jacko—?"

"Jacko was wrong, as he usually is." Behind Carolina, Yoda snorted. "We are fully booked, so . . . ." Carolina ushered Little Ed toward the large front door.

"Okay, okay. Ain't no problem here." He picked up his bag and backed up to the door. "I'm not here to cause trouble." Pressing against his back, the doorknob blocked his retreat. He fumbled with the door. "Jacko just told me that—"

"Listen, I don't want to hear about Jacko. He keeps sending his, his . . . bunkmates here. What do I look like? A warden? Does this look like some halfway house?" Carolina waved her hands in the air. "Get out, mister. I don't know you from . . . from Adam. You could be some killer, some rapist—"

"Hey, hey. Wait a minute now. Nobody here killed or raped nobody. I just came here for a place to stay while I look for work. But that's okay. I'm gone. I'm gone." Little Ed finally opened the door and quickly descended the six stained, concrete steps.

"And don't come back!" Carolina slammed the door.

Little Ed ignored the laughter and pointing from the two wasting time on the stoop and hurried across New York Avenue. He stalked away. He couldn't believe he'd punked out like that, letting some woman make him, a sixty-three-year-old man, run—*run*—from that rat hole. "I oughta . . . ," he growled, pounding his huge hands together.

But he didn't. He wouldn't do anything to go back to prison. Not today.

So Little Ed walked. And he prayed. For blocks. The sun traveled across the sky and kissed the horizon before finally, sweaty and exhausted, he braced one hand against a light post that flickered to life at his touch, and Little Ed absorbed his surroundings. His wobbly legs had carried him to Empire Boulevard.

And there, before him, stood Weisel's Bakery.

"Well, hallelujah! So Mr. Weisel ain't dead after all." Little Ed darted across the street and pushed open the heavy glass door. His mouth watered as he sucked in the smells of hot grease, butter, and sugar. His eyes raked the display case: crullers; powdered, chocolate-covered, cream-filled, and jelly doughnuts; twists; holes . . . apple fritters! He dug in his right back pocket for his wallet—and came up empty. He threw down his duffel and spent ten painful minutes searching his back and front pockets. He even discovered a tiny flap on the side of his jeans, but it barely held the lint he found in it. Investing heavily in a last-ditch effort, Little Ed unzipped the bag by his feet, right where he crouched in front of the doughnut display case, and tossed out his belongings: underwear . . . toiletries . . . shirt . . . but no wallet.

"Sir?"

Little Ed didn't look up. He was "Inmate 34821" or "Hey, you" or "boy." He most definitely was not "sir."

"Sir." The unseen voice no longer posed a question. A grizzled gentleman behind the counter peered over the glass at him. "Sir, you must collect your things and move out of the way. You're blocking my paying customers."

Things. All his worldly possessions, such as they were, were scattered about the floor between the display counter and the front door. For years, Little Ed had bought an apple fritter from this man three or four times a week. But it was obvious Mr. Weisel had no clue who Little Ed was. Fifteen years were fifteen years.

Little Ed rose to one knee. With none of the care he had taken that morning to carefully fold and tuck each article, he shoved his *things* into his beat-up duffel. He forced his feet under him. "Uh, hi, Mr. Weisel."

The man stared at Little Ed suspiciously.

"Mr. Weisel, I'm Ed . . . Edmond Agnew? I used to buy fritters from you every week? My friends called me Little Ed?" Little Ed sounded unsure about the veracity of his statements, but he was sure. Yet Mr. Weisel remained unconvinced.

"Sir, are you going to order something?"

"I'm not 'sir.' I'm just Edmond, remember? Little Ed?" He wanted—dared—Mr. Weisel to call him by name.

"Sir—Ed—Mr. Edmond, please. If you're going to order something, please do so. But I have other customers . . ." Mr. Weisel looked beyond Little Ed at the nonexistent hordes of paying people pressing their way to his counter. He walked around to stand at the corner of the glass-fronted display, just far enough that Little Ed saw the rounded top of a wooden bat. "Sir? Must I call—?"

"*Sir*, you ain't got to call nobody." Little Ed knew where

this was going. The New York Mets were either going to hit a home run against his head, or he was going to get arrested and then beat on the head. Either way, he was going down for the count—and he'd counted fifteen years already.

"I'm going. I'm going." Little Ed found himself backing toward the door for the second time that day, holding up his hands in surrender. After all, he was a strange man—some rapist or killer or armed robber—who would overthrow this *fine* establishment for an apple fritter. When the bar poked him in the lower back, he turned and, duffel first, stepped out into the muggy evening air.

"Well, I'll be a—" He planted himself on the sidewalk, contemplating his next move, recovering from his last. Finally he took one step and then another. But before Little Ed could get five steps away, he heard the same firm, accented voice call to him:

"Sir?"

Little Ed stopped, but he didn't turn.

"Sir? You dropped this. Sir?"

Little Ed hoped to see Mr. Weisel holding his wallet, but the bakery owner proffered an envelope—and a white oil-stained bag. Warily Little Ed retraced his steps. He froze two feet away and stretched to take the envelope and the bag.

"Edmond." He nodded and returned to his counter.

Little Ed almost dashed the bag to the ground, but the smell—and the thought of being arrested for littering—stayed him. Ahh, that smell. It covered up the day's indignities, humiliations, accusations. For a moment, just pressing his nose against the bag was enough. He didn't need a job. He didn't need a place to rest his head. He didn't need real food. He didn't even need his wallet. For a split second, all Little Ed really needed was a giant whiff of that apple fritter.

Little Ed carried the bag in the direction he had come, back over the many blocks he had traveled after escaping Rita's. Only this time, his load was significantly lighter: his tank of pride was running on empty. He hoped to spot his wallet somewhere along the way, and on some level, he hoped to discover his spirit, too. But he knew that neither a lost wallet nor a lost soul would last long on the hungry streets of New York.

Nearly an hour later, Little Ed found himself back at the front steps of Rita's. It was just as ugly and worn-out as he remembered. But now no one taunted him and accused him with their eyes and their fingers. Only the thin glow from a tired streetlight welcomed him back. Even the building was dark. Little Ed decided it was time to open his bag and rest his feet.

As his fingertips released the bag, he remembered his mama's letter. One hand dug in the bag for his fritter—*Oh, man! Two!*—while the other turned over the now-crumpled envelope. His teeth gripped the pastry as his fingers pulled out the pages, leaving greasy, sticky spots all over them.

Edmond,
 Son, it's your mama. You're probably surprised to hear from me, since you usually don't get more than

*a piece of my chicken after one of Sarah's visits. This
time, I thought I needed to send my own mail. I'd ask
you how you're doing, but you're doing time. That's
how. And not in some little jail but a big old prison.
I used to wonder about changing your name to Big Ed
'cause of all that big trouble you got yourself into, but I
figure now we can call you Edmond since them days are
coming to an end.*

*I couldn't keep you this time, Son. You didn't have
no woods to run to, and a good whupping couldn't
make it right. You seem to know that now by paying
that price, and not just how to do what you done better
the next time. I believe there won't be no next time,
Edmond. You know Jesus paid it all for you, and you
ain't got to steal it 'cause it's all yours.*

Amen! Little Ed thought before perusing the return address
once more. Yep, 57 Carrot Lane. Quizzically, he peered at the
writing. It sounded like his mama, but then again it didn't.

*I was hoping I'd get to see you, but the way things look,
that ain't going to happen. I can't get to you, and you
sure can't get here no time soon, least not soon enough.
Your niece Evelyn—you do remember Elisabeth's
youngest girl?—is helping me write this letter. You know
me. I can say what I need to say with no help from
nobody. She's just helping me get it on paper so you can*

understand. Although you ain't never had a problem understanding me, have you, Edmond?

I know sometimes I had to run after you so I could shout right in your face, but you always understood what I was meaning—not like some of them children. You just chose to look the other way. I know you got a big brain to match them big hands of yours, and you can understand what I got to say, 'cause this ain't some pep talk. Edmond, I'm writing this to tell you about some choices I made and some choices that been made for me.

Doctors told me that I have acute myeloid leukemia. Now, ain't that a mouthful? You'll have to talk to Sarah and her doctor husband to get an explanation, 'cause that's as much as I'm going to say about that. Now, Sarah might tell you there's some things I could be or should be doing, but you just listen to me. This is the part where I make the choices. For me to spend my time stuck in some hospital somewhere to please y'all would be like doing time in a prison. And, Edmond, you know that ain't no kind of place for a body. So the owner of this body will do just what she wants with it. I made my choice and I appreciate you respecting it. If I need something, Elisabeth is close by. Too close sometimes, like this bothersome child writing this letter.

What you can do for me is learn, boy. Learn! And that don't mean not getting caught. It means bettering your choices. You are smart and good, Edmond. And you know how I know? 'Cause I'm smart and good, and you are mine. What lives in me lives in you. Who lives in me is the same who lives in you. Yeah, you acted like one hardheaded thief—but that's what you did, not who you are. Remember that thief who hung beside Jesus? He made the right choice in the end. Be like him: Don't just make any choice, Edmond. Make the right choice. The good choice. Doors didn't close in your face—you shut them. Slammed them and locked them. Then you tried to find a way to break in when you could have walked through easy and peaceful, the right way. Boy, look out for the open door. You know it when you see it.

Take care of yourself there, Edmond, and I'll do the same. Your mama loves you—you and them big hands.

By the time Little Ed choked down the greasy mass in his mouth, he needed water—or something much stronger. His mama. He turned his hands over and over, but he didn't see the wrinkles and lines, the greasy fingertips, the ashy, pecan-colored flesh. Little Ed glared at his hands and visualized all that he'd broken and stolen, what he'd defended and whom he'd offended—all with these hands.

Suddenly he couldn't stand it. A hurt welled up from his toes and worked its way up through his stomach and chest and into his throat until it exploded. Little Ed tried to catch the hurt, to cover it with his hands, but even they weren't big enough. The pain escaped through his fingers with a gut-wrenching outcry. People passed Little Ed there on the stoop, but they ignored him.

Feeling a presence, Little Ed whirled around. "Wh—!" Clumsily he jumped to his feet. He tried to gather all his stuff—the now-empty bakery bag, the letters, his duffel—and move away from the steps at the same time.

"No—" Carolina extended a hand.

"I'm going. I'm going. I-I lost my wallet. I thought maybe it was here." He backed up.

"No, Mr. Agnew—stop!"

"I'm sorry, I'm sorry."

"Stop!" Carolina's voice had the peremptory tone she'd adopted earlier, inside the boardinghouse.

Little Ed's apology died on his lips.

"Please." Carolina approached him. In an outstretched hand she offered him a small, flat black object. "I believe this is yours."

"My wallet," he breathed. Yet he didn't reach for it.

"It must have fallen out of your pocket today when you backed against the door." Carolina continued to hold it out to him until finally Little Ed took it. "You left so quickly that I couldn't tell you—"

"You mean, you were so busy throwing me out." Little Ed squared his shoulders and raised his chin a notch. Standing there on public property, he recovered his manhood along with his wallet.

"Yes, I know. But I acted that way for a reason."

"Yeah, 'cause you—"

"Will you allow me to talk, or are you just going to slam a door in my face?"

In spite of himself, Little Ed quieted.

"Thank you. Mr. Agnew, I couldn't very well agree to let you stay here, not with Josefina sitting there. She's the owner, and she's not a very pleasant person. She's very suspicious of everybody, and she knows my brother is in jail. But I had planned to follow you out here and whisper for you to come back later, but you left so quickly—"

"Can you blame me?"

"No, I can't. But Jacko was supposed to tell you to pass me the card without mentioning his name. Usually I'm out front, but today Josefina sat at the desk while I did some bookkeeping."

"So why are you telling me this? You can't do nothing for me now."

The bald truth seemed to wound her. "No-o-o-o, you can't stay here . . ."

"Mmm-hmm, I thought so."

". . . more than a week or two. You can stay just long enough to find somewhere else to live, and maybe a job."

"But what about this Hosa—Hosi—"

"Josefina?" Carolina's laugh tickled Little Ed's much-abused eardrums. "She doesn't come here often, and she's going to Puerto Rico for a while. You'll be fine here for a week or two—but no more." She ascended the concrete steps more quickly than she had descended. She inserted a key into the lock and pushed open the heavy door. When Carolina glanced back to Little Ed, her mouth dropped open and her eyebrows furrowed together. She waved him up. "Mr. Agnew, come quickly. It's not the safest part of the city, and I need to get you settled in so I can get to Bible study."

"Look out for the open door . . ." First Edmond, then Little Ed, then Tarheel. Now, surprisingly, Mr. Agnew watched *Cah-roh-lee-na* hold open the door to the ugly hotel squatting between uglier buildings. He again tucked his belongings under his arm and mounted the steps. Carolina closed and locked the door securely behind them.

Chapter Thirteen

RUTHENA, AGE 15

"Come on, Ruthie, just one more."

"Shh!" Ruthena placed a finger over Luther's lips.

"No, I won't be quiet until you give me one, right here."

"Shh, Luther Atkins! I ain't gon' give you nuthin' if you don't hush up. You gon' get us caught," Ruthena whispered furiously.

"Ain't nobody here but—"

Ruthena clamped a hand over Luther's mouth and peeked out from behind the pew of Calvary AME Zion Church. She cast a careful eye over the pulpit, the choir loft, and up and down the right and left sides of the church. Then she looked behind them at the vestibule. Satisfied that they were safe for the moment, Ruthena decided to give Luther a little heaven on earth. *But I don't think this is what the pastor meant by fellowship,* she thought as she planted a soft—and quick— smooch on his waiting lips, both eyes open wide.

"Come on, Ruthena."

She lowered her lashes and threw a long, thick plait over her right shoulder. "Oh, hush up, Luther. You know I'm a good Christian girl, and I ain't got no business meetin' you here like this every week." Thursdays were Ruthena's days to polish the pews, the candleholders, and the molding in the balcony. "Now you just better be satisfied with this. I ain't lettin' you put yo' mouth or yo' hands nowhere else." She knew that Luther hoped to move things right along to the back of his daddy's Super Sport.

He took Ruthena's hand and interlaced his fingers with hers. "Oh, girl, you know I love you. I just want to kiss you a little bit. I miss you."

"You miss me? You just saw me."

"I know, I know," Luther said hastily. "But you so pretty and you smell so good, I just cain't thank of nuthin' else but you." He took his free hand and stroked her cheek.

Warmed, Ruthena ignored the roughness of his calloused palm. "Well . . ."

"Come on, Ruthie baby. Just one more . . ." He leaned in. His pink tongue peeked out just a bit.

"Well . . . okay. But just one." Ruthena closed her eyes and her mouth and leaned in.

"Ru-the-na Ag-new!"

Ruthena leaped to her feet.

Sister Robertson stood in the doorway leading into Calvary's narthex, her left hand cradling tiny glass Communion cups.

"S-S-Sister Robertson, I—"

The church mother stalked over to the two and yanked Luther to his feet. "Boy. I. Bet. You. Betta. Git. Yo'self. Outta. Here. Right. Nigh."

"Miss—"

But Sister Robertson brooked no dillydallying. "I. Said. Git!" She used her free hand to drag Luther to the double doors. She pushed him so hard his forward motion propelled him through the doors, where he stumbled, barely catching himself before he landed on his face on the concrete steps. "I'll see yo' mama later," Ethel Robertson warned before bringing the doors to and turning to the cowering Ruthena, who had followed them.

"Sister Robertson, I—"

"I 'spected mo' of you, Miss Agnew," Sister Robertson said stiffly. "Comin' to this church every day. I thought you loved the Lord."

"I do—"

"But you love Luther Atkins, too. Is that it?" Sister Robertson shook her head. "Take these."

Ruthena wordlessly took the cups.

"Now, clean 'em up and finish preparin' the Lord's Supper. I got some thangs to see to."

As Ruthena watched Ethel Robertson march from the church, she knew exactly what "thangs" the outraged woman was talking about. Heart heavy, yet obedient, she slowly walked up the aisle and to the kitchen in the back of the church.

Forty-five minutes later, Ruthena dried the last of the Communion cups. She was reaching for the box of wafers in the cabinet by the gas stove when a gravelly voice stopped her cold.

"I hear this church been givin' out mo' than free food to the po'."

Ruthena turned. She'd rather face the devil himself than her mama right now, but there she stood in the doorway, her eyes burning.

"Runnin' up to this place ever' day, like the Lord been callin' yo' name personal. Seems like somebody else been callin' yo' name, too."

Ruthena knew to respect her elders, so she clamped shut her trembling lips and counted the speckles in the tile floor.

"I ain't said much to yo' servin' the Lord, but when you start to servin' out other stuff—"

"No, Mama—"

"I ain't wont to hear it . . . Miss *Holy*. You better start thankin' with somethin' other than those two thangs there—" Beatrice pointed to Ruthena's lips—"or there," she finished, indicating fifteen-year-old Ruthena's chest. "'Cause if you don't, you gon' end up puttin' somethin' else to work 'fo' you ready. Ain't we got it hard enough? You tryin' to add to it?"

"No, Mama." Ruthena started to cry—from fear, from regret, but mostly from fear.

"Dry it up, girl. Dry it up. Now, it's hard enough for me to walk round Sprang Hope wit' ever'body shakin' they heads, talkin' 'bout po' Beatrice without you havin' to give 'em somethin' else to wag they tongues 'bout. I don't need nobody else feelin' sorry fo' me. And I sho as h—"

"Mama!" Ruthena gasped, looking upward, afraid that God might send a lightning bolt that would cook her mama to the bone—*praying* that God would send a lightning bolt that would cook her mama to . . . the . . . bone.

Beatrice pursed her lips and rolled her eyes at her daughter. "Oh, so yo' Lord gon' turn His eyes away from all that sinnin' you doin', but strike me down 'cause I said—"

Ruthena shushed her mama as she danced from one foot to the next.

Beatrice stomped to Ruthena. She wrapped a worn hand around one of the teen's plaits and gave it a hard yank. "You bet' not give nobody else a reason to come by my house carryin' tales or bad news. I've had enough of both in my lifetime. You hear me?"

Eyes watering, Ruthena nodded as much as her mama's tight grip on her hair would allow.

"The next time Sister So-and-So come a-callin', she better be carryin' a plate full of food or a collection plate wit' some money in it. But if all she carryin' is gossip . . ."

Ruthena used the pause to imagine the punishment.

"At yo' age I had a husband and a baby. Is that the kind

of life you wont? You best spend yo' time with the one true God than with that ol' Luther Atkins. At least God promised you a mansion in the sky. All that boy can give you is a shack smaller'n the one you live in now. Now, you best mind, girl."

Beatrice dropped her daughter's plait. Ruthena's shaky legs finally gave way and she sank to the floor. And she stayed down, watching her mother stalk from the kitchen.

"Sister Underwood? Sister Underwood!"

Sister Underwood—Ruthena—looked up from the twenty-pound turkey she was cleaning. "I'm in here!" She reached into the cavity of the huge bird and extracted the bag of giblets, neck, and other innards.

Two sets of heavy footsteps clop-clopped their way down the long hallway leading to the fellowship hall of Palmer Tabernacle Church of the Living Waters. The door swung open and a round face beamed through the crack. "Hey, you! I see you've already gotten started."

The door swung open wide, revealing Jacqueline and Caryn Allen, sisters—and Sisters—who served with Ruthena on the stewardess board of the church. Caryn pushed past her older, shorter sister into the kitchen. "We came to finish cooking the greens and the yeast rolls and—mmmm-mmmm! What smells so good?"

Ruthena leaned over for kisses from the two, all the while keeping her hands tucked inside the turkey. "I popped over here early to get the ham on—that's what you smell cooking in the oven—and I'm just getting Mr. Turkey here ready for the deep fryer. Once we prep the vegetables and set up the desserts, everything'll be all set for Pastor's appreciation banquet."

Jacqueline shook her head. "I tell you, you're like a steamroller. You do so much good for the church. You got your hands in everything—the Sunday school, the stewardess board, pastor's aid, now this turkey. When do you have time for Matthew?"

Caryn laughed. She reached for her sister's grocery bags and set them on the counter beside hers.

"When indeed?"

The women jumped and turned toward the doorway.

There stood Ruthena's husband, his serious brown eyes focused on his wife. Her niece peeked around him and waved.

"Matthew! Evelyn!" Ruthena's bottom jaw dropped open as the water flowed over her hands into the cavity of the bird.

"I hope that's a look of happy surprise." Evelyn walked to her aunt and wrapped an arm around her. She turned off the faucet as she planted a kiss on her left cheek.

At her niece's unusually effusive greeting, Ruthena's narrow back went as stiff as the thermometer she'd planned to stick into the turkey, her eyes on Matthew just as sharp. Something about Evelyn had always made her uncomfortable; her straightforward, no-nonsense manner and the way the girl's eyes unwaveringly met hers raised her hackles. Her niece tended to ask pointed questions about matters of faith rather than accepting Ruthena's biblical references as canon. Evelyn didn't even bother to suffer quietly as she suspected most of her family did, and Ruthena didn't like it. *Maybe she gets more than her name from Mama,* she thought, her lips pursed.

As if reading her mind, Jacqueline braced a hand on each of her ample hips and declared, "This child must be an Agnew. She looks just like your people!"

Ruthena's set jawbone relaxed as she nodded in the direction of her church sisters. "Doesn't she? Sister Jackie and Sister Caryn, meet Evelyn, my sister Lis's baby girl." She watched as the two women enveloped Evelyn in tight hugs, one after another. Ruthena's hazel eyes widened as the younger woman's striped shirt stretched over her rounded midsection.

"Look at you, Evelyn. Lis told me she was about to be a grandmother . . . again. I guess congratulations are in order," she choked out over the sudden lump in her throat. "Matthew, what brings y'all here? I thought I was meeting you at home later." She forced the corners of her lips to lift and prayed her spirits would follow suit.

"Evelyn and her friend . . . ?" Matthew's eyes narrowed, and he stared at the ceiling as if he'd find the name hovering over his head.

Evelyn chuckled and whispered, "Maxine."

He snapped his cocoa-colored fingers. "That's right. Maxine. They stopped by the house looking for you, and then she asked if I could lead them over here. You know I'll take any excuse to squeeze in some time with my busy wife." His look included everyone else in the room. "I think she believes God can't find her unless she's in His house." Matthew's smile was tight enough to bounce a quarter off it.

"Well, I would never refuse your help preparing for the church banquet. You know that," Ruthena murmured through clenched teeth. "So, Evelyn, you mentioned Maxine. Mrs. Tagle's granddaughter, right?" Ruby Tagle was Beatrice's longtime friend whose fried chicken and sweet potato casserole virtually put her children through college. "She's not coming in to say hello?"

Evelyn smoothed her shirt over her belly as her aunt wrestled with the turkey. "She's in the car, catching up on e-mail. We came to Charlotte to check out IKEA."

"Y'all drove all this way to shop? I know y'all have stores down your way," Caryn piped up, her head buried in the refrigerator.

"Shh, Sister! Mind your own business. Come on, we'll let these folks talk in private. Ruthena, we'll get the tablecloths and the punch bowls from the supply room. See if there's anything else we need. Nice to see y'all." Jacqueline shooed Caryn from the kitchen.

"Don't forget we're on a schedule!" Ruthena called out as the door swung back and forth behind them.

"Running for Jesus," Matthew murmured. He crossed one ankle over the other and leaned against the counter.

Evelyn peered at her uncle and seemed about to ask him a question. Then, with a soft "Uh-hmmm," she returned her attention to Ruthena. "Actually, I . . . um . . . I have another reason for coming to Charlotte. I brought you something. That's really why I asked Uncle Matthew to come along. Do you have a minute?"

"So you lied?" Ruthena washed and dried her hands to hide her impatience as she reviewed her mental checklist. *Make the broccoli casserole. Take out the ham. Heat up the oil. Go over the banquet program with Caryn and Jackie. Change clothes before our meeting.* She flicked a surreptitious glance at Matthew.

He had chosen that moment to roll his eyes heavenward. Wide nostrils flaring, he sighed through lips pursed beneath his dark mustache. "I don't think Evelyn lied to me, Ruthie. She probably had a good reason—"

"Jacob also felt he had a good reason for putting animal skin on his arm—"

"Wasn't Isaac subverting God's will by blessing Esau, when the Lord told them the older would serve—?"

"Are you saying God wanted Jacob to use trickery—?"

Abruptly Evelyn stepped in the middle of their Bible-strewn battlefield and waved a thick white envelope. "Aunt Ruthena, I have something for you. From Granny B."

Ruthena's eyes followed its movement. She huffed and went still. "Okay, I'll take a look at it tonight, after the banquet." She reached for the nine-by-twelve envelope.

But Evelyn gently set it in Matthew's hands as if it were an infant. "Uh-uh. She asked me to give this to both of you. And it's important."

"*She asked you.* Always Mama's little accomplice. Since

when does Mama need somebody to do her dirty work?" Ruthena immediately regretted her choice of words, but she refused to restate her question. She knew Beatrice might be intractable, but no one would label her words or actions "dirty work."

Her mama's "mini me" seemed to agree. Evelyn's eyes flashed at Ruthena.

Matthew spoke up before his niece could speak out. "So cooking a turkey for your overstuffed pastor is God's work? That's *church* work, Ruthena, not necessarily one and the same. We have our own laundry to air out in an hour—remember our appointment with the marriage counselor?"

Ruthena threw down her towel. She stalked over to the swinging doors and peeped through their diamond-shaped panes. After seeing no sign of the two stewardesses, she pounced on Matthew and Evelyn still standing by the turkey, its legs spread-eagled in the sink. "Matthew," she hissed, "this is not the time, the place, or the company to discuss our personal business. Just because Evelyn shows up out the blue with some mystery envelope from Mama doesn't mean I have to drop everything. When did she ever drop everything for me? I'll take care of this when I get good and ready."

Evelyn winced and drew back. Then she edged forward, the fingers of one hand splayed against her side while the others were outstretched. "Aunt Ruthena . . ."

Pregnant women always keep one hand on their bellies. Is it pride of ownership? Are they looking for sympathy or attention? Well, this girl won't get either. Ruthena only had eyes and ears for her incongruous thoughts and their subject. Gentle pressure on her wrist drew her focus to the fingers clasping it.

"I'm sorry. This day is important to you, and I should have called first. I just didn't want to delay."

Her niece's humility took Ruthena's outrage down a notch. "Well . . ."

Evelyn looked to her uncle and back to Ruthena. "Granny B and I planned to come together so she could bring this herself . . . she wasn't up to it, though. But it was so important that I created this IKEA trip with Maxine to deliver it for her. I promise there's no dirty work involved. Please, could you take a few minutes and open it? Together, like she asked."

"Why do I need to do . . . whatever this is with Matthew?"

"Because she wanted to make sure you were okay . . . I guess." Evelyn broke eye contact. She zipped up her purse and adjusted her shoulder strap.

Now *she can't look me eye to eye?* "And what do you mean by 'she wasn't up to it'?" Ruthena tried to use the power of her glare to pin Evelyn to the floor, an ability her mama had passed on. But her niece must have inherited the Agnew gene for muleheadedness, which gave her the equal and opposite power of resistance; she wasn't having it. Ruthena grudgingly accepted Evelyn's hug and kiss—though she didn't return it—and watched Evelyn back toward the red exit sign.

Good Lord, now she's got both *hands on her stomach. She's just showing off.* Ruthena shook her head.

Evelyn stopped at the door. "Don't say no, Aunt Ruthena.

You'll regret it if you do. Take it from me: sometimes it's important to read what's right in front of you." She pushed open the right door. "I've got to get to Maxine, but if you have any questions, feel free to call me or Mama—"

"Lis? What does she have to do with this?" Ruthena felt a need to move closer to Matthew. Her fingers nervously brushed the envelope in his hands.

But Evelyn was gone.

Ruthena glanced at the clock over the stove.

Matthew followed her eyes. "So does God say you have time for your mama . . . and for me?"

She faced him with a sigh. "Matthew, why am I always choosing between God and you?"

"That's exactly my question, Ruthie," he answered quietly. He brought his hands together over his heart. "I love you, and believe it or not, I love God, and He's first in my life, too. Yet I'm also aware of the other things—and people—He's blessed me with."

Stung, Ruthena replied, "That's so unfair, Matthew. I love you, and I know what a blessing you are to me. I can't help that I need to fulfill other commitments I made."

"And you made a commitment to me, too, and to the rest of your family. Isn't that the point your niece made by coming here? Also, if I recall our oneness teaching, after God, I'm supposed to be your top priority—not the stewardess board, not the pastor's aid committee, not the pastor, and definitely not this banquet tonight."

She heard the echo of the sisters' words.

"Listen, I'm not going to argue with you. I'm too tired."
He glanced at his Timex. "Those sessions cost us a fortune,
and we can't afford to waste a minute. We can continue this
argument there. At least we'll have a referee. The Allens can't
hide out much longer, so if you're going to open this with
me, we'd better get to it." Matthew handed her the envelope.

Ruthena lowered herself onto a stool, then slowly slid an
unpolished nail under the sealed flap and withdrew a set of
folded pages. "It's not like Mama to write," she said more
to herself than to Matthew. "My Lord . . . it's a letter from
Henton!"

"Henton?" Matthew tore his gaze from the double window. "Who's H—? Your *daddy*?"

Catapulted back in time, Ruthena didn't tell her husband
she'd never called Henton that.

Ruthee,

*Hey ther girl. You probly dont know wat to say
hearin from me like this. I dont ritely know wat to say
miself. Mosly, Im ritin to tell you Im livin in Jasper and
I got a job. Won day Ill send yall somthin to hep you
get by. You mite not wont to hear from me rite now but
won day you mite.*

*Wen you was a babe I wuld just stand and look at
you sleepin in that drar. You was probly the prittyest
won of all them, lookin jes like your mama. Yo daddy
wont noware to be seen. You had these beads of swet on
yo nose and youd be chewin on yo fist. You was always*

hungry. B culdnt feed you enuf. She usta cry out at nite wen you bit her. Like you tryin to git more out of her. Seems to me you lached on to that Bible so tite sinse you new it was time to give up on yo mama.

I sit somtimes wondrin wat you gone turn out to be. How will yo man treat you? Will you have chillun? Wat will you do for work? I just hope I can see for miself won day. Ruthee, Im sho sorry for havin to leav yall, but ther aint much els I culd do. Yo mam try to ty the rope roun my neck, but it aint me she shuld be huntin. Im the won who stood by her. I dint go noware wen she needed sombody—

"Oh yes, you did," Ruthena murmured.

—an I was ther for you even tho I dint have to be. I was willin to liv wit B but I aint gon suffer and like to die for doin it. Such a shame Milton had to. B can find me wen she see the lite and let up. I just hope it soon. Its cold heer, colder than home without all yall. If you get ol enuf to com see bout me, you can look me up at 23 Reedy Creek in Jasper. I imagin I hear from you for I ever hear from yo mama.

Ruthena was dumbfounded as she read Henton's name at the end of the letter. *He wondered how my life would be, if I would be happy, about my husband? Why am I learning about this now, God? Where did this letter come from?* She studied the crinkled, yellowed pages, but no clue presented itself. Ruthena picked up the envelope to note the postmark and felt its weight. *Another letter? Lord, I don't think I can take more surprises. Not today.* Ruthena carefully folded Henton's letter and set it on the counter beside her.

"Ruthena?"

She looked up.

Matthew stood a few feet away, fiddling with the measuring spoons. "What's going on?"

"I don't really know, Matthew." She pointed to the letter she'd set down beside the grocery bags. "That's from Henton. My—my father. And this—" she held up the other note she'd just pulled from the envelope—"is another. So far, I'm not sure why my niece thought I needed your support. They're just old letters." Yet her heart seemed to slow as she unfolded the two pages.

Rutheena . . .

Her mother was the only one who spelled her name the legal way. Ruthena herself hadn't discovered it until she was in the seventh grade when she'd happened upon her birth certificate.

Girl, I hope you can take some time up from those knees and spare me a minute. I imagine that after you read this and the letter from Henton you're going to fall right back down on those knees, and you might stay there for a long, long time. I guess I can use that prayer. "Just what is going on, Mama?" I can hear you asking in that long-suffering voice of yours. Well, Rutheena, the fact of the matter is, I'm dying.

Ruthena skimmed the next two paragraphs and cried out, "She's dying from leukemia! That's why she sent Evelyn here, to deliver this . . . this . . ."

"What else does she say?" Matthew stepped closer, but Ruthena's outstretched hand stayed him.

You've been doing fine keeping in touch, so don't feel like any of this is your fault. Elisabeth lives just around the corner thereabouts, and she was about knocked off her feet. I have done my share of worrying and working things out, and I'm not worried no more, to tell you the truth. I done laid it at His feet. Now, don't get the wrong idea. I don't right much care how you deal with this. Just see that you do. I've got the how part to figure out, so the way I see it, your part is a bit easier.

Ruthena gasped, a hand to her mouth, and closed her eyes. She thrust the letter at Matthew. Once she felt him take it, her eyes opened, and she watched his mouth move as his eyes silently pored over the words. After a few minutes, she picked up where she'd left off, her voice hoarse and thick as she read aloud.

"Rutheena, part of me thinks of any of my children, you'll work this out the best. Not because of that faith you put such store in, but because of that man Matthew who believes in both you and the Lord. When I see you with him, I see the real you, the one you hide behind your Bible. That need to know and be known, to love and be loved. The Rutheena that's forced to lean instead of standing straight. You're probably going to be the one who holds up the others or makes them so mad at you they'll be too busy fretting over me, and for that, I'm grateful. Thomas for one don't have that same willfulness.

But for that same reason, I wonder about you. Always have. When you were running to that church, I thought for a while you had something else going on, but you sure have stuck to it. You even found you that husband there. Maybe that's where I should have looked. That work ain't going to save you no matter how often you flip through them hymnals and rinse out them Communion cups. Remember that. I'm going to pray you find what you need and not what you're scrambling for. So stop borrowing the happiness and the sorrows that belong to other folks. Hold tight to what's yours, because it don't pay to go through life always wanting something else or looking beyond the here and now.

That's about all I can give you right now, and I hope you take it. I'm not going to say I've done what I could

*for you because I know I've done what I wanted to do,
what I needed to do. I'm just hoping to hear, "Well
done" from my Savior. I love you, even though you do
bother the hell out of me sometimes—but I guess that's
exactly what you're trying to do.*

*Take care of <u>yourself</u>, girl, by letting that good man
take care of you."*

"Oh, Ruthena, Ruthena, I'm so sorry." Matthew tried to
wipe Ruthena's face, but she brushed his hands away.

"Don't say that. There's no need for that." Ruthena hadn't
realized she was weeping. "What do the old people say? 'God
don't make a mistake.' And they're right." Ruthena rose
slowly, leaning on Matthew as little as possible.

"But—"

"I don't know why I'm crying. What kind of good-bye is
this anyway? It's just Mama's way." Her voice strengthened.
"Beatrice is in God's hands. Now we just have to pray that
one day she'll be in His Kingdom—"

Matthew took Ruthena's hands and pulled her to him.
Ruthena braced her hands on his chest and pushed back.

"No, Matthew, stop. I'm fine . . ." But her voice faltered.

Matthew pulled Ruthena to his chest. He smoothed the
wavy strands that had worked their way out of her low pony-
tail and stroked her back as she pummeled his chest with
tightly balled hands. He locked his arms around her until
Ruthena's struggles grew weaker.

"No, Matthew . . . *no*," she breathed into his neck, though it wasn't Matthew's comfort she rejected. In her heart she screamed, *No!* to God. Finally she clung to him tightly, sobbing, her stomach heaving.

When Caryn and Jacqueline flung the doors back on their hinges, Matthew waved them off, tucking his head against his wife's and whispering in a cracked voice that eventually broke on the last word, "Oh, Ruthena, God, help us . . ."

Chapter Fourteen

THOMAS, AGE 5

"Dare."

The minute Thomas let the word trickle off his tongue, he knew he'd made a mistake. But there was no taking it back. Doing so would be like trying to get back a toy or a card you'd traded. No kid wanted to hear, "Blackjack, no trade back." He could take whatever they dished out.

Or so he thought. He watched helplessly as Myron and Floyd put their heads together.

Then Myron emerged, grinning slyly, rubbing his hands together. "Okay. We decided you got to go in your house and hide in your mama's closet. Count to one hundred. Then come out."

Thomas's mouth dropped open. "But—"

"Are you wimpin' out?" Floyd sneered.

"No, but—"

"Good. Now go on. And you better brang back somethin' to prove you was really in there. Don't just hide in the kitchen." Myron pushed him.

Thomas didn't want the label of lily liver, chicken, or scaredy-cat, but . . . *Mama's closet?* Yet he knew the brothers were counting on him to back down so they'd win his pretty blue marble. They didn't expect him to do it because they thought his mama was mean as sin.

Myron cut his eyes at his brother, and in tandem they tucked their hands under their armpits and flapped their elbows. *"Bawk, bawk, bawk."* They laughed.

That did it. Thomas hitched up his pants and gathered his meager reserves of courage about him. "I'll do it," he mumbled, though in his own mind he spoke firmly, resolutely. He studied Myron and Floyd intently. "You'll watch out for me, right? You'll whistle or call or somethin' if Mama comes back from town?"

The brothers nodded solemnly.

Thomas ducked into the backyard from around the side of the house where he and the boys had been playing. Furtively he pulled open the screen door and stepped inside. There, standing in the quiet of the kitchen, he almost turned back, but once again, he summoned strength—or foolhardiness—from somewhere and tiptoed into his mama's room.

Only one small window let in the late-afternoon sun, and

with its eastern exposure, the room already had grown dim. He and Mary had been kicked out of there years before when they were barely out of diapers, but he didn't take inventory now. He ran to the closet and gingerly stepped over his mama's few pairs of carefully placed shoes. "One . . . two . . . three . . . four . . ." As he counted, he looked around him, searching for something to take as proof. *A shoe? One of her dresses?* ". . . twenty-seven . . . twenty-eight . . ."

Whirrree!

A whistle! Was that a whistle? Thomas jumped up and ran from the closet, but before he could escape through the bedroom door, he heard voices—Mama and . . . *Is that a man?*—coming from the kitchen door. The voices entered the house and moved in his direction. Thomas's heart pounded so loudly he was sure they would hear it. He raced on his toes back to the closet—first a prison and now his sanctuary—and closed the door.

And not a moment too soon.

Thomas heard floorboards creak as Mama and the man entered the room. What was Mama doing with a man in the house, in her room? It sounded a little like his daddy; then again, it didn't. And what was that click? The door—did Mama lock the door? Thomas sucked in his breath as he listened to the two of them walk farther into the room. *What . . . what was that? Did he say, "I've missed you"?* Whatever Mama said, Thomas couldn't hear. Her voice was low and husky—he'd never heard that kind of voice coming from her. He scooted close enough to the door to press his ear to it. But he heard no more voices. Instead he heard rustling and movement. The sound of bedcovers being turned back. More rustling, more movement. The bed squeaking. Thomas leaned away from the door and covered his ears.

Thomas lost track of time. All he knew was the smell of shoes, the itch on a place on the back of his neck where the clothes brushed it, and the dark that enveloped him. So focused on drowning out the noises on the other side of the door, he had no idea when the noises actually stopped. Suddenly, though, he realized it was as quiet outside the closet as it was inside. He held his breath and again trained his ear to the door, listening intently for anything, not wanting to hear anything. Silently he twisted the knob and pushed the door open first one inch, then two, then three. Finally he opened it just wide enough to squeeze through. He sucked in a lungful of fresh air and leaned back against the closed door, exhaling with relief.

"'Bout time. I almost went in to get you."

Thomas's bladder emptied itself. Balancing precariously on wet, shaking legs, he thought he would pass out. His searching eyes settled on Mama, a shadow in a darkened corner of the room. Silent tears erupted and spilled onto his cheeks, mixing with the cold beads of sweat on his face. Neither he nor Mama said anything. His right hand tried to cover the darkened spot on his blue jeans.

"Need a towel?"

Slowly Thomas shook his head one time from east to west.

"Whatchyou doin' in my closet, boy?" Mama emerged from the corner. Her arms crossed over her tatty blue robe.

Thomas shook his head again. His tongue wouldn't budge from the roof of his mouth.

"I bet you got an eyeful, didntcha?" Mama came within two feet of Thomas and stopped. She perched on the end of the bed.

Thomas hiccuped and choked back a sob. He whispered, "I didn't see nuthin'."

Mama nodded. "Oh, that's right. You was cowerin' 'hind that do'. Guess yo' ears got pretty worked over today." She studied his pitiable form. "You got somethin' to say?"

Thomas shook his head briskly this time. He just wanted out. He didn't want to say anything or hear anything else.

"Well, I guess if somebody had to be sneakin' round in here, I should be glad it was you and not none of the rest of 'em. Though for the life-a me I can't guess why you'd be in my closet this time a-day or anytime a-day for that matter."

She slapped her thighs abruptly and rose. "Well, I ain't got time to be sittin' round in this here robe all day. There's plenty of thangs to be done." She looked at him. "And I believe you need to get changed fo' you go back outside to them friends who prob'ly still waitin' for you." Mama moved around the bed, straightening the sheets and the covers.

But Thomas stood there, frozen, confused about what he'd heard and about what it might all mean. In his young mind, there were two kinds of women: the ones who were mamas and who had husbands and who took care of their children. Then there were the women he and his friends read and snickered about, the women who had their pictures and stories in those magazines Myron and Floyd's brother hid under his bed. Thomas kept going back and forth between these two women. *Which one was his mama?*

Mama must have felt him watching her. She faced Thomas, her hand fisted on one hip. Her closed face and stance told him, "You'd best leave me be." But with narrowed eyes, she asked him, "What is it, boy?"

Thomas swallowed the spit and snot in his throat. "M-m-mama? W-was th-that D-d-daddy?"

Mama said nothing for a moment. Then she answered, "That wasn't Henton." She started to turn away from him, but he interrupted her.

Tears dripped from Thomas's eyes. His nose ran. Still, he managed, "Th-then, Mama, a-are y-you a-a . . . ?" His lips couldn't form the ugly word.

Mama squared her shoulders and looked straight ahead, out the window, before she locked her immutable gaze with his confused one. "I asked myself that once, boy. I can thank of worse thangs."

———————

"That's all she said?" Sissy was incredulous. "Thomas?" She raised her voice over the wind, cupping his shoulder to get his attention. "Thomas!"

"What?" Thomas glanced at his common-law wife.

"I asked you if that was the last thing Granny B said—'I

can think of worse things'? That's all she said to you about what had happened?"

"That's it. And I never mentioned it again. To her or to anyone else. In fact, you're the first person I've ever told that story."

They rode like the wind down Interstate 95. Sissy's braids streamed out through the open window of the 1980 Porsche 930.

"How could you live there and never talk about it again? There's no way I would have let her get away with that."

Thomas laughed shortly. "Maybe you wouldn't have, baby, but you didn't live with my mama. You weren't raised the same way we were." He trained his eyes on the road ahead. "And you just weren't me. You aren't me."

"What about now?"

"What *about* now?"

"You know what I mean, Thomas. Now that you've read these." The wind rustled the sheets of paper Sissy gripped.

"Oh." Subconsciously Thomas's right foot depressed the accelerator. The ground-hugging car lurched forward.

"Thomas! Slow down! You're going to kill us!"

Thomas let up a bit—but just a little. His right hand loosely draped the leather-covered steering wheel. His left swiped his eyes as if Sissy couldn't see his wet face.

Sissy didn't speak until the car's speedometer had inched down from ninety to eighty-three to seventy-seven miles per hour. "Is there anything I can do? What can I do?"

Thomas shook his head once, twice. He swallowed

convulsively. "Have you read them? Have you read the letters?"

"No. I just know what you told me before you tore out the house."

"Read 'em."

"Thom—"

"Read them!" Thomas ordered harshly. "Read them out loud. See what Daddy has to say to me after all this time." He knew in another time and place, Sissy would have lit into him, talking to her like that. She was quick to tell him he wasn't her daddy—technically, he wasn't even her husband— and she wasn't one of his law clerks. She didn't take orders from anybody. But this was different.

Sissy seemed to think the same because she flipped to the first letter.

Thomas snapped off the radio as she began, "'Tommy—'"

"Henton never knew how much I hated to be called 'Tommy.' Tom, Tommy—they sound alike to me. I remember he'd say, 'Tommy, git on over here and hep me with this sink' or 'Tommy, g'on in and git me a cup of *waw-tuh*.' I was his fetch-it boy, too little and too scared to tell him, 'Hey, my name is Thomas.'"

"But weren't you only four years old when he left?"

"Six. I was six years and three months old when Milton was born. I'll always remember that because Mama was never the same. And Henton left soon after." Thomas looked at the blur of trees and grass along the interstate. "Are you going to read?"

Sissy sighed and started again, "'Tom—'"

"You can skip that part." He grimaced.

Sissy read slowly as she struggled with the unfamiliar spelling.

"How you doin boy? I ben thankin bout you. It ben a long time but I thank bout all yall everday. The good times we had, not bout wat yall mus be thankin bout me for leavin. Like wen we went fishin in Falk's Pond. You member? You was—"

"That was just before he left, the day we went fishing. Henton was so determined we were going to catch something, but I just wanted to get home. I knew Mama would be looking for me, but Henton wouldn't let me leave."

"Maybe he wanted to spend some time with you?"

"He didn't care about spending time with me. He just wanted to tick Mama off, show her he was the man of the house or something." Thomas's eyes checked out the scene in the rearview mirror, flicked over to the other mirrors, and then returned to the road before him. "I guess he was showing her who was boss, even though we all knew it wasn't Henton. He kept me out there all day, and boy, was I mad—I was crying, I was so mad. I mean, I still had to do all my chores when I got home, and he went off somewhere . . . left Mama and us alone as usual."

Sissy sat quietly.

"Are you going to finish?"

She only gave him the eye before once again picking up the letter and resuming:

"You member that day. You was cryin and carrin on bout them worms I made you pick up. But we stuck to it til you thredded that hook and got yoself a fish. You was so proud of yoself you dint even mind doin them chores wen we got home."

Sissy stopped reading of her own accord this time. "But I thought you said—" She looked at him. After a second she wiped away Thomas's tears with her fingertips. She squeezed his shoulder.

"I wont ther long but I tryed to turn you into a man. I tryed to show you how to treat yo sistas so youd lern how women shuld be treated. And I—"

"So *I'd* learn how women should be treated?" Thomas's knuckles were white where they gripped the steering wheel. "He was barely around, and when he was around, he was either arguing with Mama or pretending to fix something that didn't need fixing. He barely paid any attention to Elisabeth or Ruthena or Mary except to grunt orders, and he acted like he was afraid of baby Sarah. He was a worthless no-account. How can he say he tried to turn me into—?"

"But you were so young when he left, Thomas." Sissy's

low voice seemed to test the waters before wading in completely. "How can you remember things so clearly?"

Thomas didn't answer her question.

"Thomas?" Sissy's voice hovered barely over a whisper.

"Mama," Thomas answered hoarsely. "I learned about Henton from Mama. All she talked about was how my daddy wasn't worth the dirt she swept out the house each day. About how he must not have cared about any of us, leaving us the way he did. That God was the only Father we'd ever have."

"But, Thomas, I wouldn't ask your mama to sign an affidavit. She isn't exactly an objective witness about your father. Whatever she said about him was told from the perspective of a woman scorned. I mean, how could she tell you anything good about him? He left her. But there had to have been something good or decent about him. She stayed married to him long enough to have seven—"

"Really, nine. You're forgetting the twins. Of course, Mama tries to forget Milton."

Sissy shook her head slowly. "And after all that time, he left *her*. That had to hurt. I know I would have tracked him down and put a hurtin' on him. At least I would've sued him. I have connections with a great firm."

The corners of Thomas's lips twitched. "Yes, you probably would have, but that's not my mama. It's not like she needed to tell me bad things about Henton, though, because his actions spoke for him. He left me, too. He left all of us, didn't he? Henton was just as much a reprobate as she said.

That's all I need to know." Thomas heard papers rustling. "What are you doing?"

"I'm putting away the letter. I assume you don't want to hear any more."

"But that doesn't mean you can't read them."

Sissy withdrew the pages and started reading Henton's letter again—to herself this time.

"Out loud." Thomas issued the order like he was judging a court case. Upon seeing Sissy's stony expression, he amended, "Please."

"*. . . And I hope you can take wat I tawt you and make a good life for yoself won day. Im makin a life for miself now in Jasper. I got a room and a job. It aint much but I call it mine. I aint got to fite over who sposed to do wat or who dint do this or that. I can just do or not do as I pleas. Goodness knows you cant pleas B.*"

Sissy scanned the rest of the letter. "All that's left is his inviting you to come visit and his address. He signed it *Henton*." Sissy's brow furrowed. "Don't you find that curious?"

Thomas considered her and her question just long enough to make the car veer toward the right. "What do you mean?"

"That he would sign off with his given name and not 'Dad' or 'Daddy' or 'Your father.' Something like that."

"Because he wasn't a father to us," Thomas stated matter-of-factly, his tears all dried and wiped away. "He knew the truth. What kind of father abandons his children, especially

232

right when a mother is at her lowest? Maybe that's why I saw Mama with another man." He nodded toward the other letter in Sissy's lap. "Aren't you going to read that one?"

Sissy picked it up. "Haven't you read it? You want to go through this again? Frankly, I don't want to risk an accident. And the light is fading . . ."

"Actually, I haven't read it. I never got the chance. Will you read it now? I promise not to lose it. Nothing can be worse than hearing from that old man." He caught Sissy's eye for a second. "Really, you're safe. It's from Mama."

"All right. 'Thomas,'" she read.

"I still see you as my little tender bird. I practically had to throw you out this nest, even though the others all went jumping out of it on their own steam. You used to walk around here, asking so many questions. Even when you weren't asking them, you had plenty of them in your eyes, stuff you was too afraid to say out loud. You wanted to know why wheels turned the way they did. Why the sky looked pink right before sunset. Why the grass wouldn't grow and why we still had to sweep the dirt. Why your daddy left.

Like most kids I suppose you looked to your mam and your pap for answers, for explanations for why life is the way it is. But I didn't know the answers to a lot of your questions then, and I still don't, so I hope you're not still waiting on me to fill in all those blanks. Yes, I raised you out the dirt in front of my house right here in

Spring Hope, but God get the credit for knowing all the answers. And I guess, well, He should.

Consider this my last meal—you know, like those criminals sitting on death row. I know that ain't the kind of law you practice (see, I pay attention), but I figure you close enough. You have to give them whatever they ask for to eat that last time, whether it be steak or eggs and bacon or pig brain. Well, this might taste like a healthy serving of pig brain, but you got to eat up.

I can tell you, Thomas, that knowing the whys and why nots ain't always the best thing for you. Take me for instance. I was hurting and aching for a long time. I finally took myself to the doctor—and he tells me why all right. He says I got acute myeloid leukemia."

Thomas's eyes were as wide as Sissy's when they met. He swallowed hard and nodded to her to continue.

"Yep, I'm afraid it's as bad as it sounds, and it definitely wasn't the answer I was looking for. I'm not sure exactly how long I got left, but I been dealing with it. I've accepted it, as much as anybody can, knowing they about to die. I'm not taking any medicine or chemo. That's only going to put off what should happen naturally. As the lawyer in the family, trust that everything's in order, such as there is. Just see Mr. Capel in town when the time comes—and not before because he knows not to talk to none of y'all.

234

Now, don't think this letter is like one of them deathbed confessions you see in them movies, where people finally tell you where all the gold is buried or why they killed so-and-so. No, this ain't about that. Whatever I didn't think you needed to know then, well, I still think it. You know your mama, boy. Nothing much about me will change. I hear tell I popped out my mama's belly with my mouth tight shut. Well, that's the way I'm going to my grave, with my lips a straight line.

No, I'm writing you some things you <u>do</u> need to know. Things like I love you, and I'm happy for you and that woman, Sissy. Rutheena says y'all ain't really married in the sight of God, but I know being really married ain't never done much for me, and God sure enough was looking on then. He was also looking on that day when I caught you in my closet. That look on your face helped me decide some things, make some changes. Hard things, but good and right things, and I appreciate you making them plain to me.

That ain't to say I don't think you need to do right and marry that woman—you do know what God says about marriage. But yes, I am happy for you. You seemed to finally take off and fly. I used to tell you to be strong. Suck in those tears. Be a man. But turns out you is man enough—with some left over to start another. Maybe all that crying was good for you. Just don't do no crying over me. Concentrate on taking care of yourself, little bird, and that little nest of birds you done got

*yourself. I suppose you got plenty of your own questions
to answer now. You ain't got time for no more.*

"Oh, Thomas . . ." Sissy's words were heavy with the
mournfulness they carried. It was all she said . . . until she
screamed, "Thomas!" as their silvery-blue Porsche veered
toward the SUV on their left. Her hand flew to her chest
as he jerked the convertible back into his lane and slowed
almost to a crawl.

"Take the next exit." Sissy rubbed his shoulder. "Thomas,
here. Turn here."

He crept to the first available space in the rest area and
turned off the ignition. For once in his life, Thomas didn't
feel the desire to cry to relieve the pain. He just took in
their surroundings as he let his head fall against the back of
his seat. Around them, a group of leather-clad bikers leaned
against their motorcycles. A father hurried his son into the
men's room. A young woman grasping a plastic bag walked
her German shepherd in the grass beyond the restrooms. In
the silence, Thomas reached across the console and intertwined his fingers with Sissy's.

"Do you know why she called me 'little bird'?" he whispered.

"No. Why?" she responded, just as softly.

"Because she said she always had to first chew on whatever it was she needed to tell me, and then she'd give it to me
one worm at a time, like a mother bird feeds her babies. She
said I was 'tender.'" He paused and watched an antique Ford

roadster park beside them. "I used to hate that even more than being called 'Tommy.'"

He took in a big gulp of air. "But right now, I could think of worse things."

Chapter Fifteen

MARY, AGE 16

Even in the shade of the pine trees flanking the backyard, Mary's cheeks felt flushed. Her eyes were squeezed closed, but two tears still managed to eke out their corners and run down each side of the perfect O of her mouth. "Eeeewwww!"

"Hush up, girl." Beatrice expertly jabbed the needle through Mary's right earlobe.

The teen pinched her lips together, but a high-pitched "Mmmmmm!" squeaked out.

Unmoved, Beatrice raised her daughter's chin and pushed the broom straw through the new hole.

Sarah tugged on her older sister's shirtsleeve. "You can open your eyes now."

Mary ignored Sarah's muffled giggles and opened first one eye, then the other. "You done, Mama? How's it look?"

"Like some nonsense." Beatrice doused the needle with alcohol as she prepared to do the second ear.

"Then why are you piercing her ears?" Sarah took the bottle from her mama and screwed on the cap.

"Because it don't make sense for her to pay somebody else to do what I can do myself." Beatrice held a lit match under the needle. "'Sides, my mam did it fo' me."

She took your two dollars, too? Mary thought, knowing better than to let the words see the light of day.

"But you never wear earrings!" Sarah cried.

"Child, whatchyou know about *never*? You barely seen today. You thank my life started when I had 'Lis'beth? I took mo' breaths than I could count befo' that. Good, deep breaths."

Mary tried to picture her mama in something besides housedresses and a long silver braid. Her brain started to hurt with the effort.

Sarah harrumphed as if she was trying to sound wiser than her thirteen years. She leaned closer to their mama. "Mary thinks her life is starting right this moment, with this ear piercing. But I told her those straws got more use in the broom than they have in her ears."

Mary sniffed. Sarah always was a little kiss up. "Well, one day, I'm gonna have diamond earrings where these straws are now. You'll see." She didn't appreciate being laughed at, especially in front of Mama, who believed dreaming was what lazy people did for work.

Yet Beatrice seemed to be doing some dreaming of her own. "My mam called 'em earbobs, and I didn't know nobody else with a pair."

"Earbobs?" Sarah scooted over and leaned an arm on Mary's knee. Mary jiggled her leg and pushed Sarah's elbow, forcing her sister to catch herself with both hands on the ground.

"Pinch right here. Hard." Beatrice placed Mary's fingers on a spot on her left lobe. "One day when Pap was gone to town, my mam took me and my sistahs out in the woods 'hind the house—

"Like you did us," Sarah breathed.

This girl acts like she's listening to some fairy tale. Mary pursed her lips. Her foot tapped out an impatient beat on the soft earth as she squeezed her ear as tightly as she could bear.

"—and she pierced our ears. That way she wouldn't have to clean up any mess we made on her flo's." Beatrice stood there with the needle between the tips of her fingers, her faint voice sounding like she was back in the woods with the mother the girls had never laid eyes on.

"She said we was different from the rest of the world, and she wanted to do somethin' to show it. Pap had a sho' nuff *fit* when he came home and saw what she'd done. He didn't wont us looking like harlots, he said. But then, after our ears healed up, he gave us pearls to wear. Said we was like the treasure the man found in the Bible and wanted to keep close. He never could say no to Mam."

Beatrice bent over and grasped Mary's ear. She brushed away her daughter's fingers and jabbed her lobe with the needle so fast Mary didn't have the time—or the courage—to cry out. In a wink, Beatrice slid in the straw to secure the hole.

Mary let out the breath she was holding with a quiet whoosh as she watched her mama pack up her implements.

But Sarah couldn't keep her curiosity zipped up. "Do you still have them? Your pearls?"

Like she needs fancy earrings while she's on her hands and knees, scrubbing the floors. Mary shook her head at her silly sister. *Always buttin' in.*

"When my pap threw me out the house, I threw away them pearls," Beatrice responded simply. "Them earrings didn't save me, and they ain't gon' save this girl here. But at least she can look pretty in the meantime." She took the alcohol from Sarah. "Now, Mary, make sho' you and them broom straws make it back to the house to get dinner on the table."

Beatrice crunched over the needles as she left their covering.

"Well, that story sure wan't worth my two dollars, but these holes better be. Sarah, are they even? How do they look?" Mary tapped her sister on the shoulder. "Sarah?"

But her little sister didn't turn back until the screen door had shut behind Beatrice. And even then, she didn't give Mary as much attention as Mary felt she was due.

"Fine, I guess. As good as a broom straw's gonna look."

"Well . . . I'm getting ready, and you'd best be, too, little Miss So-and-So."

"Getting ready? For what?" Sarah finger-combed the fly-away strands that had dislodged themselves from the two puffs of hair on either side of her head. "There's nothing wrong with the way I look. Just 'cause I don't prance around here shaking my high-yella tail like somebody else I know . . ."

Mary, simpering, extracted the deeply buried compliment. "You're right. There's nothing wrong with you—long as you plan to live here with Mama all your life in this back-woods hole."

"Oh, hush, Mary. Ear piercings won't save you. Didn't you hear Mama—?"

Mary flicked aside Sarah's words as she would a pesky fly. "Think what you want. But I'm telling you Ruthena's got the right idea."

"With what?"

"With that song she sings. 'Mmmm-mmm . . . One of these old mornings . . . Mmmm-mmmm . . . You gon' look for me, and I'll be gone . . .'" Mary hummed the words she didn't know.

Sarah laughed as she plucked the pieces of a pinecone. "But that song is talking about going to heaven. And you ain't getting nowhere close, Mary."

But Mary kept waving her head side to side to the beat of the music in her head, her thick, wavy hair swinging.

Sarah brushed off her striped hip-huggers. "You think you're something else." Her words sounded like half-compliment, half-insult.

Again, Mary sucked up the affirmative and discarded the rest. "I sure do. And you better start thinking the same if you know what's good for you." The shadows were starting to grow longer, and Mary didn't plan to get caught out there in those woods when it was dark. She sauntered from the woods, her hips swaying.

But two seconds later, Mary was running, not strutting, back to her sister, feeling very much like a scared little girl and not the worldly young maven who had sashayed her way toward home a moment before. She dropped to her knees behind one of the pine trees and peeked out.

Sarah ducked down beside her sister. "What's wrong?" she whispered.

"It's Mama, and she's *hot*! I forgot to pick up the fish." Mary peeked through the protective cover of the trees before daring to cut her eyes Sarah's way.

Sarah covered her smile with her hands.

Mary's lips twitched, too. "Guess I'm gonna have to put them dreams on hold just a bit. What do you think?"

Sarah's eyes laughed over her fingers.

Sober, Mary stared at the house and delicately fingered her sore ears. "She really is gon' wear me out, isn't she?"

Sarah nodded slowly.

"No, that's not the right color. Hmmm. No, this is too much for a volunteer. Where's the blue—?"

Mary moved aside several outfits in search of her blue pantsuit. She just hoped it hadn't fallen into the "sell it" pile currently housed outside in the garage. Determined to find the ensemble, she pushed around clothes, shoes, pocketbooks, hatboxes, and belts. There was no room to move anything around; if she did find the pantsuit, she'd have to iron it.

An hour later, Mary emerged from her bedroom—draped in orange from her ginger-flavored lips to her carrot-colored toenails. Her sandals staccatoed up the linoleum tile hallway toward the front door. She couldn't find her purse on the table in the front hall where she was sure she'd left it. Snorting like an angry bull, she tramped back to the family room. She picked up piles of magazines and books.

"What are you looking for, Ma?"

Mary barely spared her son a glance. Simeon's six-ten, three-hundred-pound frame enveloped the love seat squatting under the small window. She grunted as she edged over a stack of unpacked boxes.

"Ma. Ma? What are you—?"

"My purse."

"It's over here." Simeon waved her leather Michael Kors bag.

"What are you doing with my purse?" She tripped over

his size sixteens as she pranced to the sofa. "And move these shoes to your closet, please, before I break a leg!" She snatched her bag and rummaged through it.

"My room doesn't have a closet, remember? And I didn't take anything from your bag, if that's why you're counting your money."

Mary tucked her five one-dollar bills back into her calf-skin wallet. "Well, whose fault is it that you don't have a closet?"

Simeon watched her check her lipstick in her compact. "Where are you going? To a job interview?"

She snapped shut the case. "You're sitting there on *my* couch, watching *my* cable—" she spied an empty bag of chips on the floor by the couch—"eating *my* food in *my* house. And you ask me if *I'm* going to look for a job?" Mary's voice increased a decibel with each *my*. "No, I am not going on an interview. I'm going to the center. To try to help people who are trying to help *themselves*." Mary headed toward the front door.

"I didn't ask to be cut from the team!" Simeon shouted from the sofa. "So I couldn't come back from my injury. At least I hope this surgery will get me back in the shape and some team will pick me up."

Simeon's words froze Mary just as she placed one hand on the knob. She clip-clopped back to face Simeon and pointed to the stack of paperwork on the coffee table. "And we have the bills to show for it. All your hoping . . ."

He pushed his considerable frame to a standing position.

He picked up the crutches that rested on the wall by the sofa and hobbled closer to Mary. "You know, I'm the one who watched his football career go down the tubes. Not you. All you had to do was give up a way of life you couldn't afford anyway."

"*I* couldn't afford—"

"That's right. *You* couldn't afford. That was my money you spent every month for that view of the river. That was my money you blew every night on those expensive dinners. You don't even know how to spell *chateaubriand*, let alone eat it. It was my money that bought all your clothes, including that orange number. And the rest of my money will pay those bills."

Mary nodded slowly. "You know, you're right. But do you know what? I put in hard time getting you where you are. Or rather where you *were*. I cleaned up the nasty mess of other people to make sure you had food on your table. I'm the one who worked nights to get you clothes for school. I scrimped and saved every penny to make sure you got to college. I asked you—no, begged you—to stay in school, to get your diploma, but no, you had to leave early and make the big time. Well, you made it, didn't you? You made it all the way back to where we started. With no degree, no money, and no knee apparently. What do you plan to do now? Are you just going to sit around here and eat potato chips and watch TV all day?"

"I don't have to apologize to you or make anything up to you. You did what any *good* mother is supposed to. I didn't see you complaining a year ago when you took all day getting your hair done and your nails polished."

"I earned it!"

"You didn't earn anything! I was the one sweating in the sun, getting beat up every day. You reaped the benefits of my hard work."

Mary took in their humble surroundings. "Well, I'm not reaping much now, am I? I think Mama's house is bigger than this."

"Does it matter, Ma? We have a roof over our heads, food on the table—"

Mary laughed. "If you knew what I knew, you wouldn't ask me that question, Simeon. I'm fifty-six years old. This is not where I dreamed I'd be living out my golden years. I can't even afford a midlife crisis!" She slammed the door.

She walked to her gray BMW parked in the drive and climbed behind the wheel. She started the ignition but didn't move. Instead, she stared at the back of the sign taped to the inside of the windshield, trying to see how many words she could make out of ƎⱢAƧ ЯOꟻ. *Seal, afro . . .*

Tap-tap-tap!

She spun, ready to face Simeon ordering her from *his* car.

"Didn't mean to scare you," the postal carrier apologized once the automatic window had whirred to rest inside the door. "Looking good today. Here's your mail."

Mary nodded curtly. After he was gone, she riffled through the small stack of letters. "Bill. Bill. Bill. Mama—?" Mary tossed the other mail to the passenger seat. She slid one manicured nail under the lip of the thick envelope. Two separately folded letters. She opened the one with the older postmark.

> *Mary*
>
> *You probly wondrin ware yo letter ben. Som of the chillun got thers a wile bak. Sorry it took me so long, but I had to get miself together. Not that you ever had much time for me. But I just dont wont you to thank you not speshal like the others. You is. I culd always see you dint feel like you fit in, but you all the same, you and the chillun and B . . .*

Mary looked at the house she and Sim had just moved into. *I'm nothing like the rest of them.* She closed her eyes. *I am nothing like them or you.* Slowly she opened her right eye, half-expecting to find herself in the parking garage of her former high-rise condominium. But there she sat, all four wheels firmly gripping the cracked concrete. Blinking away tears, she continued reading:

> *I member the day I lef. You was sittin on the front steps lookin off to somwer. I sed goodby to you and you waved but dint say nuthin. You dint know that was the last time you was gon' see me. But I dont thank you seen me that day nether. I never culd see wat you was lookin at but I can tell you saw it good and cleer. I lef lookin for somthin miself but I aint foun it yet. I got a way of*

*livin a little better than I was but I aint got no happyer.
Its just a diffrent way to be sad. I hope you thank bout
that for you run off.*

*If you ever git that ich to spred yo wings com over
this way. Its too bad you cant bring yo babe brother.
Its hard to thank I aint go never see him again. Im at
23 Reedy Creek in Jasper. I aint got much and you may
jus keep on movin, but I be glad to shar wat I got for
however long you need it.*

"Henton," she read. "Well, I'll be. My old man. From
nowhere he came and to nowhere he returned. But I know
Henton didn't think I'd really go stay with him. Well, at least
he offered, but talk about jumping from the frying pan into
the fire." Mary dug around in her purse for her iPhone.

"Hello?"

"Lis?"

"No, this is Evelyn. Aunt Mary?"

No one but Evelyn ever called her that. Even her other
nieces and nephews called her by her given name, just as she'd
insisted. No use looking old before her time. "Hey, sweetie.
Where's your mama?"

"She's at the salon. How are you? How's Sim?"

Mary cleared her throat. "Fine, honey. Listen—"

"Still enjoying that beautiful view you're always talking
about? You know, Mama tried to call you a few days ago, but
she said the number—"

"We got rid of the landline. You can reach me on my cell."

Mary cleared her throat again. "Listen, Ev, I wanted to ask Lis about a letter from your granddaddy."

This time Evelyn cleared her own throat. "Letter from Granddaddy?"

"Yes, I just read this old letter from Henton—he wrote it after he skipped out on us. He invited me to stay with him, of all things. I wanted to ask Lis about it. She always knows a little about everything going on at home." Mary listened to the silence in North Carolina. "Do you know something about it?"

"Is that the only letter you've read?"

Mary looked down at the second letter. "Actually, yes, it is. Then I take it you *do* know about this?"

"I think you need to read the other letter, Aunt Mary."

She wanted to reach through the phone and wring her niece's neck. "Evelyn. What's going on? Why am I getting Henton's letter a hundred years after the fact?"

"Aunt Mary. Read it and then call Mama. But I need to go. Kevin's calling."

"Ev—"

"I'm sorry, but it's been nearly a week since I've heard my husband's voice. I promise I'll have Mama call you back. Love you, Auntie. Bye!"

"Well, I'll be—" Mary stared at her phone in disbelief before she picked up the second letter. "Let's see what else that man had to say."

I hope this letter finds you alive and well. I haven't heard from you in some time, so I don't know what's going on in your life. Well, a lot's been going on in mine.

I know how busy you are, so I'll just jump right into it. To put it simply: I'm dying—acute myeloid leukemia. And I'm going to be pretty quick about it if these doctors got it right. What does this mean to you? Not much. I haven't hidden piles of cash under my mattress all these years, and you won't be getting any of that expensive jewelry you love to wear. God knows why, but you do. And you know I can't leave behind property and a big house. But I will leave you some experience. It'll mean something to you in the coming years, even if it ain't worth nothing to you now.

I know we didn't have much when you children were running around here. You used to ask me, "Why don't we have this?" and "Why can't we do that?" I bet you've had your fill of doing this and that, but I wonder if it's enough, if you found what was missing. I know one thing you have is a fine son. He'll probably never step a foot into this old house, with all that fine living he's used to, but you must be proud. It don't happen too often that a boy will move his mama all the way across the country and set her up the way Simeon did you.

Most of the time children up and leave and never look back to their beginnings. I don't mean to say nothing about all y'all, but it's just a fact of life. I left my own peoples, and they had a fine life in South Carolina—a big house, money.

Mary almost dropped the page she was reading and asked the empty passenger seat, "They had what?"

But money don't matter. You can have all the money and things in the world, but they won't bring you no peace of mind. I know, I know, being poor don't bring much peace of mind either, but it helps you get to the quick of things, if you know what I mean.

My memories and my thoughts are about all I'm going to leave you, so you won't have to bother about the dirt around this place here. But there's value in knowing that your mama loved you enough to scrape and scratch this old dirt to make you a home, to feed you and clothe you. It's a small house that gets dusty and dirty, but it's mine and I don't owe nobody for it. I clean up my own mess.

God trusted me to be a steward over my living children and grandchildren, and I'm grateful. No, I don't see them much, but I know they wouldn't be in this world except by me. And that settles my spirit, a feeling I didn't have when all you kids was scrambling around here.

I know you like stuff around you, but you need something that somebody can't take away when the bill come late or the money get short. Maybe you is the way you is 'cause of how you was raised, but then I put the same ingredients in you that I put in the rest of the batch and you all taste different. Well, I guess that's a good thing.

Mary, don't worry. My being sick shouldn't touch your life much at all. I know you can afford to take

*the next plane out and be here today, but I hope you
don't. I don't have to see you to tell you I love you, and
you don't need to see me neither to hear it. Take care of
yourself and that fine son of yours. Give him my best,
which is pretty good, if I say so myself.*

Mary sat in the idling car for thirty minutes while the
raindrops spattered on the glass and the birds took cover in
the trees. A sudden rap on the window snapped her out of
her reverie.

Simeon leaned on his crutches. Rain beaded in his hair.
"Mama!"

She glared at Simeon for a second or two.

He knocked again. "Mama!"

She pushed the button and let down the window—barely.
"What is it, Simeon?"

"What are you doing?"

"I'm reading the mail."

"Can't you read inside?" Wobbling, Simeon tried to hide
his bulk under his hand as the rain picked up.

"No, I can't." She reached over to the passenger seat for the
stack of unread mail and stuffed it through the crack. "Oh,
and here." Mary snatched down the Ǝ⅃AƧ ꓤOꟻ sign. She
pushed it through. It landed with a *smack!* on the wet ground.
"I may not have a home to call my own, but this is my car."
Then she put the BMW in reverse and backed out of the
drive, nearly crushing the toes on Simeon's good right foot.

Chapter Sixteen

SARAH, AGE 17

Sarah bundled up her two skirts, three shirts, two dresses, pair of church shoes, and two weeks' worth of underwear into the borrowed satchel. She tiptoed to the bathroom for her toothbrush, deodorant, and feminine napkins. She didn't have money to buy more. All she had was twenty-seven dollars, enough to get her to New York on the Greyhound bus.

But not enough to come back.

Was that a squeak? Sarah froze. Here, nothing squeaked unless it was supposed to. She wasted precious minutes determining whether it was a rare trick of the wind before she slipped back to her room, stuffed her sweater into the bag, and shimmied to the window she'd wedged open earlier. Departure at 1:30 a.m. sharp. She dropped the bag to the ground and looked back one last time.

There she saw Milton, Thomas, Mary, Ruthena, Little Ed, and Elisabeth huddled around "marbles," stones of different colors, shapes, and sizes that Thomas had taken months to collect, smooth, and polish. He was showing them how to shoot just so, but most of all, how to do it without too much excitement and alert Mama. Seventeen-year-old Sarah wished she could go back to scoop up baby Milton out of harm's way. If only—

"If you gon' git, then git. Don't be breakin' my sash wit yo' big be-hind."

Sarah immediately returned to the present, but not quickly enough to avoid falling out the window. Fortunately, she landed on the padded satchel. Unfortunately, she sprawled right in front of worn slippers that, like Mama, had seen better days.

"Better. Yo' feet belong on the ground and not up in my winda."

Numb and dumb, Sarah brushed herself off.

"So where you headed?" Mama bent down and retrieved Sarah's bag. She took her daughter's right hand and placed the handle in it.

Out of instinct, Sarah grasped the curved wood tightly.

"It look like you got all yo' stuff in there. Better not be none of mine."

Sarah finally mustered the strength to speak. "No, ma'am."

"You best be tellin' the truth. I ain't got the kinda money to be fundin' nobody's world tour." Mama took in Sarah's jeans, T-shirt, and sneakers. "So where you headed?"

"New York."

"Well, take care. I hear 'bout strange thangs from up thataway. I hope you got more'n what you got on if you hope to make it up there." Mama shook her head wisely as if she knew all about the dangers and mysteries of a big northern city. "You got somethin' lined up?"

"My friend up there will help me get into secretary school. Then I can get a job."

"But where you gon' stay in the meantime?"

"She's got an extra room."

"Well, I know she ain't gon' let you stay there for nuthin'. You ain't got money to pay no rent. She liable to slam the do' right in yo' face the minute you show up on her stoop."

"No, Mama. It's not like that! I can stay there for free. At least until I start making money. She needs a roommate, but she doesn't trust just anybody. She figures my being there will help her as much as it will help me."

"You got this all figured out, aintcha?" Mama asked quietly, lethally. "You got school lined up, even a place to stay. You been plannin' this fo' how long, this run fo' freedom? You was just gon' let us wake up and find you gone. Is that so?"

It was then Sarah saw the trap. "No, Mama—"

"Then I s'pose you tried to wake us, but we was just

sleepin' too heavy. 'Course, if you looked fo' me, I wan't there 'cause I was waitin' for you out here." Mama stared at her. "What? Was we just s'posed to hope you warn't dead somewhere?"

Sarah had a bus to catch. And she was even more determined now to make it. "Mama. I didn't want you to try and stop me. This is something I've gotta do. I was going to let you know when I got settled."

"Oh, ain't that nice. But don't worry, I wouldn'ta tried to stop you. Nobody stopped me when I got it in my fool head to do some runnin'." Mama shook her head. "But how you s'posed to make it in New York if you cain't even stand up to yo' own mama?"

Sarah wasn't sure how to answer the question, so she kept her mouth shut.

Mama watched Sarah for a moment before she sighed. "Well, it's late, and I guess now I got yo' chores to do in the mornin'."

"Look, Mama. I've got to go. I'm gonna miss my bus." She thought about reaching out for a hug or a kiss, but she thought better of it and instead grasped her mother's dry hand. Surprised, she looked down at what had been pressed into her own. "Mama? Your Bible?"

"You gon' need it more'n you need those newfound friends of yo's."

"But your mama gave you—"

"My mam gave me lots of thangs, includin' yo' name. And you ain't got no problem takin' that wit' you to New

York. You got a long road 'head of you." Beatrice stared into the darkness.

Sarah did hug her mother quickly then, before she backed away. "Like I said, Mama, don't worry about me. It's New York you need to worry about. You watch and see."

Sarah retreated a few more steps as Mama continued to stare at her with that look of hers. "I love you, Mama. Really." But she wouldn't miss her. Sarah clasped the Bible to her chest and withdrew another step before she turned and ran. The dark soon swallowed her.

Sarah panted heavily as her run slowed to a trot and then to a walk. Finally she stood still, thinking back to the day she'd made her great escape—what her husband, Samuel, called her long-ago trek to the city. Sarah never did make it back to Spring Hope. Not to stay. But after reading her mother's letter in the bright sunshine of a Manhattan summer morning, she wished that she could go back. Today. Right now. Sarah stepped off the treadmill and picked up the letter again. She skipped past the introduction and read.

> *So you made it in the big city. You should know how all the people here in Spring Hope talk about you and your fancy life with the doctor. They think you something right out the television—remember* <u>The Jeffersons</u>? *Those folks on that show didn't seem all that happy to*

*me, but you know how people is with their money. As
long as they got that, they think everything's all right.
Is everything all right with you? I hope you got more
than money keeping you warm at night in that big old
apartment. At least when y'all was young, we was warm
here in this little house even if you wasn't always happy.*

*Well, I been doing some running of my own, girl.
The doctors say I don't have much time, and believe
me, I wanted to run away when I heard it. Not because
I'm afraid of death. I just figured I had more to do here
than I do over there. But I've stopped running. God
says it's 'bout time to come home. I know your husband
might have a better understanding than the rest, so
I'm leaving word with my doctor to tell Samuel the
particulars.*

*Sarah, I been thinking a lot about that night
you left here. I bet you almost peed in your drawers
when you fell out the window and seen me. I didn't
tell you, but I understood your leaving. I was much
younger than you when I left my own mam and pap.
Sometimes I wish I had hopped on a bus to some big
city instead of hitching up with your daddy to come
here to Spring Hope. There really ain't been that much
hope here for me.*

*You did what you needed to, and I guess it turned
out all right. I know you expected me to drag you back
inside, but to tell you the truth, it's good you made the
decision to get on with your life. I didn't have money*

*to give, but I gave you all I had. I just wanted you
to think about what you was doing, what you was
getting into, and I wanted you to have the best of
me with you.*

*Nobody did that for me when I had it in my head
to get, so I wanted to do that for you. You really didn't
need me to hug you or kiss you. That might have led you
to think you shouldn't go, that your home needed you.
But you was like our Abraham, sent out from all his
peoples, and just like him you got what God promised
you. And at last count of that family of yours, you off
to a good start.*

*Sarah, we both knew you needed to go, that you had
to go. And you knew you could have come back if you
wanted to, not that you'd have wanted to. I didn't have
that choice. Much as I might have wanted to, I couldn't
never go back. Just as much as I knew what you needed
then, I feel like I know what you need now, at least
from me.*

*If you was here, I would put my arms round you.
Really, I would. I'd tell you, you done a good job, but
that you still got some traveling to do on that road of
yours. You got six children to care for and a husband
to look after. And you got some work to do for yourself.
That's the important part I don't want you to forget.
Don't get so wrapped up in what others need for you to
do that you leave out that most important part. I didn't
do such a good job of that, and I have to live with it.*

Pray on what that is and get back on the bus, girl.
You got my Bible and you got plenty of money, so you
can afford to ride a good long time. I love you.

Your mama

Sarah tucked her mother's letter back into the envelope and set it in the tray atop the treadmill, covering up the number of calories she had burned, her pace, and the miles she had run that morning. Sarah considered the words to the Frost poem—"*. . . and miles to go before I sleep . . .*"—until the activity inside the brownstone captured her attention.

Even at this early hour, the boys were at it again: Nicholas and Sam Jr., tussling on her Aubusson rug over some insult or misdeed, real or imagined. Grace and Victoria, wide-eyed, omelets forgotten. Sarah grabbed the handle of the French door, intent on breaking up the commotion before they woke four-year-old twins Evangeline and Benjamin, but then she stopped herself. "He's the one who says he wants to do this, so let him handle it." Sarah stretched, focusing on the view beyond their sunroom to tune out the hullabaloo inside.

After a few moments Sarah was ready for the rest of what her mother had to say. She positioned herself in the sun that rebelliously beamed through the tinted glass, the farthest point away from the growing din inside—*ah, there go the twins!*—and took extra care withdrawing the second letter. It crackled as she flattened it. The faded words leaped from the page:

Saragirl,

You dont member me, I spose. You only called me daddy wonse in yo year of livin wit me. I member the firs time you sed my name I was seein to the truck. You came up hind me and like to scard me to deth. I jumped a mile and you cried so. I was the won sorry makin you cry like that. Jus like Im sorry now littel Sarah. I wonder if you dun much cryin over my leavin, but you probly dun wit it by now. Yeh I magin you got yo own reasons to cry now that dont hav nuthin to do wit me. I can still see you runnin roun bare butt with B tryin to git you in the tub. You was so yung and still had that free hart. Milton jus layin ther cooin and goin on. Nether yall new wat life was realy like. Not like the rest of us. I hope you still runnin free werever you is. Even if you got to do it in yo hed like I did.

I ben thinkin bout all I had to leav. All I got in Jasper is work. No woman. No kids. No home to call mine. Jus this job and a room over the sto. The woman who hired me is like yo ma. She dont take no mess and I can trus her. But she also trus me wit her bisness. B dint never trus me wit nuthin speshally you chillun. She probly thank I proved her rite in the end. But I kep secrets. Dint never tell nobody but I the won payin for it. And that aint fare to me or my boy. I hope yall unnerstan somday. If you see roun it come see me at 23 Reedy Creek. Im here. War Im gon go now? Take care of yoself.

Henton Agnew

Daddy! He wrote me. He missed me! He hadn't wiped the dust off his feet and forgotten them. He'd taken the time to write that he wanted to see her. *Wait! Is he still alive some-where? Did he send this letter to contact—?*

With an almost-audible thump, Sarah landed on earth. *Daddy's dead.* If not, the Social Security Administration had screwed up ten years ago. Sarah squeezed her eyes shut, feeling like she had lost her father yet again. Her right hand curled into a fist.

"Sarah?"

She answered her husband absently. "What is it, Sam?"

"The little ones are up and . . . I'm not sure. They're kind of cranky. What do you usually do when you're teaching the others?"

Sarah looked up into Henton's face, at least how she remembered it. She pictured him in his clunky boots, a toolbox in one hand and his gray hat in the other. Behind Henton she saw her brothers and sisters playing on the floor, their fight resolved.

"Henton" cleared his throat. "Hon?"

Sarah blinked and her vision cleared. Of course, those were her own rambunctious bunch, not her siblings. And Sam was holding a wailing four-year-old, not a toolbox or a hat. Her husband, the brilliant doctor who commanded an emergency room. The faithful provider who had bought her this beautiful brownstone and whisked her away from a life as a waitress and a tiny walk-up in Brooklyn. The struggling father who had saved others' lives but was woefully out of place in his own family's.

For a painful moment she considered letting him suffer.

"Excuse me, Sarah, but a little help here?"

"Of course, Sam." Sarah reached for Benjamin, who was still half-asleep, and she snuggled his pillow-soft cheek. She gave Evangeline the eye, and immediately the child's screeching quieted to a whimper, then finally rolled over and died.

"How do you do that?"

"Well, dear, it's not brain surgery." Her lips hinted at a smile. "Are you sure you're up for this?"

This—Evangeline, whose copious tears and runny nose had left wet spots all over his Brooks Brothers dry-clean-only shirt. Homeschooling, running the household, the sports, the lunches, the baths. Her *life* Samuel had decided to take over for the foreseeable future until he could call her family *their* family. The relinquishing of the life he loved at the hospital, the patients who adored him, their fast-paced, well-to-do urban lifestyle.

"Of course." Sam met her gaze unflinchingly. He used his shirttail to wipe Evangeline's nose. He promised her a cookie and his iPad once she had breakfast and read *Dick and Jane.* Then he scooped her up, and she tucked her head under her father's chin, mirroring her minutes-older brother. He turned and stepped into their family room, completely out of his element.

But not for long, she prayed, she believed. Sarah loved him, this anti-Henton who'd left everything else behind for his family instead of the other way around. She knew that ten, twenty, thirty years down the road, her own children would be safe from reading their own "Dear John" letters from an absentee father, and she was grateful for God's grace in sending her this man. When she stepped into the family room and beheld the stain on her antique rug, she held on to that prayer and looked the other way. Now was not the time to fuss about the incomplete English lessons, the mess, the broken naps, or the crying. It wasn't the time to look at the past and mourn what once was. She had a new life ahead of her, perhaps a new career, something other—not more— than orchestra, soccer games, textbooks, and playdates.

Her heart filled with hope, her brain with newfound resolve, and a squirming armload, Sarah mentally tucked away her mother's letter for the moment and put Henton's in cold storage. Smiling internally, she murmured, "'War Im gon go now?'"

Chapter Seventeen

"Mama. Mama."

Beatrice's thin chest heaved one last time and her fingers stopped fussing with her hair. She couldn't stop the tremulous sigh from escaping her parted lips. Brusquely swiping her caramel-colored cheek, she expelled a sigh of a different kind. "What is it, chile?"

The girl hesitated as if gauging her mama's mood.

"What *is* it, Mary?" She clenched her teeth to stop herself from grabbing her knee baby by her frail shoulders.

"It's Thomas." Mary's voice was even smaller than her tiny frame.

At that moment, Beatrice's ears trained on her young son,

screaming his fool head off in the front room. Her brows furrowed. "What's wrong now?"

"H-h-he 'bout cut his finger off." Mary's chest absorbed her threadlike voice because that was where she'd tucked her chin.

"What?"

The three-year-old sank closer to the floor, but she looked up, revealing the panic in her hazel-flecked eyes. She held her finger aloft and pointed to its tip. "His finger. It's bleedin' all over."

"Goodness gracious." Beatrice edged Mary out of the way and stomped from her bedroom. She found Elisabeth huddled over a screeching Thomas. And Mary was right. Blood was everywhere—including the rug she had scraped together for months to buy from Fulton's. Elisabeth was working to put a Band-Aid on the situation—even if she couldn't put one on Thomas's wound—by trying to shush her panicking brother and directing Little Ed and Ruthena in their unsuccessful attempts to clean the mess.

"Lord, help. Boy, what happened?" She pushed his nursemaid aside and applied enough pressure to Thomas's index finger to make it turn blue. When Thomas yelled even louder, Beatrice slapped him, not hard enough to leave a mark, but enough to bring him to his senses.

Thomas's cries ended abruptly as if someone had lifted the needle on a record player. He stared up at his mama, his honey-colored face streaked with blood, snot, and tears.

"I said, what happened?"

"My f-f-finger. I h-hurt m-my f-f-f-finger."

"I can see that, boy. *How* did you hurt it?" She dragged Thomas from the chair into the kitchen. Elisabeth followed. The others fell into line.

"Aahh!" Thomas's cries resumed as Beatrice ran cold water over his wound. The water ran deep Egyptian river red at first, then pink, and finally clear. Thomas continued screeching, but Mama focused on her mission, her lips moving soundlessly as she prayed. She sent her assistant for a clean rag and tore it into wide strips. Roughly she wrapped each strip around his finger and secured them with masking tape. By the time she was done, Thomas's screams had tapered to whimpers, and his bandaged finger appeared three times its size.

"Is somebody gon' tell me what happened?" Beatrice wiped up the blood and water around the sink. Clenching the threadbare towel, she turned to face the remaining members of her brood. Mary, wide-eyed and tearful. Little Ed, unblinking, appearing to await the next blow or an accusation. Elisabeth, who pulled Ruthena closer.

"Well?" Beatrice decided to wrest the truth from the victim or culprit, but Thomas only had eyes for his injured digit.

"What's goin' on here?"

All heads—including Beatrice's—whipped toward the low voice at the door. She scowled at Henton's lanky form.

"What's wrong with that boy's finger?" As usual, the words seemed to drag their way through molasses before slowly drizzling from his tongue. Henton nodded the question at Thomas, still pointing his finger toward heaven.

"He near cut it off." Beatrice turned her back to the children and to Henton—and the scent of cheap alcohol that rolled off him in waves—as he stepped into the kitchen.

"How he do that?" Henton doffed his soft-gray hat and twirled it around his right index finger once, twice.

"You need to take off them dirty boots and leave 'em by the back do'." Beatrice didn't face Henton. She ignored his question even if she couldn't ignore the acrid smell of his sweat. She listened to the door squeak open and to the clump-clump of his shoes on the stoop. The door clicked closed. "And put that dirty hat somewhere 'sides my kitchen." Beatrice added ballast to the barrier she'd erected between them and secured it with the same words she told him every day.

Like always, Henton retreated. Without argument, he set his hat in the front room. When he reentered the kitchen, he squeezed Thomas's shoulder, nodded to Mary, Elisabeth, Ruthena, and Little Ed, and slipped out without saying a word.

"Well, if y'all ain't got nuthin' to say, then get on outta here. I got better thangs to do than—" But she couldn't squeeze out the order. Pressing the back of her hand to her mouth, she pushed Ruthena aside—who almost knocked down poor little Mary—and left the kitchen as fast as she could without actually running. Beatrice flicked away hot tears as she strode back and forth across the breadth of her room, her chest tight. She fought to suppress the sobs that threatened to erupt.

Through the window Beatrice saw Henton standing in his bare feet, watching Elisabeth, who'd returned to her chore of sweeping the front yard. "That fool-headed man. That fool-headed man." And the dam broke. Like a madwoman, she tore at her clothes, at her hair. Beatrice pushed away from the window as Elisabeth dropped the rake and stood, mouth agape, in the yard. Beatrice clawed her throat, her chest, her thighs.

Over the loud cries that kept coming and coming and coming, Beatrice heard Elisabeth yell for Henton. Ruthena stumbled over Mary and Little Ed crouching on the floor in her mama's bedroom doorway as she went to scoop up baby Sarah, who'd slept through all the to-do. When Mary reached for the knob to pull it closed, Little Ed swatted away her hand.

Then . . . Henton was at Beatrice's door, his eyes looking as wide and wild as hers when they met. She could do nothing but sob and shake her head as she watched him shoo away the children. Little Ed grabbed Mary and pushed everyone toward the front room. The screen door closed with a clap.

Only Thomas, forgotten, huddled near the kitchen, shivering, still holding his bloody finger high in the air. His face was the last Beatrice saw before Henton slammed closed her bedroom door. He must have heard the lock click into place.

The clicking noise worked Beatrice's nerves.

"Now, Mama, you sure you want to do this?" Lis depressed the button on the pen, in and out, in and out.

"Gal, I ain't got time to be changing my mind. 'Course I'm sure." She snatched the implement from her daughter, reached into her pocket, and took out another. Beatrice removed the cap and handed it to Lis.

"Okay, well, you know there's not much I would refuse you these days, but I'm the one who's gotta live with Evelyn."

"You mean after I'm dead and gone?"

Lis rolled around the pen in the silence. "So what do you want to say?"

Beatrice looked out toward a scraping noise across the road. She waved at Velma Johnson dragging her garbage cans. She'd decided to write this letter days ago.

"Mama?"

"You just like that chile of yours. In a rush to nowhere. How is she anyway?"

"Rounding out by the minute." Her lips curved into a smile. "Beautiful. We could just send a photograph. Let the picture tell the story."

Beatrice played with the end of her braid and chuckled. "Ain't that the truth? But I got more to say than that." She watched Velma return to her house. "Get that paper. I'm ready."

"Mama, I'm sitting here with the paper and pen. You just start talking."

"All right. Dear Kevin . . ."

Chapter Eighteen

MILTON, AGE 4

"You's a bastard!"

"You take that back!"

"I won't! It's the truth!"

"No, it ain't! You take it back!"

"I won't take it back, and it is true! That's what I heard
Daddy say, and he's big, so he knows better."

Milton didn't know what the word meant, but he didn't
like the sound of it. And if his brother was saying it with such
spiteful confidence, Milton knew it had to mean something
real bad.

He flung himself at Thomas. Thomas threw a wild punch.

Milton grunted and wrapped both his short arms around his older, yet clumsier brother, locking his hands in a fist. Thomas struggled to break free, dragging Milton all around the backyard, but the smaller, wiry boy wouldn't let go. Thomas tripped. Both tumbled to the ground. Milton's head landed square in the middle of his stomach. All Thomas's breath exploded from his lungs and escaped through his mouth with a loud *"Woopf!"* Milton's clasp loosened, and Thomas's arms broke free. Immediately he grabbed Milton's ear and pulled. Then the real fighting began.

"Eee!" Milton screamed. He drove his knee into Thomas's thigh.

"Oooohhh." Thomas rolled Milton over and plopped onto his brother's chest. He squeezed his knees together and Milton kicked and bucked, but Thomas held on. Milton pounded on Thomas's back until he pinned Milton's arms down.

Tears streamed from Milton's eyes. Pure rage drove him to buck violently one last time, knocking Thomas to the ground. With a guttural roar, he leaped onto Thomas and drove his brother's face into the dirt. "Take it back! Take it back! Take it back!"

His cries drew the others from the nether regions of the woods. Little Ed ran up and yanked Milton off his older brother.

He struggled and kicked. *"Mmmpf . . .* let me go!"

Mary ran to Thomas and helped him up. His face was smudged and dusty, his nose red, already bruising. He didn't fight to get at Milton. Thomas stood strangely quiet, staring at him.

Milton refused to be comforted by Little Ed or Sarah.

"*Shh!* You gon' get us in trouble." Little Ed shook his brother. "Hush up, now!"

Milton pointed at Thomas. "Make him take it back!"

"Take what back?" Little Ed and Mary asked in unison.

"He—he—ca-called m-me a bas-bas—" Milton choked on the word.

"A what?" Ruthena had just joined the fray. She set a basket filled with ears of corn and peas by her feet. "A what, Milton? What's got you so riled up?"

"A bas-bas—" Milton's voice hitched. Actually, he couldn't remember the exact word, but deep down, he knew it was something awful.

"A bastard," Thomas said without inflection.

Little Ed squinted at Thomas. "What'd you do that for?"

Mary cupped a hand over her mouth and leaned toward Little Ed. "What's that?"

Little Ed trained his eyes on Thomas.

"'Cause I wonted to. That's why," the normally docile Thomas responded.

Little Ed smirked. "That ain't no kinda reason."

"Well, it's my reason." Thomas tried to walk away.

"He said he heard Daddy say it a long time ago, before he left. He said Daddy and Mama was fussin' and he heard Daddy say I's a bas-bas—"

"Bastard," Mary supplied.

"And that it must be true 'cause Daddy big and all." Milton hiccuped.

All the children suddenly chimed in. Some pointed a finger at Thomas. Others told Milton to hush up. Only Little Ed said nothing. The rest just agreed with Milton. It sounded like it was something bad, and if Henton had said it about Milton, then it was something *really* bad.

"But just because Daddy *may-a* said it don't mean *you* can say it, Thomas." Mary tried to put a stop to all the arguing.

"It mean I can say anythang I wont. It must be true." Thomas poked out his chest.

"What must be true? You know what that word mean?" Little Ed finally offered his two cents.

Thomas put his hands on his hips and sneered. "It mean he ain't got no daddy. Matt-a-fact, that's what he said, somethin' about Milton not havin' a daddy and all."

Little Ed narrowed his eyes. "But that don't make no kinda sense, now do it? Henton Milton's daddy. Just like he my daddy and yours. But then ain't none of us got no daddy no mo'. Whatchyou got to say about that, Thomas?"

Milton suddenly stopped hiccuping. His eyes lit upon each face—Little Ed, Mary, Ruthena, Sarah, Thomas, and back to Little Ed. The thief, troublemaker, liar, and bully had gained another title in Milton's eyes: hero.

Thomas's mouth dropped open slightly. "I ain't no bast—" The word died on his lips.

"Well, then I ain't neither." Milton looked at Little Ed for confirmation.

"Are you sho'?" asked a voice that didn't belong to Little Ed—or Mary, Thomas, Sarah, or Ruthena.

At the sound of it, everybody took a step away from Milton, the heart of the action. Everybody except Little Ed. He put a hand on his younger brother's shoulder, and it shored him up in the face of this new, unrelenting opposition.

"I said, are you sho', boy?" Beatrice stood behind the small circle, holding a paper bag of dry goods. Her eyes, searing-hot coals in her narrow face, rooted Milton to the spot. "Well? What y'all got to say? Is you got a daddy, or aintcha?"

"Mama . . ." Milton had worked up enough courage to answer, spurred on by Little Ed's warm hand.

"Hush up, boy. Nobody talkin' to you."

Beatrice didn't sound like she was looking for an answer, and the older children seemed wise enough to know that. And Little Ed's hand wasn't meant to comfort Milton, but to keep him from doing or saying something stupid. Something young Milton divined from the press of the fingertips that kept him in place.

"I don't know who started this foolishness, but I thank y'all got plenty to do 'sides concernin' yo'selves 'bout grown folks' business."

"But, Mama," Little Ed protested, "we wan't into yo' business. We just talkin'—"

"Just talkin' when they's plenty to be *doin'* round here. Now, git." When they took too long to scatter, she planted a step forward, shoulders reared back. It wasn't like she could hit all of them at once, but that didn't seem to matter. Her threat sent them running to the woods, to the clothesline, inside the house to the kitchen.

Milton watched his superhero toss his *S* to the wind as Little Ed scattered with the rest. But before he could move his own feet, a rough hand caught him on the same shoulder still warm from the touch of his brother.

"You was 'bout to say somethin'."

Milton stared at her, his mouth open.

"What is it, boy? You all fired up to answer me. Go 'head."

As Milton faced his mama, her eyes betrayed some emotion he couldn't name. Mesmerized, he stammered, "I-I ain't n-no b-ba-bas—" Once again, his throat held the word captive.

"You ain't, huh? So who's yo' daddy?" Beatrice leaned into Milton really close, so close her breath made his eyelashes twitch.

Curiosity caused him to speak up, not bravado. "Why you askin' me? Henton. Henton my daddy."

"Then why ain't he here? The only daddy you need to be worried about is the One up there. He the only One who's here right now. They cain't tell you no more 'bout they daddy than you can yours."

When Beatrice suddenly let him go, he said nothing more. He just rubbed the pale places where her fingers had pressed into his skin. He watched her walk around the back of the house, and he waited there until he heard the back door open and shut with a screech.

"I don't know what set Thomas off that day. And I never asked. But that's the last I talked about Henton. And the last Mama talked to me, period."

"You never asked about him again?" Milton's wife, Nancy, sat to his left, holding his hand across the wrought iron arms of their chairs.

He'd tried to tell her the story many times, but he never could find the perfect words or determine the right moment. Now, it was obvious there never would be a "perfect" or a "right" when it came to unpacking his suitcase full of history. As Milton watched Nancy work through what she'd heard, he wished he'd made more of an effort years, or even months, ago, when it would've been for her ears alone.

"What about Ed or Sarah? You never talked about it with anybody? You just assumed all these years that—?"

"That I am a bastard." This time, Milton didn't stumble over the word. It still tasted bad, but he simply spit it out. "Why not? She's treated me that way all these years. Refusing to say more than two words to me whenever we're together. Not answering letters. Not calling."

He could've been describing the shades of blue, purple, orange, and red of the evening sky. Discussing the probabilities and possibilities of this, that, and the other occurring in the universe. But Nancy, married to him for the past twenty-five years, probably felt the slight tremor he couldn't restrain and suspected he saw none of the coming night's wonders, that more than likely he was as stupefied as she by his un-expected visitors.

She stroked Milton's thigh. "But now she's brought you this letter—these letters. She's here now. And in his own way, *your father*, too."

Mama. Sitting across from them in his screened-in porch, too smart not to know who "she" was, though Milton never spared her a look.

Only Evelyn sat close enough to Granny B to hear her small intake of breath. *Is she in pain?* Evelyn knew Granny B suf-fered physically, but she wondered if Milton's words had wounded her in places beyond the scope of any X-ray or MRI. She studied her grandmother's profile. *Should we leave? Is all this too much . . . even for her?* But Evelyn knew asking her would be pointless, something she'd learned after pepper-ing Granny B with questions from the second she'd put the car in reverse in her driveway.

"Why don't you ever mention his name?" Even then, on their way to visit her uncle, Evelyn couldn't bring herself to say *Milton*, he-who-shouldn't-be-named, to Granny B.

"Why I need to use his name with you? You forget what it was?"

"You know what I mean."

"And so do you." And she'd ended the discussion by clos-ing her eyes and propping her head against the seat.

Thirty minutes outside of Spring Hope, Evelyn had leaned over and whispered, "Do you think he'll see you?"

"If I didn't, I wouldn't have asked you to drive me there," Beatrice muttered, her mouth barely open and her eyes firmly shut.

"Did he mention the letters when you told him we were coming?"

"Now what sense do it make to pay mor'n a half dollar to mail him somethin' when I'm gon' see him myself?"

Evelyn nearly slammed on the brakes, right there on the highway. She stared at Granny B for a few seconds before focusing on the road that suddenly seemed longer and bumpier. She might as well; her grandmother wasn't looking at her anyway. "Are you saying he doesn't know we're coming?"

"Isn't this what you wonted me to do in the first place: drive all over creation, hand deliverin' my bad news?"

"But you decided not to. And now . . ."

"Well, I ain't got a later, do I? Last I heard, Jesus don't run a post office. I ain't takin' this with me to heaven and ain't no need of him bearin' this alone when I'm gone."

That had shut Evelyn up until they were standing, finally, on Milton's stoop, while Aunt Nancy went to locate her husband, Granny B's long-lost son who could've found his family home with his eyes closed. Then and there, Evelyn broached the question she'd never had the nerve to ask. "You've always acted like Milton is dead. Please tell me why."

Granny B had kept her head and eyes forward, seemingly fixated on the red front door. Evelyn opened her mouth to repeat the question, but before she could, her grandmother responded softly.

"Not dead. Just buried."

And then Uncle Milton had swung open that red door, and Granny B had scaled those five steps like she hadn't nearly been doubled over ten miles before. Evelyn didn't have the opportunity to help her; she wasn't as spry these days with the weight of the baby she carried and toes that looked like Vienna sausages.

Evelyn had figured by "this," Granny B had meant a figurative burden she wasn't taking with her when she died, not the letters she'd helped her grandmother painstakingly prepare. Yet sitting there on his porch, watching Milton clutch those handwritten pages, Evelyn realized that her very literal Granny B had said exactly what she meant, as always.

Beatrice could feel the weight of her granddaughter's eyes—and of her silent accusations—as Evelyn made herself comfortable in the porch swing beside her, but she didn't shift a hip or bat an eyelash. She waved off the frosty glass of tea Evelyn offered, her lips pressed to a flat line. She'd already had her say and given him the letters; nothing gratuitous was getting in or out her mouth, let alone a sip of iced tea. Somehow, Beatrice even managed to position her feet on the brick pavers in such a way they kept the rocker from creaking forward or back. She focused all her strength and attention on her youngest son, sitting across from her on his enclosed back porch.

Milton's curly hair was nearly as gray as his mama's, his eyes and mouth as lined, his gray eyes as steely. In contrast, his beard was still a rich brown, neatly trimming his fifty-two-year-old mahogany face. He held himself nearly as still, except for the middle and index fingers that played a cadence on his wife's hand clutched between both of his.

Beatrice traced that face with invisible fingers, ravenous for this long look at her boy, a luxury she'd never allowed herself, not when she nursed him at her breast when he was a baby, or fifteen years ago, when the family had come together to bury Graham. In fact, that was the last time she'd seen him—specifically, his right ear, from her perch two rows behind him in the church pew. She had forced Ruby to drive her home before the burial and repast at Elisabeth's home in Mount Laurel. While her children spoke to and visited Milton regularly, to say she *rarely* did would imply too often.

So, today, Beatrice set out to make the most of this hour with Milton, probably her last, in his home in Griffith. One hundred miles, yet a lifetime away, from Spring Hope.

"*Now* you come." Milton finally faced Beatrice, but only for a moment before he stared at the brick wall just behind his wife. "*Now* you have something to say. 'Good-bye, Son,'" he paraphrased. A bitter hint crept into his voice. "But at least you finally gave me back something you took from me." He nodded toward the letters Nancy cradled. "And it only took you forty-eight years to do it. 'Good-bye, Son.'" He looked back to the fields behind his house.

"Uncle Milton, that's not all she said, good-bye—"

"But isn't it?" Milton massaged the thinning patch on his crown. He snatched the letter from Nancy and read:

"It's been a while since we spoke last. I remember it was on a Sunday when you called, and you and Nancy had just come from church. We only talked a few minutes, but in my mind it was long enough. Looking back, it seemed like you might have had something more to say, but I didn't give you much room to say it, did I? I kinda wish I had taken a few extra minutes to let you speak your piece, but that's neither here nor there."

"You '*kinda* wish'? Just *kinda*? After what I've gone through my whole life . . . !"

Nancy scooted closer to him. "Mil—"

But he ignored her and picked up the letter.

"Today, I'm the one who needs the speaking room, and I hope you can see around it to give it to me.

Milton, when you wanted to go left, I was saying go right, and you know it's my way or no way. That's how I was raised and that's how I raised y'all. Funny thing, I left my home just for that reason, but y'all never went nowhere farther than those woods. And goodness knows you had cause. Fact of the matter is, sometimes

*I remember wishing that you would run off somewhere
or that I could. I suppose y'all did run eventually, and
you haven't looked back, have you, Milton?*

*Me? Since I heard I ain't got but a short time to play
in these woods, I've been doing lots of looking back and
a bit of looking forward, too. When I do, I see this little
boy looking up at me, hoping to get some answers. I see
a young man who barely looks me in the eyes when he
speaks to me. You might mumble, 'Yes'm' and 'No'm' on
Monday and that's all I'll hear till the next. When I
think back, I know it ain't like the rest of them talked
much, but even their quiet weren't like yours. Your quiet
said a lot. Always has.*

*I wonder what you're going to say if somebody calls
on you to say a few words over me, to break that silence.
Will you say, 'She was a good mama. She taught me to
depend on nobody but myself. She showed me how to
work hard and to be tough. My mama taught me that
love ain't about reading you good-night stories or giving
you ice cream after dinner. It's about doing what's
hard and showing you how to do it, too. Love is about
sticking around, even when you want to run off to the
woods somewhere'?"*

Milton sprang to his feet, out from under the shelter of
Nancy's arm. At that moment, his wife's embrace was a too-
painful reminder of the many times he'd needed a woman's
touch—his *mama's* touch—when he was a child. But she

couldn't be found even though she was hardly more than two feet from him in their small house. Milton wanted to rant, to rage, to throw down the pages and grind the words to shreds under his feet. Instead, he read them out loud.

"Will you even say, 'I love you, Mama'? You probably won't. But I know you do, Milton. If you didn't, you wouldn't call me even if you talk just two minutes. You wouldn't send me those cards. And you wouldn't keep sending me money even though I send it back. I know you love me and you don't really want to, but I'm your mama. And I love you, Milton, even if I tried not to, because you're my boy. My baby boy.

Milton, I just wish you some peace in this life, the same as I wish all y'all. Not everybody finds that. God knows it's taking me a lifetime to get it. And as far as answers go, yes, Milton, Henton's your daddy. I tried to give you something—Someone—better than that who was daddy, mama, sister, and brother to you, but I just think you need to know that, too. I'm not saying that because I think I owe you nothing. You can ask Thomas about that. I just don't plan to take that man's name on my cold lips when I finally rest for good. Get your peace, boy. I'm on my way to mine."

"Signed, 'Your mama.'" Milton's laugh was devoid of humor. "My mama, who wishes me peace of all things. *Peace?* That's not yours to give."

Beatrice watched Milton hold back the pain, much as she had when it had split her insides in the car. She did shift her feet then; for a split second, she thought to touch him, but his wife moved much more quickly. Nancy grabbed his hand and turned him to face her, and they stood there with their foreheads touching. Beatrice watched them until the streaks of red and orange faded into the deep expanse of midnight blue. Until one twinkling star became countless.

Finally Milton, his face haggard, stroked his wife's hair, once, twice. Then at last he looked at Beatrice, and she got to feast her eyes on more than just his profile or his forehead. He smiled wryly. "You got the last word, didn't you?"

Beatrice opened her mouth, but then she shut it, figuring they'd both said enough. She and Evelyn watched Milton push open the screen and step out, followed by Nancy. Soon, they were but shadows in the backyard.

As far as Beatrice was concerned, it was time to go. She'd done what she came to do. She grasped the chain anchoring the swing to the ceiling and hauled herself to a standing position, her arm trembling with the effort of lifting so heavy a heart. *I s'pose I am gon' take this with me to heaven,* Beatrice thought. She looked back at Evelyn.

Evelyn wasn't ready to go. Not yet. She squatted to retrieve the second set of pages that had fallen to the floor. A rough hand wrapped around her forearm and pulled her to her feet. She faced her grandmother, prepared to arm wrestle her if she had to.

But she didn't have to. Sighing, Granny B let go of Evelyn's arm and plopped her ninety-five-pound load back into the swing. It twisted and shimmied side to side and back and forth. Evelyn slowly unfolded the second letter and read it to herself.

Milton,

Boy, it ben a long time. Too long. If you ran into me on the street you wuldnt know I was yo pap. But Id know you by that Agnew nose and forhed. And you got that same mark on yo behind I got. My pap got it too. You even got my mama's name. She was a Milton fo she marryed my pap. B fawt me bout that name but I made sho she rote it down. That the least she culd do.

We the same. B dont want it that way but aint nuthin she can do even if she burn off that mark like she threten to do wen she seen it. I hated to leave you son. That nite I stared down at you layin in that box on the flo. I thot bout takin you with me but I dint hav no way of razin you. I dint have nowere to sleep and I sho dint hav no way of takin care of no babe. But I spose you mite do better sleepin in allyways like me than sleepin in that wolfs den I lef you in. All I ben doin is thinkin bout you, wondrin how B treatin you. She gotta feed you cuz the other chillun will see somthin rong. I

dont know wat she ben tellin you but I luv you Milton.
I aint ben ther to raze you but I luv you jus the same.

I hope you dont thank too hard of me. It nearly kilt
me to go. I wulda stayd jus for you. But I had to go for
you. B wuldnta let me or you have no kinda life if I
stayd. She razed cane the hole time she carryd you and it
dint get no better after you com out. You was even born
in a thunnerstorm. That rain jus pored off the house
and that thunner shook the windas. I had to run git
Miss Boyd to hep yo mam. It was jus us and Lisbet and
Thomas. Corse B dint wont me noware near her. But I
was thar by the do. You culd screem and you screemd up
to the day I lef. You put somthin on that woman, you
heer me? I jus hope them storm clowds broke wen I lef.

Im lookin to see you won day. I liv in Jasper at
23 Reedy Creek. This woman lookt kindly on me and
giv me work to do. I almost dint take this job cuz I
bout had it with all her kind but Im runnin the sto for
her. Thats how I had this munny to giv you. Now dont
spind it all at Fultons. Dont giv it to yo mam nether.
Look me up if you got the mind to. I be the won with
the gray hat on and the big smile. And you can just chek
my behind to make sho. I be lookin fo you.

Daddy

A tear wound a crooked path down Evelyn's cheek as she studied the two yellowed, faded one-dollar bills. She wondered who'd paid the higher price.

PART THREE

The First and the Last

Chapter Nineteen

AFTER GRANNY B'S LETTERS SCATTERED to the seven Agnew-scented winds, calls poured in like the rain that pelted the windowpane on summer afternoons. Lis tried to reassure her brothers and sisters that everything that could be done was being done, but they blew into town anyway, huffing and puffing against the brick fortress that was Granny B.

"She wouldn't even let me pray for her. I couldn't believe it. She wouldn't even let me step in the door and pray for her. And then I hear Little Ed is staying there!" Ruthena stood on the bottom step.

Evelyn watched her mama's shoulders lift in a sigh that seemed to start in her toes. Then she glanced at her uncle sitting beside her on a kitchen stool and smiled when he winked.

Since her uncle had been released from prison and found a new lease on life, he'd become Edmond—to all but Ruthena, who clung to the past like it was her shelter from the cold.

Lis led the way. "Come on in, Matthew. Ruthena, why don't you take it up with Edmond yourself?"

"What! Little Ed's here?" Ruthena pushed past Lis.

Lis patted Matthew's back as he followed his wife. He planted a kiss on his niece's cheek and then enveloped his brother-in-law in a bear hug. "Hey there, brother. When did you get out?"

"A few weeks ago. Big Sis over here sent me money for a bus ticket so I could see Mama."

Evelyn knew that even though Ruthena made the most noise, her aunts and uncles all looked up to their oldest sister. She'd always been their emotional go-between with Granny B, the family's second-in-command even when Henton was around.

Matthew left a hand on Edmond's shoulder. "How've you be—?"

"Why do you get to stay with Mama when the rest of us can't even see her?" Ruthena skipped all the social niceties.

"*I* see her, Ruthena," Lis responded smoothly as she opened the freezer and retrieved the decaffeinated coffee. "And so does Evelyn."

Ruthena pursed her lips and rolled her eyes heavenward, but Evelyn didn't get the feeling her next words were heaven inspired. "But the rest of us don't! Mama needs prayer, a laying on of hands . . ."

"I touch her every chance I get, Aunt Ruthena." Evelyn sipped her orange juice. She rubbed her stomach, feeling the baby kick.

Ruthena grimaced.

"And I pray with her, even when she's not looking." Edmond grinned.

Ruthena's mouth dropped open, and she aimed an index finger at her brother. "*You?* I'm sorry, Little Ed, but what do you know about petitioning the Lord, interceding on someone's behalf? You probably can't remember the last time you put a foot in church."

"What—the prison chapel don't count?" He laughed, but then he seemed to realize Ruthena wasn't in the mood for his old playfulness. Edmond snapped his fingers and pointed at his sister. "Okay, what about the apostle Paul? He carried the Church with him—in and out of prison. And I'm talking about the capital *C* church and not the little *c* you sit in every Sunday, Ruthena. He wrote Ephesians, Philippians, Philemon, Colossians . . . all from *prison*," he said, counting the books off on his fingers, "and I'm sure we can agree that my fellow former inmate was filled with the Holy Spirit and prayed . . . his . . . butt . . . off." Edmond slowly rotated back and forth on his stool, never breaking eye contact with Ruthena.

It was she who looked away first. To Lis. She aimed a thumb back at her brother and huffed, "Is he sitting here comparing himself to *Paul*?" When Ruthena faced him again, the incredulity in her eyes battled with the twinkling in his. "No offense, Little Ed, but you went to jail because you are a thief, not an apostle."

"Aunt Ruthena!" Evelyn couldn't help herself. Her stomach jostled her cup when she nearly hopped from her stool.

"Slow your roll, *mamacita*," Edmond said to Evelyn as he pressed her back into her seat. He grabbed a dishcloth and swabbed up the mess. Throughout the exchange, he'd kept his cool. If anything, his voice dropped a degree as he focused on Ruthena. "No, Sister, I *was* a thief. And Paul was a murderer of the very people Jesus came to save. That don't change the fact that Mama don't want to see you."

Matthew took his wife's hand as she stood there spluttering in the middle of the kitchen. "I don't believe it's *where* you are when the Lord calls you. It's knowing *whose* you are once He does."

Crackle, crackle, crackle . . . Lis lifted the top of the grinder. "Coffee?"

The kitchen was silent for a moment except for the clink of cups and saucers hitting the granite.

Ruthena finally spoke. "So, Evelyn, what's your part in all this?"

Evelyn took a deep breath. "I don't have a part, Aunt Ruthena."

"You most certainly do!"

"Ruthe—"

"Matthew, she does. She's the one who wrote those letters and then had the nerve to hand deliver mine!"

"Aunt Ruthena, I didn't write them. Well, I did, but not

really. Just think of me as the typewriter, the instrument—and I guess, your messenger. Those letters came from Granny B. I really had nothing to do with it." Evelyn avoided her aunt's disbelieving look by stepping down from the stool to pour another cup of juice.

Aunt Ruthena's *tsk* filled the kitchen. "Lis? What do you think about Mama's death wish?"

Mama added eight heaping tablespoons of grounds to a filter and then poured cold water into the machine before replacing the glass pot. She seemed to use the same spoon from the coffee grounds to carefully measure her words. "Is that what you call it, a death wish?"

"Well, what do you call it?"

"Her own business. That's what I call it."

"*Her own business!* She's committing suicide! Slowly but surely, she's committing suicide. And you and this girl here are just going to sit by and let her do it." Aunt Ruthena stared at Mama incredulously.

"Well, what do you expect them to do, Ruthena? Drag her to the doctor? Hold her down while they pump her with a bunch of useless drugs and chemicals?" It sounded like Edmond had already gotten an earful from Granny B.

Aunt Ruthena perched on the barstool Evelyn had vacated and turned her back on her brother. "Well, doing something might not help her physical body, but what about her spiritual body, Lis?"

"What are you talking about now, Ruth?"

"I worry about her faith, or the lack of it, and how it's

affecting her health. Does she just not believe in the healing power of Jesus? In heaven? She'll never get well that way."

Mama shook her head in disbelief. "Now I see why she didn't let you in the house. If I'd had any sense, I wouldn't have let you in either. Matthew, help me out here."

Uncle Matthew filled each cup. "Well—"

"*Well*, it's not any of your business, Matthew. She's my mama—"

"She's our mama, too, and I didn't spend twenty hours on a Greyhound to hear all this foolishness for the next two days. First of all, her faith ain't the issue. And secondly, she's not going to hell for not choosing chemotherapy. Hell is for the unbeliever, not the stubborn."

"Y'all are just running from the truth. But not me. We're calling Thomas, and we're going to ask him to draw up some kind of papers to control—"

"Don't say 'we,' Ruthena. I told you before we left the house I don't support this."

"But, Matthew, God won't—"

"This doesn't have anything to do with God but with you and your inability to accept the fact that your mama is dying. *He's* in control, not *you*. Now Granny B has always done things her way, so leave her be. You keep talking crazy like this, and Lis and Edmond will declare *you* incompetent."

Evelyn slurped down such a huge mouthful of hot coffee she scalded her tongue, but she held it, leaving her aunt to stew in impotent silence.

"Did she say she was gon' brang down the hand of God on me right then and there?"

"Oh, Granny B, you need to stop. I hope it's God's will to heal you, too—it's certainly within His power."

Beatrice heard the wistfulness, the heavenly appeal in her tone, but she didn't have time for sadness today. "No, it's Ruthena that need to stop, and you need to shake that rug one mo' time."

Snap! "Granny B, she—"

"And if you tell me she loves me, I'm gon' take that rug and pop you upside the head with it."

Evelyn vigorously shook the rug.

Beatrice took a long draw from her cup. "That girl always threat'nin' to pray fo' me. Been doin' so since she was 'bout this high." She indicated the general area around her hips. "Holdin' them prayers over folks' head like a thundercloud. But I don't thank she know God too well if she thank He just gon' jump to do her biddin'. He God all by Hisself and don't need no Ruthena to let Him know what He doin' wrong or right." She flicked her fingers. "Brang that here. Let me show you how to beat a rug."

"Uh-uh. You sit. Just keep on swigging that noxious stuff—"

"Not a what?" Beatrice's brows furrowed.

She nodded toward the mug. "That. What is that?"

Granny B grimaced. "Oh, this onion syrup. Mam used

to make us drank it when we was little. It fixed whatever ailed you."

"You mean scared it away, don't you?"

"You chillun today, with your fancy doctors and medicines. Runnin' here and there lookin' for miracles, when all they got to do is use what God gave 'em in they own backyards." Granny B pointed to a weed growing near the street. "That catnip there can make you a good tea." She held her cup aloft. "And this onion syrup? Just boil you some onion good and slow and add some honey and sugar. Better than anythang you can buy."

"According to you."

"Well, if this don't suit your taste, I can fix you up some castor oil and brandy. Thata knock them germs right out. You shoulda seent my brother Henry when Mam made him drank a spoonful—and that's all it took, a spoonful. She'd warn him, 'Open yo' mouth and hold yo' nose!' He'd take one lick off that spoon . . . !" She laughed.

Evelyn waved her hand in front of her face. "No thanks. I'm laying off the hard stuff for the next nineteen weeks or so." She draped the rug over her arm and mounted the front porch steps.

"You stayin' away from your husband for the next nineteen weeks, too?"

Evelyn froze.

"Well? You told him 'bout that baby yet?"

"Not yet."

"Speak up, chile. Any reason why you waitin'?"

Evelyn melted a bit, allowing her lips and feet to move. "It's not really something you tell over the phone."

Beatrice raised her cup and an eyebrow. "So you plannin' to hand him the baby and say, 'Well, here she is'?"

Evelyn stopped beside her grandmother's chair. "She?"

Granny B rolled her eyes. "He, she, whatever. They gon' cause you the same heap-a trouble, don't make no never mind."

"Is that why you didn't let Aunt Ruthena in last week, because you thought she was causing trouble?"

"I didn't let Ruthena in 'cause I didn't wont to, and Edmond in 'cause I did. And I know you changed the subject 'cause *you* wonted to." She relieved Evelyn of the worn-out welcome mat. It slapped the ground. "But that's okay 'cause I'm gon' lay down. Take the broom over the sidewalk."

Before she could escape, Evelyn's words snagged her.

"How have you been lately, Granny B?"

"The same."

"And how is that?" Evelyn seemed to drop the pretense as she dropped the broom.

"Not different." Beatrice resented the invasion and the help she'd had to seek lately.

"Granny B—"

"How *you* been?"

"What?"

Beatrice watched Evelyn squirm in the corner she'd tried to back her grandmother into. "I said, how you been? I see you roundin' out plenty. I guess you ain't got to hide nuthin' now."

"I-I wasn't trying to hide anything. And this isn't about me. Why—?"

"Well then, get back to sweepin'. You can use the exercise . . . and I sho' coulda used just a peek at yo' auntie's face when Edmond said he was like the 'postle Paul." Beatrice stepped into the house, still chuckling to herself. The screen door bounced against the frame before coming to rest.

———

Evelyn quietly plucked a cerulean pencil and lightly tinted the sky behind Dominick. She tried to keep the paper from crinkling so she wouldn't draw attention to herself.

"It's not right, Lis," Aunt Mary complained over her cup of Russian tea. "I came all the way across the country—"

"But she told you not to come, Mary. Evelyn, did you want some tea?" Lis blew over her cup and sank into the sofa cushion. She peered at her daughter through tendrils of steam.

Mary's narrowed eyes met her niece's before she focused again on her sister. "But I didn't think she wouldn't see me once I came all this way. And she saw Little Ed!"

Lis raised an eyebrow. "Well, when you come back home after being in prison over a decade . . . Besides, you know how Mama feels about Edmond."

Mary's cup clinked into the saucer. "But I spent more than five hundred dollars on a ticket to see that woman!"

"But, but, but. You'll have to settle for seeing me, okay? And what's five hundred dollars to you? A pair of shoes?" Lis handed Mary a slice of Ruby Tagle's carrot cake.

Evelyn hid a smile and raised her hand. "I'll take a slice too, Mama."

"I thought Aunt Mary was going to fall out of her seat. I really did, Granny B."

"That girl always been one for actin'. Her head barely reached the latch on the back do' but could she put on a show, cryin' before my switch ever touched her leg."

Evelyn laughed.

"I'm serious." Beatrice clipped the end of the clothesline and discarded the extra twine. She reached back to hand Evelyn the wire cutters. "Here, chile."

"But Aunt Mary was serious, too, Granny B."

Beatrice shook her head and wrapped the line around the nail.

"Why don't you let me do that?"

For the fourth time, she ignored Evelyn's offer to help. "What did I tell Mary in that letter?"

"Gran—"

Beatrice tried to swat away the hand on her elbow but had to lean into it as she stepped down. Once she'd planted both feet on the ground, she snatched away her shaking arm and retrieved the stool. Beatrice forced her stiff legs to move toward the screen door. "She was probably comin' to take stock of the furniture." She felt Evelyn close behind her as she took the one step up into the house.

"I don't think Spring Hope chic is quite her style."

Beatrice didn't answer, so focused as she was on trying to heft the basket of wet sheets.

Without a word, Evelyn took one of the handles. Together they ambled to the line.

Chapter Twenty

OUT OF RESPECT, Evelyn bit her tongue and let the grown folks handle things while she silently stroked Cocoa.

"What are you doing about Mama?" Thomas and Sissy sat with Lis in the living room. Granny B had turned the couple away with barely a nod at the front door.

"What am *I* going to do?"

"Yes, *you*. You live the closest to her. You see her most often."

"So?"

"*So*, you need to do something. I just can't believe her crazy idea."

"What crazy idea?"

"This—thinking she's just gonna lay down and die, go down without a fight."

"Lay down and die? *She's standing up to you, isn't she?*" Lis's eyes narrowed.

Sissy seemed to detect the heat building in the room. "Now, Elisabeth—"

"I'm not talking to you, Sissy." She held up a hand to silence her would-be sister-in-law. "I'm talking to my big-mouth brother who has lost his mind over here."

"*Mama* has lost her mind. And if necessary, I'll use my law degree to prove it."

"To prove what? And stop trying to shush him, Sissy."

"Well, Ruthena—"

"Ruthena put a buzz in your ear? I can't believe the two of you finally see eye to eye. There's no need for you to prove nothin', Thomas."

"Why not?"

"I talked to Mama's attorney myself the minute Ruthena and Matthew left—"

"And?" Sissy leaned forward.

Evelyn stopped rubbing Cocoa and stared at her mama.

"And he said Ruthena must be crazy herself. Well, not in so many words."

Evelyn expelled the breath she'd been holding.

"Well, hallelujah for that!"

All eyes turned to Sissy after her outburst.

"I'm sorry. But I never agreed with any of this, Thomas."

Thomas rubbed his hands across his face, then back over his wavy hair. "So now what?"

Lis held up one finger. "Find out what kind of insurance Mama has."

"Elis—"

Mama's raised palm stopped her younger brother short. She extended a second finger. "Ask her about the service she'd like to have. Mama might as well have her way when she dies just like when she's living." Mama raised her ring finger. "Then we're going to contact Paul Stewart's funeral home. The rest is up to Mama." She dropped her hand to her lap. "The dying and all."

"You know you should see somebody."

Beatrice grunted. "I saw Edmond. And if I see *some*body else, I got to see *ever* body else. They'll all be seein' me soon enough." She knew Evelyn wouldn't want to pick up that particular ball and run with it.

Yet her granddaughter persisted. "They're your children. They're trying to show you they care about what's happening to you."

Beatrice snorted.

"Granny B, we've been through this—"

"Exactly. We been through this. If I wan't dyin', they wouldn't be streamin' down here noway, all in a tizzy. Lookin' like a bunch of hungry rats after some cheese."

"Much as you try to fight it, they're going to come, and they're going to see you . . . whether you like it or not."

Beatrice said nothing. She just sipped her tea, enjoyed the view of the house and yard from their spot near the woods.

"How are you feeling? You look pale. Want to go inside?" Evelyn waited. "Granny B . . . I know you hear me. If you don't say something, I'm just going to keep talking."

"Surprise, surprise."

"Don't you feel a need to wrap things up with your children? To say good-bye? There might be crying or carrying on—"

"That's what my funeral is fo'."

Evelyn swallowed audibly. "Well . . ."

Beatrice held up a bony hand. "The well done run dry, gal. Now I don't wont to hear no mo' 'bout this. I said all the good-byes I'm gon' to. You got this big happy fam'ly reunion in yo' head, but it ain't gon' happen. Didn't you figure that out when we saw Milton? I wrapped thangs up all nice and neat when I wrote them letters."

Evelyn sat like a log in one of the chairs she'd dragged out.

"I can see you sittin' there stewin'."

She glanced over at her grandma. "Are you laughing at me?"

Beatrice cackled, out loud this time. "Gal, ain't I the one dyin'? We ain't like them fam'lies you see on TV. And you ain't got to work so hard tryin' to fix us. We ain't broke . . ." She paused, considering her next words. "Just a little bent, is all."

Evelyn sighed. "Granny B—"

"I had me one of them TV fam'lies once. When I was a girl in Farmin'ton." Beatrice smacked her lips together, tasting the lingering flavors of memory. "It'd be dead a-winter and them nights would make even dead bones clank together." She shook a bit herself in the warm shade. "I 'member Pap'd heat up a blanket in front of the fireplace, and when it was good and toasty, he'd throw it over all us chillun. Back then it was Henry and me, then my little sisters, Sarah Jean and Mae. Ooh, that blanket felt good goin' on. We'd run with it up to our rooms; then we'd drop it and jump in the bed.

"We was babies a long time, us chillun." Beatrice sucked up an ice cube from her glass and rolled it around in her mouth. It rattled against her teeth. "Mam would dress us in undershirts with long sleeves and we girls had to wear two slips. 'Course, it was such a long, cold walk to school, we was glad we had all them layers."

"What, fifteen, twenty miles and uphill both ways?"

Beatrice smiled. "Mo' like three and another three back. But that was pretty far when it was snowin' or rainin' or when it was hot like it is now." Her sharp teeth reduced the cube to bits. "But it didn't matter how much the wind blowed, we couldn't wait to get to school."

"You loved learning that much?"

"No, we loved *eatin'*. You shoulda seent what Mam packed in our lunch pails. Biscuit and ham. A piece of cake. You see, we was pretty well off." She could see Evelyn swallow her words as well as a big gulp of iced tea.

"I remember writing about that in Aunt Mary's letter.

You left when you were only fifteen? Why, if it wasn't to get a better life?"

Beatrice polished off her glass and set it down in the prickly blades of grass beside her chair. She wiped her mouth with the ever-present handkerchief she retrieved from the pocket of her green housedress. "Barely fifteen, and I suppose that's what ever'body thought, that I was tryin' to escape bein' po', only to find myself a heap po'er." She reached for her glass, remembered that it was empty, and sat back in her chair.

"So that isn't what happened?"

"No, that ain't what happened. We had a good life. Mam and Pap had us a big house in Farmin'ton, and my pap did good work. We never wonted for nuthin'. 'Cept me. I wanted to be grown. I got tired of warm blankets and wearin' under-shirts and thick tighties and bein' tucked into bed. And here come that man, just in time."

Beatrice's eyes sidled her granddaughter's way. "Back then, see, thirteen, fourteen, fifteen—it wan't like it is now. Girls was bein' trained for raisin' families and keepin' house, get-tin' ready for marriage. But not much in my house. Mam kept the world away from us. She hoped we'd have somethin' better, like good schoolin' and thangs." Beatrice's chest rose on a deep breath. As she let it out, she repeated, "But here come that man."

"But didn't you love Henton? Was it worth it, at least for a little while?"

"Girl, ain't nobody thankin' 'bout no Henton." She pointed at the back of the small house sprouting from the ground in front of them. "Whatchyou thank? You lookin' at the same house I am. You thank it was worth it?"

Evelyn said nothing.

"Was it worth it?" Beatrice repeated the question, and then surprisingly, she grinned. "Yep, it was worth it, 'cause I loved me some of that man *there*! I sho' did. And he loved me. At least fo' a while."

The tea Evelyn had just sipped ran from her mouth and down her chin.

"I'm a woman—don't you forget that. And I can feel just like one, too—at least I *did*. I felt the same way you did about yo' Kevin, no matter how you thank you feel now." Beatrice passed her granddaughter the handkerchief. "Here, girl, wipe yo' face. You look like you been havin' some kinda heatstroke out here."

"So what do y'all talk about?"

Evelyn looked away from the rain beating against the pane. "Excuse me?"

Lis leaned against the doorjamb. "You've been in Spring Hope every day. What do you talk about all that time? What do you do?"

We talk about our love lives. "She busies herself doing nothing. I hover until she orders me to go somewhere."

"But I bet you don't go. Right?"

"No, I don't go. When she sleeps, I sit down myself—trying

to keep up with an old lady will wear you out!" This produced a laugh, and they shared it. They sat there, enjoying the sound of the rain spattering against the glass.

"Sitting around Granny B's house, spending so much time where you were raised, I think a lot about you and my aunts and uncles. I've been wondering . . . about the letters."

Lis's eyebrows furrowed.

"You know, the letters Granny B sent out. Have y'all talked about what Granddaddy Henton wrote?"

She turned away from Evelyn then. "No, we haven't talked about Henton's letters."

"Is that what you call him now—Henton?"

"That's his name, isn't it? I mean, *Daddy* doesn't quite fit. Most of us stopped calling him that a long time ago, almost the minute he skipped town."

"Did Granny B ever explain why he left?"

"Mama? Since when does she explain anything?" She stood abruptly and walked to the dressing table. She studied the silver-framed photographs carefully placed to the right side of the mirror. "We learned early on not to ask questions."

Evelyn understood that feeling. That's why she hadn't brought up Milton's visit with Granny B despite her need to dissect all that had happened. She knew, however, that it wasn't what *she* needed that was important, not now. Still . . .

"Mama, what happened between Granny B and Uncle Milton? I get the feeling we won't be seeing him anytime soon." By anytime soon, she meant Granny B's funeral, another touchy subject.

Lis kept her eyes down as she fiddled with Evelyn's comb and brush.

Evelyn waited her out as she studied her mother's reflection in the mirror.

"When Milton's name came up, Mama would just say he broke her heart. She asked me once, 'How can you forgive somebody for tearin' your heart out and givin' it back to you?'" Lis gave her full attention to a pair of opal earrings. She turned them this way and that in the wan light.

"'He' meaning Milton or 'he' meaning Granddaddy . . . um, Henton? How could a child break your heart anyway? She acted like he was dead. We all did . . ." *Why won't she look at me?*

"And newly resurrected, the way she talks about him now," Lis finished. "Does she talk about him to you?" She finally set down the jewelry and faced her daughter directly.

It was Evelyn's turn to prevaricate. "Well, she doesn't *talk* about him, not necessarily. She does mention his name more freely, and I don't have to skip over words that start with *M* anymore."

Lis smiled, seemingly distracted.

"You know we went to see him then?"

Her mama stopped smiling. "You did?"

"We took him the letters, you know, from Granny B and Gran—Hen—the two letters." Evelyn didn't know which road to take. They both diverged into a prickly thicket, so she decided not to choose at all. "It was pretty painful, for both of them. But she seems to be better for it, somehow. Of course, *I'm* more confused. I'm curious whether she read his letters, if she knew where . . . *he* was. It's hard to believe y'all never wondered where he went, what happened—"

"I didn't say we didn't wonder where Henton went. Of course, we *wondered*." Lis wandered around the room. Eventually she settled again by the family photographs but away from the mirror, preventing Evelyn from gauging her veracity by an imperfect reflection.

Lis caressed Graham's glass-covered face. "We used to whisper late at night, asking each other if anybody had heard anything. Edmond would tell us stuff he had picked up in town. Rumors about where Henton had run off to, about problems Mama and Henton'd had. His new home in Jasper."

Evelyn's mouth flew open. "So she knew where he was?"

"There's not much Mama doesn't know." Lis laughed out loud, though it was a harsh, joyless sound. "Mama probably found him that job he wrote about and the room over the store."

"No, I didn't know exactly where he was. I just knew where he warn't."

"But how could you *not* know?"

Beatrice replaced the lid on the steaming pot and set the spoon in the bowl. She wiped her hands on the towel looped through her white apron strings. "You thank I had time to fret over the where'bouts of Henton Agnew, what with all I had to do round here? If he had it in his mind to leave, why should I waste time jaw jackin' 'bout it?"

"You know, Mama said almost the same thing the other day."

"Well, least we agree on somethin'." Beatrice continued moving about the kitchen, trying to hide that she was good and riled up. She returned spices and washed teacups. She figured Evelyn sensed her agitation because she didn't offer to help.

It didn't stop Evelyn from pressing the issue. "Did you miss him?"

Beatrice tasted the dumplings. She added more seasoned salt. "Miss who?"

"Granddaddy. Henton."

"You cain't miss what warn't never there." She tucked a few limp tendrils behind her ears. "Do you miss Kevin?"

"We're not talking about Kevin."

"You right, but you should be. I did my part, sent all them letters. And you ain't said word one to yo' husband."

Evelyn scratched her belly. "I told you I can't tell him news like this over the phone."

"So do it in person. Look at his face on that computer of yours." She immersed a dishcloth in soapy water and wrung it dry. She wiped the area around the stove.

"I don't want to Skype him or use FaceTime. Not for this."

"Not for anything, I s'pect. Anyway, you ain't gon' need no words, by the looks of you."

315

"What words did you use when you told Henton about Milton?"

Splash! Beatrice ignored the suds that sprayed her apron and arms when she threw down her cloth. "You got to go. Now. You might talk to yo' mama like you crazy, but this dyin' old lady don't have time to stand for it." Beatrice reached behind and untied her strings and tossed the apron onto the table.

"I-I'm sorry."

"Maybe so, but that's yo' mama's problem." As she stalked to the front door, Beatrice aimed her nose high in the air and gave Evelyn a wide berth. "Don't come back until you've learned some respect." She latched the screen door and returned to stir her simmering pot.

"Did you try to apologize?"

"Of course, Jackson." Evelyn pulled the car into the garage and hit the remote.

"What made you say something so off the wall?"

Evelyn threw him the keys as he emerged from the car. "Just hush and open the door. At least she told me I could come back. That's an improvement."

"What's an improvement?" Lis set down the cordless phone. She was sitting at the kitchen table in front of the newspaper's Lifestyles section.

"Your cooking! What's for dinner, Mama? You know a man's hungry after work."

"We'll see. Go wash up," she laughed as Jackson escaped to the opposite side of the house. "That was your sister on the phone, Evelyn. She says she's been trying to reach you."

"Yes, I owe her a call. We keep playing phone tag." Thing was, Evelyn had been "it" a long time, but she didn't share that with her mother as she set down her purse. "What are you doing here? It's not like you to be home this early, reading the paper, taking phone calls."

"Is it early?" Lis looked down at the thin Movado watch on her wrist. "Oh, I was expecting company. Don't clutter my countertops, Evelyn."

"Company?" Evelyn moved her purse to her designated wicker basket in the mudroom. There, she noticed a man's pair of leather shoes. "Mama, is somebody here?" She returned to the kitchen and caught Lis massaging her temples above her closed eyes. Evelyn noted the lines of strain, the tight, pinched mouth. She hesitantly stretched out a hand.

Lis leaned forward, turning her head from side to side, and rubbed the back of her neck and shoulders.

Evelyn used her empty hand to open the nearest cabinet and retrieve the popcorn popper as her mother massaged aches and pains Evelyn couldn't see. She set it on the counter and found the kernels. "What is it, Mama? Is it Granny B?"

"Yes. Well, no. It's more like everybody *but* Mama." Lis slumped down in her chair.

"Is Aunt Ruthena praying for locusts to eat us out of house and home?"

"Girl, watch your mouth!"

"What about Aunt Sarah?"

Mama opened her eyes. "Speaking of . . . you and Samuel have a lot in common now."

"With Aunt Sarah's husband? What would that be?"

"Teaching. Being unemployed."

Her words had simultaneously hooked and rankled Evelyn. "Huh?"

"He left the hospital."

"Left the—what do you mean?" Evelyn moved closer, drawn in by the tidbits of information, like crumbs dropped along a forest path. "Isn't he, like, some head surgeon–doctor–emergency room expert? He's going to teach at a medical school?"

"Actually, he's leaving work period, at least for a while. He's doing the househusband thing, you know, homeschooling the kids while Sarah goes to work. Edmond told me all about it. And it sounds like Edmond's got a girlfriend—somebody named Carolina."

"Well, that's great. Uncle Edmond's dating a woman named after a state. But what does this have to do with Aunt Sarah?"

"Nothing much. Just that he took this Carolina girl to see Sarah not long after he got out, and when he gets there, the house is all upside down." She paused. "They're leaving New York."

"Uncle Edmond?" Evelyn's head spun. She pulled out a chair and sat down at the table.

Lis dismissed her confusion with a wave of her hand, like it was Evelyn's fault she couldn't follow the story's bobbing and weaving. "No, child. Sarah and her family."

"What? Really? I thought she'd purchased a one-way ticket all those years ago."

"Yes, they're coming back home. He left his practice, said he needed to slow down and spend more time with her and the kids, write a book about his life in medicine . . . some nonsense. They feel like they can have a better quality of life down here. Of course, it would have been nice if they'd decided this *before* Mama . . ."

The sentence hung, orphaned, between them.

"Well, she's coming now, I suppose." Lis gazed into space.

"Aren't you glad? It'll be nice to have Sarah close by. Near Aunt Ruthena? In Spring Hope?"

Lis said nothing, at least not out loud.

"What is it? What are you not telling me?"

"I just imagine Sarah is going through some things right now." Lis took a sip of her diet soda and shook her head.

"Ye-es, but I'm sure she's working to keep it all together, what with the children and all." Evelyn got up and found the canola oil. She plugged in the popper and poured a table-spoon of oil into the pan. The agitator started to turn.

"In a situation like this, children can be as much a com-plication as a blessing."

As she slowly added the kernels, Evelyn weighed her words carefully to avoid hidden minefields buried in the sand of their conversation. "What complications? I thought

Uncle Samuel's purpose was to reduce the complications." As the popping slowed, Evelyn turned off the pan and flipped it, focusing on the popcorn tumbling into the stainless steel bowl instead of her mama's face.

"No, not now, now that he's decided to throw away his successful big-city medical practice for a life as a country doctor."

"I take it you don't agree." Evelyn poured melted butter onto the popcorn and sprinkled it with salt.

"Of course I agree. What's to disagree with? A man voluntarily giving up his medical career for his wife and family? I don't know anyone else who would do that. Especially when it's his job that supports the family. And he'll be home-schooling six kids at that. No, I don't have anything to say but good . . . about *Samuel*."

About Samuel. "What's the point, Mama?" Evelyn plucked a kernel of popcorn. "Because if this is about Kevin and me—"

"Nobody's said anything about you and Kevin—"

"—I don't want to hear anything more about it," Evelyn finished heatedly around a mouthful of popcorn.

"Listen, girl, don't give me orders in *my* house, especially with your mouth full of food." Mama rose.

"I'm not giving you orders, Mama, but . . . what? Do you think Kevin should quit his job?"

"Who said anything about you? Although you can learn a lesson from Sarah's situation."

"And what would I have to learn from this situation,

Mama? Marry a doctor? Move to New York? It's too late on both fronts."

"Don't get smart with me. You can start smelling yourself if you want to, but anybody will tell you it's not smart to leave your husband for months at a time, with him traveling all around the world, meeting all kinds of women. With you thousands of miles away, just getting more and more pregnant by the minute."

"Ooooohhh! I knew it! I just knew it wouldn't last."

"What wouldn't last?"

"You. Us. This. You staying out of my business."

"So it's okay for you to ask me all about me and my mama and daddy and talk all about my sister's business, but I can't ask you about what's going on in your house. That's how it is?"

"No. You just shouldn't talk about things you don't know anything about."

"I know quite a bit about it, young lady." Her mama squatted down to pick up stray kernels. "And I'm not talking about Sarah. I'm talking about what I've learned from living, Evelyn, from being a woman, from being married for longer than two minutes, from having the sense God gave a cucumber."

Since most of those points didn't apply to her, Evelyn jumped on the one brick that did seem aimed at her glass house. "So are you saying I'm stupid for trusting my husband?"

"Yes, I am."

"*What?*"

"Okay, misguided. First of all, you need to trust God, because man will fail you every time, you included. Nobody's perfect. Only God exceeds our expectations. That being said, you should be with your husband, Evelyn. You know it. He needs to tend to you and this child of his. I don't know why you refuse to go home, like you're embarrassed or scared of something—"

Evelyn's temper flared higher as Mama retrieved the partial stick of butter and returned it to the refrigerator. "First of all, there's nobody for me to go home to. Remember my imperfect husband? He's in Europe. And secondly, did you forget about what's going on right here?"

Lis slammed the ceramic bowl on the counter. Popcorn flew. "Forget what? That my mama is dying? That my daddy's already dead and gone? Or maybe you think I forgot about all my brothers and sisters and all their problems? Just what did I forget about, Evelyn?"

"Then you see why I should stay."

"No, I don't. You think your very presence wills Mama to live? To keep her one day, one *second* longer than the good Lord decides to? You know better." She jabbed a finger on the countertop. "You're here because you've got your own family crisis at home, and you think by hiding out here you can avoid it somehow. Well, you can't."

Evelyn tried to tug away her eyes, but Lis held on.

"You can't, Evelyn. So you and your baby go home."

"Yes, Evelyn, come home. Please."

Evelyn gasped and turned toward the speaker, the person she dreaded yet longed to see. "Kevin!"

He stood there, barefoot, framed in the doorway leading from the back stairs. His eyes raked her face first, then moved down to take in the rest of her. His eyes widened.

Chapter Twenty-One

"What are you doing here? Mama, what is Kevin doing here?"

"I suppose he came to see his wife." Lis picked up the bowl and dropped it into the sink with a clang. She stepped over scattered popcorn as she left the kitchen. "I'll finish cleaning up later. Jackson and I are eating out."

And so they were alone, together.

Evelyn was too tired to run—what she really wanted to do—and too tired to fight. Her mama had drained whatever emotional and physical resources the growing baby hadn't sapped. All she could do was endure his stare.

"So it's true. You *are* pregnant."

She crossed her arms over her belly, peering down at her feet. An incongruous thought popped into her head. *How much longer will I be able to see my toes?*

"Evelyn? I mean, we're having a baby . . ."

"Why aren't you wearing any shoes?"

"What?"

She pointed to his feet. "I saw your shoes when I first got home . . . *Company.* You're the company Mama came home early for!" Evelyn turned her back to him as realization sank in.

"My shoes . . . ?" Kevin looked toward the mudroom as if he was trying to catch up with his wife's train of thought chugging far and away from him.

"When did you get here, Kevin? You've been here awhile— long enough to take off your shoes, change clothes. And you said, 'You *are* pregnant.' Does that mean you already knew?"

"Whoa, whoa, whoa. Me first. I get my answers first. You don't get to take the offensive here."

"This isn't a game we're playing, Kevin. Defense, offense."

"But you're playing keep-away with my baby, Evelyn."

"*Your* ba—?"

"Kevin? Hey, bro! I didn't know you were here." Jackson appeared out of nowhere and jogged over to his brother-in-law. "So glad to see you, man!" He grasped Kevin's right hand and simultaneously embraced him with his left. After two big claps on the back, he backed up. Jackson's head swiveled from one to the other. "What's going on? Am I interrupting something big?"

"Um . . ."

"We're just trying to catch up. Actually, we were heading out to the swing. Dude, okay if we catch up later?" Kevin grabbed her hand, waved "good-bye," and dragged her out the back door.

"What are you doing?" Evelyn tried to pull her hand from his.

But Kevin held on more tightly, interlocking their fingers as he strode toward the swing mounted to the rafters of the side porch. Once there, he let go of her hand, only to wrap his arms around her and pull her close. He gently resisted her initial feeble efforts to brace her hands against his chest and push him away.

After a moment or two, Evelyn's hands crept into his hair seemingly of their own volition, and she lowered his head to her shoulder. She closed her eyes and soaked in the woody scent of him, the feel of him against her.

Kevin's shoulders shook as he cried. And it wasn't long before she soaked his T-shirt with her own tears. They clung to each other.

After what felt like hours, Evelyn pushed him away. She reached into the pocket of her loose-fitting striped dress and withdrew the handkerchief she'd begun carrying. She dried her face and leaned against the rail. She felt Kevin stand behind her, and as much as she wanted to melt against him, she clung to the post for support.

"Why didn't you tell me?"

Evelyn felt his words tickle the tiny hairs on her nape. "I-I just couldn't. If you knew, I couldn't—"

"Leave me?" Kevin placed a large, warm hand on her shoulder and forced her to turn. Then he used his long index finger to tilt her face. "You knew I'd never let you leave if I knew about the baby."

"But that shouldn't be the reason you hold on."

"I'm not the one who let go." His voice never rose a decibel. If anything, it became more hushed.

But Evelyn's heart heard him. A tear coursed down her cheek. "I couldn't stay, Kevin. You hurt me. You betrayed *us*." Her hands splayed on either side of her stomach.

Kevin didn't point out that there had been no *us*, no baby, at that time. He seemed to understand: they'd always been a family, the two of them, the children that would come one day, their vision of themselves. "I know. And I'm sorry. I need you to know how sorry I am."

Evelyn nearly muttered, *But that's your mama's problem*, but she forced her grandmother's words down her throat. She choked out, "I do, Kevin. I believe you." And she did. "It's just hard to forgive. I'm just so *hurt*." The pain wasn't quite as sharp, however. Life did feel like it would go on—that their life could go on together. But she had to know.

"Who told you about the baby? You knew before you saw me. I saw confirmation, not surprise."

"You . . . you take my breath away." Kevin's voice was hushed as he clasped her face and brought it close to his. His eyes reached for hers.

She felt him seek permission, and she nodded almost imperceptibly.

He leaned in and brought her closer, kissing her lips tenderly, then more passionately. Their cheeks were wet with intermingled tears when he pulled away. "I've missed you. I love you so much. You don't know how much I've prayed for this."

Evelyn's hands grasped his. She squeezed them as her eyes pored over his face and searched his eyes.

"It was Granny B, wasn't it?"

Chapter Twenty-Two

EVELYN AWOKE to a silent house. Jackson had dropped Mama at her salon on his way to his part-time job. Kevin had an early conference call. She didn't waste time pining for any of them.

When she pulled up at Granny B's, the house emanated abandonment. She left the Impala's engine running and the door partly open and knocked anyway. Flummoxed, she returned to the car. She rolled down her window and considered her next move.

"Watch out now!"

Gasping, Evelyn's hand flew to her chest. She turned to her left and beheld her grandmother's neighbor. "Hi, Mrs. Johnson." Evelyn smiled weakly.

"Hey . . . Sorry to give you such a fright! I saw you walkin' up to the door and I thought to myself, 'That looks like Granny B's gran.'" Velma Johnson cackled. "And then I said to myself, 'It sure is! And she's pregnant.' Then when I saw you sittin' here, I thought I'd mosey on over."

Evelyn smiled again, though she had no idea why. Mrs. Johnson drew out all her words like she was singing them, and it irritated the dickens out of her.

"So you're pregnant?"

"Yes, ma'am. How are you?"

"I'm fine, fine. You're gettin' mighty big there."

Evelyn's smile died in her heart, though it remained plastered to her face.

"You're lookin' to have that baby soon, heh?" Mrs. Johnson pushed.

"Well, right now, I'm looking to find my grandmother. Have you seen her?"

Mrs. Johnson gave Evelyn's belly another piercing stare. "Why, yes, I saw her. She was walkin' back behind the house not that long ago. Now, where's your husband?"

Pretending not to see her ashy fingers grip the window, Evelyn grasped the chrome handle and cranked it up. She turned off the car and got out. "I've got to go. Mrs. Johnson. I really need to try to catch up with Granny B."

To her consternation, Mrs. Johnson fell into step beside her. "I'm sure she'll be right back. She cain't get but so far in this heat."

Evelyn's brain sent the order to smile, but her lips refused to obey. "That's just it, Mrs. Johnson. I don't want Granny B walking around in this heat. So I'd better go—"

"I see your mama here from time to time. And I see this green car you're drivin' here a lot, too. Most ev'ry day. She hasn't ever had this kinda comp'ny."

"And you would know, wouldn't you?" The younger woman finally dug out a grin to cover her sarcasm. She drew up on the side of Granny B's house.

Mrs. Johnson seemed to hear the truth and not the spirit of Evelyn's words. "Yes, I sure would!"

"Well, I really have to go, Mrs. Johnson. You say she headed that way?" She pointed toward the woods directly behind the house.

"Yes, but—"

"Thank you, Mrs. Johnson. I'm sure you'll be seeing me later. Take care."

The forest canopy shielded her from the brunt of the late-morning sunlight. She picked her way carefully around roots, sticks, and the occasional pinecone. Evelyn had trekked ten minutes into the woods when she spotted familiar gingham material. As she sprinted forward, she tripped and sprawled. *"Ummpff!"*

"Chile, you got to be careful—you got a bellyful, 'member?" In a moment Granny B was there and helped Evelyn right herself.

"I remember," Evelyn breathed.

"Anyhow, you look fine, 'cept for that bad place on yo'

leg. Guess I'm gon' have to pack up my blackberries and take care of that."

"You walked all the way out here to pick berries?"

Granny B leaned down and retrieved her basket. "Well, I woulda picked 'em in my front room, but they don't happen to grow there. See that you stay on yo' feet till we get back to the house."

Much like Velma Johnson, Evelyn matched Granny B's pace. "Isn't the sun too strong this time of day for you to be out here?"

"Well, if it's too strong for me, it's too strong for you. Whatchyou doin' out here?" She moved aside a low-hanging branch.

"Getting you!"

"I'm the old, sick one, and you the one cain't walk straight."

"I'm glad you find it funny." This newfound clumsiness bothered Evelyn. Once, she could've run through these woods blindfolded.

At the house Granny B handed her a moistened paper towel. "Dab it while I see to these." She poured the blackberries onto a long platter. Then she washed and dried her hands.

Evelyn propped up her leg. Blood trickled down her shin. "Ooh."

"Oh, chile, hush. It ain't nuthin' but a scratch." She dabbed the sore area with peroxide and covered it with a large bandage.

Evelyn appreciated her grandma's attentiveness, even without a smear of Vaseline. "Thanks, Granny B."

She walked back to her blackberries. "You can thank me by taking yo' foot off my chair."

"May I help you?"

"You know somethin' mo' 'bout cleanin' berries than I do?"

"Well—"

"I didn't thank so." Granny B retrieved a canister from the cabinet to the left of the stove and set it down. She poured sugar over some of the blackberries she had separated. Then she withdrew several jars from the pantry and deftly unscrewed the lids. After she filled each with scoopfuls of sweetened and unsweetened berries, she resealed them. "Can you get me one mo' jar from the pantry?"

Evelyn hopped to her feet. "Sure."

Crash! Granny B fell against the sink, one hand outstretched.

"Granny B!"

She waved her off.

Evelyn's heart reached out, but she stayed on her side of the kitchen.

Two, then three minutes passed. Evelyn poured a glass of water and grabbed a hand towel from a drawer. "Granny B . . . ?"

She ignored the towel but reached for the water. "Could you get me some mo'?" Granny B looked and sounded as if she'd just run a long race.

"Are you okay?"

Granny B swallowed about half the water and set the glass on the table. "Use that towel to hep me clean up this mess."

"Of course." Evelyn restored the kitchen while Granny B got herself in order. When her grandmother returned, Evelyn asked her for the third time, "Are you okay?"

"We're going for a walk."

"A walk? It's a hundred degrees outside!"

"You gon' let a dyin' old woman get the best of you? The road got plenty of shade, and it ain't that hot."

Evelyn stared after her grandmother, openmouthed, imagining Carrot Lane, treeless. But from somewhere she heard herself agree.

"Then let's go."

———

They walked along Carrot Lane for a quarter mile before turning on a narrow, tree-lined road. Leafy, languidly swaying branches obscured much of the day's heat. Granny B's espadrilles kicked up dust and scattered loose pebbles. Evelyn's thoughts drowned out the overwhelming silence until Granny B came up for air at an abandoned, two-story brick house. Ivy grew rampant on its face. Broken windows gaped. Weeds and wildflowers warred with the grass. Still, Evelyn envisioned its former glory, with its wide front porch and third-floor dormer windows.

"That's where Miss Jeannie Boyd lived, her and her husband. They didn't have no kids. They just lived there all by theyselves in that big house his fam'ly left 'em. The chillun used ta walk out they way after school to stop by. She'd pass out candy and cookies and dranks. Sometimes they'd even get a ham sandwich. They thought she was Santy Claus."

Evelyn smiled a little.

"This where Henton run to, that night when Milton was born. Miss Jeannie had trainin' birthin' babies, you see. It was pourin' rain. Lightnin' lit up the sky like it was noonday. I thought the thunder would shake our little house right to pieces . . . but she came anyhow. All she brought with her was a cape to cover her head and some boots she thought to strap on. She just busted in the do' like one of them strong winds blowin' ever'thang round outside. Made ever'body go in the kitchen—even Henton. Not that he was much help."

"Didn't he go get her?" Evelyn asked quietly.

"The pain just kept comin'. We'd see a streak a lightnin', and the pain and thunder would hit *bam!* together. I ain't never felt nuthin' like it, not even now." She rubbed her side. "But Miss Jeannie just got on my bed with them muddy boots, and we moaned and screamed together, just pushin' until finally out came Milton. And then both of us cried. I bet the chillun didn't know what to thank."

"Was he a big baby?" She winced.

Granny B looked at the younger woman like she was coming out of a deep sleep. "No, he wan't big nor little, just yo' usual baby . . . other than his eyes."

"What do you mean?"

"They was wide-open, from the minute he got here. I 'member he looked up at me, darin' me, soon as Miss Jeannie plopped him on my belly. I couldn't take my eyes off him. I knew he was seein' what I was thankin' . . ."

A crumpled paper napkin tumbled end over end and got caught in a tall weed creeping along the road's edge. Evelyn watched it struggle free.

Granny B's eyes scaled the estate. "I was just gon' give him to Miss Jeannie. Right there. That night. And she woulda taken him, too, even bein' he was black. But then, gazin' into his eyes . . ."

". . . You could see he was your baby and you loved him?"

But Granny B shook her head briskly. One tear trickled from her left eye. "I could see he'd only come back. You know, like them birds do ever' year come sprang. Miss Jeannie just lived too close. I knew he'd find his way back."

Granny B's words, her voice, her *eyes*—they held Evelyn captive there in the road. She wanted to scream, "Granny B, how could you not love him instantly?" *So what about your own baby, Evelyn? The child growing and moving inside you that you've resented from day one?* She stumbled. Granny B's shoes were too big for her.

Granny B kept her from falling. "That makes two times today."

Evelyn caressed her rounded belly.

"When you pregnant, you don't give up nuthin'. Yo' body does the work, not the heart or mind. But bein' a mama mean *choosin'* to do stuff you don't wont to do or maybe doin' stuff you shouldn't even be doin' at all. You might have to turn yo' back on whatchyou love and wrap yo' arms tight round whatchyou don't. But that's a choice you make up here." She tapped her head. "Not always in here." She jabbed her chest. "God knows my heart didn't even recognize Milton. Not then."

Granny B waved a hand at Evelyn's waistline. "It's easy now, carryin' round somethin' you ain't got to work yo' butt off to feed or clothe . . . and then they look at you with eyes still hungry and cold. They look like the very person you hate even more'n yo'self."

Evelyn couldn't dispel the image of baby Milton, gazing with brand-new eyes at his mother and seeing . . . despair. She remembered the grown man, broken, supported by his wife, gazing at his mother and seeing the same thing. "Poor Milton," she mumbled.

"Poor *Milton?*"

"Yes, poor Milton. He was born with the weight of the world on his tiny shoulders. He could never carry that! Give him away to some woman down the street? He was innocent, Granny B! *You look at raising children as a job, a punishment even. Where is the joy?* Sure, you had it hard, but a lot of people have it hard. At least you had your husband—"

"No, I didn't have no husband. He left me."

"But that wasn't until after Milton was born. Why didn't he just take Milton with him when he left, like he mentioned in his letter? He could've taken all of them once he found a place."

"How could my husband take Milton somewhere? He was long gone 'fo' Milton was born. 'Bout a year in fact. Not that he woulda taken Milton somewhere since he left his own chillun behind, too."

Evelyn's head swam.

Granny B smiled with her mouth, not her eyes. "You thank you know it all, and you just cain't wait to share it with ever'body. 'Granny B, go to the doctor. Hug yo' chillun. Talk to me. Mama, stop tellin' me what to do.' You don't know how to find yo' be-hind with both hands."

Evelyn stepped away from her.

Granny B headed in the opposite direction.

Evelyn didn't know if she wanted to follow her. Then suddenly she did. "Granny B, wait!"

She was talking before Evelyn reached her. "When I was thirteen, Hewitt Agnew stopped at my mam and pap's house for a drank a-water from the well. My sisters and I were s'posed to be workin', but when I heard that voice, I dropped them eggs and ran to the side of the house where I could peep at him. He was somethin' else, with that wavy hair and them green eyes. My sister tried to pull me back to them chickens, but I knew that my days stealin' babies from them stupid hens was 'bout to end."

Granny B quieted and they both moved aside for a passing car. When the last bits of gravel stung their legs, they resumed walking. "Hewitt came back to the house three, fo' mo' times over the next year and a half, askin' fo' work. My pap thought he was a nice young man, so he hired him on. But he didn't know Hewitt. Pap sho' found out when Hewitt ran off with his baby girl.

"Hewitt drug me to a justice of the peace—I was raised right, you see. Then he moved us 'bout two miles from Farmin'ton and he set me up in a boardin'house over a shoe-shine sto'. We stayed there 'bout two weeks while Hewitt tried to get my pap to take him in as his second son." Granny B laughed derisively.

"You see, I didn't know it, but Hewitt had come up with this big plan to marry some rich man's daughter and then set hisself up. Well, he didn't know my pap. Turns out I didn't know him either. Pap bent my spoon and turned over my plate when I left like I did. I was no mo' his daughter—so Hewitt surefire wan't his son and wan't never gon' be.

"Hewitt saw he was stuck with a young wife who didn't know nuthin' 'bout lovin' no man. And he came to see she didn't know nuthin' 'bout stoppin' babies from comin'. One day he moved us to Sprang Hope. And this where I been ever since." Granny B clamped her lips together in that way she had of saying, "And that's the end of that."

"But what about Henton—?"

"You thank this some fairy tale I'm tellin'?"

"I just don't understand."

"Goodness, chile, all that education . . . Henton is Hewitt's older brother, his only brother. The house on Carrot Lane? That was Henton's 'fo' Hewitt brought me there. Henton stayed there all by hisself, tendin' to them weeds, movin' from room to room like a shadow. At least until we got there."

"But what about the kids? Didn't they wonder . . . ? I mean, they think Henton's their daddy—I thought he was my *granddaddy*. Granny B, what are you telling me?" Evelyn stumbled to the grass and sat down.

Granny B took a few more steps before she slowly joined her granddaughter and lowered herself to the ground. "Hewitt . . . he . . . well, he worked fo' the railroad and he came and went with it, maybe two, three times a year. He'd just show up and then be gone by mornin' 'fo' the sun could get a breath, if he even stayed, especially when the chillun was younger. Henton, he worked most nights and caught a nap in the day.

"The chillun . . . well, they was too busy stayin' outta my way, though Thomas s'pected somethin'. He was hidin' in my closet one day, Lord knows why. Hewitt caught me by surprise and we . . . Well, when I found him hidin' there, I thought all the words been scared out of him. He never asked me plain, and I . . . I let it go. I guess you know why the chillun spent summers in Booker's garden."

"So you let Hewitt use you?" Evelyn couldn't imagine her grandmother living at the whim of some man.

Granny B's eyes flashed fire. "Use *me*? I was usin' him. I had a house. Henton was nuthin' but a ghost round there. Hewitt brought money when he could. But say I left. Where was I to go, a woman with a baby—then another baby and another? My mam and pap wouldn't have me, so you can be sure nobody else would." She shook her head as if she'd considered and discarded this option. "No, Hewitt didn't use me. My chillun had a roof over they head and a man they could point to and call Daddy."

"But the man who was their father wasn't, a-a-and the man who wasn't their father was!" Evelyn ran her fingers through her short, sweaty tendrils. "And you had to sleep with him . . ."

"Had to?" A real laugh rumbled up from her belly. "Mo' like *wonted to*. It won't like I was doin' nuthin' wrong—he was my husband. And he could touch me and make me forget 'bout them rusty pipes and cracked walls and wailin' chillun."

"If it was working out so well for everybody, why'd he leave?"

Granny B's smile slinked back to where it had escaped. "My heart just got tired, is all. I told him to leave."

"His own brother's house?"

"Awww, Henton was mo' mine than his. That fool Henton woulda done anything fo' me I asked him to. Turns out, he did mor'n I asked him to." She swallowed.

"But, Granny B, Henton left you, too."

The field before us captivated Granny B. "Yeah, he left. And not 'fo' leavin' me somethin' to remember him by."

"Milton . . . but how?"

Granny B pushed herself to her feet and brushed off the back of her dress. "The same way with you." She nodded toward my midsection.

"But—"

"We done talked enough." She peered up at the bits of sky peeking through the leafy canopy overhead. "I smell rain. We'd better head back."

Clear blue skies and fluffy white clouds winked at Evelyn as Granny B set off for home. Yet by the time they reached the house, the wind had picked up and the heavens had turned gray. Evelyn waited at the porch until her grandmother inched to the top step.

Granny B slid in the key. Thunder rumbled as she looked back over her shoulder.

"I'll let you get some rest. It's been a long day."

Granny B merely nodded and walked inside as the first heavy drops splashed onto Evelyn's forehead and coursed down her nose.

"Hi, Evelyn. How's Mama?"

"What do you mean?"

"I mean, how is Mama? I assume that's where you're coming from." Lis dropped a pack of frozen ground beef on the island. Ice crystals melted on the countertop.

"I'm sorry. I'm just tired and soaked. She's fine. Tired, I guess, but fine." Evelyn popped a grape and looked for something else to occupy her mouth besides words.

"Tired from what? What did you do today?"

"Well . . ." Evelyn pieced together a reasonable facsimile of the truth. "We gathered berries, or rather she did. I just helped her around the kitchen." Her eyes zeroed in on the mole on her mama's chin. *Who does she get that from? Granny B certainly doesn't have any moles.*

"What is it?" Lis studied Evelyn's face.

"Nothing. I just noticed your mole."

"Mole?"

Evelyn pointed to her chin.

Mama's fingers brushed her lower jaw. "Oh, my beauty mark? I've had it all my life!" She tried to peer at her face in the stainless steel refrigerator.

Evelyn poured a glass of water and took a sip. "I know. It's just that I've been thinking a lot about family characteristics and traits, stuff like that. Where did you get that mole? Does your dad, Grandfath—Henton have a mole like that?"

"Noooo. I don't think so. What makes you think of something like that?"

Evelyn choked on a grape stem. Quickly she sipped more water. "Well . . . you know . . ."

"What? Is it the baby? Is having Kevin here making you finally think about this baby?" Mama turned her back to the refrigerator.

"I guess I should, huh? Where *is* Kevin?" She slinked toward the kitchen door.

"He waited around for you after his call, but then Jackson came home and asked him to play basketball."

"Okay . . ." Evelyn's voice sounded as distant as her thoughts. She started walking away.

"So have you?"

"Have I what?"

"Been giving some thought to the baby? What you're going to do."

"What do you mean? I'm going to have a baby—that's what I'm going to do."

Mama looked out at the rain. Then she studied her daughter again. "I imagine you and Kevin had a lot of catching up to do. Did you two have a good talk?"

Evelyn's fingers played a concert on the countertop. "Fine."

"I remember how you and Kevin used to talk during your visits. But from what I could tell, you never called him. All these weeks, never once. Now that he's here and knows about the baby, I would think you'd have plenty to talk about." She paused. "Was he angry?"

"Was *he* angry?"

"Yes. Was *Kevin* angry? You've been holding back some pretty important information from him, your husband, the reason you're in this situation. This affects him, not just you. Pregnancy changes everything."

"So I'm pregnant. My life didn't change." Evelyn reached for more grapes.

"Your life didn't change?" Lis's chuckle was short on mirth. "Girl, of course your life changed. You're sleeping differently, you're eating differently—you need to dress differently. I'm surprised Mama hasn't lit into you yet."

"Granny B? She'd have some nerve."

"What's that supposed to mean?"

Evelyn suddenly focused on peeling her grape. "Nothing."

Mama walked over and snatched the fruit from her. "You

always mean something, Evelyn. And this is no different. Did y'all get into it again?"

"Get into it?"

"Yes, get into it. Like you did before."

"No, Mama. Granny B and I did not *get into* anything. It's just that I'm tired—"

"There you go with that lame 'I'm tired' excuse."

"I'm *tired* of you defending Granny B. I mean, who is she? Just some ordinary person like you or me. She's had her own problems to deal with, just like I've had."

"Ordinary? Ordinary! You're going to stand there and call my mama some ordinary woman? So you think you could give birth to nine children and bury two of them, starting when you were fifteen years old?"

"Mama—"

"You think an 'ordinary woman' can raise up seven children by herself? And do such a job most of them become accomplished, God-fearing people—lawyers, business owners, teachers, parents? Do you think an *ordinary* woman could live so distinguished and upright that even white people back in the sixties gave her respect? Do you think you could live and *die* with such dignity, Evelyn? That you'd still come out of it loving the Lord?" Lis's chest heaved.

"Mama, listen. I really don't know what I'm talking about."

"You're right this time, Evelyn. You most certainly don't know what you're talking about." She shoved the grapes at her daughter. "When you can summon up one-tenth of the character of my mama, the courage she had to own up to her responsibilities and do what needed to be done . . . well, then you'll be doing something. But until then, yes, I will continue to compare you and everybody else to her. And you'll come up wanting." Lis stomped from the kitchen.

Evelyn started to run behind her mama and tell her a thing or two about her dignified mother, but she went to her room instead, glad that Kevin was playing basketball with Jackson. She threw herself across the bed. Before she cried herself to sleep, Granny B's voice asked her, *"How can you forgive somebody for tearin' your heart out and givin' it back to you?"*

Chapter Twenty-Three

KEVIN SHOOK HER GENTLY. "Evelyn?"

Evelyn rolled onto her side away from him.

"Evie?"

Though she still clung to sleep, Evelyn retreated physically and emotionally at his pet name. His touch forced her to open her eyes. She blinked and flopped onto her back.

"Good morning, Evie." He smiled and touched the mound her midsection made beneath the sheet. When she recoiled, he withdrew his hand. "I'm sorry. Did I do something wrong?"

She regretted her reflexive movement. She reached for his hand and held it to her belly. "I'm just waking up, that's all." She cleared her throat and tried to smile. "You know I'm not a morning person." Ignoring his questioning eyes, she squeezed his fingers, threw back the covers, and moved away. "It seems quiet. Where's everybody?"

"Lis and Jackson left for church some time ago. Then they're going to Granny B's. How about we join them? I haven't seen her yet."

She and her mama had tiptoed around each other the past thirty-six hours, and she hadn't spoken to Granny B since she'd fled her home. "I'm not up to it today. But please don't let me stop you." And she really meant *please*. She ached for some time alone.

Evelyn stretched, causing her pink flowered nightie to lift higher on her thighs. Feeling his eyes on her and knowing the house was practically empty, Evelyn straightened and pulled down her white lace hem. She flicked aside the curtain to avoid his hungry look. The drops that had sent her scurrying for the car two days before were nothing compared to the torrential downpour outside. "What a difference a day makes."

"Why don't we have breakfast and hang out? We can spend some time catching up and maybe watch a movie or cuddle on the sofa."

"Mmmmm." *I wonder what he means by "hang out" and "cuddle"?* Evelyn left the window seat and headed toward the door. "I'm going to wash up and get dressed. You want to start with breakfast and see what happens from there?"

Kevin reached for her hand as she passed him. "Want an omelet, coffee, or me?"

"Why don't we go with door number two? I'd love some coffee. Decaffeinated." Evelyn kissed him lightly on the cheek and dug out denim shorts and a flowered T-shirt. Then she hastily found refuge in the bathroom. Once inside, she leaned against the closed and locked door and squeezed her eyes shut on a prayer. *Dear Jesus, help me. I can't live without Kevin, but it's hard to live with him. Show me how to trust him, to forgive him, to love him as You want me to, flaws and all. His sins against me, against You, O Lord, are no greater than mine. Please, please, please help me remember that. I know I want You to forgive my trespasses, so help me forgive his. Amen.*

Evelyn heard the landline ring just as she stepped from the shower. A moment later, there was a soft tap on the bathroom door.

"Evelyn?"

"Yes?" The T-shirt muffled her voice as she pulled it on.

"Telephone."

Evelyn turned the lock and peeked around the door.

"I'm going to join Lis and Jackson and visit Granny B." Kevin thrust a phone at her through the opening before he abruptly about-faced and headed toward the stairs.

I guess he was going for door number three, she thought, only slightly chagrined. "Hello?"

"Evelyn?"

"Oh, hi."

"'Oh, hi' to you, too. I won't hold you long, so don't worry."

"No worries, Yolanda. Kevin just didn't tell me who it was."

"I've been trying to catch up with you for a while, to talk about Mama's birthday party. Did you get my text about switching gears? With everything going on, I think it's a good idea."

Evelyn smacked herself on her forehead. "Right, right, I did. I'm sorry. And I agree: a family dinner sounds best, and now Kevin can be there since he's changed his travel itinerary."

"Yes, I've heard. I've talked to him more than I've talked to you. So, no more jet-setting for him?"

"Nope, looks like he's homebound for a minute. Listen, thanks for staying on top of all this and for chasing me down. Life has been crazy."

"Sure. You know how I hate loose ends. Maybe this will take one thing off your plate."

What plate? Yolanda had no idea Evelyn hadn't spared a thought for her mama's party. At least now she wouldn't have to feel guilty about avoiding her sister's calls or faking excitement in a roomful of people. Soon enough, she'd be faking grief. The baby kicked her, and she jumped.

Evelyn cleared her throat. "I appreciate your taking the reins. I'm sure you have enough on your own plate. How are you?"

"Tired, but good."

"I'm sure. Keeping up with the family and your responsibilities at the firm must keep you hopping. How *are* the kids?"

"Getting on my nerves. Wonderful as ever. You know, Monica starts school this fall."

"That's right! She just turned five, didn't she? With all that's going on here, it slipped my mind. Did you do it up in a big way?"

"Of course! We had a tea party. Complete with ten little girls in flowered hats, dripping red fruit punch on my carpet." She laughed. "I lost a plate, but it was lots of fun. Phillip Jr. blew a gasket when they trooped into his room, but I promised him a game for his computer, and he settled down."

Evelyn quickly calculated her nephew's age. "He turns eight this November, right?"

"Yes, though you'd think he was thirty-eight the way he tries to boss people around here. Phil treats him like the sun rises and sets on him. I keep saying, 'You'd better take a hard line. We're going to have a mess on our hands.' But you know men are hardheaded, old and young."

She sounds so much like Mama. Is this how I'm going to sound in a few years? Evelyn looked at her belly.

Yolanda seemed to hear her thoughts. "But what about you? You'll have your own soon. I haven't talked to you since you found out you were pregnant."

Since everybody else *found out I'm pregnant.* "Yes, I know. A lot has happened, but . . . I'm good. You talked about the kids, but you left out my brother-in-law. How is he?"

Yolanda paused. Then she took a breath. "Phillip is better. *We're* better. Actually, Phillip and I just got home from a marriage retreat."

"A marriage retreat?"

"Sponsored by the women's ministry at our church. It was

beautiful—but you know it took the Lord to get me into the wilderness! I don't do bugs. I had to suck it up, though. Phillip and I really needed this."

Evelyn took the phone into her mother's room and stretched out on her chaise longue. "Y'all good?" She heard her sister sigh again from hundreds of miles away.

"We're getting there. It was iffy for a minute."

Evelyn was unsure how to navigate these uncharted waters of her sister's vulnerability.

But Yolanda continued, unprompted. "I'm just grateful God blessed me with this loving, patient man. If He hadn't, I don't know, Ev . . . I guess I'd be on my way to single motherhood."

"*He's* loving and patient? Did you—?"

"Have an affair? No, it wasn't something that black-and-white. But really, it's not what I did. It's more about what I didn't do. I pretty much checked out. I couldn't manage more than the bare minimum. You didn't notice you weren't hearing from me?"

Evelyn cringed. She'd thought she was avoiding Yolanda, not the other way around.

Her sister must have sensed her chagrin. She cracked up. "It's okay, Sis. We never talked much anyway. Life just got to be too much for me, and . . . let's just say I stepped away from myself for a bit. From Phil, the kids, work. Everything. I just wasn't quote-unquote happy, and I thought I deserved it, or some such nonsense. But Phil held on to our marriage, to our family, to me. He waited until I got it together. Shoot, there's lots of ways to be unfaithful in a marriage."

Don't I know it? Evelyn rolled to her side, overwhelmed with the awareness that this was God. She felt more shock than judgment. She and her sister hadn't talked in almost a month about something as banal as the weather, let alone life changers like this. "Yolanda, I didn't know . . ."

"No one did—well, no one but me and Phillip and Mama. And I wouldn't be talking about it so easily now if I hadn't just left the retreat and told the group. This isn't something I'd normally share so easily with anybody, including you, Baby Sister. But God showed me how being real about my own marriage, my own limitations, helps others."

"Mama knew?"

"Who do you think I cried my heart out to when Phillip confronted me? And I really think if it wasn't for the children—and God, of course—he would have moved out. And I couldn't blame him. Shoot, Mama's got a whole bunch of my secrets buried in her backyard! She really helped me find my way back home. We're not perfect, but we're like new—and not like Target-opened-box-returned-television new. I'm saying *brand-new*."

"I don't know what to say, Yo."

She sighed. "That's because we never say more than two words to each other, let alone the deep stuff. Maybe that can change. We're about to have lots more in common when you have that baby! Mama told me how good you look. I was as big as a house when I carried my babies."

"She said that?"

"Mmm-hmmm, she said you could barely tell you're showing. Why'd you wait so long to tell somebody?"

Because I hadn't even told my own husband, Evelyn almost blurted out. Instead she answered, "There was so much going on around here. It just seemed like one more thing to discuss."

"'One more thing to discuss'? That's good news, something we needed to hear. It's not like you had to tell somebody you're sick or dying . . . Oops, I'm sorry. That was thoughtless."

"Why are you apologizing?"

"Well . . . you know. Granny B."

"She's your grandmother, too."

"True, but you have to admit she never could stand much of me or Lionel."

"Yolanda! That's not—" Actually, it was true. But then Granny B couldn't stand much of anybody, and Evelyn told her that.

"Maybe, but you and Granny B have this special chemistry."

"I just bully my way in. Everybody else is too afraid to."

"But that's just it. You two are so alike."

"Just because we share the same name doesn't mean we're alike."

"No, it's just one more thing. The way you speak your mind—"

"So I'm honest. At least I'm nice about it."

"But when you pretend you don't hear a question or politely change the subject . . . same thing. And you know how Granny B remembers even the smallest offenses? Well, that's you, a dog with a bone. I'm sure you still remember why you got in trouble when we were at Maxine's that day—"

"Because you disobeyed Mama and I got the blame for it! You know that was your fault—"

"See? That's what I mean. Like I said, just won't let things go," Yolanda giggled. "And you're both so closemouthed. Look at how Mama found out her own mother was sick, from a friend. That's you. Granny B all the way . . . Evelyn? You still there?"

"I'm here."

"You're not mad, are you? I'm sorry—"

"*Now* why are you apologizing?"

"I thought—"

"I'm fine. I'm glad to hear your voice. I needed this. Did you call to talk to Mama?"

Yolanda didn't answer for a moment. "Actually, no. Like I said, we walked in the door, and the Lord said, 'Call your sister.' So I did. You're really all right? And Kevin? I imagine he's ready to get y'all back home."

Evelyn made a quick decision. "Kevin . . . well. I'm really glad he came back early. We have stuff to work through. The baby, for one."

Yolanda said nothing for a few seconds as if she was listening to all the unspoken words between them. Then she seemed to reach a decision, for she abruptly shifted her tone from warm-and-fuzzy to back-to-business. "Speaking of babies, I should go. Mine have been awfully quiet for too long, and you know what that means."

Evelyn drew from her teaching experience to chime in with her: "Trouble!"

A few minutes later, they ended the call with a promise to talk again soon. Evelyn replaced the receiver and tucked the conversation into the back of her mind. She'd bring it out later, turn it over, and poke at it, but for the moment, the rest of the day yawned before her.

Then she spied her mama's closet. Not thinking twice, she opened the door wide and stepped inside. Lis's walk-in closet was just as neat and organized as Granny B's, just bigger—nearly the size of Granny B's extra bedroom. She pushed through clothes, accessories, and other odds and ends. When Evelyn couldn't find anything interesting above, she ducked under the skirts and shirts. And there in the back she found yet another box, *the* box, what her subconscious mind had sought the whole time. She dragged it into the open and lifted its lid. Inside, hundreds and hundreds of photographs fought for space.

Lis had always promised to "do something soon" with all the photographs they'd taken, but her "soon" spanned more than three decades. Evelyn plowed through, briefly reliving the life history of their family: Lionel and his first and only puppy. A tiny Yolanda, sprawled on the sidewalk in a pair of clunky skates. Evelyn holding a screaming Jackson the day her mama and daddy brought him home. Graham holding their laughing crew in his armchair. Her mama kicking up a leg, brandishing a one-dollar bill outside her salon.

The photographs depicted fruitfulness, productivity, blessings. Evelyn considered their accomplishments, what her aunts and uncles had striven for. Was it all based on a lie? She had half a mind to scratch off the coating to find the ugliness their smiling faces concealed.

Evelyn gathered her energy and dragged the box to her room. There, she upended it, watching images cascade onto the floor. She rubbed her hands together, relishing the project ahead of her.

For the next few hours Evelyn threw herself into grouping them based on the year they were taken. Sometimes she guesstimated, studying their clothes, where they were, or the subject. Lionel's Members Only jacket got him thrown into the 1980s pile. A photograph of her posing with her parents and Yolanda on the steps of the Capitol was placed in the 1990s because Lionel had graduated from George Washington University in 1999. Jackson's baby pictures landed him in the new millennium stack.

She was grooving along when she happened upon a large copy of one of the two photographs hanging in Granny B's front room. In it, Granny B commanded center stage, her hand clutching the head of a doe-eyed Sarah, pinning her to a spot just to Granny B's left. Little Ed stood partially behind his baby sister and his mama, his arms intertwined with a statuesque Elisabeth, a young woman of seventeen. For once, she and Little Ed refrained from punching or chasing each other. To Elisabeth's left Ruthena, with her long plaits, clung to the fringes, looking as if she would rather be somewhere else—perhaps crouching on bended knee at the church. On Granny B's right Thomas held a slight four-year-old Milton, who always seemed small for his age. Mary's toothy smile shone just beside Thomas's right shoulder. They all grinned at the unknown photographer, the day Elisabeth finished high school, the day before she graduated from the Spring Hope school of hard knocks and left home for good.

Evelyn peered at the differences in hairstyles and hair textures, the aquiline noses and flaring nostrils and skin tones that ranged from fairest Mary to bittersweet chocolate–flavored Milton. She wondered about what Hewitt looked like and which of his children looked most like him. Did Ruthena's wavy hair remind Granny B of her lost love? Or did Thomas's mellifluous voice that served him so well in the courtroom strike a discordant note in her grandmother's ear? Most likely it was Milton's sturdy frame and jawline that caused her the most pain.

She caught Cocoa scooching under the bed with a small photograph between her teeth. Evelyn gently dislodged a black-and-white close-up of Lis, decades later, kneeling under a large tree. Her hands were tucked beneath her large belly, and she was laughing at the photographer. Evelyn smiled with her beautiful mama, imagining her daddy teasing her in that easy way of his.

"We took that at Holden Park." Lis peered over her shoulder.

Evelyn gasped. "When did you get home?"

"Just now. I left Kevin and Jackson at Mama's." Lis reached down and gently took the photograph. "I remember I was about seven months pregnant, and I was feeling it. Your daddy got a babysitter and we headed over to the park. It was a beautiful park—and it was the perfect day for a picnic. He'd seen some movie—hmmm . . . what was it? And he had the idea to buy all these gourmet foods for us to eat—stuff only people in movies eat, you know what I mean?" She sounded like she relished the day.

Evelyn nodded.

"Well, I took one look at the basket and thought, 'Ooh, fried chicken and potato salad!' But when I opened it, I saw runny cheese and goose liver and these crackers that looked like they had seaweed in them! You should have seen your daddy when he took a bite of that pâté. It was so funny. We laughed the whole time, but boy, were we hungry!"

Evelyn soaked in the splendor of their long-ago day.

"We spent hours at the park, in spite of being hungry and all. He rubbed my feet and massaged my neck. I'd been so achy the whole pregnancy. He just pampered me. Then we held each other, and he rubbed my stomach. We discussed having another girl or another boy . . . I was so big."

"You were so beautiful." Evelyn took the photo from her. Then her mama's words struck her. "You were pregnant with me."

"Of course. Didn't you read the back?" Mama turned the picture over.

Elisabeth, with baby #3. She blinked away tears. "Oh!"

"Yes, I was pregnant with you. And let me tell you, you kicked my butt the entire time."

Should I apologize? Laugh?

But her mama didn't seem to pick up on her discomfiture. "What are you doing? Where did you find this picture?"

"In the box in your closet. I'm organizing them." She pointed at what she'd already started.

"What are you planning to do once you're done?"

Evelyn sat back then. "Well . . ."

"I'm going to need more than a dozen albums to hold all these. Do you mind if I work with you?"

Evelyn had expected her mama to have her head before giving her a hand. "Sure, that'd be nice."

They dove in. Every now and then they laughed over a picture or Lis explained the circumstances. More than two hours passed before they heard the chirp-chirp of the security system announce the guys' return.

Lis leaned toward the door. "Jackson! Kevin! We're up here!"

After the thud-thud-thud of footsteps, Jackson poked his head inside. "Mama, Granny B cooked up a storm and sent most of it with us. It's downstairs if you're ready to eat. What are you doing?"

"Stepping back in time," Evelyn responded smartly.

"Why don't you and Kevin go ahead? We'll be down." Once he withdrew, Lis faced Evelyn. "You haven't asked about Mama."

Evelyn suddenly busied herself with brushing off her shorts. "How is she?"

"She's fine. Wondering how you're doing."

Evelyn stopped brushing. "Wondering about me?"

Lis held her daughter's gaze and dug in. "Yes. She's worried how you're taking the news."

"What news? That's she dying?"

She smiled slightly. "No, that she's a woman. She's human. Just like you and me."

Evelyn struggled to find her voice. "What are you talking about?"

"I imagine we're talking about the same things, Evelyn." Lis inclined her head slightly. "Mama told you about my father. About *Hewitt*. She told you about all his comings and goings, and she told you that Milton is really my half brother. That Henton is his father."

Evelyn sat as stone.

"It's okay, Evelyn. Mama told me."

"It's okay? It's *okay*?" She finally scooped up her voice from between her toes. "How can you stand there and say, 'It's okay'?"

"Because it is. Here, come sit down." Lis took Evelyn's hand and led her to the window seat. She tugged gently. "Sit down, Evelyn. Please.

"Evelyn, there are so many things that can happen to a person, things that other people can't understand—even the person involved sometimes doesn't understand. Imagine it." She entreated Evelyn with her free left hand. "Thirteen.

Mama was *thirteen* when she first met Hewitt. And then two years later, there she was, living with a man, yes, her husband—"

"Of her own free will, to hear her tell it."

"Yes, but how much free will does a girl that age have? I don't care if it's 2040 or 1940. She was a teenager, and she'd never been off her daddy's farm, at least not long enough or far enough to speak of. And here comes Hewitt Agnew. Fine as wine to hear her tell it." She grimaced. "And she was caught up, like so many girls are caught up today. She marries him and her family spits her out like something that tastes bad. She's living with another stranger—his brother, Henton—and the man she loves who loves her maybe twice a year. What would you have her do?"

She had no idea what she would have done, but then she wasn't Granny B, the strongest, meanest, most faithful and honest woman she knew.

"You're looking at your grandmother through eyes that see her as she is today—not as she might have been, as she was years and years ago, when she was less than half the age that you are now! Who do you think made her who she is? What shaped her life? Her experiences made her who she is today, and I'm proud of her for it."

"What?"

"Yes. She stuck it out when my own father left her, left us. And he never looked back. She made mistakes, but my mother was a faithful wife, a strong mother who didn't take nothing from nobody, Evelyn. She protected us fiercely from a town that could have run her out on her ear. We could have been labeled all kinds of names. But she wouldn't have it. She stayed there and waited for him, and yes, he took what he wanted from her. But she needed him, too."

Evelyn listened as Granny B's words flowed from her own mama's mouth.

"As far as any outsider really knew, Hewitt was just Henton's brother, and he came home from time to time. She was living in Henton's house and her last name was Agnew, so naturally most folks assumed Hewitt was our uncle, not our daddy. I'm sure some nosy people could have timed her pregnancies with his visits, but living was pretty hard then, and who had time for that?" She seemed to consider it. "Well, maybe Mrs. Johnson, but she didn't move there for a long time.

"Meanwhile, we had a roof over our heads and food to eat, and we went to school. And she protected us, too, by keeping us so busy and distracted, we didn't know any better. We would have had none of those things if Mama had followed your modern way of thinking." Lis swallowed.

"So Mama stayed there, having six children and burying two, until finally, God gave her the courage to kick my sorry daddy out. Over time, she became the Granny B you know today." She squeezed Evelyn's hand.

Evelyn thought she could accept all that. But not everything. "You left out *one*. What about Milton?"

Two tears seeped from the corners of Lis's eyes and trickled down her otherwise-calm face. She blinked and broke their gaze for the first time. "Milton's another matter."

Then it was Evelyn who did the squeezing. "What do you mean?"

Lis blew out a breath. "Well, Mama didn't have anywhere to go then, after Hewitt left. So she stayed there in Henton's house."

"Are you going to tell me they fell passionately in love and that he left her, too?"

"No, they didn't, or rather, *she* didn't. I don't know if Henton loved Mama from the moment he saw her or if he just grew to love her. We can't ask him. They spent a lot of time together in that house, and I do believe he loved us children, and she probably felt something for him, but she fought it with all she had." She shrugged.

"But one night, the night Thomas nearly lost his finger, Mama was beside herself. She'd been looking backward and forward, blaming herself for staying with Hewitt so long and kicking him out too soon. Missing him, loving him. Hating him and herself. Just out of her mind with heartache. And that night—" Lis swallowed hard as more tears chased the others—"Henton came home drunk. When we heard Mama crying, I called for him to go see to her . . ." She brought a hand to her mouth.

Evelyn's heart was a slowly moving stone. "Did he assault Granny B?"

Lis wiped her eyes with the back of her hand. "No. *That* she could've moved past, strangely enough. But what she couldn't forgive is her own part. She blamed herself for everything, especially for the sin in seeking physical refuge in Henton. And then she had Milton.

"At first, he reminded her of her weakness, the mistakes she'd made. But later, I think Milton stood for the love that got away—Hewitt's and Henton's. One man she loved who she couldn't keep and another who loved her. I think in his own way, Henton loved her, really loved her, in a way that Hewitt never did. But for Mama, loving had caused her nothing but pain, loss, and suffering—her parents, Hewitt, children, Henton. Oh, Milton."

Then Lis wiped her eyes again, and Evelyn could tell it was for the last time. Yet the words continued to well up and over.

"Milton symbolized all of that heartbreak, and she poured it into all of us, all the bitterness. She wouldn't risk loving another thing, another person, or even God, who allowed it to happen. So more and more, love became this work you *do*, not a joy or a gift you feel or extend. Henton stuck around for a while after his son was born. But then I guess he assumed the blame. He probably knew Mama couldn't take him anymore either, so he left. Leaving her the house and the land—everything."

"So the Social Security that Granny B gets—"

"Is from Hewitt. She was his wife, not Henton's." Lis's now-dry eyes searched her daughter's. "Are you still angry?"

"I never said—"

"You were angry. And hurt. Disappointed, too. But there

was no need. It's sorrow we should feel. I hope you see that now."

Evelyn looked away, but a finger forced her head back.

"And I hope you see some other things."

"What things?"

"Why I've been so concerned."

Evelyn laughed shortly. "Concern. That's what you call it?"

"Yes. You are so much like Mama, Evelyn. Holding things in, creating your own hell."

Evelyn thought of Yolanda's words.

"Yes, you are like her." Her hand gripped Evelyn's, and her eyes devoured her daughter's face. "And as much as I love her and admire her, I don't want you to be like her. I don't want you to live like she did, all alone, with a child she viewed as punishment, a life she had to endure. I want you to look at this baby as an opportunity, as a blessing, and not as a rope tied round your neck."

"You look at raising children as a job, a punishment even. Where is the joy?" Evelyn's own words haunted her.

"Have you even talked about the baby with Kevin since he's been here?" Lis released her hand to grasp both shoulders. "What Mama went through? Each pregnancy, each baby, tied her inextricably to Hewitt, even to Henton. And I don't know what I would have done. Probably resented each nappy-haired one of us."

"And she does."

"Yes, she does, or at least she did. But she loves us, too, more than she can even say on a piece of paper. But you,

Evelyn, you're not living Mama's life. You have a loving husband. He did something terrible, almost unforgivable—"

"Mama!"

"—but he's a good man, I know. And this life you're carrying is just as special as each of you is to me. And you need to act like it."

She brushed away her mama's hands and rose. "I know all this."

"Then act like it." Lis remained seated.

"I just didn't plan any of this." And by *this*, she meant Kevin's unfaithfulness, the separation, Granny B's illness, the pregnancy.

"So what? Neither did I. Not Lionel or Yolanda or Jackson either."

Immediately Evelyn pictured helping Granny B gather linen at the clothesline. It felt like years before but was only weeks. *"Getting pregnant was not in my plans, and being a single parent most definitely isn't."*

"You think dyin' was in mine?"

Evelyn shrugged off the image. "But you wanted to have children, even if you didn't know when. I didn't plan to have children at all."

"So what? Now, I've sat back and let you and Kevin—"

"Sat back?"

"—act like nothing strange was happening, but I can't let you ignore what's going on."

Evelyn studied the floor, the bed, the wall behind the bed, and the window behind them that framed the pewter skies outside. But that didn't seem to stop Lis from approaching Evelyn. She again took both her daughter's hands and cradled them. "Evelyn," she whispered.

Evelyn stared at the clock on the nightstand, willing the second hand to stop and freeze everything in the room—everything but her, allowing her to escape.

"Evelyn Beatrice, look at me." Lis didn't raise her voice. She obeyed.

"Child, child," Mama groaned, pulling her close.

How long had it been since her mama had held her tightly enough to squeeze the breath from her? How long since she'd wanted her to? Evelyn clung to her and poured out her sorrow for Granny B and for herself. Her mama tenderly ran her fingers through Evelyn's spiky strands and held her. When Evelyn pulled back slightly, it wasn't because she wanted to. She desperately needed a tissue.

Lis reached into the pocket of her jumpsuit and offered her ever-present handkerchief. She placed a hand on each of her daughter's shoulders. "Better?"

Evelyn nodded.

"Girl, I've tried to blaze the trails before you. I don't want you to waste time making my mistakes. My mama's mistakes. What would be the point? I remember when I found out I was pregnant with Lionel. I was scared to death! And I was scared to death with Yolanda, and with you, and definitely with Jackson since I was nearing fifty years old. And I know you must be out of your mind, too."

Lis nodded toward the handkerchief and was quiet until

Evelyn wiped her overflowing eyes and nose. "I know you're mad, too. Mad at yourself for allowing this to happen. At your husband for forcing your hand. At me for buttin' in . . . Everybody! But that's okay. *Be* mad. Mama stormed around the house every pregnancy. But when the time came, she did what she had to do, and so will you. Because of *love*, Evelyn. *Love*. That's the only reason I put up with your sassy tongue—hush, now."

Evelyn closed her mouth.

"That's the reason Mama put up with what she had to, and I'm sure it's why she's giving us all such a hard time now. She's trying to do what's best for us and for herself, and just like children, we're fighting it. But joy is wrapped up in the love God gave us. Mama didn't hold on to it, but you can. You will. You have a responsibility as God's child, my daughter, and that baby's mother."

Lis sighed. "Now, I'm going down to see if my eighteen-year-old left us anything for dinner. And I'm sure that husband of yours, who stomped around Mama's house all afternoon, is dying to know whether we've finally killed each other."

Lis looked at her squarely. "I'm sure you have things to do. Right, Evelyn?" Her mama kissed her on the cheek and patted her softly on each shoulder. Then she let Evelyn go.

Chapter Twenty-Four

THE IMPALA'S TIRES consumed the road. With each mile, the rain that had steadily pummeled the ground over the past few days lightened, disappearing altogether by the time Evelyn turned onto Carrot Lane. She skidded to a stop in Granny B's drive and dashed across the sodden ground to the door. Several minutes later, she realized that again, Granny B was gone. Evelyn descended the steps slowly, wondering if she was up for another berry-picking adventure.

"Where you runnin' off to, child?" Velma Johnson, wearing a wide-brimmed straw hat, knelt among the weeds in her flower bed.

Evelyn's fingers twitched weakly in greeting.

Mrs. Johnson used her hoe to push herself to her feet and walked closer to the road, not that she had to. Her strident voice carried. "Lookin' for your grandma?"

Evelyn bit her sarcastic "Obviously" in two and swallowed it. *May God bless widows and children,* she prayed. "Yes, ma'am."

"Well, I saw her walk that way just as the rain was stoppin'. Toward town." Mrs. Johnson brushed mud and wet grass from her knees.

"Thanks, Mrs. Johnson!" Evelyn hastily pulled the handle to open the door.

"She was lookin' good today—"

Evelyn turned on the engine and backed into the street. As she shifted into drive, she risked a glance in the rearview mirror. Velma was waving her hoe wildly back and forth. For a second, Evelyn considered pretending she hadn't seen her, but God made her press the brake, jerking the car to a halt.

"Yes, Mrs. Johnson?"

"She told me to tell you she's at the Skillet."

Granny B, why do I keep underestimating you? "Thank you, Mrs. Johnson. Be careful out here in this sun."

"Gal, you'd best believe I'll catch that sun before it catches me." She waved the hoe one last time as she touched her hat with one gloved hand.

Evelyn ignored the Speed Limit 45 signs, making the ten-minute drive in eight. She slowed down once she reached downtown, an area so designated because it had a Piggly Wiggly, a few storefronts with uneven lettering hand-painted on their front windows, a Shell gas station, a drugstore, the Skillet, and Mr. Fulton's general store centered around an octagon. Evelyn parked in one of the many empty spaces along Main Street. An old truck clunked by. When it passed, she spotted her: Granny B in the Skillet's picture window, enjoying an early lunch.

———

From her perch in the booth to the right of the door, Beatrice watched Evelyn look both ways as she waddled across the street. She took another bite from her plate of rice, steak and gravy, and black-eyed peas as her granddaughter scooted in across from her.

Beatrice nodded hello to an older couple leaving the restaurant. "What took you so long to find me? I had to start without you." She took another forkful and spared a glance at the slender watch on her left wrist. "It's past time for my nap."

"You're right. But I had some—"

Just then a server set down a plate of steamed cabbage, fried pork chops, and macaroni and cheese and a glass of lemonade. "What's this?"

"I thought I'd order you some food, as it is after—"

"Noon, yes, you told me. But you never eat out." She picked up the utensils wrapped tightly in the paper napkin.

"Why pay for somebody else to cook what I got in my own house?" Granny B tucked into the remaining bit of food in front of her. She'd been waiting a long time.

Evelyn sliced the crunchy yet succulent chop. "Mmmm."

"Yes, these folks can sho' nuff cook." Beatrice smiled to herself as Evelyn put down her utensils and used her hands. She slurped her sweetened iced tea as her granddaughter enjoyed her bite. "You know, this is where the church got them plates of food they used ta send me. As much as I hated to see that preacher when he came callin', I couldn't turn him away for fear he'd stop lettin' Ruthena bring me a plate." She sipped again, her fingers playing in the ring of sweat the frosty mason jar had left on the table. Beatrice would pay for this splurge later, but her stomach was just going to have to sit tight until she got home.

"So why are we here today?" Evelyn drank from her own jar.

"'Cause we celebratin'." Beatrice watched Evelyn chew.

"Celebrating what?"

She pushed away her plate and from nowhere a hand whisked it away. Another refilled her tea. She raised her freshened glass to her granddaughter. "Let's call it a home-goin' party."

Evelyn rested her fork on her plate and stared at her grandma's raised glass. "You expect me to toast to your leukemia?"

Beatrice set down her mason jar. "Girl, this *yo'* home-goin' party. And if you ain't gon' drink that lemonade, at least finish your lunch." She nodded at Evelyn's fork.

"How'd you know I was going home?"

Beatrice picked up her tea. "I didn't. I was just hopin'." She closed her eyes in appreciation as she swallowed another mouthful. She could feel Evelyn's eyes on her.

"You think you know a whole lot about a whole lot, don't you?"

Beatrice gazed out at the tableau on the other side of the window. "I ain't sayin' I know 'bout a lot. I just happen to be right about what I do know." She snickered a little, confident about the truth in her words. Evelyn joined in as a truck bound for the Piggly Wiggly ambled noisily by. "Just how long you been here?"

"Six or seven weeks."

"Then I'd say 'bout a month too long."

Evelyn held her tongue—and her fork.

"I know you don't thank so, but 'Lis'beth sho' do."

"So Mama's been talking about me, huh?"

"No mor'n usual. But I been thankin' 'bout the reason you stayed round here so long." She paused as Evelyn took another bite of pork chop. "'Cause you know I'm gon' do or die whether you stay or go." She held her granddaughter's eyes prisoner as she looked up from her plate. "You must have other reasons why you still hangin' round."

"Isn't it enough I'm leaving now?"

"But you was leavin' then, too. Leavin' Kevin. This baby stopped you from what you was plannin', didn't it? 'Bout to throw yo' life away for what? What dreams you thank he keepin' you from?"

Evelyn fiddled with the knife and fork like she was ready to carve her grandmother into tiny pieces. "Maybe the same dreams Hewitt stole from you!"

Flames licked the corners of Beatrice's eyes.

Evelyn looked down. "I'm sorry—"

"No, you not."

"You wear me out, Granny B. I came down here to say good-bye, to apologize, not to get riled up by—"

"By the truth? You know my story, and now I know yours, at least some of it. Was he beatin' you?"

Evelyn shook her head vigorously.

"Drugs?" She peered intently at Evelyn for a telltale sign— a twitch, a blink, a sideways look. "Was he messin' round?"

Evelyn crisscrossed her utensils over her remaining food. Her arms followed suit over her chest.

"Oh . . . so that's it." Beatrice's heart was like tiny pebbles scattering about in her chest. She measured her grand-daughter's pain. "But now you goin' home, so that means . . . what? What done changed?"

"Me." When Evelyn said it, her eyes didn't waver. She even smiled a little.

Beatrice smiled then, too. She wouldn't spoil her grand-daughter's mood by admitting she'd had a heart-to-heart with her Kevin. "Seems you found somethin' it took me most my life to put my hands on."

"But you've been saved a long time, Granny B."

"I ain't talkin' 'bout salvation. I'm talking 'bout grace, chile. Somethin' I didn't know how to accept or give, even to myself. But I'm learnin'. I'm glad you didn't wait as long as I did."

Beatrice reclined against the leatherette cushion. "Now I ain't makin' no excuses 'bout what I done in my life—or what's been done to me. I ain't gon' tell you God says this or that. But you got some sense, gal, or I been wastin' my time with you all these years. Whatever you was plannin', you got different plans now. I don't care if Kevin been travelin' round the world without so much as a postcard—you somebody's mama and somebody's wife. You hear me?"

"I hear you."

"You better. 'Cause I can tell you there wan't gon' be nuthin' waitin' fo' you on the other side of thangs. Hewitt found that out, and Henton sho' knowed it."

"How do you know Hewitt found that out?"

"He wrote me a letter and told me so hisself." Granny B inclined her head Evelyn's way. "You got the letter. Read it and see fo' yo'self." She watched her granddaughter's thoughts travel back. Beatrice wanted Evelyn to know it was okay to read it now.

Evelyn flushed. "Granny B—"

"Hush now, gal. We ain't got time for all that. That's over and done with. I just hope you learn that they ain't no value in runnin'. I know you fed up wit' me fo' stayin'. I'm fed up wit' you for leavin'."

"Keep my vows like you did, come hell or high water?"

Beatrice didn't hear any condemnation, just curiosity. "No, not like I did, but yes, keep your vows. Looks to me yo' hair a little burnt and yo' feet wet already."

Evelyn inclined her head. "Well, I'm not going anywhere, Granny B. Trust me. It was just an idea, a way I thought I could learn about myself."

Beatrice brayed. "You wan't tryin' to learn nuthin' 'bout

yo'self. You was tryin' to teach that man of yours a lesson. But he'll learn, Ev'lyn. That Kevin seem like a smart enough fella, even if he don't always think wit' the head on his shoulders. Ain't nobody perfect. Give him some time—and a whack upside the head with a broom. He'll learn."

Evelyn sat there looking at her Granny B and then she laughed, too. She laughed until she cried. And then she couldn't stop crying.

"Now stop that. I brought you up here so you couldn't do all that," Beatrice hissed. Evelyn could scream and laugh and shout all she wanted, but as far as Beatrice was concerned, out in public was no place to cry.

This seemed to make Evelyn laugh again. "How did you get so wise, Granny B?"

Beatrice's eyes again consumed the scene beyond the window. "You know how, Ev'lyn. And I don't never wont you to get as wise as I am." *Yes, you through laughin' for now, but I prob'ly got mo' tears on the way.*

It was time to go. Beatrice pushed her way to the counter and insisted on paying the $11.45 for their meal. As she led the way from the Skillet, she felt a tentative touch on her shoulder. She turned to her granddaughter.

"I *know*, Granny B. Really. I know. And I'm sorry. Will you forgive me?"

Anyone else might have inquired, "Sorry for what?" But not Beatrice, because she didn't have to. This was the second time Evelyn had asked her, but this time the girl knew what needed to be forgiven. Beatrice could feel the weight of her regrets, the sincerity of her repentance. They balanced her own. Beatrice stretched to her full height and grabbed the young woman by her chin. She pulled Evelyn's face closer, leaned in . . . and thumped her on her forehead. As hard as her bony fingers could manage.

"Ow!"

"That's for not mindin' yo' own business!" She reached into the front pocket of her green skirt and extracted an envelope. "This is for you, too, but it shouldn't hurt as much. Now get on home. I got thangs to do in town."

Evelyn cradled the letter to her chest. "I planned to drive you home."

"You know and I know that you need to take *yo'self* home." She held up a hand. "It's the truth, Ev'lyn. I don't need no car and driver. I got here on my own two feet, didn't I?"

"But you didn't have any business walking all the way here."

"And you thank I need you here to tell me that?"

"Well—"

"And since you know that, stop wastin' my time."

Evelyn shifted from one foot to the other.

"Go on, now." Beatrice waved her on.

"Oka-a-a-y. If you're sure . . . ?" At Beatrice's curt nod, Evelyn inched in the direction of the Impala glowing on the opposite side of the street. "I'll be back. I'll see you soon."

Just then, a car loaded with Spring Hope teenagers whizzed between them. Evelyn missed Beatrice's hushed "God willing."

Chapter Twenty-Five

"PLEASE, GOD, don't let Daddy die. Please, God, don't let Daddy die . . ." Evelyn huddled in the second pew. She'd run to the tiny hospital chapel to escape her mama's stricken face and Yolanda's and Lionel's wide eyes. Even baby Jackson looked frightened, all bundled up in his puffy red snowsuit. Neither the emergency room nurses nor Grandpa Willis could pry the youngster from her mama's grip. Evelyn couldn't catch her breath, staring at Daddy, all covered in tape and bandages, tubes hanging everywhere. The iron bed railings imprisoned her larger-than-life hero, keeping them from him and him from them. He couldn't move in that bed. And she couldn't keep her legs from moving, churning their way to the only safe place she could find. "Please, God, don't let Daddy die . . ."

"Gal, you need to get up from there and come with me."

Evelyn's eyes flew to the altar, where a wooden Jesus had been glued to the cross. *Why does God sound like Granny B?* But the gentle pressure on her shoulder was of earthly origin. She met her grandmother's calm, clear gaze.

"Come on now, chile." Granny B's supple, low voice belied the firm command in her tone.

Evelyn stood. "Is—?"

"Yo' mama lookin' fo' you. You had her worried sick, wondrin' where you was." Granny B's hand steered her from the chapel. "I know you ain't meant to cause her mo' worry, but when you left, that's exactly what you did. Now we need to get back—"

The girl stopped walking and shrugged Granny B's hand away. "What about Daddy, Granny B? Did he wake up?" Evelyn ignored the unabashed, understanding looks of white- and green-smocked hospital personnel.

Granny B's cool, steely fingers cupped her chin. She leaned close. Her eyes imparted worlds of truth. "If you need to kick and scream, you go on 'head and do it now, gal. In there you gon' need to be strong. Yo' mama fallin' apart, and yo' sister and brothers ain't doin' much better. Now, y'all got the right to act the fool 'cause yo' daddy was a good man and this don't seem fair. But you won't help nobody if you lose yo' head, and I know yo' daddy would be mighty surprised to see his girl actin' that way." Granny B smoothed her hair.

If Evelyn had been older or wiser, she would have recognized a comforting touch, but she wasn't older or wiser. She was fourteen. "Don't touch me!"

This time, her wild cries drew more than curious stares. Granny B drew herself up and frightened Miss Muffet away. Then she stood there, her face devoid of emotion, as Evelyn wept. She didn't try to touch her. Yet her solid presence calmed Evelyn. Somehow Granny B conveyed that as much as things were changing, some things would not.

"You ready to see yo' mama?" Granny B did not mention her daddy at all.

Evelyn nodded quickly.

They strode down the hall toward the intensive care unit. It wasn't until they reached the wide double doors that Granny B lightly touched her again on the shoulder. Evelyn turned to look into her gray eyes.

"You make yo' daddy proud. Don't you grieve him none. You hear me?"

All Evelyn could do was nod. She pressed her now-sodden handkerchief into her grandma's hand, and bracing her shoulders, she pushed through the heavy doors. Evelyn left her standing there on the other side.

Sudden great gusts of wind and rain drove everybody inside. Ruthena and Matthew huddled in the corner in the front room near the photographs on the wall. Lis, Jackson, Yolanda and her family, and Lionel and his family retreated to the kitchen with Thomas and Sissy. Sarah, kneeling by the front door, straightened Nicholas's tie while Sam Jr. gazed at first one unfamiliar face, then another. His sister Grace hovered at her mother's shoulder, arms crossed and wide-eyed, because her dad had remained in Mount Laurel with her three youngest siblings. Edmond wasn't there yet, but his children and all *their* children were. They studied the various odds and ends with Mary in tow. Even now, everybody looked tired of hearing about Sim's life as an injured free agent. Voices remained at whisper level, although Evelyn heard a few questions about Milton as she and Kevin scooted through. She wondered if Milton and his family would show.

In the kitchen, Kevin and Evelyn went to work organizing food from Manna, the catering company run by Granny B's longtime friend Ruby. They stacked aluminum containers of fried chicken, barbecued pork shoulder, and country-fried steak on the counter and put the potato salad, fried corn, and banana pudding in the refrigerator. Ruby's efforts were superfluous because Granny B had stored away casseroles, canned fruits, and vegetables just for this day.

Yolanda touched her younger sister's elbow and whispered behind her hand. "Did you know that Granny B washed clothes for needy women and their families?"

Evelyn's mouth dropped open.

"Well, Uncle Thomas just told Mama. Granny B wants to leave the house exactly as it is so young mothers from her church can use it."

Evelyn looked out toward the clothesline, now empty save a dozen or so wooden pins.

Ruthena's voice carried from the front room. "If it isn't the apostle himself!"

"Edmond?" Lis rose from the table. Evelyn and the others trailed her from the room.

Her uncle stood by the door with his arm around a beautiful woman with flowing curls. Evelyn watched him hug, shake hands, and make introductions.

"So this is Carolina." Lis drew out the long *i* as she embraced them.

"Yes, this is *Cah-ro-lee-na*." Edmond drew his friend closer as Sarah pushed through to kiss his cheek.

"Edmond, you made it. Carolina, good to see you again."

He looked down at the boy at Sarah's hip. "How's your dad, little man?"

Sam Jr. responded soberly. "He's losing his mind. Isn't that what you said, Mama?"

The crowd around them hushed as Sarah flushed and opened her mouth. But before she could speak, a man in a black suit opened the screen door and tipped his dripping hat to Lis.

Finally the limousines had arrived.

Evelyn and Kevin watched the standard jockeying for position. She wanted to ride in her own car. She hated the curious stares of passersby. No one knew the person being buried today the way Evelyn did. At least, nobody living.

"You know, I don't need you to hold my arm. I can make

it to the car." Evelyn fiddled with her buttons before stepping off the porch.

"You're helping me. These are new shoes." Kevin held up his foot to show her his unscuffed soles.

She rewarded him with a glimmer of a smile as they slogged to their car. *If he thinks I'm going to roll on the ground in paroxysms of grief, he still has some digging to do.*

She was grateful for Kevin's steadying hand, for her heart quaked behind her impassive demeanor. All weekend she had dutifully greeted people. She'd accepted platters of chicken, lemon pound cakes, regrets, and condolences, until she was sated and ready to vomit. But Evelyn expressed her appreciation for their useless gifts, nodding solemnly and shaking hands until her neck and fingers were as stiff as their wooden platitudes. And probably Kevin's hand on her elbow and her mama's eyes trained for any sign of Milton kept her from losing her composure.

Jackson fell into line with them. Yolanda and Phil already sat in their Suburban along with Lionel and Muriel and all their kids. But at the last minute, as Elisabeth prepared to climb in the first limousine, Evelyn squeezed Kevin's hand and broke away—and not to roll around in the muck. She darted through the rain to sit beside her mama. If she had to go, she wanted to ride as closely as she could to the two most important women in her life.

Granny B was finally going somewhere with her children.

Evelyn stared at the back of the hearse as they crawled past Mrs. Jeannie Boyd's decrepit house, which seemed to have fallen into itself since the walk with Granny B. *"The day you come here and find me with my feet up on a table takin' one of them afternoon naps is the day you need to call the undertaker—'cause I won't be sleepin', I be dead."*

"What?" Mama leaned toward her.

Evelyn squeezed her mama's right hand. "Nothing, Mama. Just daydreaming."

They arrived at the redbrick edifice about ten minutes after the line of cars first pulled away from Granny B's house. As they cruised around to the side of Shiloh Baptist Church, Evelyn leaned forward to peer through the tinted window, shocked at the number of cars already there. Their driver parked at the walkway that led to the church steps. The rest of the family stopped in succession. Doors opened and shut. One by one, they emerged. The driver of the hearse and his assistant opened the wide back door. Evelyn turned away from the cascade of white roses and freesias adorning the mahogany casket.

"Watch your step, Evelyn." Kevin reappeared at her elbow. He grasped her right hand and her left hand clutched her mama's. Together, with Jackson, they trooped toward the doors of the church.

Mary suggested they line up according to age, oldest to youngest, and proceed into the church. Lis objected. She didn't want the grandchildren to walk in last because that meant she couldn't sit with Lionel, Yolanda, Jackson, and Evelyn—and then of course, all of *her* grandchildren. Sissy agreed, which seemed to prompt Ruthena's protestation. But then, at the last moment, Edmond, with Carolina in tow and flanked by his progeny, assumed his patriarchal role. He shushed them all, and Mary, pushing herself to the fore, pranced inside, her Chanel-scented black lace handkerchief placed just so to her nose. Watching them all file in, the hushed congregation probably read their angry, set faces as sobriety, their pained, put-out expressions as grief.

Granny B's children, their children, and some of their children's children shuffled into place on the hard wooden pews as the seven-person choir rose. While the family filled most of the left side of the small church, the three men and four women opened their mouths and crooned, "'Steal away, steal away, steal away to Je-sus . . .'" Somewhere in the back, someone coughed. A baby wailed.

To Evelyn's left, Jackson fiddled with the program. "'. . . to sta-ay he-eerre.'" She stole another look at Jackson's program as the choir sat down. By now, Granny B's replicated face had more wrinkles than the real one. Jackson winked at his sister. Evelyn winked back as the minister rose from his purple-draped throne and approached the pulpit.

"Let us pray," Reverend Farrow intoned. After the resounding "Amen," he reflected, "I'll never forget what Beatrice told me the day I asked her what brought her to Shiloh. She said, 'I been lookin' fo' true love all my life. Never found it with no man. Well, one day, some women come by speakin' 'bout a Man who was the best Lover they ever had—well, with them words, I just had to know 'bout Him! And they introduced me to Jesus.'

"Now, I don't know exactly who introduced her to Jesus,

but I know Beatrice Agnew introduced me to a whole new way of thinking about Him . . . Anybody out there looking for true love?"

"Amen!" the whole church chorused again.

Well, almost the whole church. Evelyn faked a cough to mask her hysteria. Kevin glanced at his wife and leaned in close enough that his words tickled her ear. "Are you all right?"

She nodded, giggling more, until her shoulders quivered.

"Look at Evelyn. She's overcome, poor thing," Sarah whispered.

Evelyn wanted to turn and reassure them that she was fine, but Lis leaned over Jackson and hissed, "Stop that laughing. What would Mama think?"

Evelyn worked hard to restrain herself. Then suddenly, she really was overcome, and she sobbed. Kevin enveloped her and she leaned into him, drawing still closer. Her mama nodded, approving either her proper funeral behavior or Kevin's response to it.

Dear Evelyn Beatrice,

I know your mama use your full name when she got something important to tell you, so I best use it now too cause I need you listening with your ears, eyes, toes, head, your whole self.

I was sitting out here on my front step cause I didn't want nothing tween me and the sky God made. Of course without that screen I had my fill of swatting bugs. But that's okay cause being out here put me in the mind of you and watching you staring at them lightning bugs. And then I heard God tell me write that girl.

Evelyn, you ever with me. Even when you was little and you was playing hide-and-seek in them woods out back, I felt God had a call on you. I didn't know what it was then and I don't rightly know what His plans are for you now, but I can hear Him speaking just like tonight. I hope you listening, child. I didn't always. Maybe He gon talk to you through that baby. He might use your work. He sure trying you in your marriage and with your mama. Just press toward the mark of that high calling.

Your Granny B loves you. And you know I don't waste them words like blowing wishes on dandelions. Evelyn, I feel like you mine just like the troubles and pains I been bearing all these years. Yes, we got the same name, but these my own heartaches and blessings and nobody can feel them or share them like me. Now blessings a person tend to crow about. But that ache and pain gets kept close, deep in the heart. It might feel like they gon kill you but you get stronger in the end. You learn from it. Well, that's you in my life. You make me stronger, girl. You build me up. You also get on my nerves but you done more good than harm. And I thank you for it.

I been seeking the Lord for you. I know you got your own pain and God knows what it is. I ain't saying share it cause you got to let it go. God's grace is sufficient—and that don't mean it's enough. His grace is more than enough for you and whoever you need to give some to and it's full of love, forgiveness, and strength. The peace that come with it was a long time comin' for me but I got it now. I wish I'd had it to give when my children was running round here. I was too busy feeling shamed and sorry and thinking that they stood for all the wrong that I done in my life. Specially Milton. That wan't right. They was blessings God gave me when I didn't have too many to speak of.

You got a blessing on the way, Evelyn. Share it. You also got pain coming. Hold it dear to your heart. I'll be holding you a little while longer but be glad for God's got you always.

Granny B

Evelyn looked away from the tearstained, well-read pages and rested her head against the sunbaked pane. She could almost say the words by heart. She'd read the letter almost every day since Granny B had slipped it into her hand outside the Skillet. Evelyn focused hard on the memory, so hard she could see her grandma's reflection in the glass. *"I'm talking 'bout grace, chile. Somethin' I didn't know how to accept or give, even to myself. But I'm learnin'."*

"I'm still learnin', too, Granny B," she murmured in the empty room.

Evelyn straightened her legs and stood. It was her last full day in Mount Laurel, and it was time to focus on the new life she was carrying rather than her past mistakes and miseries she'd buried with Granny B. She stepped into the hallway. Her mama's genteel lilt and Kevin's deep voice floated from downstairs. Within seconds, Evelyn placed a sneakered foot onto the hardwood kitchen floor.

"Good morning."

Lis glanced quickly over her shoulder before turning her attention back to the griddle. "Mornin'!" She awkwardly flipped an omelet. "I did it!"

"Good work, Mother." Kevin winked at Evelyn and mouthed a kiss. "Hi, hon."

She smiled at him as the baby kicked a greeting to Daddy. They both were still adjusting to life with Kevin—but her heart definitely felt more at home with him than without him.

"Kevin shared his secrets." Lis beamed.

Evelyn took in the cheese, eggshells, empty sausage roll, peppers, onions, and other materials dotting the countertop and peeked over her shoulder. "And what does *he* know about cooking?" She listened to the quietness of the rest of the house. "Where's everybody?"

"This *is* everybody. Jackson drove Yolanda's kids to the store to pick up some things. As for Lionel and Muriel and Yolanda and Phil, they're still sleeping."

"What about everybody else?" Evelyn nibbled on some cooked sausage.

"Well, after a lot of fussing and a lot more reminiscing, they drove to Spring Hope and stayed at Mama's last night."

"What? How did they fit in there?"

"The same as before."

Evelyn shrugged and walked toward the mudroom.

"Where are you going?" Kevin pushed back his stool. Elisabeth, watching, slid the omelet onto a plate.

"To the graveyard."

"Didn't you just say yesterday how you hated it? And what about breakfast?"

"But I have something I need to do. I won't be long." Evelyn grabbed the keys from the wicker basket. She walked back to Kevin. She clasped his face between her hands and pressed her lips to his. "I love you, and I'll be back as soon as I can."

Once seated, she plugged the directions into the navigation system. Kevin was right. She'd said her good-bye to Granny B. Evelyn headed to the tiny town of Jasper, where Henton and Hewitt once lived, according to Granny B. And where the brothers were buried.

It took her all of thirty minutes to drive there. After stopping to ask for directions, Evelyn turned right off the main street and onto a bumpy dirt road. She angled her car between two others. The cemetery was old and not as well-kept as Hillcrest. Cracked headstones leaned this way and that or were missing altogether. Dead or dying flowers dotted the plots. Evelyn studied headstones and markers for about fifteen minutes before she found what she was looking for— as well as something she wasn't.

"Uncle Milton?"

When the lean, square-jawed man faced her, Evelyn noticed that even though his hair had grayed, he looked very much like the baby boy in the picture on Granny B's wall. His lips broke into a familiar smile, a smile so like her grandma's it triggered a sudden painful ache in her heart.

"Evelyn."

She stepped into his arms, and they embraced briefly, yet deeply, something they hadn't done at their last meeting.

"I see you're taking the plunge."

"The plunge?"

"You're having a baby." It was obvious he hadn't noticed during that emotional visit.

"Yes, Kevin and I can't wait." She paused. "I'm surprised to see you here."

"*You're* surprised? No more than I am. Why are you here anyway?"

Evelyn shrugged. "The same reason you are, I guess. So that's where they're buried?"

Uncle Milton's brow furrowed. "They?"

"All the secrets," Evelyn improvised.

Uncle Milton stared at his niece for a moment, but then he knelt at the grave, arranging the fresh flowers he must have placed there. "You're probably wondering how I knew to come here."

"Just a little bit."

He fiddled with the flowers. "I talked to Mama the day before she died."

Evelyn gasped.

"Actually, I visited her, and we talked a long time. It was probably the most I'd talked to her in . . . well, ever, I guess." Uncle Milton finally stood and brushed off his knees. "She looked good and strong. She sounded healthy. Mama looked happier and more peaceful than I'd ever seen her. We talked about her condition . . . her dying. Thanks for writing me . . . and for bringing Mama to see me."

She shrugged off his thanks.

He glanced back to the grave, which was simply marked by a nameplate pushed into the ground. *Henton Agnew.* "For some reason, I asked her where Daddy was buried. I don't know why I did—I just wanted to know, and I had a feeling she knew. But what shocked me is she told me."

He looked at Evelyn and smiled wryly. "You know Mama was good for keeping things to herself."

Evelyn shook her head wistfully, secretly grateful.

"Anyway. When Lis called the next day and told me Mama had died, I just didn't know what to do. I couldn't come to her funeral. After all that time, I'd finally started to feel like I was getting a mother and a father, and then just like that . . ." He closed his eyes. "I wanted to remember her the way I'd last seen her."

Evelyn pretended to study the grass at their feet. Instead, she peered at the nameplate on the grave to Henton's left: *H. A. Agnew.* She quickly calculated that Hewitt had died the same year Uncle Milton was born. She didn't point out the grave or her ironic discovery to Uncle Milton. After a while, he opened his eyes. "Ready?"

"Well, actually, not really. I'd like to stay for a moment longer. But don't wait for me," Evelyn offered quickly, "because we can catch up at the house. Where is Aunt Nancy?"

"At the hotel. I guess it's time for me to pick her up and face the music with everybody."

"Brace yourself. But don't worry. It's just like a bee sting. It hurts a lot but just for a moment."

He laughed with Evelyn and hugged her again, even more tightly this time. He took a step away before he looked at her hand. "Hydrangeas?"

"Oh yeah!" Evelyn looked down in surprise, having forgotten the pot of flowers she had purchased. She crouched at Hewitt's neglected spot.

"What are you doing?"

"Well, it looks so empty, and you've already taken care of your father's."

"Those will require some work, won't they? They can grow to a pretty large size."

Tenderly she set the container of flowers down and reached for a nearby stick. "I know, but I don't mind."

"Well . . . okay. I'll see you then."

For a moment, Evelyn watched Uncle Milton pick his way around the gravesites before she returned her attention to the two buried at her feet. She brushed away the crushed leaves and broken limbs covering *H. A. Agnew* and thought about what she would have said to him if she'd had the chance. Then she plucked the resealed, yellowed envelope from where she'd hidden it among the blooms and wondered at those words meant only for her grandmother, written long before Evelyn's time. She sighed. There'd been enough said.

Kneeling, she used the stick and her bare hands to scoop out clumps of dirt. After she'd made room for the hydrangeas, she withdrew a miniature box she'd bought at the last minute and pushed it open.

Evelyn struck a match and held it to the corner of the rectangle. At first, the edge glowed bright red before turning black and fading to white. More smoke than flame, the heat crept over the paper until finally nothing but a fragment was left. She dropped it, but not before the tiny flame licked the tip of her thumb, a tender red blotch admonishing her for holding on a little too long. Rising slowly, Evelyn brushed off the ashes, leaves, and dirt that clung to her knees and hands and followed in the footsteps of Granny B's baby boy.

A Note from the Author

In the words of Michael Crichton, "This novel is fiction, except for the parts that aren't." Yes, there actually is a Spring Hope, North Carolina, but that's where all similarities end and creativity begins. None of these folks walk and talk except in my mind and heart—and in yours now, too. Also, while I'm not sure if my mama adds green peppers and onions to her ham hocks, I add them to everything, so I wrote those in. There were no bugs killed in the writing of this novel, though I tried.

Acknowledgments

To say I acknowledge God may be stating the obvious, but this is my rooftop, and I'm shouting His name from it. He is my inspiration and the fulfillment of it.

I couldn't have typed *The End* without my beginning, my dearest husband, Eddie, and my middle, our precious children. There's nobody like my crew. God led me to "write the vision," but they were the ones who helped me "run with it." They filled my coffee cup; prayed with and for me; listened to me rant, rave, and read; kept the laundry flowing; loved on me and cheered for me; made me laugh; became amateur social media specialists, publicists, and personal assistants; and sat dusty in the corner while I holed myself away. I may have been responsible for homeschooling them, but they taught me more than any textbook or literature anthology. While I didn't get it at first, they made the children's book *I'll Love You Forever* my over-the-top personal testimony. Eddie, thank you for being my safe place. Nick, Kate, Benjamin, Faith, Hillary Grace, Hallie, August . . . my quiver and my heart are full.

But this story wouldn't have blossomed without strong roots to grow it and anchor it. My parents made sure my sisters and I spent lots of time with our grandmothers, who taught me to hold faith and family dear, no matter how hard it got. My parents always supported me as their daughter, and they never stopped believing in me, the writer, even when my hands were buried deep in a sink full of dirty dishes or cradling one sweet, sleepless baby after another. My sisters and I wouldn't be who we are—to each other and to our own families—without them. Of course, I wouldn't have my own peeps without my father- and mother-in-love who produced this amazing man I get to call my husband. They welcomed me as a second daughter and made our children theirs. These two are always there in a pinch and will even pinch us back if we need it. I love them all from the top of my head to the tips of my toes.

Of course my family includes those people who also call me friend, across the country and at my church. No way am I as funny or as faithful as they make me think I am, but I always know they're laughing with me and not at me. They've served as trusted resources and early readers, provided comforting shoulders and comfort food, and prayed for, with, and over me. They've waited for me to call, and they didn't hang up when I finally did. When we text, we can use proper punctuation because we get that a period doesn't mean we're angry; it's just the end of a sentence, not the friendship. They know who they are, and what makes it better, we all know whose we are. That makes it so much sweeter.

Since I'm talking about punctuation, here's an exclamation point for Cynthia Ruchti, my fearless and faithful agent! She and Books & Such Literary took a chance on me and Granny B when other agents were afraid to dip a toe in these unknown waters. She has gripped my hand and patiently led me along, and not just leading but walking alongside, even dragging me when necessary. I appreciate her prayerful intercession and skillful mediation. She is my friend, confidante, and warrior, even if she does put syrup on her grits and voluntarily eats beets. She always knows what to say and when to say it, wisdom and discretion at work. And of course, I must thank her for connecting me with my Tyndale team . . .

Jan Stob is a dream. She made sure what happened in North Carolina didn't stay there by welcoming me to her Tyndale House family. This project has been a long time comin', but working with her made it worth the wait. She really listened and then put hands and feet to all she read and heard. I count her as a friend and an unanticipated blessing—the best kind. Caleb Sjogren, my editor, is truly next level. He has sharpened my thoughts and my words, ensuring they were fit for flight as arrows soaring to their designated target. If he has any new wrinkles, he should consider them smile lines that spell my name. And Eva Winters . . . that cover! Just like Granny B, her behind-the-scenes work made such an impact, right there front and center. She was gifted with a beautiful eye for design that totally nailed it.

While I can't capture it all, I praise God, who can.

About the Author

ROBIN W. PEARSON'S writing sprouts from her Southern roots. While sitting in her grandmothers' kitchens, she learned what happens if you sweep someone's feet, how to make corn bread taste like pound cake, and the all-purpose uses of Vaseline. She also learned about the power of God and how His grace led her grandmothers to care for their large families after their husbands were long gone, rearing children who became business owners, graduates, ministers, parents, and grandparents themselves. Their faith and superstitions, life lessons, and life's longings all worked together to shape and inspire her, leading her to write *A Long Time Comin'*, the first in a three-book series about man's timeless love affair with God. This story shares an African American family's experiences in a relationship that crosses generations, cultures, and geography.

While her family history gave her the story to tell, her professional experiences gave her the skills to tell it effectively. Armed with her degree from Wake Forest University, she has corrected grammar up and down the East Coast in her career as an editor and writer that started with Houghton Mifflin Company twenty-five years ago. Since then she has freelanced with magazines, parenting journals, textbooks, and homeschooling resources.

At the heart of it all abides her love of God and the family He's given her. It's her focus as a wife and homeschooling mother of seven. It's what she writes about on her blog, *Mommy, Concentrated*, where she shares her adventures in faith, family, and freelancing. And it's the source and subject of her fiction—in her novel *A Long Time Comin'*, in the new characters currently living and breathing on her computer screen, and in the stories waiting to be told about her belief in Jesus Christ and the experiences at her own kitchen sink.

Follow Robin at robinwpearson.com.

Discussion Questions

1. No one would say Beatrice Agnew is warm and fuzzy, yet Evelyn could cozy up to her in other important ways. For example, she could trust her to deliver the truth without any sugarcoating. Is there a Granny B in your life? Describe this person and your relationship.

2. Evelyn and her grandmother have more than their names in common. How are they alike? How are they different?

3. Did Beatrice's resistance to cancer treatment demonstrate faith or fear? Why?

4. Granny B has been walking with God a long time, in a very real, practical way that impacts her day-to-day interactions with others. How does her spiritual walk compare to Ruthena's? Edmond's? How does their relationship with God affect their personal relationships?

5. What clues do the letters Beatrice hid in her closet reveal about her life? What big revelations has God shown you in tiny steps along the way in your own life?

6. Kevin said he didn't "let go." How did he hold on, and why might Evelyn agree or disagree with his assertion?

7. Beatrice had to make some hard decisions about who needed to know what about her diagnosis and how she should deliver the information. Evelyn respected Granny B's wishes enough to help her carry them out. Was there any information you believed her children had a right to know? What would you have said or done differently in Beatrice's shoes? In Evelyn's?

8. Did Kevin's right to know Evelyn's secret justify Granny B's interference, or did her grandmother jump the gun?

9. Evelyn believes there are many ways you can be unfaithful, in your heart and in your actions, to God and to others in your life. What did Granny B's life teach you about faithfulness?

10. Do you think Evelyn ever read the letter she took from Granny B's house? Explain why you agree or disagree with what she did with it.

11. What does Granny B mean by Ruthena's "white God in the sky"? What are your own perceptions of God?

12. The Agnew siblings are their best friends and their worst enemies. How do their sibling dynamics compare to your own?

13. Why do you think Granny B resisted a family reunion?

Turn the page
for a preview of
Robin W. Pearson's
next novel set in
Spring Hope, North
Carolina, releasing in
spring 2021.

Watch for it in stores and online

Chapter One

"YOU KNOW DIVORCE ain't catchin'." Ruby's dark eyes flicked in her granddaughter's direction. "Nobody's goin' to sneeze and give it to you or Theodore."

"Are you listening to your grandma, Maxine?" Vivienne stood on her toes and stretched to retrieve a small jar from the kitchen cabinet. It skittered away from her.

"Yes, ma'am, but I never said I thought divorce was contagious," Maxine smiled a little and shook her head as she hopped down from the stool. She reached over Vivienne and set the glass container on the counter. At five-six, she had her mother by three inches. But that was the only thing about Maxine that outmatched her mama.

Vivienne opened the pimientos with a *pop!* and spooned some into the bowl in front of her. "Then what do you think this is all about? You've been having these crazy dreams for weeks now, ever since you set that appointment. Then you hear about your friends' separation. That's not going to happen to you and Theodore." She stirred the potato salad, using one pink-gloved hand to hold on to the bowl.

"I didn't say it was, Mama." Maxine moved her shoulders to the beat of the Jackson Southernaires, crooning from the Bluetooth speaker, to mask the shiver snaking through her. Maxine wished she could blame her chill on the clouds cloaking the pale-blue sky, but she knew it had nothing to do with the below-freezing temperature, unusual for North Carolina. The three women had been going back and forth for over an hour, since Maxine had shown up on her mama's doorstep holding her box of silk chrysanthemums.

"The thought just breaks my heart, Mama, that's all, that she couldn't talk to me about what she was going through. Pregnant, in broken pieces, trying to avoid the whispers, pointing fingers, the dissection of her problems, the gossip from church folk." Swallowing hard over a lump that suddenly lodged in her throat, Maxine took a step closer to the flames flickering brightly in the fireplace behind her. She fiddled with the ribs of her gray corduroy skirt. "Evelyn's having a little girl."

Vivienne frowned and shook her head, dislodging a strand from her silver-streaked bun. "Is that what this is about? *Her* baby girl?" She aimed a gloved finger at her daughter. "If so, you need to keep in mind that it didn't have anything to do with you. Baby or no baby. Besides, her marriage is fine now." Vivienne returned her attention to the bowl.

The chair creaked as Ruby propped an ample hip on the stool Maxine had abandoned. "Goodness gracious, Maxine Amelia, you don't know your end from your beginnin'. You ain't even married yet. Your weddin' is months away and you're already in divorce care." She pointed to the speaker. "And turn down that music. Cain't even hear my own thoughts, let alone help you with yours."

Maxine obeyed.

Vivienne scooped out a teaspoonful of the creamy mixture and turned to her daughter. "Here, taste this for me. What does it need?"

"Mmm. Nothing."

Vivienne nodded in response and sprinkled kosher salt over the bowl and swirled it around with her mixing spoon.

Maxine pursed her lips and inhaled a sigh. She watched her mama finish off the potato salad with paprika and cover the sixteen-inch melamine bowl with plastic wrap. "Like I said, it's just sad. For them, not me. I'm too nervous about premarital counseling to worry about divorce."

Ruby wrapped an arm around her granddaughter. "Don't let your mind play tricks on you, awake or asleep. Their problems ain't your problems. Stop thinkin' of this pastor as some one-man inquisition. I hear Reverend Atwater is good people."

Her grandma was squishy in all the right places. Accepting

the comfort of her embrace and her words, Maxine planted a quick kiss on her velvety cheek. Then she opened the long, rectangular box on the quartz countertop and lifted out one flower after another, setting the counter ablaze with purple, cranberry, and orange blooms.

But she wasn't so focused she missed her mama rolling her eyes in Ruby's direction. Vivienne picked up the pumpkin-colored dish, hefted open the vacuum-sealed door of the refrigerator, and stowed it on the second shelf.

Ruby cast her eyes heavenward. "Trust God's authority and care, not just your spouse's—that is, your *future* spouse. That's what's kept me and Lerenzo married. And that's what keeps Manna in business."

That's easy to say when you've been married for decades and you run a catering business together. I'm just trying to keep a fiancé. Maxine snipped stems and leaves and arranged them in the olive cut-glass vase. "All I know is I'm going to struggle at playing truth or consequences during these seven sessions with the pastor."

Vivienne huffed. "Maxine, just be yourself. You're thirty. It's been thirteen years since . . . It's time to let go of this guilt and do something. It's bigger than you and Theodore. Now, I'm done with this."

"Done with this." Really, Maxine didn't think she'd ever be done with *this*, the burden she'd been toting around half her life. It had grown heavier since adding the weight of her engagement ring. Sunlight danced through the picture window overlooking the backyard, setting fire to the cinnamon

ringlets framing Maxine's face. *It's been thirteen years, but it feels like yesterday. Is Mama right? But what if my "self" isn't good enough for Teddy?* Maxine twirled a curl around her finger and looped it around her right earlobe.

Vivienne squinted at Maxine. "I don't know what you're tuckin' in your heart's back pocket, but I should tell you John and I talked about it, and he thinks it's high time, too." Vivienne stared at her daughter a few seconds before she shrugged as if giving up. She strode from the sun-splashed kitchen, throwing over her shoulder, "Just know you have your daddy's blessing."

John Owens became her stepfather three years after a sleepy teenage driver had blindsided her biological father, David Clark, on an inky Union County road. John had officially adopted Maxine to hush Vivienne's clamoring, not to fulfill Maxine's own burning, personal need, before he'd uprooted his new family for a temporary work assignment in Alabama. It had taken some time, but eventually she and her stepfather got along like mayonnaise and mustard. Still, more often than not, Maxine respectfully—and teasingly— called him "First John" and his namesake, her little brother, "the Second." One thing she never called her stepfather was "Daddy."

Maxine glanced at her grandmother and whispered, "That's all well and good, but there are bigger things to consider than First John's blessing."

Ruby held up her hands in the universal sign of silent

surrender. She walked to the double wall ovens and fiddled with the dials.

Vivienne clip-clopped back from the storage room in her daisy-covered clogs and set her handful on the counter. She peeled off plastic wrap and aluminum foil, revealing a frozen pound cake. She usually baked three or four at a time and pulled them out to order. Then she'd add a freshly made glaze.

Maxine swiped Vivienne's discarded wrapping and dropped it in the trash. She leaned against the counter, twiddling with her flower trimmings. "Evelyn was always so focused on her work, teaching and writing, not on being a mom."

Vivienne peeked over her glasses at her daughter as she set the cake aside and consulted her iPad. "Having a baby doesn't end the world. It didn't end mine."

"Well, it almost ended mine." Maxine held her mama's eyes. Neither blinked for a moment. But Maxine looked away first as she muttered, "And you're not a seventeen-year-old."

"You're not seventeen years old . . . now." Vivienne closed her tablet with a decisive click. "Just what *are* you doin' with those flowers?"

"I'm trying out colors and arrangements for the bouquets." Maxine repositioned a flower. "I have a feeling Teddy wouldn't take the news that he's a father quite as well as First John did."

"Your Theodore ain't becomin' a daddy. So no need to send out birth announcements." Ruby opened a bag of dark-brown sugar and spooned some into a small pot bubbling away on the gas cooktop.

Vivienne opened the refrigerator and drew out a large, glistening ham covered in pineapple slices. She set it down. "I like the purple and cranberry. Are you sure about the orange?"

"You know orange is my favorite color, and it's perfect for my fall wedding." Maxine shifted a stem. "And as far as birth announcements go, that's exactly what I'm doing, Mama Ruby, sending information out into the world it doesn't have the right to know. This is mine. I'm not holding on to this just for my sake . . ."

Ruby stopped stirring and raised an eyebrow that proclaimed her disbelief.

"Your weddin' is December 5, which feels more like the Christmas season than the fall." Vivienne plucked two orange mums, leaving only one in the center surrounded by a mixed spray of purple and cranberry, like the setting sun on the horizon. "There. Better. See?" She turned the vase toward Maxine. "The fact is, tellin' Teddy the truth might be the right thing to do."

"You're right, Vivienne, but there's a right time and place for it. That's a lesson I learned as a young girl." Ruby never looked away from the brown sugar mixture she'd pour over the ham once it was ready. "I remember when my brother planned to leave with Mr. Baker to sign up for the Army. At first, Mama didn't say nuthin', but not too long after he left, she sent me to get him off that bus. She didn't want him to go because she knew if he ever left Spring Hope, he wasn't ever comin' back.

"As much as I hated to, I did as I was told. I didn't even ask Daddy what he thought of the matter 'cause nobody got in the way of my mama. Billy and I was thick as thieves, and I knew what that trip meant to him. So I took the long way round gettin' to Mr. Baker's, hopin' that bus would be long gone. I even went by Fulton's and bought myself five cents worth of candy. But sure 'nough, that bus was still sittin' there when I came walkin' up, lickin' my peppermint stick."

"Couldn't you have told your mother how you felt?"

"Child, didn't nobody care how I felt. It was my job to obey. Young people these days . . ." Ruby shook her head at Vivienne.

Vivienne laughed as she took the spoon and stirred the glaze.

"Besides, that's not the point. Follow where I'm leadin', girl. Now when I got there, Billy was already on the bus. You should've seen his face when he saw me walk up. His eyes just got bigger and bigger, wellin' up. Mr. Baker must have suspected I'd be comin' 'cause he opened up those doors straightaway and asked me, 'You come for Billy?' Well, I looked from him to my brother sittin' in that window, and I couldn't do it. I just could not break his heart and pull him off that bus in front of all them other boys."

Maxine stopped spinning the vase. "So what did you do?"

"I put a hand on my hip and said, 'Mr. Baker, Mama sent me to see to Billy. She'll have your head if somethin' happens, so you'd best take care of him.' He looked like he didn't quite believe me, but he closed them doors and drove away. Billy was still wipin' his face when he waved good-bye. I can still see him grinnin'—and lickin' one of my peppermint sticks."

"What did you say when you got home, Mama Ruby?"

"At first, I reported I was too late to stop Billy from leavin'. Which was mostly true, if you want to pick through the meat to get to the bone. It was too late. His heart was long gone, and he needed to follow it. But that wasn't the whole story. Tellin' that lie ate me up until I confessed it to my daddy. He made me tell the truth, and then I got the whuppin' of my life. That was okay though. Forgiveness don't always soften the consequences."

"Excuse me. I don't mean any harm, but what does all that have to do with Maxine?" Vivienne set the spoon down in a dish on the counter and lowered the flame.

"Everythang. I could've told Mr. Baker that I was sent there to get my brother, but that wouldn't have been right. I didn't lie. I did go to check on Billy, and Mr. Baker surely would've been eaten alive if somethin' bad had come of my baby brother. But it wouldn't have helped nobody to make him get off that bus. My mama had to let go sometime, and Billy did too." Ruby readjusted the dial on the stove as Vivienne walked back to the island. She lifted a finger to her lips and shook her head at Maxine.

She wiggled her eyebrows and nodded in response as her grandmother, the sous-chef, continued.

"That truth you've been carryin' around all these years?

When to tell it is just as important as what to tell and who to tell. That decision will affect a lot of lives, like the one I had to make. Only God knows what the right decision is, although you'll have to deal with the consequences, painful as they may be. But it's for you to determine the what, when, who, and how, Maxine. Not me. Not your mama." Ruby shrugged. Then she reached into her apron pocket and withdrew a pad of paper and a Sharpie. She marked off an item on her list.

"I just don't know what the right decision is! If I tell Theodore, I have to tell—"

"Hey, y'all! Ooh, pretty . . ."

Ruby's green marker clattered to the floor.

Maxine's whole body froze. She turned incrementally, like the second hand on a clock. It seemed like a full minute passed before she faced the high-pitched voice coming from the mudroom that connected the kitchen to the storeroom. "Celeste . . ."

The thirteen-year-old girl clad in a denim miniskirt, pink-and-orange long-sleeved tee, and pink leggings was nestled between the two doors leading outside. She pulled the storm door closed and backed into the glass-paned wooden door, pushing it to. "Oh, Maxine, your flowers came!"

Celeste bounded into the kitchen, her low-top blue Chuck Taylors squeaking happily on the hardwood floor. She leaned over and kissed Vivienne's cheek. "Mmm-mwah. It smells good in here, Mama. What's going on?"

TYNDALE HOUSE PUBLISHERS IS CRAZY4FICTION!

Fiction that entertains and inspires

Get to know us! Become a member of the Crazy4Fiction community. Whether you read our blog, like us on Facebook, follow us on Twitter, or receive our e-newsletter, you're sure to get the latest news on the best in Christian fiction. You might even win something along the way!

JOIN IN THE FUN TODAY.

 www.crazy4fiction.com

 Crazy4Fiction

 @Crazy4Fiction

CP0021